IRISH LINEN

IRISH LINEN

A Nuala Anne McGrail Novel

ANDREW M. GREELEY

A TOM DOHERTY ASSOCIATES BOOK

NEW YORK

IRISH LINEN: A NUALA ANNE MCGRAIL NOVEL

Copyright © 2007 by Andrew M. Greeley Enterprises, Inc.

Map by Heidi Hornaday

A Forge Book
Published by Tom Doherty Associates, LLC
175 Fifth Avenue
New York, NY 10010

Forge® is a registered trademark of Tom Doherty Associates, LLC.

ISBN-13: 978-0-765-31586-1

Printed in the United States of America

For Colm

— Author's Note —

All the Chicago characters, lay and clerical, in the Chicago story exist not in God's world but only in the world of my imagination. All the characters in the German story, except Annalise, Paul, and the Ridgeland family, existed in God's world.

The Irish Free State (Eire) immediately established full diplomatic relations with most European countries because that was assumed to be part of being "A Nation Once Again." The Irish Embassy in Berlin remained open until the arrival of the Red Army in the spring of 1945. It was not, however, a one-man operation, as is my Irish embassy in the story. Nor was the embassy necessarily on the Friedrichstrasse. Nor was its ambassador, as far as I know, engaged in activities like those of Tim Ridgeland. The posture of Ireland in the war, absolutely and totally neutral but pro-England, was much like that in the book.

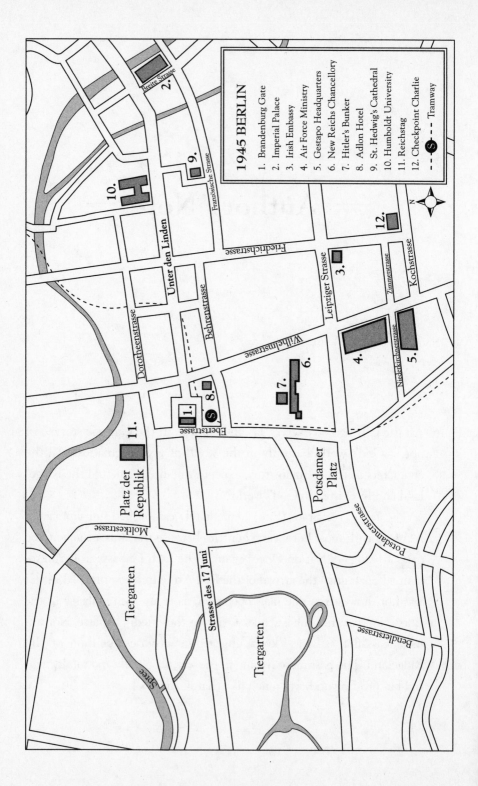

1945 BERLIN

1. Brandenburg Gate
2. Imperial Palace
3. Irish Embassy
4. Air Force Ministry
5. Gestapo Headquarters
6. New Reichs Chancellory
7. Hitler's Bunker
8. Adlon Hotel
9. St. Hedwig's Cathedral
10. Humboldt University
11. Reichstag
12. Checkpoint Charlie
- - - - Tramway

IRISH
LINEN

— 1 —

AFTER A certain number of books, even folly-driven mass horror becomes boring. All right, I had to read them for my wife's current case, a search for a nice young man from our neighborhood who had disappeared in the Middle East, maybe in Iraq. There was, I thought, not a chance in the world of Nuala solving this one without one or the other of us flying to Kuwait or Dubai or some such place. That we would not do. Since she would have to stay home to take care of the kids, I would have to fly to Kuwait and she wouldn't let me do that.

I pushed aside the stack of books about the world from 1914 to 1945 and began a dialogue with my six-month-old son Poraig Josefa (Patrick Joseph) Coyne aka "Patjo."

"We have a lot in common, young man," I informed him. "We are both large, good-looking, gentle blonds who are also lazy, mostly undependable sensualists. One might even use the adjective 'useless.' We make our way through life not by hard work but because we have a happy smile, an appealing laugh, and lots of barely resistible Irish charm. We both have breast fixations, indeed about the same pair of lovely breasts, if for somewhat different but related reasons."

He smiled enthusiastically.

"You must never tell your mother I told you these truths, because she becomes furious when people assert them about me and she'll go ballistic if she should learn that I'm saying that about you."

He laughed.

"Herself, mind you, is a brilliant woman altogether, to use the Irish superlative and, if you don't mind my using male talk, a wonderful lay. She has a friggin' ton of talents and she feels obligated to be perfect at all of them—singer, accountant, actress, detective, wife, mother, lover. She's the alpha person in this house and the sooner you learn it the better off we'll all be. You four young 'uns, the two wolfhounds, the nanny, and the housekeeper work for her. As does your poor father. The only reason you're here is that she had to prove she could have a normal, easy pregnancy. The red-haired woman in the house, your big sister Nelliecoyne, required a lot of effort to bring into the world, your big brother Micky plunged her into a terrible fit of PPD as they call it these days. Then the little imp who presides over you like she's your mother showed up awfully early and barely made it. Your mom thinks these events were somehow or the other her fault. Well, she knows better, but deep down in her bronze-age Irish soul, she's still convinced she did something wrong. We conceived you in a memorable night of orgy so that she'd finally get it right and we'd also have a neatly balanced family, two boys and two girls, which appeals to her accountant's love of order. I shouldn't mention it to you but I will. She knew your gender and that it would be an untroubled pregnancy at least a month before your conception. I don't know how she does that and I don't want to know."

He frowned. Hungry again. I offered him one of the bottles of milk that I had stockpiled for him. As his mother would have said, he destroyed it altogether and discarded the bottle like a fifteen-year-old male would discard a beer can. He then closed his eyes like he was thinking seriously about sleep.

I glanced out the window and considered Sheffield Avenue, which on this mild, wet, and dark April morning looked like a set for a horror film. Everything—trees, lawns, homes, the church and school—was dank and barren, fog hovered just above the church steeple, it seemed, and drizzle was touching the ground with its faint hint of corruption. I imagined I could even smell corruption, the corruption of an old graveyard.

"Don't misunderstand me, young man, your mother is an astonishing woman. My lust for her varies from intense most of the time, to mild and that only after she's exhausted me in bed. If your man Freud is right, you feel the same way about her. Well, she's mine, do you hear!"

In fact, he didn't hear because he was sleeping soundly.

"With any luck, your mother and Socra Marie will return soon from her weekly voice lesson with Madame down at the Fine Arts Building. The little terrorist needs an afternoon nap to replenish her energies. The two of you would thus be asleep and your mother and I would have the house to ourselves until the older kids return from St. Josephat's school across Sheffield Avenue. I could take advantage of that situation to fuck her right and proper as they say in her native land . . . and as she herself has said on occasion."

These salacious words did not upset the woman's son in the slightest. So I began to sing the Connemara lullaby,

> On the wings of the wind, o'er the dark, rolling deep
> Angels are coming to watch o'er your sleep
> Angels are coming to watch over you
> So list to the wind coming over the sea
>
> Hear the wind blow, hear the wind blow
> Lean your head over, hear the wind blow.

I shouldn't have been singing it. The lullaby was my wife's. Indeed it had been the lead song on her platinum disk *Hear the Wind Blow: Nuala Anne Sings Lullabies*. Nevertheless, even in my whiskey tenor voice (not created by drinking whiskey, which I rarely do and only when me spouse wants the two of us to have a splasheen before we progress to other matters), it puts Patjo to sleep for a long time.

"Och, don't I have a rival in me own house!" said a voice which always reminds me of church bells ringing across the bogs.

'Twas herself in a tightly fitting blue summer suit, her pale face and deep blue eyes in a leprechaun mood. I tend to gasp and blink every time I see her, a mix of desire and adoration which has been with me ever since I first saw her in O'Neill's pub just off College Green in Dublin.

"Ma, doesn't Da sing real good?" our sleepy-eyed toddler asked.

"Da does lots of things real good," her mother responded. "I'll put this one down in the nursery, Dermot love," she said. "Why don't you put himself in the bedroom, where our conversation won't wake him up?"

"Conversation be damned, woman! I have other plans!"

"Do you now?" My wife, always a modest woman, blushed.

Fiona, our elder wolfhound, rose up from her own afternoon nap and padded down to the nursery while Maeve ambled into the master bedroom where Patjo still ruled. I never understood how the two dogs divided their child protection responsibilities.

In a very few minutes Nuala Anne returned to my office, several buttons on the front of her suit open and a robe draped over her arm. Very gently I claimed her in my arms. She leaned against me and sighed loudly, "Well, if you want to fuck me, I suppose, I have to let you do it."

Nuala is very careful with her language under most circumstances, having learned, much to her dismay, that "your Yanks are not relaxed about words, are they now?" She is also careful about such matters when there are little ears around. However, privately she reverts to the West of Ireland traditions when we're alone.

"Sure, Dermot Michael," she added, "isn't it yourself that owns me altogether? You look at me that way and don't I want to take off all me clothes?"

That's not the way it really works. Most of the undressing is left to me. I had learned early in our marriage that there was no upper limit to the amount of foreplay my wife could absorb.

"We'll talk about the war afterwards, won't we, Dermot love?" She sighed as my lips sank to her breasts to taste a bit of her milk.

"Woman, we will, but only after I've reestablished my reputation as a Viking ravager of Irish matrons."

She laughed.

"If you were really one of them dumb Vikings, I'd already have me knife in your heart . . . Och, Dermot leave some for poor Patjo . . ."

I will not describe what me wife looks like with all her clothes off, save to say that she is lithe rather than voluptuous and that she looks like a naked Irish goddess, not one of your buxom Greco-Roman though, mind you, I've never slept with a naked Irish goddess, nor even set eyes on one. My Nuala was not one of your hefty, slow-moving classical goddesses like Juno. Rather she was a slender, quick-flowing powerful goddess like the River Shannon. She was also determined that four pregnancies would not change her figure, a goal which both genes and rigorous exercise sustained.

Nor will I give you any of the details of our little afternoon romp, except that we were improving through the years at the signs and the signals, the constantly changing art of the rhythms and the negotiations and the strategies a husband and a wife, if they're sensitive to one another, slowly acquire.

"You're getting better at ravishing the matron." She sighed, a great West of Ireland sigh, like the advent of a major asthma attack, when I had finished with her. Or she with me.

"'Tis yourself," I said, struggling to regain my breath, "that leads me down the path to terrible sin."

"Just like I thought when I first saw you at O'Neill's, that's the kind of man I want to undress me and fuck me for the rest of me life. I'm old enough now to know better, but I haven't changed me mind."

Nostalgia as postcoital reinforcement. The subject would soon change to my readings. Och, didn't you have to pay a price for everything?

Yet she gave me five more minutes of gentle caresses before it was time to get down to business. Then she bounded off the couch on which I had taken her and threw on her pale green robe. She folded her suit and her lingerie in a neat little pile on my desk.

"They'll be after coming back in forty-five minutes," she said, nodding in the direction of the parish school across the street. "I'd like to continue this for the rest of the day, but . . ."

"But," I said, getting off the couch but not exactly bounding, "we can continue these amusements tonight."

She blushed again.

"Ever since I brought that clone of yours into the world, I've been a pushover for you, Dermot Michael Coyne."

" 'Tis the other way around, woman."

"Tell me what you learned this afternoon." She turned into her schoolmarm persona.

Me wife has a couple of dozen different personae, from one to the other of which she moves with the speed of light—this time from the sexual playmate to the serious scholar. I couldn't move that fast, even among my far more limited repertory of masks. So I had to look away from her green robe and disarrayed hair and concentrate on me . . . my notes.

"It was only one war," I began. "It started in 1914 and ended in 1945, with a twenty-year intermission. Germany against England and France— and Russia. Germany started it and then restarted it. The Austrians used the assassination of Franz Ferdinand and his wife as an excuse to slap Serbia down. The Germans thought it provided an excellent excuse to try out their plan for mobilization of their armed forces, a plan which predicted that on M Day plus thirty they would be in Paris. Such was their contempt for the military ability of the French that they saw no reason to take them into account. Get your troops on the trains, send them to the front, push across Belgium, and that was that. They had beaten up the French forty-four years before and figured that there was no reason why they couldn't do it again. Both they and the Austrians were convinced that the war would be over in two months, regardless of what the Russians did. To put frosting on their cake, an outnumbered German army in East Prussia wiped out the Russian forces."

"It wasn't a short war, was it?"

"Not at all. They almost made it to Paris but were stopped by the French at the Marne River on M+30. The Germans pulled back, both sides dug trenches and the war settled into bloody attrition for the next three and a half years. In January of 1915, the German chief of staff, one Erich von Falkenhayn, went to the Chancellor, a certain Bethmann-Hollweg, and told him that the war had settled into a stalemate and that Germany should seek some kind of peace deal to prevent the slaughter of its young men. At that point, Nuala Anne, you see what had happened. They hadn't won their quick victory, the military knew it, and wanted to end the slaughter. The Chancellor said that such a deal would embarrass the Kaiser and the war must go on. Thus sealing a death warrant on a whole generation of French, German, and English soldiers."

"Wars being easier to start than to end?"

"That's the overriding lesson of this Thirty-One-Years war. To the point of our investigation, there were many attempts to end it, but finally the one that worked was the destruction of Germany in the spring of 1945."

"But these other attempts might have worked?"

"Most made excellent sense, but no one had the intelligence or the courage to combat the war fever and the patriotism and the desire for vengeance."

"Dermot Michael Coyne," she interrupted me, "stop leering at me like an eejit and get on with the work."

"Sure, woman, I'm doing the best I can, but it isn't that easy with someone like you in me classroom."

She blushed, covered her face with her hands and doubled over.

"Isn't that a grand compliment altogether and meself an onchuck for not being flattered."

She drew her green robe more closely together and held it at the collar, a frivolous precaution against my admiring eyes.

"By 1918," I went on with some effort, "none of the three armies were capable of going on with the war. There were not enough young men to throw into one more big battle. Then the situation changed when Woodrow Wilson found an excuse to involve the United States in a war that at that point was none of our business. That meant millions of more young men to feed into the machine guns and the poison gas and the artillery shells. The Germans tried one more massive offensive, reached the Marne again, and were turned back again. They retreated and the retreat was almost a rout. The German people were rioting. The General Staff insisted on an armistice. The Kaiser abdicated, and the shooting stopped. Though the English and the French would never admit it, the United States had saved them, not for the last time."

"How many million dead?"

"Fifteen anyway."

"And the Kaiser was embarrassed anyway!"

"The German, Austrian, and Russian Empires were destroyed and the British Empire fatally weakened. The Communists took over Russia. And nothing had been settled, at all, at all. Except the establishment of an Irish Free State and some artificial nations like Yugoslavia and Czechoslovakia and the reestablishment of some old countries like Poland and Lithuania."

"And didn't the Irish set about killing one another and then half a dozen years later, didn't de Valera settle for what he could have had without the Civil War? Och, aren't we humans terribly daft?"

"The French and to some extent the English wanted revenge. At Versailles, they imposed a harsh treaty on the Germans and Mr. Wilson, not in good health by then, was unable to stop them. He hoped that the League of Nations would prevent more war, as naïve a notion as you could imagine. The United States gained absolutely nothing from the war. The Germans sulked and their anger increased as their economy collapsed. A decade later Hitler came to power and Stalin was in control of Russia. The two most powerful countries in Europe were now led by madmen, brilliant madmen perhaps, but still off-the-wall insane."

"All because the Germans had wanted to test their mobilization plan?"

"All because they wanted to demonstrate how brilliant was their military planning. Does that sound like another nation today?"

Nuala rose from her chair, leaned over me without any regard for the parting of her robe, and kissed me fervently.

"And all those poor kids who were killed had wives and maybe kids of their own. I don't want you in any eejit war like, do you hear me now, Dermot Michael Coyne?"

"Woman, I do."

Large paws scratched at both doors.

" 'Tis themselves. Sure, I'd better be collecting the kids."

I looked out the window. No sign of kids piling out of St. Josephat's. But the doggies knew it was time to cross the street and collect them. Me wife dressed quickly, a ritual that I enjoyed as much as watching her undress. She opened the door to our bedroom, placed the green robe on a chair, and emerged with Maeve in tow.

"Would you see to himself, Dermot love?"

"I will."

I watched the ritual as Nuala with the two huge white dogs on leashes, walking docilely at her sides, crossed Sheffield and waited for Nelliecoyne and Micky—no raincoat for the Galway woman on a soft day. Her light blue suit—the perfect color for turning heads on Michigan Avenue—was a beam of radiance in the schoolyard. A horde of kids rushed up to play with the hounds. Then, waiting for the approval of the crossing guards, dreadfully serious sixth-grade girls, my entourage crossed the streets. I collected my clone, who would have rather continued his nap but who laughed happily when he heard his siblings tramp into the house.

"One more thing, young man. I've known her for almost twelve years and slept with her for almost ten years and I haven't begun to figure her out. Maybe I should turn our conversation into a poem and send it to *Poetry*."

— 2 —

ME WIFE solves mysteries. There's some dispute whether she or the little Archbishop down at the Cathedral are the better detective. Both claim that the other is. Nuala, however, is fey. She sees things. Like battles being fought at Fort Dearborn almost two centuries ago. And the Haymarket Riot. And the dead bodies of the Union soldiers floating into Lake Michigan where Lincoln Park is today. And an airplane crashing into the Lake. And an old man trying to punish his son for happiness that was stolen from him. And like the burning of a manor house outside of Limerick in 1920.

I knew what I was getting into when I married her. Hadn't she pointed out to me that the grave next to my beloved grandparents was empty? But, such was my infatuation with her, that I didn't much care. I still don't, though sometimes the detecting puts extra burdens on me since I'm her Dr. Watson, a useful spear carrier and research assistant.

My family will tell you that I don't work for a living. The implication is that I live off Nuala's success as a singer of popular and standard songs. That's not altogether true. After I had failed to earn degrees at the Golden Dome and Marquette, my family decided to do what similar professional class Chicago families do with a ne'er-do-well in the making. They bought me a seat on the Board of Trade, where I was an abject failure until one day, when I bought when I had meant to sell, I won almost two million dollars. I paid back my parents for the capital they had invested in me, sold my own seat, turned the cash over to the smartest investor on LaSalle Street and went on the Grand Tour of Europe, ending up in O'Neills just off the college green, where my future wife dismissed me as a "fucking rich Yank."

Even apart from her earnings, I don't have to work, which suits me just fine. I write some poetry, which gets published, and an occasional novel about a dolt married to a brilliant woman, which also gets published. But in my achievement-oriented yuppie family these successes don't count.

Anyway I got involved in the study of the history of the War because Nuala was looking for a young man from our neighborhood who disappeared in Iraq and I had found, in the archives of my brother George's parish, a manuscript about a young Irish diplomat who had disappeared in Germany in the more recent act in the Thirty-One-Years war. Such MSS were more or less expected to turn up when Nuala needed them. I don't even try to understand why.

Desmond Doolin, the lad from the neighborhood, had graduated from Marquette in 2000. I had played basketball with him at one of the neighborhood parks. He was a nice kid, a good half foot shorter than I am, but quick. Like me his family had destined him for financial services. Like me he wasn't much good at it. So he signed up for the Peace Corps and went to Eritrea of all places. He came back with shining eyes and a knowledge of Arabic and whatever it is that the Ethiopians speak. His family and his friends, almost all of them financial service gnomes, wanted him to settle down and get a job at McCormick Blair, for example. His knowledge of Arabic, they said, would make him a hot property.

Instead he enrolled at Illinois-Chicago, in Arabic and Islamic studies. He had finished all the required courses and begun his dissertation when

Mr. Bush decided to protect the United States from terrorists. Desmond called his mother, an MD at a Catholic hospital, and told her that he was going to Iraq to stop the war. That was the last anyone had heard from him.

His father was executive vice president of a very important bank and a major contributor to Republican fund-raising. Yet the Pentagon refused to provide any information. The military refused to deny that they had ever heard of him or confirm that they knew about him. The Honorable Company, as the CIA used to be called, wouldn't even return their phone calls. His mother was a Democrat with a record of generosity to good liberal causes, but she couldn't get any satisfaction from our two Democratic senators or our Democratic representatives. The State Department admitted that he had a passport but denied any knowledge of his leaving the country.

What had happened to Desmond Doolin?

The elder Doolins did not go to the media, partly because they did not want publicity and partly because they feared that media attention might endanger their son's life. So they came to see us, that is, to see Nuala Anne. We had heard vague rumors of Desmond's disappearance in the Middle East, but they seemed too flimsy to take seriously. I had said, "He's probably gone CIA."

My wife frowned but did not comment.

Then Thomas John Doolin phoned us one evening to ask if he and his wife, Grace, might visit us the following evening. I passed the phone over to me wife, excuse me, my wife. She listened, nodded sympathetically, and said that they would be most welcome.

The next day she consulted with our neighbor down the street, Commander Cindasue Lou McCloud Murphy of the Yewnited States Coast Guard, mother of Katiesue Murphy, inseparable buddy of our Socra Marie, and a wild infant son called Johnnie Pete Murphy. Cindasue was an intelligence officer for someone in the government.

Nuala returned from the Murphy house with a grim frown on her face.

"I couldn't pry anything out of her, Dermot love. That's not like Cindasue. She kept saying that she didn't know anything about Desmond Doolin and couldn't talk about him."

"The Feds have their reasons for pretending that he doesn't exist and have spread the word to all their spooks."

"Come on, Dermot Michael Coyne, Cindasue isn't a spook even if she's talking like one." My wife sighed. "She knows something all right . . . Is this frigging president of yours scaring everyone?"

"He's your president as well as mine and I didn't vote for him and I don't like him any more than you do."

"We're stuck with him, Dermot Michael, it's not friggin' right."

"We'd better watch our step, woman. The Feds might come looking for us."

She grinned in happy memory of her previous successful battles with the men in dark suits.

"Let them try it."

That evening Grace and Tom Doolin climbed the stairs of our pre-Fire house and entered through the second-floor doorway—the house, like all its neighbors having been pumped up out of the ooze, a good four feet above the level of the backyard. When they were admitted to the house, both of them—slender handsome people in their late fifties—marveled at the wonders we had worked on the old place and admired the two snow-white hounds who greeted them, as they greeted everyone who came through the door, with paws extended in friendship.

"What lovely dogs," Grace Doolin said, "so well behaved."

Having played their game, the pooches took their leave to return to the playroom to frolic with the kids.

I had no idea why this ritual was important. However, Nuala, in an elegant black dress with silver jewelry, believed firmly that it was necessary to impress new clients. Hence I wore a blazer and a shirt and tie she had selected.

ALPHA PERSON ALL RIGHT, said the voice of my Adversary, who lurked in one of the subbasements of my brain.

Could anyone seriously believe that this charming Irish countess (whose brogue became thicker every time a "client" arrived) could actually solve mysteries? Or that she was fey, blessed with what the little Archbishop called a "neo-Neanderthal" vestige which enabled her to "see" things?

"I gave a considerable sum of money to Bush's campaign," Tom Doolin began the serious conversation after I had poured each of them a "splasheen" of Middleton's Special Reserve. "I regret it now, but he won't even talk to me about Desmond. I'm sure they know something. I don't think they give a damn."

"Never trust a politician who won't let you pick up a marker," I remarked with the solemnity of a Hindu wise man.

"I think they have him in one of those horrible detention centers," Grace Doolin added, "that we've been reading about in the papers. If we knew which one it is, our lawyers could go into court and seek a writ of habeas corpus. They have been warned by federal agents not to do that, but we've learned in recent years not to trust federal agents, haven't we?"

"The men in dark suits," I murmured.

"Which federal agents warned your lawyers?" Nuala asked.

"They claim to work for the government, but they didn't say which agency."

"Sounds like the CIA to me!" Tom said, struggling to keep his temper.

"If he isn't in one of their prisons," Grace said, dabbing at her eyes with a tissue, "then he may be working for them. If only they would tell us that."

"And," Tom joined in, "he may be dead. Sometimes we are convinced that he is dead and that we will never know what happened to him. So many people have died over there. Who would notice if a roadside bomb blew up one more idealistic and naïve American boy."

Poor people, I thought to myself. Nice, hardworking, churchgoing, successful Americans, products of a world where your lawyers and your doctors and your priests could be expected to protect you from disorder and confusion and crime—so long as you lived in the right neighborhoods. They could not comprehend the utter and absolute fragility of all of us, whether it be the men and women in the World Trade Center or riders on English buses or Jordanians at a wedding party. Those things didn't happen in our neighborhoods.

"Would you ever mind telling me about Desmond?" Nuala asked in a tone of gentle compassion. "Me husband played basketball with him once or twice, but we'd like to hear about him from you."

The couple glanced at one another and Grace began.

"He was an ordinary young American Catholic. He went to SS Faith, Hope, and Charity grammar school up in Winnetka, Loyola Academy, and then Marquette. He was barely five feet ten, the shortest of our three kids, bright and a great reader, but I'm afraid he didn't take his academic responsibilities seriously . . ."

"He didn't take anything seriously," Tom Doolin cut in. "He could have played varsity sports in high school, track anyway. He could have made the dean's list. He could have gone to summer school. He could have worked as an intern in any of a dozen financial services firms. BORING! was his favorite word. He didn't want to grow up."

I resisted the impulse to say that every male was entitled to a Peter Pan interlude and I had one too. That would leave open the question of whether I had ever grown out of mine.

Grace passed two graduation pictures of her son to me—one in academic robe and hat and the other in blazer and slacks. Typical financial services kid with a wonderful Irish grin . . . Not a hint as far as I could see of craziness. I handed them over to Nuala.

"Sure, doesn't he have the glint in his eye?" she said with some surprise.

"The glint?" Tom asked. "What do you mean by that, Mrs. Coyne?"

"Mrs. Coyne is me mother-in-law. I'm Nuala Anne . . . He was an impish little lad, wasn't he?"

Grace laughed, with a tone of pain and sorrow in her voice.

"It was so long ago that he was a little boy that I forgot that we always called him our little leprechaun. Even Conor and Jenny laughed at him, though sometimes he drove them crazy with his jokes and his silly tricks and riddles."

"Sure, and of course he grew out of that phase, didn't he now?"

Tom leaned forward and rested his elbows on his knees, forming a tent of fingers under his chin.

"I'm not sure he ever did. Shovie, the girl he dated, told us often how he could keep a whole crowd of drinkers sober because they were laughing at his silly stories."

"One of them kind, was he now . . . Was it serious between him and Shovie?"

"Her real name was Siobhan, of course . . . We hoped it was serious because we thought she might settle him down. On the other hand, as Tom often said, she just encouraged him to be goofy. She urged him to join the Peace Corps after we had bought him a seat on CBOT."

"Remember, Tommy, when we visited him in Eritrea? He was telling his stories in three different languages and everyone was laughing. He was teaching them English and supervising a clean water project. They all adored him. You even said he was kind of like a priest for those handsome black people—and most of them Catholics too . . ."

"The most vile place on the face of the earth," Tom responded. "Hunger, poverty, disease, misery, everyone speaking their own language and an economy ruined by stupid civil war. We flew from Frankfurt to Addis Abba on an old DC-8 and then up to Asmara on an older DC-4. The stench was terrible even before we left the plane. And there was our son, in jeans and a Marquette tee shirt, having the time of his life."

"I thought of that short story we had to read in college," his wife added, "*The Darkness of the Heart,* the one about Mr. Kurtz. I wondered if our Desmond was Mr. Kurtz for these people."

Heart of Darkness by Joseph Conrad. I restrained my correction because it was worthy only of a prig. Anyway, Desmond Doolin sounded like the exact opposite of Mr. Kurtz.

"And more Catholic Churches than there ought to be," her husband protested. "I thought there was just one Catholic Church, the Roman Catholic Church. In Eritrea there are Egyptian and Greek and Ethiopian and Roman Catholic Churches and no one seems to be able to tell the difference. I can't understand why the Pope tolerates such stuff!"

Probably because Catholic means here comes everyone.

"And whatever their language or religion, they all loved our poor Desmond. He wouldn't translate some of the nice things they said about him."

"Did he break up with this young woman," I asked, "when he came home from the Horn of Africa?"

They both were silent for a moment.

"I don't think they actually broke up," Grace replied. "It was hard to tell. He enrolled in the Arabic program at UIC and she had a fellowship out at Creighton in psychology. I think they saw each other occasionally. He was always very mysterious about her."

"He would be now, wouldn't he?" Nuala said.

My wife sniffed something.

"Did he call her before he left for Iraq?"

"We've never asked her," Tom said sorrowfully. "He didn't even talk to us. He called the house. Had a quick conversation with my older son and said he was off to Iraq in the name of peace. That was the last thing we heard from him. We know he flew from Chicago to Frankfurt on American and then on to Dubai on their airline. Then he disappeared into the desert sand."

"Did he tell his brother that he would be back?"

They were both quiet for a couple of moments.

"Our sons were not close to one another," Grace finally replied. "But there was no animosity between them either. They were so different from one another. Conor of course tried to talk him out of it, but he said that Desmond was being his usual goofy self. He thinks his last words were something like 'If I don't see you, I'll see you.'"

"Typical goofiness," his father said, shaking his head.

Poor guy. He'd been a good father. He didn't understand. Just like my family never understood me, though I was not as much an amadán as Desmond was.

"He was very interested in Islam and Arabic?" I said, a foolish question I realized as soon as I asked him.

"He went up and down Lawrence Avenue," his father told us, "talking to every Arab shopkeeper he could find and made friends with a lot of their clergy, imams or whatever they call them."

"But he never became a Muslim, did he now?" me wife said, a statement more than a question.

"We became worried about that," Grace admitted. "He thought that was very funny. 'Mom, he said, I'm an Irish Catholic from Chicago. How could I convert to Islam?'"

"That would be the kind of thing he would say," Nuala nodded wisely.

"Do you think he's alive, Nuala Anne?" Grace was crying again.

Me wife sighed her loudest Connemara sigh.

"I don't know, Grace. There's too much that's still a mystery. I don't want to raise your hopes when there's all that mystery. All I can say is that I wouldn't be surprised if he were."

That was a big leap beyond the evidence for our Nuala Anne.

After they had left, grateful for our time and interest and encouragement, me wife and I sat silently in our parlor (or "living room" as she calls it). The Doolins promised that their son and daughter would talk to us and that they would ask Desmond's best friend Ryan Dorsey and Shovie and the Newman chaplain at UIC to call us.

"Do you think they'll call us?" I asked finally.

"Give over, Dermot Michael! Of course they'll call. Young master Desmond is the kind of person about whom people love to talk."

"One of those with the glint in his eye, like meself?"

"Och, you have a couple of glints, Dermot love, especially when you look at me and doesn't it embarrass me something terrible. 'Tis the other glint that I'm talking about."

"Is it now?"

"'Tis, and those poor good people don't really understand him, do they now?"

"I know the experience," I said.

"Indeed you do and your family still not quite understanding what you are, but then, if they did understand you, you wouldn't have gone to Ireland seeking an innocent Irish virgin to bed, would you now?"

"I thought the said Irish virgin was looking for a focking rich Yank!"

She bounded across the room and cuddled up next to me on the couch.

"Well, I was the winner, wasn't I now?"

"I never had a chance," I replied as I tightened my arm around her.

"Sure, doesn't your family have enough sense of humor to laugh at you? Those poor folks are humorless altogether."

"I was surprised that you encouraged them to believe their son is still alive."

"Were you now? I wouldn't be sure that he wasn't still alive, Dermot love . . . And whatever are you doing now!"

"I think I'm feeling up your thigh."

"And the childer still playing downstairs and Ethne and Brendan playing with them!"

Ethne was our nanny and Brendan, a rich young artist with whom she was keeping company.

"I wasn't planning an immediate assault on your matronly virtue."

"I'm glad to hear that," she said with considerable insincerity.

"You think he's alive?"

"Wouldn't it be just like one of them kind to be alive and well?"

"One of your fellas with a glint in his eye?"

"Just so . . . it's hard on his family, but I couldn't help thinking that they'll be so happy when he comes back they won't mind . . . and that's true enough though they'll never understand why he did whatever he did in the first place, will they?"

She rested her hand on my knee.

AH THERE'LL BE SCREWING TONIGHT. THE WOMAN IS GETTING WORSE.

She's not. She's just more confident in herself.

Laughter.

In truth, however, herself was acting more confident and aggressive in every aspect of her complicated life. Perhaps even pushy. She would never before have suggested to anyone that their missing child might be alive and well and stirring up trouble somewhere in the Middle East. Now I was the one who had to return to the subject we were supposed to be talking about.

AND YOURSELF STARTING THE GAME!

"We have to find out where he is first," I said.

"Ah, no, Dermot Michael. First off we must find out why he went there."

There was a roar and the thunder of footsteps from downstairs—the "childer" coming up, either to demand adjudication of a conflict or to present something of which we must be proud.

We drew discreetly apart.

Fortunately it was the latter.

Nelliecoyne took command of the situation, as she usually did.

"We've learned to sing 'Lord of the Dance,'" she announced. "And we call ourselves the Coyne Chorale—that's alliteration!"

She produced a pitch pipe, set the key, and they began to sing. Herself and Micky were in perfect tone. Socra Marie made up for her inability to harmonize with her vigorous enthusiasm. Nelliecoyne swayed the grinning babe in tune with the music. The dogs sat on their haunches and listened attentively. Brendan and Ethne beamed proudly. There would be a lot more family theatricals in the years ahead.

We applauded enthusiastically. The pooches barked. Nuala hugged and kissed everyone.

The noise did not prevent Patjo from falling sound asleep.

"Should I put himself to bed, Ma?" Nelliecoyne asked.

"That would be lovely, dear. You could even sing a couple of lullabies for him. Doesn't he like them something terrible?"

"Cool!"

"Don't I see a little girl and herself looking pretty sleepy too," me wife observed.

"No!"

"I'll tell you a story," Ethne promised.

"Cool!"

"And I'll sing a lullaby for you," the Mick added.

"Isn't himself becoming domestic?" Nuala demanded when the horde had disappeared, save for the two dogs, who had decided to curl up and keep us company.

We talked for another hour about Desmond Doolin.

"I wonder if he kept a journal?" I asked.

"Of course he did, but we'll never find it unless the young woman knows where it is."

"Shovie?"

"In this house," me wife insisted primly, "we don't use nicknames. We'll call her Siobhan."

"As I remember our resident music director is called Nellie."

"Sure, if we called her Mary Anne outside of school, she wouldn't know who that was."

That settled that. No points for you, Dermot Coyne.

"Do you remember, Dermot, that journal we found over at His Riverence's church by the Irish diplomat that disappeared during the war?"

"Vaguely."

George the Priest, my brother, was always His Riverence. The Cardinal of Chicago was simply Cardinal Sean. The coadjutor Archbishop was simply Blackie. But my brother, so far devoid of either purple or crimson, was treated with more respect than either of them.

"I'd wager that he had the glint in his eye too."

"Even in that unpredictable land of your origins, my love, they don't make people with the glint into diplomats."

"'Tis true, but he was some kind of English lord, wasn't he?"

"Lord Ridgeland, as I remember."

"That might overcome the glint . . . Would you ever go over to them archives of his tomorrow morning and see if we can have a look at it. Maybe it will give us some insight into that kind of person."

For some reason that I never fully divined I was always given that assignment.

— 3 —

"THE WITCH stirring up another one of her pots?" Prester George asked as we walked down to the basement of his little old church on North Park Avenue.

"We're interested these days in the psychology of men with the glint in their eyes."

"The Holy Madman?"

"Something like that."

"Francis and Philip Neri and that bunch?"

"Arguably."

"You sound like our Most Reverend coadjutor Archbishop . . . Does he have the glint?"

"Herself has never suggested that."

He opened the door to a small, dusty, dimly lit room in which piles of manuscripts were neatly stacked.

"I'll have to get these all archived at the historical society someday. At least we have them indexed."

"Because herself insisted."

"And paid for it, God bless her . . . I can't figure out how they help her in her searches, but what do I know . . . Here is the one by Lord Ridgeland. As far as I can tell, no one has ever told his story."

Unlike the other manuscripts we had rescued from this center, this one was neatly typed, though by an old-fashioned typewriter. The label on the black, loose-leaf cover announced "Some reminiscences of Timothy Patrick Clarke, Lord Ridgeland, of the Second World War."

Timothy Patrick Clarke, an odd name for a laird, but there were Catholic lords in both England and Ireland. "Ridgeland" suggested Northern Ireland. A Catholic remnant of the old Ascendancy? Not completely impossible.

I opened the binder. Before the first page someone had included two pictures of Milord Ridgeland, one where he was wearing what had to be the Oxford Blues, the other of the same young man, a year or two younger perhaps, with a hurling stick, in a green-and-white outfit. He played both Irish and English sports, did he now?

In both pictures his face was solemn and serious, game faces as we'd call them today. I would not want to face the hook of his hurling stick. The eyes? Ah, the eyes!

In both his English and Irish manifestations, they glowed with mischief or perhaps with divine madness. Otherwise, he reminded me of Desmond Doolin, slender, medium-sized, dark, curly hair—an utterly harmless young man despite his dangerous stick. And his dangerous eyes.

"Is he your man?" Prester George asked.

"Looks like it," I replied. "Herself will have to judge . . . By the way, what can you tell me about religion in Eritrea?"

"I've never been there, as you well know. It was part of the great Abyssinian Empire back in the old days. It was founded by Semitic peoples who migrated across the Red Sea and united all the local tribes under one rule, long before the Romans were building an empire. The Egyptians came down the Blue Nile and were consistently beaten back. Their great emperor was a certain Aksum, who had a daughter named Sheba, who may have been the Queen of Sheba who visited King David and may have been his mistress. With the coming of Christianity, Ethiopia became Christian, part of the Church of the South, and then inclined in the direction of the Monophysite heresy which more or less denied the humanity of Jesus while the Church of the East inclined to the Nestorian heresy which denied his divinity. Both churches were intensely missionary, the Nestorians spread out from Antioch through Persia and Afghanistan, in the wake of Alexander's kingdoms and into China while the Monophysites went south into Ethiopia and what we now call the Sudan. In both cases they were out of touch with what was happening among the barbarian tribes who had inherited the remnants of the Roman Empire. Nor did they pay any attention to Byzantium, which they figured was the Church of the West. It is unlikely they even knew there was a Pope."

"Ah," I said. "Nuala said I should ask you."

Once you asked my brother something you'd better be ready to listen to the lecture, one of the few traits we have in common.

"Then along came the Arabs and Islam. They were driven back from the borders of Abyssinia about the same time that your man Karl the Hammer stopped them at Tours. Various less dangerous tribes drifted in from Africa and Arabia and the Indian Ocean, including the Eritreans who never much liked the Ethiopian emperors but more than they liked the Arabs who just kept on coming. A young emperor named John reasserted the control of the empire and drove away the Arabs once again. It is said that he was also a priest. Rumors reached Europe in the twelfth century about this Prester John, as they called him, and his rich and deeply cultured empire. It was said that he would come with great armies and join the Crusaders in driving the Arabs out of the Holy Land."

"He never arrived, I guess."

"He was not entirely a legend. Art and religion did flourish in Ethiopia in the Middle Ages. Scores of monasteries all over the highlands, with precious manuscripts from ancient times, including the Bible, many of which have yet to be recovered. What we have of their art is lively and creative. Eventually the culture waned, but religion—their version of Christianity—survives even to this day. The Jesuits came in the sixteenth and seventeenth centuries and tried the same game that they played in India and Japan, enculturating themselves into Ethiopian culture just as Ricci did in China and deNobili did in India. It didn't take there, and the Dominicans, who had more clout in the Vatican than the Jebs, eventually snuffed it out."

"Too bad!"

"Indeed, yes . . . Then came the colonizers in the late nineteenth and early twentieth centuries. Ethiopia lucked out and got the Italians, who were, as in other matters, the least efficient of all. They annexed the Eritrean north, whose people were only too happy to be rid of the Ethiopians. Then they took over Somalia, which was the southern part of the country and mostly Muslim. Finally, in the nineteen thirties, they took over the whole country and proclaimed the king of Italy as emperor of Abyssinia, which in retrospect was high comedy. The Brits drove them out during World War II and restored the emperor. The local Socialists drove him out and established their own version of the Soviet Union. Eritrea seceded again and established its own Marxist regime. They fought a bitter war which left Eritrea free and Cuban troops, of all people, in place in Addis Abba. More recently they both have typical African governments, relatively democratic, incompetent, corrupt, and unable to deal with the periodic famines. Sad end to three thousand years or so of history. Yet Christianity in its variant competing forms still survives. When you hear Third World poverty, think not of Nigeria wasting all its oil income but of Eritrea and Ethiopia, without any income to waste and still willing to go back to war about their border disputes . . . Can you remember all of that, Dermot? I wouldn't want you to provide any inaccurate information to herself."

"I'll take notes in the car, before I drive home."

I wasn't about to tell him that I had a photographic memory and could rehearse his lecture verbatim to my good wife.

"I don't know"—he sighed—"how Prester John and Lord Ridgeland fit together."

"They both had the glint in their eyes," I said.

Meanwhile back at the ranch, that is the headquarters of Nuala Anne McGrail, Inc., on Sheffield Avenue, I found that worthy woman, dressed in dark brown slacks and light brown blouse (and gold jewelry), sitting at the desk in her workroom (as distinguished from my office) poring over computer output. She was wearing her glasses, which meant this was very serious business.

I kissed the back of her neck.

"'Tis yourself," she noted. "I'm trying to think . . . How is His Riverence keeping?"

"He's in grand form."

"Putting on weight."

"Woman, he is not!"

"And himself without a wife to keep an eye on his diet."

"Are we going somewhere?"

"We are. Your man over at UIC is too busy saving the souls of the young to come to our house, so we have to see him at two this afternoon . . . Danuta is bringing up some Irish tea and bean soup and Polish salad for our lunch."

Polish salad!

"No ice cream?"

"It's Wednesday."

That settled that. She didn't look up from her papers.

"Does he know who you are?"

"I spoke with his associate, a woman, a former mother superior I should think."

"She was rude to you?" I demanded with unfeigned outrage.

"She said I would have to wait three weeks for an appointment so I called Cardinal Sean. Chicago is a city that understands clout, isn't it, Dermot love? Just like you always say?"

She looked up from her papers and winked at me.

YOU'VE CREATED A MONSTER, DOCTOR FRANKENSTEIN!

"Did the good young priest tell you much about this mess in Ethiopia?"

"A bit."

"Well, sit down and tell me about it! You don't have to stand up just because I have clout with Cardinal Sean, do you now?"

I sat down and recited almost verbatim my brother's lecture about Prester John and the monasteries with priceless manuscripts and these handsome dark folk who had fought off the Egyptians and the Arabs and the Turks and the Eye-talians and the Jesuits and now were almost starving to death all the time.

"'Tis the same thing with your Chaldees or Assyrians or whatever you want to call them, only now they're getting gassed by your man and blown up by suicide bombers but have made peace with the Pope after fifteen hundred years, give or take. Just the kind of place that a daft idealist would have a grand time altogether!"

"We're getting to know him better?"

"Better than his parents anyway . . . Did you remember to pick up the manuscript of Lord Ledgermain or whatever he was called?"

"Woman, I did."

"Lemme see it!"

I passed over the loose-leaf binder. She flipped open the cover.

"Brigid, Patrick, and Colmcille and all the Holy saints of Ireland!" she exclaimed in wonderment. "Would you ever look at him, Dermot Michael Coyne!"

"I have already. Even I recognized the glint."

Why there always were connections between her games and the manuscripts in the archives at old Immaculate Conception Church (on North Park, as you had to say in Chicago because there are so many parishes with the same name) remained a mystery to me, one which I did not want to explore. Danuta arrived with our Polish lunch—bean soup, Polish potato salad, and iced Irish Breakfast Tea.

"Ethnic lunch," she said. "Eat!"

"Good stuff," I said. "But ice cream would have fewer calories."

"Och, haven't you been getting enough exercise lately that it shouldn't be any problem at all, at all! Eat letcha!"

"Letcha" is not a food, but another one of them, er, those tricky Irish subjunctives, I suppose one of polite command. It stands for "let you eat" and does not suppose that you are not eating.

She destroyed her lunch despite my warning that she would give a bad example to the childer if she kept on eating that fast.

"Well, you're not eating for two and a half, are you now?"

She went off to feed the other one and a half and put him to bed. Socra Marie was already deep in her energy-renewing nap. For my part, I turned to the memoirs of Timothy Patrick Clarke, Lord Ridgeland.

When I say that I am a marginal man, I am not complaining. I've been on the fringes for my whole life and have learned that you accomplish a lot more if you're not tied down by the ordinary boundaries and restraints. The uncertainties increase, of course, but so do the opportunities — and little time is often available to consider the various opportunities in the detail that one would wish.

This pompous observation is an attempt to explain to whoever might read these notes that I am not totally mad. If you happen to be an Irish Catholic lord in County Down, the most Protestant part of Ireland, it is assumed that you act a little mad and even enjoy the shock your actions create. To put a finer edge on the matter, oftentimes you don't really give a damn what people say or think and on the contrary rather enjoy the dismay you have created.

That's how I became the Irish ambassador to Germany during the war and in fact a spy for the English government and how I was involved with the efforts of the German resistance to kill Hitler and end the war.

In any event I was born in 1910. My father was the thirteenth Lord Ridgeland and, I believe, the fourth Roman Catholic to hold the seat. He took it, if the legends are true, by main force from his Protestant brother whose behaviour towards our tenants shocked even the most ruthless of the local gentry. Perhaps because our historic seat was on the border of a solidly Catholic county in what would later become the Republic of Ireland, the gentry were not greatly concerned with the man on the fringes.

If the boundary commission's definition of "Northern Ireland" had been less a farce and the resulting rump state had been at least half-Catholic, my father would have been a great man in Irish history. He had the will and the wit, the brains and the brawn, the intelligence and the industry to have created a tiny state that was not owned by the Orange Order and then combined the two segments of Ireland into a strong—and much more tolerant and even liberal—new nation. As it was, there was no opportunity to play that game. He washed his hands of the Protestant leadership after warning them that they would eventually lose to the gunmen from the south who, he said, "Are as hard as you are and much more creative."

That was my father. They didn't understand what he was talking about of course. He turned his attention to modernizing our linen mills, providing wages which the emerging Labour Party would not have believed possible, and playing the role of a slightly daft but brilliant lord of the manor. During the Great War he had commanded the Royal Irish Fusiliers with ingenuity and courage. Then when Dougie Haig, as he always called him, sent most of that distinguished regiment to the world to come, he handed in his resignation papers to the War Office and returned to Ireland. What do you do to a nobleman and a brilliant leader who quits because he says his commanding officer is a butcher?

You don't do anything to him.

As Winston Churchill said in my presence, probably in 1923, "James, if we had made you viceroy here—as I strongly argued we should—none of the troubles would have happened and we would have had a nice little dual monarchy here on this glorious island."

"Winston," James Joseph Clarke, Lord Ridgeland—tall, strong and with flaming red hair—said with a sigh he had learned from his Black Irish Galway wife, "you're often mistaken about this glorious island as you call it and not without some reason. On that matter, however, you are absolutely right, but not because I'm not an idiot, but because the men you and that damnable Welsh bastard sent over here are worse idiots than I am."

That's how we would speak in the House of Lords on the few occasions when he deigned to enter that "coven of fools, fags, and fakirs."

He got away with such outrageous comments because such were almost expected from the Irish lairds, especially if they happened to be Catholic. I was taking it all in, of course, not consciously learning, but absorbing.

My mother, a black-haired beautiful Galway woman, was certainly fey, and probably a witch of some sort. But she was a warm, passionate person of whom the neighbours said that she laughed far too much ever to be considered a Lady. However, my mother, the good Lady Ridgeland, was smarter than all of them put together, smarter even than His Lordship as the latter was eager to admit.

I need not say that I had a happy childhood in such an environment. My four younger siblings were not from the same bolt of Irish linen. As the oldest I was the most responsible and the most cautious. I would warn the reader that I caught up with them after I turned thirty.

I was sent off to Congreves in Dublin to study with the Jesuits, and was there on Easter Monday 1916, having just returned from the Easter Holiday. The people of Dublin were furious at the eejits who had tied up the streets and made it unsafe to walk around the center of the city for several days. They also resented the cannonading of the English gunboats in the Liffey. Destroyin' the Easter peace, they complained. The Jesuits were unanimous in their disdain for "dreamers and gombeen men" with guns.

So the English tried these silly fools for treason and decided to execute them, a typical mistake the English always make here. My father argued mightily that this would enflame the country. Lloyd George said that we could not tolerate treason (a tune he would change later). So they were all shot. James Connolly propped up on chair because his legs had been broken in the battle. At Westminster, Lord Ridgeland thundered that they had turned a minor incident into a war that would never end.

When I left Congreves the war in Europe was over and me Old Fella thought not so much that I needed Oxford as he said but that Oxford needed me. I was the first in our clan to go there instead of Trinity. Again I was the odd man out, nobility of course, but Irish and Catholic and curiously quiet about the "troubles" in the South. Because I was the son of my mother and father and hence what the former calls a "shite-kicker" I would introduce myself as Viscount Ridgewood, sometimes adding "of Ridgeland" as if to distinguish myself from other Viscounts Ridgewood that might be around somewhere. My friends were content with "Timothy" or even "Timmy Pat."

I liked Oxford. No one made you study. You worked with your tutors, went to a few lectures, and studied occasionally for exams. It did not take me long to figure out how to charm everyone I needed to charm. I "read" European his-

tory which was a pleasure and drank very little. I was polite to the young
women who were about, but wasn't ready to be involved, an Irish bachelor in
the making. I answered foolish questions about my life plans by murmuring
"foreign office" or "diplomatic service" or even "MI 5."

"Which diplomatic service?" someone asked, a recruiter it later developed.

"Why not both?" I said. "The Free State grants citizenship to everyone on
the island."

"Even to a British laird?"

"The question does not arise."

On that issue I had, however, made up my mind. I might be a British Lord
but I was also Irish. I was not Free Stater exactly, but neither was I on the side
of the "Irregulars" who were foolishly trying to destroy the Free State. However, I would certainly embrace the role of a citizen of the "nation once again."

I read Modern European History—which meant after 1700—and wrote
my paper on the cooperation between England and German states after 1750.
I had the vague notion that despite the folly of the Great War the two "Anglo-
Saxon" nations were natural allies and that the English and the French were
natural enemies. I don't remember as I write these notes what I meant by "natural." I do know, however, that an alliance with France meant that we would
have to pick up the pieces whenever the French Humpty Dumpty fell off the
wall. I managed to gather a "first" despite the indifferent quality of my efforts.
My father expressed some disapproval of that achievement. "Sure aren't you
disgracing the family by doing so well."

Ireland was a political mess then. The boundary commission had created a
rump state which it called Northern Ireland whose boundaries were drawn in
such a way that it would be dominated by the Protestants and their Orange Order. It accomplished this miracle by excluding three of the nine counties of historic Ulster and thus imposed on the island a conflict that goes on even as I
write these words. In the Free State the bitterness created by the civil war continued, though in 1927 de Valera had taken the oath to the king and entered the
Dail as we called our new parliament.

"That man will be Ireland to the world for the next thirty years," my Old
Fella insisted. "And himself looking like a fucking bishop . . . If only they

hadn't killed Mick Collins, we would have become one of the most important countries in Europe."

My mother sighed loudly, as she often did at the folly of men and especially when they were politicians.

When he had read my thesis, the Old Fella was impressed.

"Damn good stuff. Where would England be without the Prussians or the Hessians? What would Jack Churchill have done without the Austrians or Art Wellesley without the fucking Prussians?"

The Dukes of Marlborough and Wellington were always discussed as if they were still alive and our neighbours.

One was not expected to answer such questions.

"You gotta understand," he went on, "that not all Germans are real Germans."

"Ah," I said.

"They only put the country together fifty years ago. The Prussians have been running it ever since. Their General Staff, which almost won the Great War, are not your typical Germans. You go to a place like Bonn or Cologne or into the Black Forest and you'll find a much different kind of man."

"How so?"

"Converted by Irish Catholic monks! I spent some time at Heidelberg before I fell in with this Galway woman. You learn the language, observe how they're recovering from defeat, keep an eye on the politics, you'll come back with a much broader understanding of our former enemies."

"To what purpose?"

"They'll be back. They don't believe they really lost the war. They'll want revenge. The Bolshies will try to take over the country, like they almost did in 1918. And so will people like Mussolini. That madman in the brown shirt who staged a make-believe Putsch in Munich last year is insane but brilliant in his own way. There'll be another war, or maybe only a continuation of the last one."

"The Irish will sit it out this time."

"I hope to God they will," my mother agreed. "And I don't want you to be in it, you hear, Timmy Pat."

I promised that I would not. I didn't stay out of it, but I played a very strange role.

Anyway, Heidelberg sounded like fun. Why not. I was in no rush to "settle down," whatever that means. So off I went. And changed my life irrevocably.

— 4 —

"ISN'T THERE a parking place in the next block below?" my wife suggested.

You must understand that, while my wife uses more interrogative sentences than declarative, she is often not asking questions but giving instructions. Also that her "th" sounds are spoken as though they are "T" or perhaps "D." As in "Isn't dere a parking place in da the next block below." Finally, on matters like parking places she is never in either doubt or error.

Nor is that, as far as I can tell, a result of her devotion to St. Anthony. The good patron of lost causes is not involved in her "intuitions"—for lack of a better word. She simply knew where the empty space was. "Why would I ever bother the poor man when I already know where the parking place is?"

We had driven around several blocks in the area near the University of Illinois at Chicago—an aggressively ugly modern campus—and even found the Newman Center, which looked much like a modern Catholic rectory, grim and tasteless. We were driving in my car, an ancient but re-silient Benz (herself's car is a massive Lincoln Navigator SUV). I was at the wheel which was an unusual event. No matter which car we might be in, Nuala Anne was almost always at the wheel, because as she asserted, "I'm a much better driver than you, Dermot Michael Coyne, and yourself teaching me how to be a safe driver."

My wife was still fuming about her initial conversation with Father O'Halloran, the director of the Newman Club. At first, through his as-sistant, he had refused to meet with her at all, at all. He was too busy with his responsibilities, the woman had told him. So Nuala had called the Cardinal. Shortly thereafter the assistant had phoned her.

"And wasn't she the snippy one? And didn't she say that we should let the dead bury their dead? Fine Catholics they are!"

The door to the Newman Center was locked and we had to push the doorbell. After the kind of long wait that one normally endures at a Catholic rectory, a dour woman in her late twenties opened the door and regarded us suspiciously.

"Ms. McGrail to see Father O'Halloran," my wife said tersely.

"The Cardinal only mentioned one visitor."

"Me husband drove me over."

"Can't he wait in the car?"

"No!"

We were ushered into a barren office with a desk and three chairs. Out-side the single (dirty) window the cloudy sky seemed to threaten snow, though it was April and too warm for snow. Indian summer was years ago. We waited a half hour after our assigned two o'clock appointment.

"Isn't the place swarmin' with unruly galoots?" Nuala demanded. "And themselves taking up all your man's time?"

"Most kids are probably in class now."

"Or riding home on your CART," she sniffed.

The Dublin rapid transit is called the DART, Dublin Area Rapid Transit, so the Chicago system should be called the CART, right?

Finally, we were shown into Father's office with the courtesy deserved

by someone with an infectious disease. I could tell that Nuala was working up a head of steam.

The director was a tall, broad-shouldered man in his middle forties,
with an egg-bald head that he patted often in the course of our conversation. He wore a cassock with a sash and a biretta rested on his big oak
desk. His large, square face radiated the good health which marks a man
for whom exercise is close to an addiction. A flat screen television was
mounted on the wall. He stood up when we entered the room, sending a
whiff of something like Old Spice cologne across the room.

"Ms. McGrail," he said, not offering to shake hands, "do come in.
We're very busy around here. In fact we have more Catholic students
than any Catholic college in the state. So we're very busy protecting
them from the secularist faculty."

He sank back into his plush CEO's chair.

"A grave responsibility," my wife replied, arraying herself in one of
the folding chairs.

"Dermot Coyne," I said, forcing him to shake hands.

"Father Coyne's brother?" he replied in a tone suggesting that if I had
any sense, I would not claim that relationship.

"George is my brother," I replied, taking my place in the other folding
chair.

I noted that the bookshelves, the carpet, the drapes, the refrigerator
were appropriate for a corporate executive though one innocent of good
taste. Somewhere there was a cabinet with expensive Scotch.

"Actually," he began what seem to be well-rehearsed remarks, "there
are so many young people around here and most of them commuter students from parishes which do not exercise any pastoral care for them,
that we often find it difficult to remember them. However, God rest him,
Des was the kind of young man that is hard to forget. Frantic energy,
great charm, intensely religious, perhaps in some ways a little too intense. He certainly ran us ragged around here, but it was impossible to
say no to him. At some point we had to draw the line, especially when
we received complaints from parents of our students. You must understand, Ms. McGrail, that most of our students are ethnics of one sort or

another and first-generation college students. Their parents are deeply concerned about the secular influence on their lives here at a pagan university. So I must be sensitive to their complaints."

"I attended Trinity College," my wife said, "and I'm aware of such circumstances."

"In Washington, D.C.?" he asked.

"Ah, no. In Dublin and meself an innocent child from the rocks of Connemara. Didn't I manage to hold on to my faith, but only by receiving the Eucharist every day?"

This was a highly edited version of herself's student days.

"Des went to Mass here every day too. He appointed himself sacristan, mass server, lector and leader of song. He made himself indispensable and indeed brought many students to church with him. I feared that he might be neglecting his studies, but I gathered that he was doing very well in his field. The lecture series he established after barely giving me a hint about it was very well attended, I must say. Too well attended, as it turned out, I fear."

He did not look at either of us as he talked; rather, his face was tilted to the right and his eyes elevated towards the ceiling as though the teleprompter for his remarks was up there somewhere. He was being careful because he suspected that his every word might be repeated to the Cardinal and perhaps to Father Coyne, who was a known friend of the little coadjutor Archbishop.

"Was it now?"

"The idea was to bring in non-Catholic students from other religious traditions, permit them to talk about their faiths, and then call upon our students to ask questions. I became uneasy about these dialogues, though to give him due credit Des presided over them with great skill. Even I was fascinated by the Muslim and Buddhist and Sikh and Hindu young people and indeed by the ability of our own young people to hold their own in these discussions. Some of them, unwisely I should think, reported these discussions to their parents, and I began to receive letters. It was the fire-eaters that were the final straw."

"Fire-eaters!" me wife exclaimed with some dismay.

"Zoroastrians?" I asked.

"Persians, I think they call themselves." He looked at me as though I were a disagreeable rodent who had been allowed into his domain.

"Parsee, more likely," I said, showing off my knowledge of such things. "They use fire in their sacraments, but they don't eat it."

"Perhaps that is true, but I was inundated with parental complaints. Some people even wrote to the Pope. I had no choice but to terminate the series."

"Ahura Mazda," I went on, "is the good God of that tradition, God of light, warmth, and wisdom. He is so beyond humans that we cannot even imagine him. Fire is only a hint of what he is like. He is engaged in an almost but not quite eternal battle with Angra Mainyu, the God of evil. Mazda wins in the long term, though it is very long. They don't take converts so they were no threat to your ethnics. Much of their thinking was later appropriated by our heritage."

"Really? And I thought that a Mazda was a lightbulb or a Japanese car!"

"Ah, see how much you learned, didn't you now?"

I realized as the conversation went on that Father O'Halloran did not know who my wife was. At one point in our marriage I was astonished by how often she was recognized—and flattered. Now when people didn't recognize her, I was furious.

"I suppose so." He suppressed a yawn. "But I am responsible for the thousands of Catholic students on this campus and I must take a conservative stand on many matters to preserve their faith."

"So you stopped the series?"

"As I have said, I had no choice . . . Des went along with it and continued his religious ministry around here . . . I hardly know what else to call it. I suppose this zeal was the result of his Peace Corps experience. I have reason to believe that he continued these dialogue sessions in his own apartment over on Taylor Street. Indeed I warned him that I could hardly approve of such conversations. However, he was evasive. I was seriously considering my duty to issue a cautious warning in our bulletin. Then he disappeared on this strange venture to bring peace to Iraq. I'm told his dissertation was virtually finished. This was quite typical of poor

Des, I'm afraid. A lot of talent and charm and even zeal, but regrettably poor impulse control."

"No one here has heard anything from him?"

"Not to my knowledge," he said with some hesitation.

He paused as though to consider another revelation.

"To complete the story, I suppose I should tell you that government officials—I do not know from which agency—have visited me several times to ask about him. Different officials each time. Obviously they had some fear that he might have gone over to the other side in Iraq. I tried to reassure them that in my judgment his Catholic commitment was too strong for that. He might well try to have a friendly conversation with a suicide bomber and be blown up for his troubles, but that was as far as I could see the matter going."

"Did they think he was still alive?" Nuala demanded, ignoring the obligation of a West of Ireland person to be indirect.

"I don't know"—he shrugged—"they were most circumspect . . . I had the impression that they were perhaps collecting information about him in case he might emerge as a terrorist. I tried to explain to them that I did not find such an eventuality likely. I am convinced that he disappeared into the desert and we will never hear from him again. He was, in the final analysis, a lightweight."

Nuala Anne nodded solemnly.

"So," he continued, "I can only conclude that your quest to learn more about him is doomed to failure. I hope that you don't raise any futile hopes with his parents. They are, I believe, contemplating a donation of a badly needed new chapel for this center to honor his memory."

"I hope they do," my wife said, rising from her chair. "I'm sure he'll be here for the dedication."

He stood up too.

"That's most unlikely, Ms. McGrail."

"Are you a betting man, Father O'Halloran?"

"On occasion."

"I'll bet you a hundred dollars that he is still alive. If he doesn't return to Chicago within two years, I'll owe you that money."

His laughter, I thought, was unpleasant. But then I didn't like him.

"You have a bet, Ms. McGrail, though I would be happy to lose it."

"I've known me wife for over a decade, Father," I said. "I've never won a bet from her."

He showed us to the door of the center.

Three young women, hardly more than eighteen, pushed their way in.

"Good afternoon, Father. We're here for Mass . . . Good afternoon ma'am . . . You're NUALA ANNE . . . Are you really?"

" 'Tis meself," she admitted with a modest blush.

"Sing something for us . . . Sing the Connemara lullaby! . . . PLEASE."

"Wouldn't it be easier now if I had brought the little gossoon with me, but sure, I'll pretend he's here! Dermot love, would you ever hum along with me."

Spear carrier and accompanist!

> On the wings of the wind, o'er the dark, rolling deep
> Angels are coming to watch o'er your sleep
> Angels are coming to watch over you
> So list to the wind coming over the sea
>
> Hear the wind blow, hear the wind blow
> Lean your head over, hear the wind blow.

The youngsters joined in the repetition of the chorus.

"Will you be doing your Christmas special this year?"

"Haven't I after been agreeing to it already?"

"Can we have your autograph, PLEASE!"

She withdrew from her huge purse three CDs of her lullabies and autographed them for the delighted kids.

"Good-bye, Father," she said, as we walked down the steps. "Remember we have a bet!"

"You knew those three little groupies would be waiting!" I said, as we got into the car, herself in the driver's seat. Where she belonged.

"I did NOT, Dermot love. But wasn't I glad that they did and wasn't he a dreadfully stuffy and self-important priest altogether?"

"Scared by the kids and especially by your bet . . . Why did you make the bet?"

"Give over, Dermot Michael! I only bet when I know I'm going to win. Poor Desmond is still alive. Otherwise, why would your friends in the suits be asking questions about him? He's up to some divilment over there and they want to figure out what it is."

"So we stop worrying about him?"

"Och, Dermot Michael, don't be an amadán! Doesn't the poor lad need our help in getting out of there when he's ready to come home!"

"And how are we going to get him out?"

"We'll figure that out! I'll not be letting you go over there by yourself, do you hear me!"

"I hadn't volunteered."

"One gobshite of a hero is more than enough."

"Woman, I understand!"

— 5 —

Heidelberg was a grim place in the early nineteen thirties. So was Belfast, so was Dublin, so was London. The economies of both victors and vanquished had been throttled by the war and peace and victory. The Neckar River was still lovely. The great old ruined castle on the hill and the quaint old fifteenth-century university were down at the heels. The people were shabby and often freezing in bad weather. Wounded war veterans on crutches begged in the streets. The students in their uniforms were grim and discouraged. They still drank in the pubs and sang their songs, which reminded me of the Irish rebel songs. I guess they fought their duels, but I didn't see anyone with saber scars. The young women were worn and lonely, so many had lost their husbands and lovers in the war and looked forward to grim and unhappy lives. It was not, I reflected, all that much different from London, though Labour leader Ramsey McDonald was hardly what my Old Fella would have called a Bolshie threat. The Germans also suffered from the reparations demands imposed by the Versailles treaty, though more from the threat of the demands than the actual payments. The Yanks, who had won the war and bungled the peace treaty, went home and forgot about Europe.

Heidelberg in the thirties, as I've told my children, wasn't much like The Student Prince. It was not a good decade to be young. Yet hope and love persist among the young, no matter how foolish their hopes are and how blighted their loves will be. Conditions in Germany would improve and then become much worse, and then in the long haul when most men I knew in Heidelberg were dead, they would get much better. Why? I tell anyone who will listen to me that the reason is this time the Yanks did not go home.

So I looked out of my one room in a building overlooking the Neckar every morning and wondered about my own future. I would eventually return to the Free State, which hardly needed a diplomat who could speak fluent German and had learned a little bit about German culture. Well, I could always go back and direct the family linen business. I studied German with a private instructor, attended concerts, inspected the museums—Germans have an obsession with museums—admired the music at Sunday Mass in the old churches, listened to lectures I did not understand, and sang with the students in the pubs, as I called them. I laughed and joked with them, even though I didn't quite understand all the jokes, smiled at the barmaids and pretended I was still young. I still possessed my crazy Irish charm and once I had established that I hated the English as much as they did, I was tolerated as a strange but interesting manifestation of the lost Celtic civilization.

Heidelberg, I told myself, was like Oxford but with a language barrier.

Then one afternoon in spring I was sitting outside a Bierstube, drinking a pint (as I would call it) of their terrible German beer, wishing for a taste of Guinness, and feeling sorry for myself—as we Celts are entitled to do most of the time. A tall, handsome man with jet-black hair sat at the table, stuck out his hand, and said, "Stauffenberg, Claus."

He would turn out to be the most remarkable man I would ever meet.

"Ridgewood, Timothy Patrick," I replied, not ready for such vitality in this dying city.

It was, as I would later understand, also the most important moment in my life.

"English?" he asked in English with not a trace of resentment.

"Irlandese," I replied. "And I would wager (I added in my best German) that it is Claus Graf von Stauffenberg."

He laughed happily.

"Actually Claus Philipp Maria Graf Schenk von Stauffenberg."

"Naturally."

"You Irish," he said, "are a fey people. How did you know that I was nobility?"

"I'm a viscount," I said, "son of Lord Ridgeland. I understand such things, though sometimes I don't like them."

He smiled and his whole face came alive.

"You are Catholic nevertheless. I see you in church when I attend on Sunday."

"There are some Catholic lords in Ireland. Strange breed."

"So I see you at the museums and the lectures and the concerts and in the taverns and in church. Yet you are not quite part of the environment. What brings you to Heidelberg in these terrible times?"

"I may want to enter the Irish foreign service which is just beginning. I wrote a paper at Oxford about the old alliances between England and the German states. My father said I ought to learn more about Germany. He said the war would continue."

Claus nodded solemnly.

"Please God it will not. It will only mean more dead. Our General Staff were fools to get involved and you were equal fools to come to the aid of the French."

"The English did, we didn't. We were in the process of breaking away from England, though some of us did fight. My father commanded a regiment in Flanders. They were destroyed of course. So he resigned. I would never fight in another war. What are you studying?" I asked, changing the subject.

"Architecture, music," he waved his hand dismissively. "We have a military tradition in our family. I fear that I may have to join the army to prevent another war with England or France. Someone must resist the Junkers on the General Staff."

"And to fight off the Bolshies?"

"They would never attack us unless our own madmen should attempt to re-peat Napoleon's mistake."

"Is that likely?"

"We went to war with the French merely to test our mobilization plans, we could do anything."

"And it is your vocation to become a soldier to prevent the madmen from making similar mistakes?"

"One must follow the directions of the Holy Spirit," he said with a shrug. . . . "However, you need some German friends. . . . Would it embar-rass you greatly if I invited you to visit my family at Easter?"

"It is difficult to embarrass an Irishman, Claus. I'd be delighted to meet your family."

This was interesting stuff, but why was I reading it? What did it have to do with the long-lost Desmond Doolin? Foolish question. Me wife in-sisted in her fey modality that there were parallels in events from the past and what was happening in the present.

"Sure, Dermot Michael," she said on more than one occasion, "isn't every thing present with God?"

That irrelevancy settled the matter as far as she was concerned.

"Does the name Claus von Stauffenberg mean anything to you, Nuala?"

"A German."

"He was the man who almost killed Hitler in 1944. The German re-sistance to Hitler—they called themselves the Widerstand—was not very large and not very effective but it was very brave and mostly very Catholic. He was shot the same day."

"So your man was getting mixed up with German Catholic assassins."

"Tyrannicides they called themselves. Your good friend Thomas Aquinas said that sometimes it was all right to kill tyrants. In this case a couple of million lives might have been saved if they had succeeded."

"And your man says it was the important event in his life. Was he part of the plot? And what was he doing in Germany in 1944?"

"Spying, no doubt."

"For whom?"

"For Ireland, who else?"

She sniffed. Ireland did not spy on other countries, except England.

"A little crazy, still . . . Maybe like your man over in Iraq . . . Good crazy."

"Catholic crazy."

"Sure, there's nothing wrong with that, is there now?"

"Among the Irish, nothing at all, at all."

She went back to her notes.

"The kind of man who picks up a foul-mouthed bitch in a pub and marries her against all common sense, is it?"

"Wasn't he seduced by her?"

"He was NOT," she said firmly.

"He was just minding his own business when she sang this song and he never recovered."

"He was too busy ogling her boobs to hear her songs."

"Well thanks be to all the holy saints of Ireland he doesn't do that anymore."

"Now he wants to go beyond ogling and play with them all day and all night."

This banter between us was endless. I could never win.

"Now if you stop lollygagging, isn't it time to go down to the local and meet your man Ryan Dorsey."

"Plenty of time to lollygag tonight," I murmured, as I struggled to my feet to begin the walk down to Webster and Sheffield, where there was a tavern named Sean's which Nuala considered our local pub. It was also a useful meeting point for some of our interviews, especially when the subject was the kind of man who might frighten our children.

I kissed her cheek and cupped a breast in my hand.

"It's not night yet, Dermot Michael Coyne." She sighed. "You'll have to wait."

But she didn't brush my hand away. Rather she sighed with a hint of complacency in her tone.

"Sean" was Polish and his tavern was hardly an Irish pub. But as Irish yuppies began to take it over it was drifting in that direction. One could for example purchase a "jar" of Middleton's Single Malt just as one could in Dublin.

I ordered one such and began to sip on it as I meditated that even under the protection of a Chicago Cubs sweatshirt and a bra, her breast was pure delight—and after ten years of marriage. Moreover she enjoyed my "fooling around" as much as I did, something that was not at all true of many of the matrons of her age.

Ryan Dorsey, who had played the drums in Des Doolin's Irish band, was indeed the kind of person who would scare the living daylights out of our kids. He was a big guy, some of it fat, but some of it hard muscle, with uncut hair and a wild black beard and permanently red face. Move back a couple of centuries and he'd do fine as an example of a Viking berserker or in the present age a defensive lineman on the Minnesota Vikings . . . His clothes had never seen a laundry or a dry-cleaning establishment and he smelled of woodsmoke. Under his arm he carried a Bodleian drum which he fiddled with through our conversation.

"Ryan Dorsey?" I stood up to shake his hand.

"Dermot Michael Coyne." He tried to squeeze my hand like he was a linebacker. However, my grip was at least as strong as his. So he gave up and sat down.

"A sip of Middleton's?" I asked.

"That's good stuff," he agreed. "I'm surprised they have it here. Just one swallow. I have a gig tonight at a real Irish bar. One that doesn't have Middleton's."

His laughter seemed to shake the bottles behind the bar.

We toasted each other with our jars and he began the conversation.

"You want to talk about Desi D?" he asked. "Mind if I ask why?"

"His parents want to know whether he's dead or alive?" I said cautiously.

"Well, if he is alive, it's not their fault." He sneered as tears formed in his eyes. "They've been ruining his life since he was born. He went off to Iraq to get away from them. At least they couldn't go over there to make fun of his work like they did when he was in Africa . . . Dermot, he was one of God's great creatures, filled with charm and intelligence and talent and they wanted to remake him into a dull stockbroker. They just never got it, never, never, never."

He pounded the pockmarked table at which we were sitting and "Sean" looked up from behind the bar and frowned. Noting Ryan Dorsey's size, he decided not to make an issue of it.

"As much as we loved him at Marquette, he should have gone somewhere on the other side of the continent or even the ocean. They were up there every other week, checking him out. They complained about the mess in our room, they looked for booze—never did find any—talked to his professors, even went to see the president because they were worried that he would flunk out. And him with a four-point average. They sat in on his theology classes and criticized the professors because they weren't orthodox enough. Even went to the Archbishop . . ."

"He majored in theology?"

"Yeah, he said that he wanted to know the big answers to the big questions. He drove the professors crazy with his questions, but they loved him because he kept the other students awake. He won a departmental prize for one of his essays. The dean wanted him to go on to graduate school at the University of Chicago Divinity School. His parents scotched that idea and made him go to work at the Board of Trade . . . You put a frigging genius in that nuthouse, can you imagine anything that crazy?"

"Des was a genius?"

"He told stories, he danced, he played every musical instrument, and he sang like an angel. We put together an Irish band and performed at one of the bars in Milwaukee, a German bar at that. His parents caught us there one night and called the police. Can you blame him for running off to Africa? They even tried to persuade their contacts in D.C. to wash him out of the Peace Corps."

"Sounds a little daft."

"And all the time they're comparing him to his 'big brother,' a bald, lazy drone with an MBA. Why can't you grow up and be a man like Conor! Conor's an idiot too. Always lecturing Des about how great it was to be a settled married man, married to a good stable wife!"

"Ah?"

"I met the woman once. Castrating bitch. But they insisted that Des take such women out on blind dates. He was perfectly polite to them but never called them back. I told him that if he did, I'd disown him."

"He fought with his parents?"

"Not once. He'd listen, smile politely, nod and then do what he wanted to do."

"Solid Irish male response!"

"We moved into an apartment up in Lakeview when we graduated and I started my band. He played with us at night and we really had a lot of good gigs. They called the police on us a couple of times. Cops left us alone. Then he ups and joins the Peace Corps. He thought he'd get away from them that way . . ."

"Did he ever say that?"

"Not once. He was always telling me that they meant well . . . No, thanks, Dermot, I've had my drink for the evening. Just a Diet Pepsi if you don't mind."

I treated myself to a second jar of Middleton's, aware that if I came home fluthered, I'd be banished from our marriage bed. Well, that had never happened, because it takes at least three jars to fluther me. But I had been warned often enough.

"He didn't expect them to follow him to Eritrea, did he?"

"He sure did. I'm like they won't visit you over there? He laughs and he goes, 'I'm sure they will and they won't approve and they'll write to the senators and congressmen and to the president that the Peace Corps endangers the health and morals of American young people.' Then he laughs and laughs and laughs. That's the kind of guy he was. We all miss him so much . . ."

More tears on that rough, bearded face which I began to realize was a mask.

"And I suppose that they didn't approve of his young woman, Siobhan, wasn't it?"

"He kept them away from her. She's like totally gorgeous and sweet too, not like these bitches who try to prove they're tougher than any guy.

I don't know what went on between them because he wouldn't talk much about her. She went off to Creighton to do her doctorate. They kept in touch, maybe went out a couple of times when she was back in Chicago. He might have written her, I don't know. Never saw any letters in our mailbox from her. Maybe he wrote to her from that African place . . ."

"Eritrea?"

"Yeah, asshole end of the world from what I hear. He came home from his two years, bought a condo over near UIC and signed up for a program in Arabic, if you can believe that. Along about then his parents finally gave up when he refused to date some creep they had discovered for him. They didn't want him around the family for fear he'd give bad habits to his little sister, who had attended New Trier and was going to Notre Dame."

"Kind of washed their hands of him?"

"Well they poked around UIC a bit, but yeah, they wrote him off."

"So he really didn't have to go to Iraq, did he?"

Ryan paused to ponder that.

"I guess not. But you have to understand Des, if something wild and crazy and exciting came along and he thought he could help and he had some talents, like maybe knowing the language, he'd be off on the first plane. I guess"—he strummed his drum—"he was a bright candle who had to burn and burn out if necessary."

An insightful observation from our itinerant Irish drummer, not quite the latter-day hippy whose mask he was presently wearing.

"Doomed by his talents and charm as much as by his parents?"

"Even without his parents," he admitted, "he probably would have gone to the Peace Corps—and to Iraq too. One of the girls in our group up at Marquette said she thought he was doomed to a short and glorious life."

"You think that's what happened?"

He thought for a moment.

"Yeah, Dermot, I think he's dead. Some kind of hero probably, but we'll never know how he became a hero."

He glanced at his watch and rose from the table.

"Thanks for the drink, Dermot. Good stuff. I gotta get on with my gig. I hope you find out what happened. He deserves to be remembered."

"Yes, Ryan Dorsey. He does indeed deserve to be remembered."

I walked back to our house, shivering from the cold which was creeping back into Chicago from Canada and from the cruel fate which had afflicted Desmond Doolin. What might he have become if his parents were not such eejits?

"Dermot Michael Coyne! Have you been drinking too much!"

"Woman of the house, when did I ever drink too much?"

"Well there's always a first time!"

"Two jars of Middleton's!"

"Why did you climb up the stairs so slowly?"

The witch never missed a thing.

"Because I felt sad."

"Why don't you sit down on me bed and tell me about it?"

She flipped the switch on the bed table lamp and patted the bed. She had the sheets drawn up around her neck which meant she had dispensed with a nightgown. It was my fault I had started the foreplay earlier in the evening.

"Ryan Dorsey is a nice young man who in his current mask is pretending to be a gross Irish Bodleian drummer. He had only one jar of Middleton's because he had a gig at some Irish pub later on."

"And?"

"And he thinks that Des Doolin was a brilliant candle doomed to burn himself out."

Me wife shivered.

"How very Irish."

I went through our conversation in all its sad detail. She shivered again.

"'Tis terrible altogether." She sighed. "His parents are awful eejits."

"Ryan Dorsey thinks he would have burned out no matter what his parents and his brother might have done."

"Poor dear boy."

"Indeed."

"Dermot Michael . . . I'm sorry I was mean to you when you were climbing up the steps. I was worried about you and yourself almost never coming home late."

"And yourself all ready for lovemaking and meself never late for that."

"There was good reason to be sad."

I caressed her bare shoulder.

"So much goes wrong in this world, Nuala Anne, no matter how hard people try."

She sighed quite loudly.

"And don't I worry about ourselves making such mistakes about our kids and not even knowing it?"

" 'Tis true."

" 'Tis true," she agreed. "Of course we know that Des is still alive, don't we?"

"Woman, we do! Now all we have to do is save him."

"Or help him save himself."

" 'Tis true."

"So," I said, folding back the sheet to uncover her delectable torso, "we should celebrate the power of life over death."

"Aren't you the brilliant man, Dermot Michael Coyne."

" 'Tis true."

I admired her loveliness for a long time. In a world where there is such beauty, there must yet be hope.

— 6 —

"So you have a Schloss on a hill outside of Ulm?" I asked Claus, as we drank our traditional afternoon glass of their execrable Deutsch beer. "Look like a place in the fairy tale?"

It was a lovely early-spring day with warmth creeping back into the earth and back into our bloodstreams.

"Well, a German fairy tale anyway," he said with a chuckle. "It's quite attractive up there on the hill. Tourists love to take pictures of it. Some parts of it may date to the ninth century. It's in ruins now of course. We live in a manor house down in the valley, lovely picturesque place. Nineteenth-century construction around a twelfth-century core. We call it a Schloss though it really isn't. . . . And your castle?"

"The Vikings and the Brits knocked down our towers and castles. Our term for a Schloss is The Big House, nineteenth-century manor house, probably not unlike yours, big, drafty and cold with plumbing that doesn't always work."

"In Germany we would not tolerate that," he said with his broad grin. "Everything is always in order here. Ja, Ja. Well, in Prussia anyway . . . Here in Swabia we are a little more relaxed. We are part of the Secret Germany."

"Secret! You sing as loud as anyone in your pubs!"

"Not that kind of silence. We Swabians have been soldiers in this part of the Old Empire, the First Reich if you will, for a long time and fervent Catholics for all that time too. We are very serious about our faith, though we feel free to criticize Church leadership."

"No bishops in the family?"

"If there were, we keep it a secret," he said with his contagious grin. "We feel that we are better Catholics than most bishops and indeed better Catholics than the Pope."

"Funny that's the way we Irish feel too."

"My father, Alfred Schenk Graf von Stauffenberg, was the last Oberhofmarschal of the kingdom of Wittenberg, which disappeared in 1918. Naturally he fought in the war and was wounded twice in Flanders. He walks with a cane, and at first will seem very stiff and aloof. In fact, he is, as you will discover, a delightfully humorous man. He hates war and sometimes says that Swabia should leave Germany rather than fight in another Prussian war."

"You folks have a different military tradition than the Prussians?"

"We would like to think so, Timmy Pat. We are the Secret Germany in part because we are also the real Germany. The Prussians," he said with another grin, "are merely recently converted Teutonic Knights, semibarbarians from the shores of the Baltic. Yet we have intermarried with the Prussians, though not recently. August von Gneisenau who designed the strategy for the battle of Waterloo is some kind of ancestor of mine. He was not exactly a Prussian since he was born in Saxony, but he was a general in the Prussian army. Now we tend to marry other Swabian nobility, though that has its own risks. Our family does not marry cousins because we are so Catholic."

"Our aristocracy doesn't go back that far," I said, "and is much less distinguished. Mostly land grabbers. You'll explain to your family that I am really little more than an uncouth lord of a hill fort."

He chuckled again, as he often did.

"They'll love you, Timmy Pat. We are serious, very serious people. Serious *about our faith, serious about our tradition of service, but not really serious about ourselves."*

"'Tis said that in England the situation is always serious but never desperate, while in Ireland it is always desperate but never serious."

He laughed again.

"Our Schloss is never desperate . . . We will have some other guests for Holy Week, I hope you do not mind, some of them will be women."

"I've never been known to object to women," I admitted.

"Yet you seem to avoid beautiful women in the pubs, as you call them."

The comment was very gentle. He was always gracious even when he was offering a blunt insight. The man was, I told myself, too good to be true.

"I become dizzy at the sight of a beautiful woman, Claus. I'm afraid that I'll fall in love too soon."

"What, Timmy, is too soon?"

"I don't know."

"Both women who will be with us during Easter Week are beautiful . . . Baroness Nina von Lerchenfeld is from Bamberg. Our families have been friends for generations. Both families are convinced that we should marry, my mother especially since my two older brothers already have spouses. She is quite attractive, very calm, very brave . . ."

"And you are in love with her?"

"I think so . . . You are not to fall in love with her."

"Holy Week is not a time for falling in love, Claus."

"Yet when the Christ rose from the dead, did he not seal his love with us forever?"

This mystical side of Claus was very attractive because it was utterly sincere and unself-conscious. He belonged to a "circle" of young German students and aristocrats who had gathered around a poet named Stefan Georg, a group which the couple of times I was with them were entirely too otherworldly for the tastes of this Ulster farmer and linen maker. Now I realize that he was an Irish equivalent of Willie Yeats, only much stronger.

"And does she love you?"

He shrugged and blushed.

"She gives some signs of it, I think. We must make some progress this week.

I have made up my mind to join the army. There are many among the officers
and even the General Staff who are part of the secret Germany. We will resist
this madman who wants to destroy the Germany that we love."

"The Secret Germany?"

"Of course."

As best as I could figure out, then and much later, this was the noble ideal
of German culture contained in its religion, music, literature, and art. It had
nothing to do with Prussia or Frederick the Great, or the Kaiser or the pagan-
ism which, as the Georg circle believed, lurked in the eastern regions of the
country.

"We don't have a secret Ireland," I said.

"I'm sure you do . . . the other woman is Annalise von Sternberg who
is Nina's cousin. Her father and three brothers were killed at Verdun. Her
mother later died of the flu. Nina's family have taken her in. She is perhaps
sixteen . . ."

"Too young for the likes of me, Graf von Stauffenberg."

"She is blossoming into a woman. She has now returned from school in England. She is brilliant and has very strong opinions. She loves to argue and says
many outrageously humorous things. She is a fine athlete too."

"Not my cup of tea," I said.

"She is also unbearably beautiful, but, as my mother, Gräfin Karoline says,
she lacks mature sense. She needs to grow up for a few more years."

"That sounds like a perfect match for me," I said ironically.

"You may fall in love with her. Even worse she may fall in love with you.
Now would not be the proper time."

"I'll take your word for it, Claus."

I promised myself that I would avoid this delectable young woman. She
sounded like someone I did not need, not in a Germany with the power of
Adolf Hitler growing. Anyway, I was not the kind of person who fell in love
with a kid.

I wondered what the Galway woman, who married my father at eighteen
and herself sixteen would have to say about all of this. I resolved not to consult
with her.

"Our Easter customs are traditional," Claus pointed out to me. "We begin with a Palm Sunday celebration and enjoy recreation and exercise till Wednesday. That evening we do Tenebrae and enter the Holy Week Triduum on Thursday. We try to devote Thursday and Friday to prayer and to eat no food at all, at least on Friday. Our chaplain, a wonderful old priest, will preach each day. With the Gloria of Saturday, Lent is over, the purple hoods come off the statues and the bells ring again. We have a big feast on Easter—a really big German feast and then leave the Schloss perhaps on Tuesday morning."

"Sounds pleasant," I said, lying just a little. I don't mind fasting but we Irish don't like such rigid schedules.

"Good," he said, happy that he had imposed Teutonic order on my disorderly, as he saw it, Irish life.

"Ja, ja!" I said.

He laughed at my making fun of his German need that everything be in order.

"You do exercise, don't you, Timmy?"

"Rugby, soccer, Irish football, rowing, and a little of a violent game called hurling."

This answer was greeted with another one of his contagious laughs.

"We do have a lake in which you could row, even a boat with oars," he said with a teasing wink. "Perhaps you could ride in it with Annalise."

"No," I said firmly. "We Irish males tend to be celibates anyway."

"You will be a priest?"

"In Ireland you don't have to be a priest to be celibate. All you need is to be afraid of women."

"But the young servingwomen in the taverns dote on you!"

"That's why I'm afraid of them . . . what other recreation do you have besides pulling the oars for this young Brunhilde."

"Tennis, horses."

"I can do those too," I said confidently. "I hope I don't have to play tennis with this Teutonic goddess."

"It would be rude not to, Timmy."

"I thought you didn't want me to fall in love with her."

"Oh, no, I did not say that. I said that she is too young now, too inexperienced, too grief-stricken over the death of her family. Someday it would perhaps be advisable. It should not be hard for an Irish celibate to wait a few years."

His grin this time was a little sly, which for Claus was not very sly. "You and she would be well matched in five years."

"I warn you that my Old Fella, the current Lord Ridgeland, married the Galway woman when she was sixteen and he was eighteen. When we Irish celibates fall in love we do it dramatically."

"You are making fun, Timmy," he said cautiously. "Yes, of course you are! It is the Irish in you!"

It was indeed. I did not bother to tell him that curiosity was a special weakness of us Irish males. I would fantasize about this Bavarian paragon till I met her—and then be sadly disappointed.

"What does your family think of Herr Hitler?"

"He is the Antichrist. You read about the so-called Night of the Long Knives last week? He ordered the elimination of those in the party who disagreed with him. He denounces the Jews on every occasion. He is vulgar, disgusting and mad. We in the Secret Germany must resist him, to death if necessary."

It was quite a change from teasing me about the yet unseen Annalise to threatening revolution.

"Is it that bad?"

"May I recite Stefan George's poem about the Antichrist? You must remember he wrote it in 1907. Stefan was all too aware of the infection that lurks in the German soul."

How can an infection lurk in a soul? I wondered. Damn German mysticism!

"Sure," I said.

> He comes from the mountains, he stands mid the pines!
> We saw it ourselves! He transforms into wine
> Clear water, and trafficks with dead men!'
>
> Oh could you but hear how I laugh in the night!
> My hour is now struck, my snares are all sprung
> And fish fill my nets, thickly swarming.

Wise men and dullards, the mob, frenzied, reels,
Tramples the cornfields, tears up the trees.
Make way for the flock of the Risen!

No wonder of heaven but I can't perform.
A hair's-breadth impure, but you'll not note the fraud
With your stunted and stultified senses.

In place of the arduous and rare I invoke
The Facile; from compost I make things like gold,
And perfumes, and nectars, and spices.

And what the great prophet renounced I extol:
An art without ploughing or sowing or toil
Which yet drains the soil of its essence.

The high Prince of Vermin extends his domains;
No pleasure eludes him, no treasure or gain.
And down with the dregs of rebellion!

You cheer, mesmerised by demoniac sheen,
Exhaust what remains of the honey of dawn,
And only then sense the debacle.

You then stretch your tongues to the now arid trough,
Mill witless as kine through a pasture aflame,
While fearfully brazens the trumpet.

"Book of Revelation turned around," I murmured.

"Precisely," he said grimly. "Now you see why I must kill him."

"You personally?" I said, hardly able to believe what he was saying.

"Not immediately, of course. Eventually we of the Secret Germany must assume our destiny. Each of us must be ready to do his duty when it becomes necessary."

We were riding through the Schwartzwald, picturesque hills and forests and fields just coming into spring's first rebirth, neat small towns, freshly painted homes, occasional working men and women tilling the soil.

"Is this land the Secret Germany?" I asked.

"If one needs to give it a geography," he said softly, "Swabia is as good a place as any. We have protected the Church and the Reich here for over a thousand years. We will continue to do so, no matter what the cost nor how vile the enemy . . . I am being too serious, am I not, Timmy? We are on holiday, no?"

"You feel you have to carry the burden of a millennium on your own shoulders?"

"What is the responsibility of a lord in Ireland?" he replied.

"Make money on the land, stay alive, see that the people are safe and well fed, though most of the Protestant lords are really English and care very little about the people whom they consider an inferior race."

"Your Old Fella too?"

"Ah, no. He wants a free and just and peaceful Ireland. Periodically he lectures the House of Lords on the subject. They don't listen."

"We feel, some of us more strongly than others, that by tradition and training and faith we are destined to lead. In war if necessary, but reluctantly. We are not Prussian Junkers who are war leaders and little else. We are leaders of religion and vision. So sometimes we must be ready to die to save our people. Does that seem arrogant?"

"Not when you say it."

"Thank you, Timmy."

"But this permission to kill a local Antichrist whenever he comes along?"

"An obligation . . . You have read Aquin on tyrannicide? Sometimes the beast must be slain. Our Protestant brothers have learned from Martin Luther that they have great respect and tolerance for our leaders. We Catholics are prepared to say 'no' a lot earlier than they are."

Ten years later, in July of 1944, I would remember every detail of that conversation on the train from Heidelberg to Stuttgart. Even today I'm not sure I fully understand them. Or fully understand Claus.

Then we arrived at the Hauptbanhoff in Stuttgart, the old capital of the

kingdom of Wittenberg, where Claus lived till 1918. Then the kingdom became a republic and his father, no longer the senior marshal to the king, had to
move back to the family Schloss in Jettingen between Munich and Stuttgart.
We had time between trains to visit the Altesschloss, a forbidding pile of
bricks.

"You liked living in that place?"

"It was all I knew. When we arrived in Jettingen, I thought I had found a
place like heaven."

We boarded the train to Ulm and Munich, having made it just in time. I
sensed that Claus had calculated the time of our walk to his childhood home so
that we would return to the Hauptbanhoff with not a moment wasted. A
mystic who bore the responsibility of a thousand years of history and still kept a
close eye on his wristwatch. Herr Hitler didn't know what kind of an adversary
he would have to face.

"Do people swim in this lake of yours?"

"Naturally, it is a small and shallow lake. It will become quite warm in another month. Some may want to swim this weekend."

"So perhaps this legendary woman will swim?"

"Have you fallen in love with her merely because of my description? Shame
on you, Timmy!"

"I think you want me to fall in love with her, Claus, so you yourself won't."

For a moment, an expression of sadness flickered across his face.

"That would not be proper. She is too young and I am virtually engaged to
her cousin. If there is a war, I may be killed. I would want to leave some children behind . . . But to answer your unspoken question, she is most attractive
in a bathing costume. She is also quite progressive in her choices, much to the
dismay of my mother and some of the townsfolk. I myself find no fault in her in
this matter, however. Nor, I believe, would you."

"She rejects their complaints?"

"You don't understand Annalise, Tim. All love Annalise too much to complain."

"So," I said.

My interest, I told myself, was ridiculous. I had resisted the charms of En-
glishwomen at Oxford and German women in Heidelberg. Why should I fall in

love with a woman out of a medieval Germanic myth. I should return to Ireland soon and find myself a proper Celtic spouse. As the Galway woman herself would have said, I should not be swept up by a springtime daydream in this fairyland where the Emperor Otto might still be lurking in preparation for a battle with the Antichrist and his Teutonic nights.

We were the only ones to leave the train in Jettingen, a small and pretty little town, little more than a village, in a valley surrounded by high and somewhat forbidding hills, behind which the sun was already creating statues. There were no servants there to meet us.

"Our Schloss is right down the street, Tim," mein host informed me. "It is that buff-coloured home next to the church."

In the land of my ancestors the Schloss would have been considered a medium-sized manor house, too big for the town, too small for the countryside. Sedate and comfortable, but hardly as monumental as my own Big House in Ulster. Petty nobility at best—with a magic princess whom the count wanted to peddle to me as an investment in the future, Parzifal indeed!

The old stationmaster embraced my friend.

"Ja, ja! Claus!"

"Ja, ja, Freddy!"

Then as we walked towards the alleged Schloss, a swarm of kinder saw Claus.

"Unser Claus!" they screamed, and ran down the street towards us.

Claus beamed happily at this mob, shook hands with all of them, and called each by name.

"We live very close to the families of the village, you see."

"All very seventeenth century—if the Thirty Years' War wasn't going on."

"If we go to war again with France and England and Russia, there will be more devastation in Germany than there was at the time of the Peace of Westphalia."

Nothing like a grim cloud of warning on this warm and mystical spring day.

— 7 —

ME WIFE was sobbing when I entered my office. The two hounds were pawing at her in vain efforts at consolation. Timmy Pat's first segment lay on my desk. It was Saturday afternoon and I had spent much of the morning over in Lincoln Park interviewing Conor.

"Och, Dermot, isn't this the saddest story you've ever read? Those poor young men and the women they loved! All killed in that terrible war! And everything so beautiful that spring! Just like August of 1914!"

August 1914 was alleged to have been the most beautiful summer in a hundred years. How did my Nuala know that!

"Well," I said, playing to my designed role as the sensible and insensitive male, "Timmy Pat lived to write this memoir, so he wasn't killed in the war."

"I wonder if he's still alive . . . He should have brought that young woman back to Ireland with him, still."

"Maybe he did!"

"And I'm the one who is obsessed with happy endings!"

"How old would he be now?"

"In his nineties."

"Timmy never mentions his mother's name, does he now?"

"I thought it was Galway woman, and don't you have a monopoly on that name?"

"Silly! She must be a relative of your children, through Nell Pat your grandma! Isn't that wonderful. We must find out her name and her home town in Galway. I just *know* that it's Carraroe!"

Carraroe was the hometown of Ma, as we called our grandmother, and of Nuala Anne herself. Me wife was convinced there were all sorts of mystical connections among the lot of us. I never debated the point.

"There were many red-haired women in Galway in those days, even today."

"Give over, Dermot Michael, with your pedestrian Yank imagination. I know that we're supposed to be involved with this story."

"I thought it was the story of poor Des Doolin."

"Go 'long with you Dermot, you're having me on."

I sat down on my couch and reflected that according to the implicit bylaws of the house my wife could enter my office whenever she wanted to, but I couldn't enter her workroom when she wasn't there.

Maeve, our younger hound, curled up at my feet, as if to console me for this injustice.

"You are telling me, are you now, woman of the house, that Tim Clark's story and Des Doolin's cross lines somewhere. I'm sure they never met one another."

"Never be sure of anything, Dermot Michael Coyne, until you have the facts!"

"Just like you!"

"Just like me," she replied calmly. She had, however, the good sense to giggle. "Now tell me about poor Des's big brother . . . what's his name?"

"Conor . . . He's about as unlike Des as anyone could be."

Their home was over in Lincoln Park, to the east of us near Clark

Street. We were in DePaul or West Lincoln Park, which is a notch or a notch and a half down on the status ladder. It was a major center for Chicago yuppies with expensive tastes and the money to support such tastes. I was dispatched to walk to their home on Saturday morning and, among other things, study their interaction with their kids, of which they had three about the ages of our top three. That was impossible because their kids were nowhere to be seen. Their house, just a block south of Fullerton, had been rehabilitated, stood out from a street of gracious old brick homes. It still looked old, but grace had decamped, presumably in disgust.

I commented that they had obviously done a lot of work on their home.

"You have to maintain the property in this neighborhood," Conor drawled with a slight yawn. "This property is the best investment in the city because of its locale near the Lake and L and the intrinsic value of the housing. A lot of our neighbors don't seem to understand that location is not enough to maintain property value. You have to keep the housing up-to-date, especially with electric and electronic and plumbing resources that the next generation of investors will demand. The current investor will lose some of his wealth if he does not constantly renew the resources."

He yawned again.

Values, resources, investors, wealth—all words applied to a house. Not once did he call it a house, much less a home. The jargon of big-time finance applied to a family dwelling sounded almost subversive.

Conor Doolin was about my age, tending towards too much weight which with his hair loss and absence of vigor made him look ten years older.

"A property like this place must be viewed as an important dimension of the owner's wealth and money invested in it conceived of as a wealth enhancements endeavor."

"You have an investment over on Sheffield, don't you, Dermot?" his wife, Mattie, asked. "A wooden place, I believe?"

She was her husband's age, I figured, but sufficiently out of condition to look much older.

"Pre-Fire," I said.

"There is certainly," Conor said solemnly, "some wealth inherent in such a building, but the age of a property is a fairly fixed value. It does not advance the wealth at a reasonable upward curve. I tried to explain to my neighbors that we saw the necessity of remodeling here purely as a matter of enhancing our future wealth beyond the future value of the building as it was. In the case of your own, the proper question is how much the land is enhanced by the presence of the building and how much its wealth potential is separate from the presence of the building. Separate the building factor and you would not lose much wealth but then you would have the possibility of immense enhancement by putting a new and more attractive building on it."

"You went to the University of Chicago Business School?" I asked.

"Of course." He yawned again.

"We believe that one must do everything possible," Mattie insisted, "to enhance the wealth of our children. Sentimental attachment to a given building does not contribute much to enhancement."

"It's worth something surely," I suggested, making trouble, "that one's children need merely walk across the street to their school."

"I didn't know there was a good school over on Sheffield," Mattie said, her face easing in a puzzled frown that seemed habitual.

"St. Josephat," I said, ratcheting up the trouble bar.

"A *Catholic* school?" Conor asked, more puzzled than shocked. "I admit that they do good work in poor neighborhoods, but certainly not in this neighborhood."

"We believe that we owe our children the very best in educational resources," Mattie added. "Schools like Chicago Latin or Frances Parker are the kind of schools to which our youngsters are entitled, until we move back to Hyde Park and are able to send them to the Lab School at The University."

Mattie seemed to believe in an awful lot.

I had found out about all I needed to know about the Conor Doolins. Nuala would love my stories. However, I'd add one more bit of evidence and then get on to the Dangerous Des.

"I noticed that the children are not around today," I said tentatively, fearing that I might be wading into deep water.

"Mattie is a stay-at-home mom, and we think that this investment is a prudent one. But we also believe that it is sensible to provide a day when the children and the mother can be free of one another."

"We believe that too much togetherness," his wife said, adding yet another belief to their dogma system, "negatively impacts on family well-being."

Their dogmas were a caricature of the Business School faith, but obviously it had worked for them so far in life, if the expensive modern furniture, heavy drapes, and faintly grotesque art were to be believed. That it was a tasteless mélange that might cause acute nausea in a sensitive guest did not matter.

"Those are very interesting theories on which I will have to reflect," I said, "but I'm here, as you know, to ask for details about your brother Desmond."

"Desmond's life has been a tragic waste." Conor suppressed a yawn and began to recite his carefully prepared script. "He was a young man of enormous talents, the most delightful child I have ever encountered. He entertained us when he was a kid every night at the supper table. He sang, he danced, he told stories—most of them, I might remark, not altogether true. He made us all laugh. I warned him when he began to attend school that his teachers would expect him to be more serious, that he would have to apply himself to the serious business of learning. He just laughed. Since then he laughed himself from one madcap escapade to another, without, if I may say so, ever acquiring good judgment or maturity."

"The poor kid," Mattie took up the cause, "was a Peter Pan. He did not want to grow up, he refused to grow up, he bragged to us that he would never grow up. He was smart enough and clever enough that for a long time he got away with not growing up. You could call his tragedy, 'Peter Pan goes to Iraq.'"

Nice line. Not Mattie's I was sure, but nice just the same.

"In a way," Conor said, this time not suppressing his yawn, "I have to blame my parents. They encouraged his craziness as a child and then, by the time they began to see its serious effects, it was very difficult to turn him around."

"A lot of boys," Mattie added, "go through a phase of sowing wild oats. The best cure for it is a serious young woman who makes them settle down. We did our best to find such a woman for Des. He turned on all his charm for them and then danced away. I said to Conor, 'that's the last girl I will try to persuade him to date.' He was not mature enough for a serious relationship."

I wondered how often such conversations had occurred in the Coyne family about me. Then I came home with Nuala Anne and they were astonished. Since then they try to protect the poor kid from me, a game which herself enjoys enormously till they begin to criticize me. Then Katie bar the door.

"I had gathered," I said, "that he had good grades all through his education."

"Without any effort." Conor shook his head. "That was infuriating. Other children had to work for their grades. He led his class with native intellegence, quick wit, and charm. He thought that life would be like a classroom at Faith, Hope. He never grasped that life was a serious business and that success would come only to a mature and responsible person."

"Faith, Hope," is the name of a parish on the North Shore—actually a shortened form of SS Faith, Hope, and Charity. It is often called "Faith, Hope, and Cadillac," though that is hardly fair because the Lexus has become the auto of choice up there, just as the parish, albeit the wealthiest in the Archdiocese, has taken up voting Democratic. "A miracle of divine humor," the little Archbishop claims.

"He never said 'no' to his mother and father," Mattie said, "not once. He just listened politely and then went and did whatever he wanted to."

"My parents made up their minds to send him to New Trier Township High School. You know, of course, Dermot, that it is perhaps the best high school in America. I had done very well up there. We all agreed that the rigorous academic discipline at New Trier would settle him down. Instead, he went over to the Jesuits at Loyola Academy, where he had a wonderful time, earned several athletic letters in sports like lacrosse, and was still an emotional ten-year-old."

"Con and I were dating at Princeton. Every time I encountered Des, I laughed myself sick. Until Con pointed out the terrible effect an audience had on Des."

"And how worried my parents were that Jennifer, our little sister, would follow after him."

"Has she?"

"I don't think so," Con responded promptly.

"I'm not so sure, dear." Mattie permitted herself a dissent. "She's still in college. She's quiet, but she chose Notre Dame when she could have gone to Princeton."

Mortal sin!

Well she could have chosen Marquette.

"And," Mattie continued, "she's talking about Notre Dame law school."

God forbid.

"I'm afraid that she might follow Des into the Peace Corps." Conor sounded worried, but he still managed to yawn. "That's when Des went into his 'Mr. Kurtz' phase. He became a god to those poor, ignorant natives. He came to believe that there was no crazy thing he could not do . . . He called me just before he left for Iraq. I begged him not to go. I warned him that it might kill our parents. He just said something foolish and hung up."

Tears actually appeared in Conor's eyes.

"I'm sorry, Dermot, in my world men don't cry. Yet I loved the little punk. You couldn't help loving him. I asked myself every night if there were anything else I might have done."

"You did all you could, dear." Mattie touched his hand affectionately. The first hint of emotion that I had seen between them. "You did all you could, we all tried. Nothing seemed to work. He really thought he was Peter Pan."

"Mom says that your wife thinks he's still alive. Do you agree, Dermot?"

"Nuala Anne operates on a different wavelength than most of the rest of us. I make it a practice never to write off one of her insights."

I thought that was a pretty good dodge.

I could hear herself say, "Give over, Dermot, you know I'm right."

"Was your family astonished that he chose to major in theology at Marquette?"

"We were all dismayed. Theology is what priests do! He had no business in that program. What would it equip him to do? Besides, my parents did research and discovered that it was a hotbed of radical religious ideas. I suspect that it was in that climate that he decided that he could save the world all by himself."

I shook hands with them both as I left. Tears were now in both of their eyes. They thanked me for my interest and said that it had been good to talk to me. They meant it, poor dear people, as Nuala would have called them.

I never thought that I could save the world by myself. I just wanted to be left alone. Did anyone in my family weep when I went off to tour Europe with my commodity exchange profits (earned, like I say, by mistake)? I didn't think so.

My wife insists that God sent me to Europe to find her and take care of her and protect her for her whole friggin' life. She believes that as though the Archangel Michael had told her it were so in a personal conversation.

What the hell do I know about how God works!

Even financial services creeps love, I told myself as I began the walk back across Halsted Street. What could they have done to protect Des from the drummers to which he was marching?

Maybe, just maybe, however, if they had valued his drummers a little more or had been more sympathetic to the mysterious workings of the Holy Spirit, his brief life story might have had a different ending.

If I were to believe my wife, however, the final chapter of that biography was yet to come.

The drizzle turned to rain as I walked down Webster Avenue. I jogged home and arrived at the top of the steps leading to our second-floor entrance wet and winded and sad. No, I would not tear down this house and build something on it to enhance the wealth of my rug rats.

The front door was open. In the bowels of the house the kids were shouting, the dogs were barking, and me wife was singing some kind of Irish song. Bedlam was after all a place in Ireland. No it was Donnybrook. Saturday morning at the Coynes.

The pooches, always alert to someone coming in the door, especially when he had been away for a time and in their perspective might not return, ignored my arrival.

"Quiet, guys," my wife said, "Da's here and he is in a BA-AD mood."

She could smell me even more quickly than the pooches could. Small chance I had of sneaking up behind her and having my way with her—unless she wanted me to.

The dogs charged up the stairs, eager to make up for their dereliction of duty and almost knocked me down. I stumbled into the playroom and the three mobile kids assaulted me and the nonmobile one on the floor screeched with delight. My wife in exercise shorts and a wet tee shirt embraced me. I held her a little longer than was strictly speaking proper in the context.

"Da's home," I confirmed the announcement. "And he's in a great mood . . . Ethne, can't you control this mob of Galway miscreants?"

"Haven't I given that up long ago!"

"Da isn't in a bad mood," Socra Marie assured the assembly. "He's never mad when he hugs Ma!"

"Dermot Michael Coyne! You're soaking wet and you're shivering with the cold! Won't you be catching that virus that's going around!"

"Woman, I'll not! I've come home to report on my work this morning."

"Well, upstairs with you anyhow!"

"I'm on me way."

"Take off your wet clothes, Dermot!" she ordered me. "And into the shower with you."

"How can I report about the young Doolins when I'm in the shower?"

"Won't I be there with you?"

That put things in an entirely different perspective.

I'll not tell you how I rehearsed my adventure in the shower with me wife. It's none of your business.

— 8 —

"POOR DEAR people!" my Nuala Anne said predictably.

"Poor dear creepy, misguided people," I agreed.

We were sitting in my office. My wife had made huge plates of fruit salad for both of us. She was wearing her official uniform of jeans and a sweatshirt, the latter celebrating the Chicago White Sox, though I had distinctly forbidden such memorabilia in my house. The two younger kids were sound asleep in the nursery, under the watchful eyes of the hounds. Ethne was down in the playroom, working on her dissertation, while the older kids worked on their artistic efforts.

"Your man," I said, "really is a little daft."

"And himself going off to Iraq without talking to his parents . . . I'm tired of this stuff, Dermot Michael Coyne. I don't want to be a detective anymore."

"I'll call over at the zoo and see if the other leopards are changing their spots."

"Why can't I be just a wife and a mother and someone who sings in public occasionally? Why do people have to bother me about the messes they've made in their family lives? Why can't they leave their blather to your man Jude?"

"Maybe he has too much to do and himself under contract to your Claretian fathers anyway!"

"Des Doolin really was immature and irresponsible. If our Patjo were ever to run away like that, wouldn't it break me heart altogether?!"

YOUR WIFE, DOLT, IS GOING THROUGH SOME KIND OF MIDLIFE CRISIS!

She never is!

YOU DON'T HAVE TO TALK THAT FUNNY IRISH WAY WHEN YOU'RE TALKING TO ME.

"We'd never be so clueless about Patjo if he turns out to have the glint in his eye."

She pondered that.

"And meself hinting to them poor folks that he's still alive."

"I thought you said you knew that."

"There's knowing and there's *knowing*, Dermot love. I'm worn out from my friggin' instincts. Are they any better than guesses?"

Was Nuala losing faith in her own fey insights? Life around Sheffield Avenue would be a lot quieter. Also a little dull?

"They work well enough so far."

"They seem to be fading away. Maybe a fourth pregnancy is too much for them. Maybe the hormone cocktail erodes them. Maybe it's time I grow up and myself with four children to take care of them."

"Five counting meself!"

She laughed at that.

"Sure, you're easy altogether . . . A little loving every once in a while is no work at all, at all . . . But seriously, Dermot, it's not fun anymore. I'd leave as soon spend Saturday playing with me childer and romancing me man."

"You seem to have accomplished both of those tasks this morning."

"Only because I made you do the work."

THAT ANSWER IS IRRELEVANT.

"You're not sure that Des is still alive?

"Desperate Des? . . . Well, part of me kind of knows that he is, but what good does that do? Here in Yank land, don't we fairy folk turn pragmatic?"

THAT WAS A GREAT LINE.

I don't need an eejit like you to tell me.

"And how do I get him out of Iraq if he is still alive? Write a nice note to Mr. Rumsfeld? And I won't be after sending yourself over there to find him! This one is beyond me, Dermot Michael Coyne!"

"Isn't the other man some help?"

"Dermot, Lord Ridgeland is long since gone from this world . . . No, I'm wrong there. He's still alive too, even if he is ninety-five or whatever, but we don't know what crazy things he's going to do and himself falling in love with that German hussy even before he meets her."

My wife was in a very bad mood.

"I suppose we have to try to wrap this one up before we retire from the business," I offered.

"Och, 'tis true, Dermot love . . . Well what did we learn this morning?"

"That our Des didn't fit what his parents and his brother and sister-in-law thought was the paradigm for maturity and responsibility. Mattie compared him several times to Peter Pan."

"Yet didn't your man spend two years in Ethiopia, didn't he all but get himself a doctorate in Arabic, and didn't he organize an interfaith group of students at the university down below?"

"Your man" refers to almost anyone. A listener has to figure out who the speaker means. "Down below" is the way the Irish cope with geography. In this case it means University of Illinois at Chicago or UIC—almost always called the Pier by my parents' generation when GIs back from the war went to Navy Pier for their first two years of higher education. "Down within" means downtown or sometimes the Loop or other times Michigan Avenue. Nuala's point is that P. Pan didn't do much constructive with his life. Des Doolin's madcap life did not suggest an inability to set goals and achieve them.

" 'Tis true," I said. "He wasn't just playing games for the pure fun of it."

"Are we missing something altogether, Dermot Michael? What was he up to? What demons drove him? If he were just running away from his family, there would be better ways to do it, wouldn't there now?"

"You have the right of it, Nuala Anne."

THERE YOU GO AGAIN, TALKING FUNNY TO HER. HOW OFTEN DO I HAVE TO TELL YOU THAT YOU'RE NOT AN IRISH IMMIGRANT?

West of Ireland immigrant.

"You went to Marquette, didn't you, Dermot love?"

"Woman, I did and had a wonderful time and learned a lot, even if I didn't put enough credits together to graduate."

"Why did you have such a brilliant time?"

I thought about it.

"Everyone has a brilliant time at Marquette," I said.

"Beautiful campus?"

"Pure ugly."

"Lovely city?"

"The joke is that it's a nice place to live in but you wouldn't want to visit there."

"Are those gobshite drinking laws you Yanks indulge in easier up there?"

"They used to be but not anymore."

"You're not making sense, Dermot love," she said.

"Wonderful community spirit," I said, not altogether clear as to what that meant.

"Well, that's better. Now what about his studying theology? Do you think he wanted to be a priest?"

"I took a lot of theology and I didn't want to be a priest."

"Why?"

"Because it was a fun department, great priests and great lay teachers. They made religion exciting."

"That broke all the rules, didn't it? Any special priest?"

"Father Bob O'Donovan S.J., a Jesuit who was run out of Ireland. He made God fun."

"Well, as you would say, Dermot Michael, maybe he had the right of it."

"Most popular teacher on campus."

"And himself still alive?"

"Very much."

"Any particular part of Ireland?"

"Come to think of it, the County Galway."

"Give your man a ring on Monday morning and tell him you're driving up with your Galway wife to pay your respects and thank him for putting up with you."

"You think he will be able to explain what made your man tick?"

"If he's from me own county, he'll be able to make up an explanation even if he doesn't have one now."

"I wouldn't doubt it for a minute."

"Dermot," she ordered, "don't wait till Monday. Call him now. Maybe we can have lunch with him on Monday."

"You don't want to visit Milwaukee?"

"I do. Maybe we can visit that great art museum they have up above."

I dialed the Marquette number and asked for the direct line to Father Robert O'Donovan. He was the kind of celibate faculty member who worked all day Saturday in his office before he went off to some dorm to say the Saturday Mass for the kids.

"Bob O'Donovan," he said briskly, answering on the first ring.

"Hi, Father, I'm sure you don't remember me but I'm Dermot Coyne."

"Dermot Michael Coyne, if I remember correctly. I always remember the troublemakers."

"I just liked to ask tough questions."

"Good questions generally, if my memory serves me right . . . What can I do for you, Dermot?"

"Well, I'm married now, in fact to a Galway woman."

"I read the newspapers and watch television. I know whom you married."

"Do you now . . . Well we were talking about Galway this afternoon and I mentioned that a Galway man protected me from heresy and immediately she wanted to drive up on Monday and meet you because she was certain you were from Connemara."

"Clifden."

" 'Tis strange altogether," I said, "we have a place up in Rynville."

"I'd heard that too . . . Well, I'd certainly like to meet the fair Nuala Anne, find out what she saw in you."

"Doctrinal orthodoxy, I'm sure."

"Come into the Student Union, ask for the private dining rooms, and then for Fr. O'Donovan's room. We'll see you both then."

Me bride could scarcely control her giggles.

Inside the entrance to the Schloss Stauffenberg, two aged male servants hugged Claus and carried our luggage upstairs. We walked through a big solid oak door and into a parlour that must have been the old Schloss which the new manor house had enclosed. The high walls were covered with armour and weapons and paintings of earlier Count Stauffenbergs, of some of which Claus was a photo-perfect image. The furniture and rugs and lamps which, however, were late Victorian, the latter with electric bulbs. The people in the room, mostly tall and graceful, rose respectfully when we entered. Claus took over the introductions smoothly.

"Family and friends," he said in German with his most gentle charm, "I wish you to meet a new friend I have brought from Heidelberg. He is Irish and you will find him very amusing. He claims, accurately I think, that Irish monks converted our ancestors thirteen hundred years ago. I present," he went into English, "the Right Honorable Viscount Timothy Ridgewood of Ridgeland. I believe that 'Sir Timothy' would be the appropriate mode of address."

"Call me Timmy," I said and then continued in German. "It is a pleasure to visit this historic Schloss, which represents a great tradition of Catholic and German humanism and especially in the company of the son of the house, who is the finest Catholic gentleman I've ever met, un chevalier parfait, if you will excuse my using another language."

All right it was excessive. At least it would have been excessive back home. Here with these formal but not stiff people, it might just go down.

It must have, because they applauded—knocking on tables and chairs and any wood available.

Claus slipped a glass of sweet Rhine wine into my hand.

"From the Jesuit Garden," he said.

I raised the glass, "Prost! And as they say in my native land, 'God bless this house and all who live in it! And may Brigid, Patrick and Colmcille and Killian bless you when you have to leave it.'"

The shite was getting so thick that they'd have to shovel it out when I was finished.

Claus took me around the room and introduced me to his family. I had some blarney for each of them. I noted that, though he was the youngest of the three sons, he was treated with the respect due to the head of the family. Nina, blond, tall, and well proportioned, was not exactly pretty, much less beautiful. But she was striking and would become more so, I thought, with the passage of time—a perfect lady for the perfect knight.

"Claus has spoken often of you," I fibbed. "He did not exaggerate your presence and your grace."

"Danke, Herr Viscount," she said lowering her eyes and blushing.

Then we came to Annalise, the Gothic empress who had distracted my eyes from the moment I had entered the room—a perfect Blanchefleur for Parzifal. Long, pale blond hair, dancing blue eyes, tall, willowy with a flawless body. I wanted to take her into my arms and hold her forever.

"Annalise," I said in German, as I bowed to kiss her hand, "Claus says that it will be necessary for you and I to argue. I must say at the beginning of our arguments that I have never encountered such a radiant adversary, one with whom it will be a joy to argue and a pleasure to lose."

A wicked grin appeared on her face.

"Blarney is an Irish word," she said in perfect upper-class English, "isn't it Herr Ridgewood?"

The rest of the savages laughed and applauded. My face grew very warm.

"Touché, ma'mselle," I said with a bow. "As we say on the tennis courts, c'est à vous!"

"We will see later about the tennis courts," she replied aloofly. "I will, of course, win."

"As God wills . . ."

The child, I told myself, is spoiled. She has been rude to a guest and gets away with it. They all adore her. Still, there is magic between us. Someday I will marry her.

Over the huge Teutonic meal—seven courses and four kinds of wine in a room glowing with candlelight and candles—we talked about Ireland, not at my initiative, but at the choice of the guests. Germans, I had learned in Heidelberg, were always eager for learning.

Gräfin Karoline, Claus's mother, wondered about the condition of the arts in Ireland.

"Ireland became a nation once again only in 1921," I said. "The arts have only begun to flourish. However, the Irish art has typically been verbal, stories, poetry, drama, not all of it the kind that the good Annalise dismisses as blarney. We did, after all, invent rhymed verse, a couple of centuries after we brought Christianity to the Swabians. We seemed to have succeeded fairly well in the latter task."

His father, Graf Alfred, asked about the economic conditions in Ireland. I told him that they were mixed, somewhat better in the North where the English permitted the development of manufacture. In the South there had at least been no return of the famines which wracked the country in the last century. Nonetheless, as a poor country, Ireland suffered especially from the worldwide Depression.

I explained to Gräfin Nina, Claus's love, that I hoped to join the Irish diplomatic service when I returned from my studies in Heidelberg and to Baron von Uxküll, Claus's uncle, that though we were a poor country we would have a foreign service because all nations did and now we were a nation. That notion of a "nation once again," was, I told him, very important to the New Ireland. Berthold, Claus's brother, said that Ireland would certainly remain neutral if there were another war between England and Germany and that its status as a "Dominion" like Canada or South Africa, gave it the right to remain neutral.

Annalise had patiently been waiting her turn, next to me at the table, a delicious presence at which I stole an occasional furtive glance.

"I went to school in England for two years, Herr Ridgewood . . ."

"And speak excellent English, if I may offer a compliment . . ."

She waved it away.

"They told us there that the Irish nobility live in caves and paint their bodies blue."

"That is true, Annalise, but only on the first Monday of every month and on the rogation days every leap year. However, we normally do not eat our own children, at least not anymore. Truth to tell, however, there really are no Irish nobility left. The English killed them or drove them away long ago. Most of those who remain are Protestants and their titles are English titles, which the new country recognizes. Our family Schloss is in Northern Ireland which the English still occupy, but we have citizenship in both Ireland and England."

"So you are not really an Irish noble?" she said, raising an eyebrow.

"On the contrary, lovely one, I am both Irish and English. It is very convenient."

"But is that not a contradiction?"

"We Irish don't worry about such philosophical details."

The savages around the table were enjoying this contest between their lovely princess and the Auslander from the Celtic fringe.

"In Ireland," Annalise said crisply, "the principle of contradiction does not apply?"

"It never has," I replied with equal crispness.

Laughter and applause from around the table, the latter from knives against goblets.

"Your point, Herr Ridgewood. Match point tomorrow morning on the tennis court."

"By all means."

There was a chemistry between us which seemed to be noticed with approval among the guests. Were they hoping I would carry her off and free them of the responsibility of protecting her? Dizzy from the wine and the conversation and her beauty, I thought that might not be a bad idea.

As Claus and I went to our rooms much later, he said, "I warned you about Annalise."

"Claus, old fellow," I said, "I have the impression your family and Nina's would be delighted if some appropriate man carried her off and freed you from the responsibility of protecting the little brat."

"*So long as it is the right man and he waits a few more years. She is still too young.*"

"*Do you think I could cope with her, say, in four or five years?*"

"*You already are thinking of that? It didn't take long.*"

"*It's the wine and the candlelight talking,*" I said.

"*I hope not.*" He opened the door to my room. "*Sleep well.*"

I woke up the next morning, furious at my presumed friend Claus von Stauffenberg because he was attempting to trap me in a union with an obnoxious child. I told myself I was being enticed into the local fair to purchase a promising heifer who the owner admitted would be difficult to keep in line.

Then I remembered that I must attend the Palm Sunday Mass down in the Schloss's tiny chapel, also part of the old citadel enclosed in the manor house. I was the last one in and arrived just as the ancient priest tottered out on the altar, which is early for your Irish male. Morning light streamed in through the small stained-glass windows on one side of the chapel. Here the Stauffenberg men must have prayed before they went out to battle whatever invaders were washing up on the far end of the Empire in the region where both the Rhine and the Danube began and flowed in opposite directions. Here their women wept over the lifeless bodies brought home after the battles. I glanced around the chapel, searching for my beloved. She was up in front, head bent in fervent prayer.

I was out of my mind crazy to think that she was the woman for me based on one evening's confrontation. All right, she was the most beautiful woman I had ever known. Moreover she was an orphan who needed protection, parents and brothers dead in the war and of the flu. She was too smart for her own good and too grown-up physically for her age. So she seemed to find me attractive enough to banter with. As good as the von Uxkülls were to her, she must crave for her freedom to act like an adult. But she wasn't an adult. Yet she was old as the Galway woman was when my Old Fella carried her off and himself a lot younger than I was. Why should I lack the wild courage that had driven the Old Fella's whole life?

If you fall in love, the Galway woman had said, and you're sure that she's the right one, what are you waiting for?

But how could I be sure on the basis of a single evening?

We sang Gregorian chant during the Mass, Claus conducting of course. After the Gospel, the old priest preached movingly, but in a Swabian dialect that was utterly unintelligible. I noted that many members of the congregation were nodding, perhaps with headaches much like mine.

I admit that my imagination filled up with images of Annalise in various stages of undress. Shame on you, I told myself. Then I replied that if God had not wanted men to have such images of women, he wouldn't have created us male and female.

If I told Claus that I wanted to take Annalise back with me to Ireland, he would have tried to broker the deal. He would persuade first of all his parents, then Nina soon to be his betrothed and her parents. There would be little resistance from either party. Good riddance. Then he would talk to Annalise. She would tell him that if I were interested, I should talk directly to her. That was as good as if she said yes. It would all be easy.

What would my parents say when I brought her home? They would be astonished that I had found a wife, especially one so decorative. In all probability she would bond with the Galway woman and they would make common cause against me.

Would my new wife like Ireland? How would she react to life in a foreign country? Especially with her own country caught up in the bloody war which seemed probable? Who could say?

She also doubtless loved Claus, from as close a distance as he would permit, which was not likely to be very close. How would I stand up in comparison with un chevalier parfait?

Not a chance.

Not a good idea, I told myself as we left the chapel.

I now tell myself that I caused sadness for many because of my Irish bachelor's fears.

I noted that she remained for more prayer. How would I fare with a pious wife? The Galway woman, God knew, was pious in her own half-mystical, half-superstitious style.

I realized that this Easter week would be decisive for claiming Annalise as my wife. Claus might well join the family's traditional regiment—the Seventeenth Cavalry—in the summer. I would be back in Ireland for Christmas, ready for my first assignment, doubtless in some dark hole in Africa. It was now or never.

My last-ditch argument paraded as unselfish. Annalise had the right to grow up to be her own person, to continue her education, to make her own choices in life. If she married me, no matter how much she liked me, it would not be a free choice but one imposed by her well-meaning family and friends. It would be intolerable of me to take advantage of such a situation.

Yet she would escape from Nazi Germany before the next and more terrible war began.

Servants were distributing a monumental breakfast on the dinner table. I ate lightly. I had a serious tennis match to face. However, since I had won the Oxford tennis tournament during my last two years there, I didn't feel in all that much jeopardy. I noticed a picture of Annalise on a shelf. She was standing with a very handsome man in an army officer's uniform, complete with the spiked helmet, and three children, two strapping young men, also in uniform, and a little girl with a silly grin, just barely able to walk.

"Was not my mother beautiful?" Annalise asked behind me.

"No more beautiful than her daughter," I replied, realizing for the first time that this was a picture of the family she had lost.

"More blarney, Herr Ridgewood, but thank you."

She was wearing a black skirt and a white sweater which molded itself around her delicious breasts.

"Do you want to talk about it?"

"Why not?" she said unemotionally. "A month after that picture, my father's regiment, under the command of the Crown Prince himself charged the village of Douaumont. It was almost completely destroyed. The men in my family were killed within a half hour by French artillery. Our custom was always to have all our men in the same regiment so they could take care of one another. At one time it seemed to make sense. Not anymore. A great tragedy for me and my mother perhaps, but also for a quarter million men on both sides. The strategy was to bleed the French white and end the war. It bled us too. The French army was close to mutiny afterwards, but the Americans entered the war and they had many more men to lose."

She shivered but she did not weep.

"I am sorry, Annalise, very sorry."

"Thank you, Herr Ridgewood. Now I must eat breakfast because I have a difficult tennis challenge this morning."

"I assume you were praying this morning for victory."

She glanced at me and then looked away.

"I was praying for many things, Herr Ridgewood."

The grass tennis court behind the Schloss was in good condition, the white lines fresh and the grass neatly cut. The custom was that those who did not play sat on a porch under big gold-and-red umbrellas, sipped coffee or tea or lemonade and cheered the contestants.

Alexander von Stauffenberg provided white tennis togs, shoes, and a racquet for me, all of them better than my equipment at Oxford. The procedure was "winner continues to play"—thus the final winner, on the verge of exhaustion no doubt, had defeated all the others. We drew for position and the lucky mick would be the last one on the court. I would face an exhausted Annalise. That wasn't fair either.

Best out of three sets was a victory.

Annalise disposed of Nina, Berthold and Alexander in three quick matches. I reveled in the twists and turns of her body as she served, raced across the court, and then, killed a return at the net.

She would be a big success in Ireland.

"She does that all the time." Nina collapsed next to me on the verandah and sipped at a glass of lemonade. "The only one who gives her trouble is Claus."

The match with Claus went the full route. He lost in the third game of the third set when she broke his serve.

"Claus says that you are not perhaps an effective player."

"Nina, I take it easy on the others up in Heidelberg. I won the Oxford All-University championship two years in a row."

"Poor Annalise." Nina sighed, not exactly troubled at the prospect of her cousin's losing.

My foe kissed Claus briskly when the set was over, with a little more feeling than she had shown for her other victims. He walked off the court, clearly distressed.

"She is much too good for a woman." He sighed as he sat on the other side of Nina.

"You should be proud of such a strong cousin, Claus."

"Herr Ridgewood, it would not be a humiliation if you withdrew," she shouted at me.

Arrogant little bitch.

"Well, I'll have a try at it anyway."

I walked out on the court, a little slippery under my feet compared to the indoor court at Heidelberg. For a moment I was tempted to let her win. If she ever found out, however, she would not forgive me.

"Some practice volleys, Herr Ridgewood?"

"That wouldn't help me at all," I said in the tone of one conceding victory.

"Your serve." She tossed the tennis ball to me.

I felt very foolish. Claus would recognize that I had never really tried in Heidelberg. I hoped he would understand why. But in these circumstances, I really had no choice, did I? The honour of Ireland was at stake, was it not?

So I used my strongest serve.

It zoomed right by her.

The crowd, such as it was, cheered.

Annalise stood as if she were suddenly paralysed. She lifted her racket in salute and smiled. She hunkered down, determined to return my second serve.

I aced the game.

She should have been very angry, especially because her family was cheering enthusiastically against her. Instead she laughed.

"You are a bad man, Herr Ridgewood," she hollered at me. "Very bad!"

Well, I lost one point to her in the sixth game.

Everyone was laughing now, except me.

Timmy Pat, you are one mean son of a bitch.

After I volleyed a backhand right past her and put the match away, she strode to the net, embraced me and kissed me with disturbing vigor. Her clothes were soaked in perspiration. Her family cheered.

"You were a champion at Oxford?" she demanded, still holding me as if a prisoner.

"Twice," I admitted.

"You did not tell me."

"You did not ask me."

There was general enthusiasm for my victory as we collapsed in chairs under the verandah.

"Annalise would have done much better," I said, "if she had not worn herself out in the early matches."

"Ja, ja." Claus chuckled.

"Claus, why did not you tell me that he won the championship at Oxford? Twice!"

"He never told me. He was nice to the rest of us at Heidelberg. You made fun of him."

"I will never do that again." She continued to laugh. "He is a bad, dangerous man . . . Come let us bathe in the lake."

"It will be too cold," Nina warned.

"It's been a warm spring," she replied. "Claus?"

"Very well."

So the three brothers, Annalise, and I, robes over our swimsuits, walked fifty yards behind the house, through a thin line of trees, to the shore of a small, narrow lake, peaceful under the strong summerlike sun. I strode down to the small pier where a rowboat was tied, dipped my foot in the water, decided that it was no worse than Galway Bay, tossed aside my robe and dove in.

"'Tis grand altogether!" I shouted, once I had regained my breath. "You're not afraid of a little cold water, are you now?"

Annalise discarded her robe and revealed a two-piece black swimming costume. I gulped for the second time. Mind you, the costume was as extensive as a corset and a bra . . . Still it revealed a lot of that wonderful body.

She dove in, surfaced almost at once and swam towards me.

"Herr Ridgewood tells the truth," she sputtered. "It's wunderbar!"

The other males jumped and yelled in protest.

Annalise caught me by surprise, grabbed my head, and shoved it under water.

I came up sputtering.

"That is because you beat me in tennis."

Then she dunked me again.

"That is for staring at my bathing costume."

I grabbed her and restrained her arms.

"The bathing costume is meant for staring."

She struggled to free herself from my grip which I was beginning to enjoy.

"Beast, pig!" she protested.

"You started it."

"All right! Dunk me twice and then let me go!"

"Promise me you won't dunk me again?"

"Yes!"

I let her go.

She seemed surprised.

The Stauffenberg brothers had already climbed on the pier. I helped Annalise up the ladder and then turned around and swam out into the lake. It was very cold, but not as cold as the Irish Sea or Galway Bay. Was I showing off to impress the young woman?

No, I was once more upholding the honour of the Irish race.

In accord with the goal, when I had returned to the pier I did my best not to shiver.

"Much warmer than Galway Bay," I assured my friends, as they huddled inside their robes.

"You are mad, Timmy!" Claus insisted as he helped me on with my robe.

"Only Irish, Claus."

"We must go back to the Schloss," he insisted, "put on warm clothes, and drink a glass of schnapps. It is very good for frostbite."

As we walked across the lawn, Claus whispered to me, "I must apologize, Claus, for Annalise. She is most forward. Too aggressive for a woman. Her bathing costume was outrageous."

"Did you really think so, Claus? I thought it was lovely!"

"Of course! Very lovely indeed, but . . ."

"If she is protected from too much more tragedy in her life, she will always be very lovely—and as innocent as she is now."

"Please, God, Timmy, that you are right."

"And as for the bathing costume, Claus Philipp Maria Graf Schenk von Stauffenberg. Don't pretend to be Protestant. It doesn't work."

He laughed, loud and long.

Even today, many long years later, memories of that laugh as well as the swimsuit that occasioned it, haunt me.

In the walls of the old fort, Claus served the schnapps—as clear as if it were alpine water—in shot glasses like he was administering a sacrament.

"Ja, ja, this is very good for one's health! It cures most serious physical diseases and all mental diseases. It is said that it even heals a broken heart!"

"It looks like poteen," I said as I sipped from the glass. "Sure it is the poteen, with a touch of cherry flavour in it."

I thereupon swallowed the whole glass. I felt that I might have swallowed a glass of liquid fire. I smacked my lips.

" 'Tis very like the poteen," I agreed, "not quite so strong. I'm sure, Claus, that it cures everything but a broken heart."

"You are a fraud, Herr Ridgewood," the dethroned tennis queen said, with a smile that might have been affectionate. "You were just as cold in the water as we were and the schnapps burned to the bottom of your soul—if you have one."

She was wearing the same white sweater that she had worn in the morning, but with a gray skirt.

"The sight of your glorious bathing costume has dulled my sensitivity to heat and cold."

Everyone laughed, even Annalise.

"Match point," she said again, as her face turned red.

"And I would add that we Irish are very tolerant of such matters. I found it very modest and appropriate in the circumstances and, if I may make bold to say it, quite innocently delightful."

I was fibbing again.

"You are still a fraud, Herr Ridgewood, but a very nice one." *She enveloped me in a radiant smile that was even warmer than the poteen. I figured that I had been a fine credit to the Irish race.*

"We should all perhaps take a nap now so we will be awake at dinner and not miss the ongoing battle between Annalise and Viscount Ridgewood."

"Will I not be granted a respite because I say nice things about her?"

They all laughed because it was obviously a silly question. I poured myself another glass of schnapps and downed it, against the chance of filthy dreams during my well-deserved nap.

As the angels would have it, I encountered Annalise in the corridor.

"Why did you not push my head under the water, Herr Ridgewood?" she asked. "You had the right to do so."

"In my country, Annalise, women have the right in such games to force a man's head under the water as a matter of principle because he deserves it. But men have no right to retaliate in kind."

"You were being a gentleman?"

"Well something like that . . . But I must apologize for not taking more appropriate action. In truth I didn't want to shock the good Count Claus, who as we both know has a touch of the prude in him."

It was the demon rum speaking in my voice. I never should have issued such a challenge. It would only get me in trouble.

"And what would that more appropriate action have been?"

I put my arms around her and drew her close.

"It is wrong in my country if a man holds a woman in his arms like I did and he does not kiss her."

I kissed her several times, forcefully. After the first one, she responded in kind. It was the poteen that was making me do it. She did not struggle as I thought she would. Rather, she rested her head against my chest and sighed.

Oh, oh. I was in trouble now.

"Those are very nice kisses, Herr Ridgewood," she whispered. "You are no longer a fraud."

Gently she disengaged from my arms.

"'Twas the poteen that made me do it," I exclaimed.

"I'm sure that it was."

She turned and walked slowly down the corridor, like a cloud was wafting her away.

I staggered into my room, told myself that it was indeed the poteen which had carried off my sanity and that I shouldn't worry about it. I fell asleep too quickly to experience guilt. When I woke up I told myself piously that it had never happened. However, Annalise's shy smile at dinner told me that it had.

The meal consisted of a wide variety of cold cuts, meat, cheeses, sausages, and Bavarian beers. I wasn't sure that my stomach, disarranged by the drink taken and the taste of Annalise's lips, would tolerate any food.

"We hear, Sir Timothy, that you were not shocked by my cousin's bathing costume."

Oh, oh. Trouble!

"Claus did not express shock," I said, pretending to be puzzled, "nor did Berthold or Alexander. I saw no reason why I should protest. We Irish, puritans in so many ways, are quite tolerant in such matters."

That was, of course, an absolute and total lie.

Annalise's face was crimson, her head bowed. So this was the sort of stuff with which she had to put up. Perhaps I had better, after all, take her away.

Gräfin Karoline frowned. "That is kind of you, Sir Timothy, but you understand that we must apologize to you."

"I thought it was quite appropriate in the circumstances, Lady Karoline, and perfectly innocent. After all it was a domestic swim at a private lake. Moreover, and despite my pretense that the water was quite warm, there was no danger of anyone's passions being aroused. In fact, if I may say so . . ." I paused as I had found a way out . . . "I personally found Lady Annalise's great beauty, I'm sure a durable gift from God, more appealing as she scampered around the tennis court this morning, even when she was swinging that wicked racket of hers at me."

This was not an altogether false statement.

The men around the table applauded, even Graf Albert.

"So long as you were not offended, Sir Timothy . . ."

"I assured you, ma'am, far from being offended I was delighted as I always am by Lady Annalise's youthful charm and vigor."

"Game, set, match, and tournament to you, Herr Ridgewood," Annalise murmured.

"Well done, Timmy," Claus said to me later after we had listened to his mother and Annalise play for us on the harp and piano. "I believe you have created a minor revolution here. I'm sure that my almost intended will join it before the week is over."

"Those negotiations go well?"

"Smoothly enough. The decisions will be made sometime tomorrow. In the morning, however, you and I and Annalise will ride around our lands, if you wish. I may have to return early to finish the negotiations. Perhaps you could take her for a ride across the lake."

"Perhaps I could."

I did not sleep immediately that night. It had been an exciting day. I had problems to consider, decisions to be made, futures to ponder. All right, she was still very young, but she was intelligent, determined, witty, and, ah, so beautiful. And her lips burned like fire and smoothed like silk.

— *9* —

THE FIELDS of Wisconsin were brown and boring under a dismal gray sky as we rushed up the interstate to Milwaukee on Monday morning in Nuala's Lincoln Navigator SUV, a car as graceful as an M1-A3 tank.

"In another month, everything will be turning green," I explained to her.

"And then it will look like the County Meath, the most boring place in the whole of Ireland, with the people to match."

"If you say so."

"And what did you think of himself?"

"Patjo? Was he misbehaving again?"

"No, your man the viscount?"

"I thought he handled those krauts very well."

"Smooth-talking gombeen man," she said.

"Oh, all of that. Yet what he told them was the truth and, it would seem what they wanted to hear."

"And that terrible stupid war just down the road."

"Do you think he ought to have taken her home with him to Ireland?"

"On the basis of a romance during Holy Week in 1934?"

"Would you have done it?"

"I didn't take you home from Ireland, Nuala Anne."

"'Tis true and meself having to come after you."

"She was too young to flee to Ireland."

"Two or three years younger than I was."

YOU WOULD HAVE LEFT HER THERE IN GERMANY TO DIE IN THE WAR.

I thought about it for a few silent minutes as we hurtled towards Milwaukee.

"If I knew what would happen in the war, I might have taken the chance. Otherwise, I'd probably persuade myself that she wouldn't go anywhere and I could return in five years or so and see if she were still interested in me. I would have been a fool and never forgiven myself."

"Irishmen," my wife said, "are notoriously reluctant suitors."

"His father wasn't."

"'Tis true."

"What do you think he should have done, Nuala Anne?"

"The problem is that none of us know exactly what the future will be like."

That was all my wife, stern critic of male behavior that she was, would judge. Timmy Pat would have to live with his decision and regret it for the rest of his life, even though it was certainly sensible and reasonable.

"Well, maybe he'll get another chance," I suggested.

"Timmy Pat is a good and thoughtful fella," she said, "even if he is a bit of a gombeen man. He didn't take advantage of her, like many would have done. Maybe God will give him credit for that."

Nuala had set her global locator for the address of Marquette and navigated into the University with her accustomed skill. She even found a parking spot near the Student Union that was big enough for her beast of a car. Naturally she knew exactly where it was before she pulled into the campus.

She had put on the mask of the successful, though sexy, professional woman—black suit, black hose, high heels, hair piled up, black leather jacket, large black briefcase with copies of all her CDs, "for the poor exile priest from me home county." I could count on it, the brogue would get thicker and thicker before the day was over. I compromised and wore a sport coat and a tie with the Marquette colors—red and gold of course.

I felt irrationally proud when I walked into the Student Union and the young women and the young men turned for a second look at my wife. Some of them frowned a little—they thought they remembered the face, but they weren't quite sure about the name that went with it.

"Father O'Donovan." I shook hands with my teacher.

"Dermot Michael Coyne," he replied.

"Father O'Donovan, this is me wife, Nuala Anne McGrail."

"I figured as much," he said with a big grin.

Thereupon the Irish language flowed like butter melting at a picnic on a hot summer day. The two Galway people ignored the poor, semiliterate Yank. Nuala Anne did not stop talking even while she was hanging up her black leather jacket.

As far as I could tell the only change in my Jesuit mentor was that his tight curly black hair, parted in the center, had turned silver. If he had put on any weight, the shapeless Jebby cassock with its floppy sash covered it up. The light of mischief on his face was as bright as ever.

"Does Dermot have the tongue?" He turned to English as we sat at a table in which the dishes and the silver had been laid out with the neatness we used to expect from nuns.

"He does not, poor dear man." She rested a sympathetic hand on my arm. "When we're back home, the childer translate for him."

Out of the black bag there appeared an eight-by-ten picture (in a frame) of the childer and the dogs.

"The lads favor Dermot as you can see, and Nellie, the oldest, looks just like his grandmother. The little girl, our tiny terrorist, favors me."

"Dermot," said the priest, "you've done well for yourself, a lovely celebrity wife, four grand-looking kids, and all the time yourself continuing the image of the lazy lad to whom all these wonders just happened."

"You have the right of it, Father Bob," Nuala agreed. "That's the image. Isn't the reality of it very different?"

"'Tis," he replied.

Thereupon me wife opened her black bag, removed the six platinum CDs and autographed the sleeves with words in green ink—Irish words of course. Then she pulled my four books out of the bag and gave me the pen with the green ink. I signed them with the greeting "Father Bob." Nuala made a face of displeasure. I should have been more elaborate.

A waitress began serving our soup. She leaned over the table and whispered in the priest's ear and then departed with a giggle.

Did I know what was coming? Certainly I did! I'd been there before.

"Nuala Anne," he said, "we have a very polite request for you to sing, just one song before you go back to Chicago. Would you ever be able . . ."

"I would, Father, and be happy to do it, so long as they can find a harp or a guitar."

Truth to tell, she would have been brokenhearted if they hadn't asked.

Father Bob wanted to know whether Archbishop Ryan was really running Chicago now that he was coadjutor with right to succession.

"Isn't there a lot of talk about it?" Nuala replied. "He claims that nothing has changed. Cardinal Sean says that he himself is on a permanent vacation. I don't believe either one of them, at all, at all."

"I agree with me wife, though I would express it differently. I believe both of them."

"'Tis the same thing," Nuala admitted.

"Chicago continues to luck out," he said. "You two know both of them well, I take it?"

"Nuala is a full-fledged member of the North Wabash Avenue Irregulars, the crowd of people that help Blackie to solve mysteries. They both claim that the other is better at the puzzles. Again I believe both of them."

"Well, Father," she segued to the work at hand, "on the odd occasion don't me husband and I wrestle some small puzzles . . ."

"I'm the spear-carrier, and she's the thinker. She's just a tiny bit fey . . ."

"No one's just at tiny bit fey, Dermot," the priest said grimly.

"The little Archbishop says that it's a neo-Neanderthal vestige and I'm not really a witch."

"If Blackie says it," the Jeb said, "it has to be true."

"Anywho, we've been asked to see if we can find young Des Doolin and aren't we a bit confused about him? Some folk say he was immature and irresponsible and others that he knew what he was doing and his family didn't support him."

Father Bob sighed, not as spectacularly as me wife could, but still it was an impressive protest against the folly of the human condition.

"He baffled me too, Nuala Anne, almost as much as this fella you picked up in Dublin. Dermot was always thinking and dreaming up questions. Des . . . well, Des was running around all the time doing things . . ."

"No one ever accused me of doing that . . ."

"Hush, Dermot love, we're being serious now."

WELL, I GUESS SHE PUT YOU IN YOUR PLACE.

'Tis the way of the world.

"I'd say that, like your fella, Des was solidly and unshakably Catholic. We get a lot of kids like that these days—absolutely dedicated to the tradition, shaped by the Vatican Council reforms, turned off by the leadership, but deeply committed to being Catholic. For Des that meant going to Mass, singing in the choir, acting as a lector or a Mass server, volunteering to work with the poor, saying the Rosary, nudging his friends back into the Church—any Catholic activity he could find, old, new or perennial. Like I say we get more and more such kids. They couldn't be anything but Catholic and they want to be more Catholic. After all the scandals and the horses' asses in the saddle they are a breath of fresh air, maybe a hurricane of fresh air."

"The leaders don't know about them, do they?" Me wife beat me to that question.

"Well, from what I hear about Chicago, Cardinal Cronin and Blackie know about them, but they're not typical . . . Mind you, Des was not a fanatic, not a fundamentalist, not a pusher, he was much more sophisticated than that. Most of his nudging was his contagious enthusiasm. He got his class work done, earned his 3.95 average—a bit higher than yours, Dermot—didn't drink too much. I know his parents thought he was immature . . . They complained to me and denounced me to the Archbishop . . . But he was far more mature and more responsible than they were."

"Were you after telling them that?"

"Not in so many words, Nuala. We Jebs are a bit more subtle than that. I told them that their son was a fine young man and they should be proud of him. His mother said that they knew he was a fine young man, they only wished he'd settle down. I suggested that the young might need some time to test their wings and she said something about their mistake was letting him go to Loyola Academy . . ."

"Blame the Jesuits," I intruded. "Why not? Where was he headed, Father Bob?"

"I don't know and I think he didn't know either. Peace Corps for sure and Africa for sure. Beyond that? No plans. Play it by ear. Go with the flow. He had a great time over in Eritrea. Loved the people. He came up here to see me when he returned. Asked my advice about learning Arabic. I told him it was a great idea."

"Any young women in his life?"

"A lot of them would like to have been. They told me that he was adorable, but he fended them off. One kid, Siobhan, hung out with him a lot, but I had the impression that she didn't push him very hard."

"Your typical Irish bachelor," I observed.

Look who's talking.

"Wouldja look who's talking," my wife said, echoing as she often does the Adversary who hides in the subbasement of my brain.

"His mom said that she wished he'd find a nice young woman who'd settle him down. My guess is that their idea of a nice young woman and Des's would be very different. At that stage in his life he wanted mobility, freedom. Then this damnable war started and he disappeared off to Iraq."

"You haven't heard from him?" Nuala asked.

"Not a word. He was smart enough to know that it was very danger-ous. He also knew enough Arabic and enough about Islam to lose him-self in the country if he wanted to—for a while anyway. He's a very clever guy and moves very quickly when he wants to."

"You think he's still alive?"

He sighed, a Galway man again.

"A roadside bomb, an exploding car, a suicide bomber, a stray Ameri-can bullet—that could have been the end of him and we'd never hear. If the terrorists kidnapped him, we'd have seen him on television. I don't think he's working for the CIA or any of that bunch of gobshites."

"They won't talk about him, which makes me think they know about him," I said.

"Or want to make us think they know about him."

The waitress, having served the ice-cream sundaes which were our dessert, leaned over Father O'Donovan and whispered again.

"Ah, they've found a harp!"

"Brilliant! Would you ever tell them, dear, that I'll be out in a few minutes to sing a song or two."

IRISH SUBJUNCTIVE OF POLITE REQUEST, STILL OCCASIONALLY HEARD FROM SOUTH SIDE IRISH.

I know that.

"Better you than Britney Spears, Nuala . . . And what will you two do when and if you find him?"

"It depends. We're not on retainer, we almost never are. So if we find out that he's alive and well, we tell his parents that he is and that he loves them and leave it at that. If he's in trouble, we see what we can do to get him out of trouble—which does not mean sending Dermot to the desert."

"I'm glad to hear that!"

"So am I!"

"For all his enthusiasm," Nuala said, "he sounds like someone who has sense to come in out of the rain still."

"You mean that you'd bet," the good Jesuit responded, "that his trip to Iraq may not have been as spontaneous and impulsive as it seems?"

"Something like that . . . I have the feeling that he's still alive, but I keep telling meself that I'm out of me mind. You can't trust the feelings all the time, ya know . . . I'd never change our investment portfolio on one of them."

"You'd not be all that far from wrong," Father Bob, who was slipping into more brogue as he listened to herself, said, "if you continued to search for him."

"Me very thought."

I had finished my ice cream and Nuala's too.

"We're very grateful for lunch, Father," I said. "And it's been good to see you again. You've confirmed our impression that Des is not the flaming idiot that his family thinks he is."

Nuala nodded solemnly.

"We just have to work harder and dig deeper . . . Now if you excuse me for a minute, I have to check on the childer."

She walked over to the corner of the room and flipped open her cell phone.

"They DID! He DID! She DID! Let me talk to HER! . . ." She rolled her eyes at me. "Miss Coyne, Ethne tells me you won't take a NAP! Right NOW! No NOT in a little while! NOW! You understand NOW!"

She returned to the table, produced a set of her disks for the waitress from the black bag and set about autographing them.

"Dermot, your daughter refused to take her nap. You'll have to deal with her when we get home."

"Sounded like you dealt with it already . . . Notice, Father Bob, when they do something wrong, they're my kids."

She gave the disks to the waitress.

"YOU'd never do anything like that, would you now, dear?"

"All the time, Nuala Anne."

"All you kids are alike!"

We all laughed at her.

"And all men are kids . . . Dermot, would you ever carry me coat?"

There was a huge mob of Warriors (as Marquette students still call themselves) waiting for us in the lobby of the Student Union. A harp and a mike were set up in a corner.

She sat next to the harp and lovingly strummed it, tightened the strings, strummed it again, and sighed.

" 'Tis good of all youse to cut class to hear me sing! I'll do only a few songs, so youse won't miss the next class. I'm going to sing the song about Molly Malone. 'Tis a very sad song. Molly was younger than most of you when she died. Most poor kids in Ireland her time died young. However, up in heaven Molly knows that she's immortal up there and down here too. Wherever in the world there are Irish and some of them sing—and that will be up midnight on the day before the last judgment—they'll remember her. It's my favorite song because one night in O'Neill's just off College Green, a big dumb Yank listened to me sing and I knew that I'd have to marry him someday."

Somehow every time she sings it tears form in my eyes. The song is both so sad and so glorious.

Then she did "When Irish Eyes Are Smiling" and "Galway Bay" ("Because Father O'Donovan and I are both from Galway"). Then she concluded with the "Connemara lullaby" ("Because we're both from Connemara").

"She's magical, Dermot," my old teacher whispered.

"Sure, you're grand folk, but don't I have to get home to me four childer before they tear the house apart."

"Did you marry the big dumb Yank?"

"I did and isn't the poor dear man a livin' saint altogether. If it weren't for him, I wouldn't be a singer at all, at all."

Cheers and applause.

We worked our way through the crowd of autograph seekers, shook hands with Father O'Donovan, and climbed into the Navigator.

"Would you ever drive us home, Dermot love? I'm an emotional wreck."

"Sure," I said, "though I don't think I've been cleared for jet aircraft."

When she goes into those emotional wreck situations, the best course for me, I have learned, is to keep my big mouth shut till she works her way out of it.

We were thirty miles south of Milwaukee when she signaled the end with an extra loud sigh.

"I'm all right now," she said. "It was all so beautiful and so sad."

"Marquette?"

"And those wonderful, fresh-faced childer and you there and the poor dear Galway priest and meself a Yank now . . . do you take me meaning?"

"Woman, I do."

"With each new kid I get more sentimental . . . The generations turn, don't they, Dermot Michael?"

"They do indeed . . . Maybe we should rethink these spontaneous concerts . . ."

"Ah, no. If I were doing that, I wouldn't be meself anymore would I? What did you think about your man?"

I guessed she meant Des.

"Well, I'd say that the poor dear Galway priest thought he was a lad with his head screwed on right."

"You have the right of it, Dermot. He was neither immature nor irresponsible, even if he had the glint in his eye. What does that tell us?"

"That his brother and parents are creeps."

"It also tells us that his trip to Iraq wasn't impulsive or sudden. Something must have been in the wind before your man ordered the invasion."

That was my Nuala Anne being insightful instead of fey.

"'Tis true."

"So, he's up to something over there!"

"'Tis true also."

Would you stop saying that!

"We have to find out what it was and then we'll know where to look."

"That won't be easy."

"At least, Dermot love, we'll know what we're doing."

I didn't see that quite as clearly as she did, but I wasn't going to get into a pointless argument.

"I'm sorry I was so emotional like and meself making you drive me car."

The Navigator was "her" car. My Benz was "our" car.

"I've always wanted to drive a tank."

"Des was plotting with someone. All we have to do is to find out what he was plotting . . . I wonder if the childer are all right."

"Call Ethne on your cell phone."

"Brilliant altogether."

It turned out that the little childer were just waking up and the big ones were coming out of school.

"I feel like I've been away from them for years," she admitted to me. "Whom would he know in Iraq?"

"Maybe some Iraq-Americans."

She sighed. "'Tis a deep puzzle altogether . . . Don't drive too fast, Dermot. It's raining."

"I'm driving the limit, which is ten miles an hour slower than when you were driving."

She giggled.

THE NEXT MORNING our investigation ran into more trouble.

I was in my office reading about the youthful adventures of Viscount Ridgewood with an increasing sense of doom. The kids were in school, except for Patjo, who was sleeping soundly. Nuala was downstairs reading the draft of Ethne's dissertation and telling her that it was ded friggin' bril.

The doorbell rang, always a warning signal. Then a cacophony of angry sounds swirled upstairs. Nuala screamed, the doggies howled, Ethne screamed and Poraig Josefa wailed, the bell continued to clang as someone outside pushed the button insistently. I grabbed Nuala's canogi stick (Irishwomen's field hockey, like) and thundered down the stairs. Herself was pressed against the wall, still screaming. The dogs were scratching against the door, eager to get out and kill or maim the invader. Periodically, they paused in their efforts to vent their rage with their lost-soul-in-hell cry. Ethne was trying to console Patjo.

"There's one of them suits outside, he tried to push into the house and meself nursing poor Patjo. I screamed and shoved him out. The doggies went wild! Get rid of him, Dermot."

"Woman, I will."

I searched in a table drawer and found a card which would be useful.

"Doggies, downstairs!" I ordered in my most authoritative voice.

Two white heads swiveled in astonishment. I never ordered them to do anything. Did I really mean it?

"I said DOWNSTAIRS!"

Obediently they went downstairs.

"Close the door on them and lock it, Ethne," I commanded. "And you brat child, QUIET!"

Poraig looked at me in astonishment. I was breaking the rules. Nonetheless he shut up.

I put my arm around a still-weeping Nuala.

"I'll take care of him, Nuala love."

"Don't be hitting him over the head with my canogi stick!" she sobbed.

"It's a shock and awe weapon. Don't worry."

I opened the door and ambled out on the porch.

The man indeed wore a dark suit and a dark raincoat (even though the sun had made a token appearance) and rain-spattered horn-rimmed glasses. He looked sufficiently shabby and disconsolate that he had to be from the Bureau.

"I'm Dermot," I announced genially.

"Are you Mrs. Grail's husband?"

"That's an issue which need not detain us."

"Do you intend to abuse me with that stick?"

"It's a canogi stick, Special Agent. Used by women in Ireland in a version of hurling which is distantly related to our field hockey. I'll use it on you only if you attempt again to force your way into this house or if you ring the doorbell one more time."

He flashed his badge and ID card at me.

"Federal Bureau of Investigation," he said in an attempt at terseness.

"Forgive me for not being impressed," I said, caressing the canogi stick. "You look and smell like Bureau."

"Are those big white dogs dangerous?"

"They're sweet and gentle and well behaved, unless they perceive you as menacing Ms. McGrail. Then your throat and genitals will be in grave danger."

"I will charge her with attacking a federal officer and you with threatening one. I could arrest you now on both charges."

"Do you have a warrant for Mrs. Grail or to enter her house?"

"I don't need a warrant to arrest both of you."

"Think very carefully, Special Agent, about what you want to do. We will sue, you, the Bureau, the United States Attorney, and maybe even the vice president on the grounds that you used physical force to gain entrance into a private home without a warrant. Moreover, since I assume you are one of those hacks whom the Bureau sends out to check on National Security Agency wire taps, we will also sue them and everyone else for violation of privacy. I don't think you want to have given the civil liberties organizations an opportunity to go after the all the snoops in the Beltway."

"Mrs. McGrail has been making long-distance calls in an unknown foreign language. She may be a threat to national security. It is imperative that I interview her."

"Could you guess what language it might be, Special Agent?"

"The FBI doesn't guess, sir."

"I am delighted to know that. Let me say on the record that Ms. Mc-Grail will be only too happy to discuss her phone calls with you in her lawyer's office. Her lawyer is one Cynthia Hurley. You may want to phone Ms. Hurley for an appointment. You may now go back to your superiors at the Everett McKinley Dirksen Federal Building and tell them that is our response. They are, I should think, not unfamiliar with either Ms. McGrail or Ms. Hurley."

"You haven't heard the last of me."

"In all candor I think we have, but who knows. We may meet again in federal court. Now I urge you to leave our property."

He glared at me, turned, and stumbled down the stairs.

The trouble with the security apparatus of the United States was that it wasted so much of its time on stupid intrusions into the lives of innocent Americans that it had no time left to find the dangerous people.

Why not tell them that my wife's phone calls were in the Irish language to her parents in the County Galway? Because they had no right to be snooping on her calls and because anyone with any sense would know who she was and why she would be speaking an "unknown foreign language" in an overseas call to Galway.

No one in the government had common sense anymore.

"'Tis all right," I said as I returned to the parlor. "Ethne, please let the doggies upstairs."

I sat down next to Nuala on the couch. Patjo was sleeping contentedly in her lap.

"The gobshite says that you might be a terrorist because after all don't you make overseas phone calls in a strange foreign language which might be Arabic."

She laughed.

"Are they that dumb, Dermot Michael?"

"Woman, they are! But I think they—not this guy but his bosses—are not so dumb as to take Cindy and you on again."

"Why me?"

"Somewhere in the bowels of the federal government there is a database with your name on it from previous struggles. They pick up your conversations in the general wiretapping of the country. Then they compare it to their lists and they send a hack out to intimidate you . . ."

The hounds rushed into the room, sniffing obsessively. They had to kiss Ethne and me and Nuala and nuzzle Patjo before they settled down at Nuala's feet, panting heavily from their exertions.

Beautiful big dogs, but, oh, so big!

"I'll call Cindy," I said as I pushed the button on my cell phone which symbolized my sister.

"Hi, sister, Dermot. I have thick red meat for you."

I told her the story.

"Nuala was nursing that big lazy punk that looks like you when he tried to force his way into the house?"

"He's lucky she shoved him out before the beasts got him."

"I think I will make a phone call to my very good friend the United States Attorney for the Northern District of Illinois and suggest that before the end of the day I will seek an injunction against everyone in sight to cease and desist and a press conference to ask what the federal government has against my client."

"Sounds cool."

"Tell her that asshole and all his fellow assholes won't be back."

"You know how me wife is shocked by that kind of language."

"And tell her that I'll get that red flag off her name . . . Dermot, this country is truly becoming a police state."

"One more thing, we are investigating the case of the young man who disappeared into Iraq, trying to find out for his parents if he's still alive. That may have stirred them up."

"So it's against the law to search for a missing person? If it comes up, I'll take care of that too . . . Is he still alive?"

"Me wife says he is."

"That's good enough for me, brother. Give my love to my most beautiful client."

Nuala collected the hounds and went across the street to bring the three kids home from school for lunch. It was always a great event for Maeve and Fiona because there is much more adoration and affection to be absorbed. There wasn't any time to talk about my conversation with Cindy. After the kids went back to school and Socra Marie and Patjo went to bed and the pooches curled up for their afternoon naps at their respective stations, I poured her a jar of Middleton's and put her to bed.

"The whole family needs a nap, except me," I said.

"You'll be reading about your man in Germany?"

"I will."

"Thank you, Dermot."

Cindy called back while she was asleep.

"Your good friend the United States Attorney for the Northern District apologizes in his name and in the name of the Agent-in-Charge. He understands that Irish is not a Semitic language. He will insist NSA drop the red flag after your bride's name on its database. He also knows that there will be a major suit if it ever happens again."

"Well done."

"My pleasure to hear him eat crow. He'll get it in writing by next week. I will, as a matter of principle, reject it as not strong enough, then he will redo it. No more of the men in suits will climb the steps to your house."

"After all she's been through, Nuala will be glad to hear that."

"She probably won't believe it . . . The United States Attorney for the Northern District also knows about your investigation of the Desmond Doolin matter . . ."

"He does!"

"He makes no claim that you have no right to look for the young man. He thinks it would be better if you did not, however."

"Does he now? Does he say why?"

"I don't think he knows. Someone higher up told him to pass that on."

"What do you think?"

"You ask me, I think the poor kid is dead and was killed by our side. That's top probability."

"What's second probability?"

"That they have fouled up badly and they want to keep it a secret. The kid is still alive and they don't want him to get out to tell his story till the Iraq mess is over."

"As the little Archbishop says, 'fascinating!' "

"Will herself back off?"

"I don't think so."

"I told him to tell his bosses not to count on it."

After all the kids were safely in bed, Nuala joined me in "my" office. I poured her a large goblet of Bailey's Irish Cream on ice for dessert and recounted my conversation with Cindy.

She sipped slowly on her Bailey's and thought for a few moments.

"Well, if you ask me what I think, I think that they know a lot more about Des than they're telling anyone and that your man is up to something pretty interesting."

"Like?"

"Like something we have to figure out, somehow. In the meantime, we continue to poke around . . . Did your man tell Cindy that it was dangerous?"

"He did not."

"Well, then we'll see what Siobhan has to say next week, won't we?"

"We will."

— 10 —

The next morning we went riding—Claus, Annalise and I. As befit rural aristocrats, they were both superb horsemen, as good as I was but not better.

"You ride a lot in Ireland, Tim?" Claus asked me. "You certainly seem at
ease on a horse."

"I'd rather ride a motorcar," I said, "like one of your Benzes or our Rolls.
But horses are fun too."

That wasn't exactly true, but I was up to my old tricks of making trouble,
kicking up shite as the Galway woman would say.

"Herr Ridgewood likes to argue, does he not, Claus?"

"I think it is an Irish trait, Annalise."

"Everyone learned in the last war," I continued, "that cavalry is useless in
battle."

"Many countries still have them," Claus observed. "Even the German army."

"Only until they build enough Panzers. If you do sign up for your historic
Seventeenth Cavalry, you'll be riding a Panzer into Poland and France."

"*That is not funny, Herr Ridgewood,*" Annalise protested.

"*You will learn, Annalise, that the Irish change from comic to serious and back in a single sentence . . . There are brilliant writers, our Heinz Guderian, the Frenchman Charles de Gaulle, the Englishman Liddell Hart who argue that tanks will make wars shorter. I don't believe that. We won't kill as many horses and we'll probably need fewer horses anyway.*"

"*Do your people listen to Guderian?*"

"*More than the English listen to Hart, and much more than the French listen to de Gaulle. To fight a war without horses seems almost immoral.*"

"*And what do you think, Claus?*" Annalise asked.

"*I think that you may need cavalry to train leaders, but that Timmy is right. The General Staff is intrigued by one of Heinz's phrases—Blitzkrieg, lightning war.*"

"*I hope there is never another war,*" she said fervently.

The horses came to a stop as Claus reined in his great stallion.

"*I hope so, Anna.*" He rested his hand on her arm. "*There are many in this country who want to settle scores with France and England. And even with America. Including Herr Hitler and his band of ruffians. I think that many of the officers, however, fear that another bloodbath would indeed lead to a Bolshevik revolution that would succeed this time. If I join the army, I will ally myself with that side. Never another Verdun, liebchen.*"

"*I certainly hope not,*" she said.

We rode on in silence.

We had circled around through the trees and the meadows and were back by the edge of the lake. Again, Claus drew in his reins.

"*I'm afraid I must return to the Schloss,*" he said with resignation. "*There are some delicate negotiations which have to be carried on today before we go into the heart of Holy Week. All hope that a happy announcement can be made after Mass on Saturday when we sing the Gloria and the Alleluia again and Lent ends.*"

"*Surely, there can be no doubt, Claus, about the outcome?*" Annalise said.

"*Hardly. Nina and I already pledged ourselves. However,*" he said with a shrug, "*there are certain dignities that must be honoured, certain formalities maintained, certain symbols respected.*"

"Of course," I said.

He tipped his hat to both of us and cantered off towards the Schloss.

"You have been to my Bamberg, Herr Ridgewood?"

"Certainly. I love the town hall in the middle of the River Regnitz between the Bishop's town and the Berger's town and the water pouring around it on all sides."

"It is a very old town and very important. It really is part of the Secret Germany that Claus speaks about so often."

"It is quite beautiful," I said.

"You have been to the cathedral?"

"Naturally."

"And you remember the statue?"

"Der Ritter? I'm hardly likely to forget it. The perfect embodiment of knighthood."

"We have ridden with him today, have we not? Even to the lovely cleft in his chin?"

"It is uncanny," I said, shaken by the fact that in appearance and manner, Claus von Stauffenberg was the Rider.

"His family has been in this part of Germany for centuries. It is not unlikely, do you think, that one of his ancestors was the model for the sculptor?"

"Not unlikely at all . . . Does Nina see the similarity?"

"Naturally . . . Though I saw it first."

"You are in love with him, are you not, Annalise?"

She sighed, like the Galway woman sometimes sighs.

"How could I not be, Herr Ridgewood? It is what my colleagues at the school in England would call a 'schoolgirl crush.' "

"Perhaps not."

"As a young woman without a family, Herr Ridgewood, I cannot afford to be anything but realistic. Moreover, Nina is a good friend. She protects me from the well-meaning supervision of her parents. She is the kind of strong, loyal woman that the Rider must have as a wife. I am happy for both of them . . ."

"And unhappy for Annalise?"

"That is my fate. I could never be the Lady that he needs. Herr Ridgewood, he is the last knight of Europe."

She did not so much weep as permit a few tears to slip down her cheek.

"The last and lingering troubador, to whom the birds have sung that once went singing southward when all the world was young."

"The last and the best."

"But, Annalise, you are young. Give yourself a few years and you will be such a woman."

"Perhaps. But now is the time that the Rider must marry."

"You think he will survive the war."

"No," she said lightly. "He is too good, too generous. He will be swallowed up in the Blitzkrieg . . . Now, Herr Ridgewood, I thought you were going to row me down the lake?"

We hitched the horses to a tree and climbed into the boat, both in our riding clothes. I fastened the oars in place, removed the line that tied us to the pier and cast off.

"You are very good at it, Herr Ridgewood. There is a lake near your manor too?"

"A couple of them," I said, "with rowboats for fishing and a dory for sailing and on the River Bann a sailboat with a motor for going down the river and out on the ocean."

"The Atlantic Ocean!"

"Sure, one can sail that without any fear, as long as one is careful."

"I do not think I would like that."

"I suspect that it is just the sort of reckless thrill that a woman like you would come to love."

"Perhaps, Herr Ridgewood, perhaps. Yet today I am happy to know that my rower here on the Stauffenbergersee is an accomplished and brave boatsman."

Stauffenbergersee? Typical German. Both the Nordsee and a tiny lake in the Bavarian mountains were "sees."

"I'm not sure about the brave part."

It was a perfect day for youthful romance—a clear blue sky, a smooth mirror of a lake, hills and mountains all around, some with pine trees at the top, and a breathtaking woman lounging gracefully in the stern, a woman who indeed was sad and lonely.

It was also a very warm day, under the springtime sun. I was sweating heavily as we sliced across the waters of the Stauffenbergersee. The worship in Annalise's eyes made me even warmer.

I resolved solemnly to myself that whatever romance there would be at the other end of the lake, it would not do violence to this brokenhearted and inexperienced girl. I was not the last knight of Europe, but still I was a gentleman and an Irish gentleman at that. Sometime later I would come back to claim Annalise, that I knew with certainty—or at least I thought I did. I wanted her to have only pleasant memories.

We pulled up to a small landing at the far end of the lake. I helped her out of the boat and onto the wooded shore. She continued to cling to my hand as we walked a few yards into the forest and found a small, weathered bench leaning against a big pine tree.

"This was built long ago so lovers could view the full length of the lake," she said.

"Lovers and anyone else," I added, putting my arm around her.

"It is not really a very big lake," she said, leaning against me. Her heart was pounding. Poor kid, scared and not sure about my intentions. I wondered if she still played with dolls.

"Our lakes in Ireland," I said, "are usually bigger, but not so beautiful. Someday you and I will sail on them and maybe down the Bann in the big sailboat."

"If you are there, I will not be afraid."

Her pounding heart calmed down. She trusted me.

"Monday I will go back to Heidelberg and then in the autumn to Ireland, but I promise you, Annalise, I will come back to Germany someday for you."

"I will wait for you," she promised.

We remained in our embrace for a long time, silent in the magic of the lake and the forest and the mountains and our own love, whose sweetness permeated my body and promised me long years of happiness.

I knew even then that there would be a terrible war and that it would be a long time before we'd see each other again, if ever. I would probably survive the war because I was Irish and would not enlist in the English army no matter what happened. Her chances of surviving, a young woman with invading armies sweeping back and forth, were more dubious. We both meant our solemn promises at that magical moment on the side of the Stauffenbergersee. I understood that the fulfillment was somewhere in the distant, misty, and mystical future. Did she? At least the promises would console her a little in the hell that the future might bring.

We Irish like to luxuriate in a mix of darkness and light, despair and hope, death and life that created in our souls bittersweet memories before the fact. Caught up in that exquisite blend of gloom and joy, time stood still. I was in temporary eternity, a pure Celtic delight, in the mystical moment. I began to kiss her, gently at first and then passionately. She surrendered to my emotions and then after a time gently eased me away.

"Your kisses are wonderful, Herr Ridgewood," she gasped, "but they take my breath away."

"That's what they're supposed to do, Annalise."

I told myself that I would permit one more such exchange and that would be that.

"I love you, Annalise," I murmured.

"I love you too, Herr Ridgewood."

We had said the sacramental words, we had plighted our troth, just as much as Nina and Claus were doing back at the Schloss.

I would never forget, I told myself, this glowing moment, no matter how long I lived.

Thus thinks the Irish romantic who substitutes daydreams for action.

We embraced and kissed again, this time pushing the job as far as I thought we safely could. I touched her breast through the protective armour of blouse and brassiere. She sighed contentedly.

"We had better return to the Schloss," I said. "Claus will worry about us."

"Perhaps," she said, standing up and brushing dust off her riding clothes. "And perhaps not. I believe all his thoughts will be on Nina."

I shivered at the grim anticipation that Nina would be a young widow before the war was over.

Please, God, NO!

"Did we sin, Herr Ridgewood?" she asked, as I helped her into the boat.

"Surely not, Annalise. Perhaps we were tempted, but God understands love between young people."

"You also are un chevalier parfait, Herr Ridgewood."

"And you are a perfect lady for such a knight," I said.

I was not a knight at all, but on that day on the Stauffenbergersee, I felt like one.

"It is all arranged," Claus said to us as we entered the Schloss, "but do not tell anyone. It is a secret till after the Mass on Saturday."

"A secret that everyone knows," Annalise said. "Therefore, I will not congratulate you till Lent is over. You look very happy and I am very happy for you. Now you must excuse me. It was very hot on the lake and I must bathe before dinner."

"So you fell in love with her, Timmy," he said to me later, "just as I foretold."

"Enough in love so that I would not take her away now, as appealing as that prospect might be. I did promise her that I would return someday."

"Such a promise might be difficult to honour . . . So much could happen."

"That must be left in God's hands, Claus."

"Naturally . . . I had hoped you would carry her away. However, that would have been an error for both of you."

"She promised to wait for me."

"In the terrible days ahead that might be an impossible promise . . ."

"Again, Claus, that hope must rest in God's hands."

At the melancholy Tenebrae services that evening, I spoke to God about these matters.

How does one know what one is to do? Should I have cast my caution aside and taken her as my betrothed today? Everyone here would be delighted at a second engagement on Saturday. Would you be? Or would you think that I was an unfeeling brute? Or would you not care much either way?

I do love her, and I do want her. I fantasized about joining her in the bath when she left us. But it is the desire of a hungry young man. Is it really better for both of us to wait? That is my explanation, my excuse, my confession of cowardice. Will I hate myself for the rest of my life for my loss of nerve? Or will our joy be greater because of my restraint? The Galway woman would blame me for my English prudence. My Old Fella would shrug. He always believed in careful calculations with his linen mill, but he was surely heedless when it came to love.

The situation is different.

Isn't it?

I could still change my mind. I could speak to her during the darkness after Tenebrae tonight, or tomorrow night, or the night after and ask her to come back with me to Ireland.

I made up my mind that I would do just that.

But the next morning, in the bright light of the Bavarian spring, I changed my mind. Each time I saw Annalise, she wrapped me in her radiant smile and I changed my mind again.

Holy Saturday morning came too quickly. I did not invite her to come for a sail on the Bann. We did not announce a second engagement. We still had the Pasch to rejoice over the Lord's return and to rejoice at a new, young, and perhaps reckless love. I let that chance slip through my fingers.

On Monday morning, a rapturously happy Nina and a quiet Annalise accompanied us to the railroad station. Claus and Nina would marry at harvest time in August. For both of them the months seemed like years. As I kissed Annalise and promised that someday I would return, the years looked like months.

The rest of my time on the bank of the Neckar River was empty. I worried about all my friends from Jettingen. Claus would eventually do battle with Hitler and, I thought, lose. Nina would be a very young widow. My beloved was probably doomed and it would be my fault. I was a fool.

Claus left in June to join his regiment. Before he left he invited me to his wedding in Bamberg. I declined with the excuse that the Ministry for External Affairs wanted me back in Dublin to train me for my first assignment—Vice Consul in Chicago. He understood the stern demands of bureaucracy. He didn't realize that the Ministry was in no hurry, Irish bureaucracies being much more relaxed than Germanic ones.

At Ridgeland, the Galway woman immediately caught my Weltschmerz.

"Some bitch of a young woman broke your heart, didn't she, lad?"

"No. I fear I might have broken her heart."

"And left her without a word?" she frowned darkly at me.

"We left each other with promises."

"Which you don't intend to keep?"

"I certainly do."

"And herself?"

"She will if she's still alive."

"Why would she die? Is she sick?"

The Old Fella put down his copy of the Financial Times to listen to the catechism.

"No. There's going to be a terrible war and millions of young men and women will be killed."

"How old is she?"

"Sixteen."

"A little young."

"You're a fine one to talk, woman."

"I'm Irish," she said waving him away with a grin.

"What's her name?"

"Annalise."

"That's a foreign name."

"She's a foreigner, Ma."

" 'Tis true . . . Well, I'll be looking forward to meeting her and I'll be after calling her Annie and won't I be praying for her every night."

Chicago is a fascinating city. The Consul General was an elderly man, a delightful raconteur, a tolerant boss, and drunk by noontime. All the work was left to me, but he never checked up to see if I had done it. My venue was everything west of Pittsburgh. I saw a lot of the United States in the midst of the Great Depression. Despite the poverty—which was not as bad as that in Dublin or Belfast or even London, it was still a vast, fascinating, and hopeful country that I couldn't help but like.

Shamed by the Galway woman's promise, I prayed for Annalise every night, but my memory of her faded with time as memories do.

I received the occasional letter from Claus, written in German. There were many Germans in Chicago. I had continued to work on my German with some of them because I did not want to lose whatever skill I had. Censorship of German mail had not yet begun.

Timmy,

Hitler is very popular just now. He has solved our depression problems by pouring money into preparation for war, he reentered the Rhineland without any opposition from the English or the French, who are still demoralized by their losses in the last war, he has taken over Austria, and is threatening Czechoslovakia. It seems that all of Europe is open to him for the taking. My mother's brother took me aside to tell me that I must organize opposition to Hitler in the officer corps, especially because of Hitler's rabid hatred of the Jews. I tell him that I'm too young and too junior to do that just yet, but I will eventually organize such a group. I already make my opinion known by walking out of every anti-Semitic harangue from the SS men who appear here sometimes to indoctrinate us. I am the only one that does, but almost all my colleagues praise me for it. I tell them that our family has put down pogroms since the time of the Crusades. Jesus and his mother were Jews. I suppose they still are. We must respect their relatives. Jews are good Germans like the rest of us.

You have surely read about *Kristallnacht.* The Nazis blame the Jews for the fire that destroyed the Reichstadt and organized a pogrom against the Jews. Many were beaten, some killed, their shops vandalized and some destroyed. The Nazis celebrate this as proof that the German people wish to purify themselves of degenerates. The Nazis are scum. Hitler is mad and those around him are incompetent fools. Soon we will have to act. I hear that von Beck, the Chief of the General Staff, plans to arrest Hitler before he forces a war with England and France over the Czechs. But both countries are weak, worn-out from the war, as I have said. We lost the war and had terrible casualties too. But our desire for revenge is apparently stronger than their desire for peace. There will be no peace until Hitler is dead.

I now have two children and am very happy. Nina sends her love.

Claus

Not a word about Annalise. That had to be deliberate. Was she married? Was she dead?

I almost never drink too much. As I drank myself to sleep that night, I cursed myself as a stupid fool. I still prayed for her, however, because I knew the Galway woman did.

His next letter had more bad news.

Timmy,

The English and French are fools. We had sent word to them that if they stood up to Hitler, we would remove him. They must not have believed us. We also told them that the *Wermacht* was no more ready for war than they were, probably less. The French army could have moved into the Rhineland overnight and met almost no resistance.

Yet they appease him instead of resisting. Mr. Chamberlain, a pathetic fool, waves his foolish little piece of paper when he gets off the plane returning from Munich. And says that Herr Hitler promises no more expansion. How can he not understand that a piece of paper means nothing to Antichrist. Chamberlain and Deladier have left all of Europe open to the Nazis, who will be stopped now only at the English Channel, if there. Guderian is already making plans for a *Blitzkrieg* through France.

I am now Q officer of the Sixth Panzer Division. We will be the head of that *Blitzkrieg*. The mistakes of 1914, we hear, will not be repeated. France will be destroyed.

Nina and the children—there are now three—are well and send their love.

I must tell you Annalise is engaged to be married to *Luftwaffe* General Paul von Richthofen. He is not a Nazi and is a good man. He is a cousin of the famous Red Baron of the last war and flew with the Flying Circus at the end after his cousin was killed. He commands the Stuka wing of the *Luftwaffe*—those odd divebombers with gull wings and landing gear that does not retract. The plans for the invasion of France require a thousand of these to fly in close support of our Panzers. Militarily that is exciting. Personally I dread what will happen to the French. No humiliation, however, will weaken their arrogant self-confidence.

Goering, who is a pervert and a drug addict and not half the man he was when he was in the Flying Circus, admires and respects him and will protect him and Annalise from all the evil men who want her. She had to marry to find someone to protect her. They will marry next autumn after the war with Poland and before we invade France.

Paul is twenty years older than Annalise, a widower who lost his wife in the stillbirth of his first child. I regret the marriage, but she could have chosen someone who is much worse.

I will give this letter to my brother Alexander, who goes often to Switzerland on business matters. He will mail it in Berne. From now on all my mail will be censored. God bless you and protect you. Pray for all of us.

Claus.

I read the letter late at night in my apartment in the Tower Neighborhood on the Near North Side of Chicago in August 1939. I was exhausted because of a long and very bumpy flight from San Francisco. This time I did not drink myself to sleep. Rather I wept myself to sleep. I had been a stupid fool. I would regret my cowardice the rest of my life. I told God that I would no longer pray for the woman who had broken our pledges. Nonetheless the next night I mentioned her in my prayers. Fool that I was, I still loved her. What choice did she have?

The next day, Germany announced a "nonaggression" pact between Berlin and Moscow, the so-called Ribbentrop-Molotov pact signed in Moscow. Poland was doomed. Even before the Panzers rolled into Poland and slaughtered the Polish dragoons who charged them with lances, the Ministry recalled me to Dublin to prepare for assignment as Irish ambassador to Berlin.

— 11 —

"WELL," NUALA Anne observed, "their story isn't over yet. He's returning to Germany, just as he promised."

"He'll probably be there for Claus's *Putsch* against Hitler."

"In which Claus will die?"

"Yep."

"And he will meet Annalise again?"

"Maybe. You can't have happy endings all the time in real life, Nuala Anne."

"Why not?"

"That's the way of the world."

We were in our room dressing for dinner at the Cape Cod Room with Siobhan, Des's sometime date at Marquette. She was coming to Chicago for an interview at Children's Hospital about her internship in child psychology, the subject of her doctoral work.

"I don't mind talking about Dizzy Des," she said. "He's a fun subject.

I'm not sure I can tell you very much, however. He's always been a mystery to me."

She would come to our house after the interview, meet our childer, and then we'd take her to the Drake for supper and drive her back to her home in Oak Park.

Spring having made an unexpected arrival, me wife was dressing in her "light blue" outfit, which she affirmed was her best color, an observation with which I could not argue.

It meant totally light blue—lingerie, nylons, knit dress, hair bow, shoes, all emphasized with silver jewelry, including a Brigid Cross and a Newgrange pin.

"Would you ever stop staring at me while I dress," she demanded. "Letcha get dressed yourself."

"No," I said firmly. " 'Tis the privilege of the husband to ogle his wife while she's dressing."

"I never heard that rule," she protested, not altogether displeased with my attention.

" 'Tis true just the same . . . And remember you can't read ahead in that manuscript to find out how it ends."

"Haven't I promised?"

"You have."

"I won't cheat, Dermot Michael, and would you ever hook up me bra."

"Wouldn't I be delighted?"

I hooked it and kissed her neck. She shivered with delight.

"He promised to return to Germany, and he'll be doing that, won't he?"

"So it would appear. And his lover married to a veteran of the Flying Circus."

"And that means that Des will return to Chicago, doesn't it?"

"We don't know that he has a lover in Chicago and I've never accepted the parallel between our stories."

"Is this the same Red Baron that fought with Snoopy?"

The ultimate historical fame is to be identified with Snoopy.

"Annalise's husband is his cousin."

"Why do they call it a 'Flying Circus'?"

"The planes were all those three winged Fokkers painted different colors. The pilots lived in tents to back up the circus image. It was not a circus for those English and French pilots they shot down. They had developed a tactic of flying around with a massive number of planes, cornering a single enemy pilot, and forcing him into a position were von Richthofen could jump on him and shoot him down. It piled up eighty victories for him and apparently provided a boost for German morale, which was in sad shape in those days."

"He was shot down himself eventually, wasn't he?"

"Killed by a single bullet from an Australian gunner on the ground."

"War is stupid, evil nonsense, a silly game played by men with high testosterone levels and led by old men trying to make themselves famous."

"You won't get me to disagree."

We arrived in the parlor just before our guest, who was on a high because she had aced the interview at Children's.

"I'm so happy that I'll be back in Chicago next year," she told us. "I miss it so much, and it's more beautiful every time I come back."

She was an attractive young woman, not quite as tall as me wife, with brown hair and eyes and an elfish grin.

"I couldn't believe it was you on the phone, though actually you sounded just like yourself . . . That's an Irish Bull, isn't it?"

"'Tis close enough," Nuala admitted, deciding that she would bond with this exuberant you woman. "These canines are respectively Fiona and Maeve. We work for them. They like to meet everyone who comes in."

Each of the snow-white doggies presented a paw and then curled up on the floor.

"Gorgeous creatures! Will one of them come home to Omaha with me?"

"You have a deal," I said, "but you'll have to take the four kids along or the pooches won't leave."

Said kids straggled in, Patjo in Nellie's arms, and were solemnly introduced. They politely greeted the guest as they were told to do. Socra Marie, her glasses askew, tried, as always, to steal the show.

"Patjo is my baby brother. I'm not a baby anymore, I'm a little girl!"

"And a very pretty little girl too!"

That was all she needed to make her night.

The kids and the doggies returned to the playroom and we went down the stairs to my Benz. I opened the front door for both young women and assigned myself to the backseat as I was expected to do.

"The little one is the preemie?" Siobhan asked, apparently having been informed about her on the phone.

"Twenty-five weeks."

"She seems fine . . . Tiny but filled with vitality."

"More than enough of that. The doctors say she might even outlive the glasses still."

"You worry about her all the time, I suppose?"

"Not that it does any good!"

"She fades a little at the end of the day," I said, "but which of us doesn't."

"We're getting much better at working with them," Siobhan commented. "The neonatal care people are more cautious about making grim predictions."

"But the trick of it is to prevent premature births, isn't it now?"

"It certainly is . . . What did they tell you when she was born?"

"That the odds were against us ever taking her home, but it was our call."

"And you called for life?"

"We did and never regretted it."

"Good for you!"

"Don't we take her over to the unit every couple of months and meself singing for them. Herself comes along and tells the small ones that they'll be all right just like her."

"So it's a mark of pride to her?"

"If you had stayed five more minutes, she would have told you the whole story," I said.

It was good for Nuala to hear the opinion of a professional, though she had heard many such opinions before. Every new one was still a help.

We turned to the subject of Des—or Dizzy Des—only after we had ordered dinner at the Cape Cod Room. Herself had not explained to me why our interview with Siobhan was solemn high, herself in her trademark light blue, meself with a suit (brown) and tie, dinner at a classy restaurant. Such decisions were usually instinctive and unassailable. Sure weren't the reasons obvious!

"We're trying to find out what he's like," Nuala began after she had ordered a bottle of Cakebread Chardonnay, "and why he might have gone off to Iraq at the beginning of the war?"

"I'd say he had cooked up some kind of deal over there and, being Des, wasn't about to back off just because of Donald Rumsfeld."

"Weren't we thinking the same thing?" Nuala said. "Only one glass of wine for you, Dermot love! Won't you be driving home."

"He's the nicest boy I ever dated," Siobhan observed. "And the most unpredictable. I don't believe he's dead, not Dizzy Des. He's too clever for that."

"You wouldn't be hearing from him now, would you?"

"No, but I wouldn't be surprised to get an e-mail from him any day now, just like he'd written last week. A roadside bomb or an exploding car might have caught him, but I don't think so. His luck is legendary and his ability to talk himself out of trouble is fantastic. He could win over even Osama himself.

"I'll never forget the night in Milwaukee when his parents sent the local cops to a bar where his Irish band was playing. It was a pretty seedy place, filled with pugnacious Irish drunks, some of them from the old country and all of them looking for a fight. Dessy and I were the only sober ones in the place and I was scared silly. He cooled the whole scene and when the cops came there was not the slightest hint of disorderly conduct. Just the same we got out of there in a hurry. I made him promise never again."

"His parents wanted to put him in jail?"

"They're nice folks, but creepy and dull. His mom tells me that she hopes I'll settle him down."

"And what were you after saying to her?" Nuala asked.

"I said that Des was who he was and I liked him the way he was. What else could I say?"

"You were in love with him?" I asked.

"I didn't say that. I liked him a lot. I had a crush on him. I could have fallen in love with him, but his signals said not yet, maybe not ever. Dessy was still exploring."

"You thought that was all right?"

Siobhan was exploring with obvious delight the Bookbinder soup.

"I liked him enough to want him to have all the time to explore that he needed. He was a special guy, you see . . . Besides I was in no hurry for permanency either."

Herself was quiet. So I figured it was my turn to ask a question.

"You admire him very much?" I said lamely.

"What's not to admire? He sent me a thousand-word letter every week while he was in Eritrea, publishable stuff. Hilariously funny at his own expense and a very sensitive depiction of the Horn of Africa. I edited it and sent it to an agent. We have a publisher, all we need is his signature on a contract."

"And he didn't object?"

"See, that's the problem with trying to describe him. Most guys wouldn't want their personal mail turned into a book without someone asking their permission. And they'd be right, I suppose. There wasn't much personal in the letters anyway and I knew Des. He was delighted when I told him. Loved it. Said I was wonderful, even kissed me."

"Did he now?" Nuala asked with a wicked gleam in her blue eyes.

THE BRAT IS ALWAYS MAKING MATCHES.

Comes with the gender.

"I'm not waiting for him, Nuala Anne," Siobhan said, serious for a moment. "I waited through the Peace Corps years, because I was busy anyway with my studies. Then he came back and he was magical as ever but still frying his own fish and marching to his own drums. He wasn't ready to be serious and I figured it might be a long time before he would be. So I made a decision in my head that I should be open to other options. So I've been dating guys out in Omaha, which isn't a whole ton of fun, and even found a nice boy here in Chicago, who is a little like Des, but sane."

" 'Tis sad," me wife said.

"Oh, Nuala Anne, guys are like L trains; you miss one there's always another one coming along."

"That's what me Dermot told me when he went home from Ireland and left me there!"

"I said no such thing!"

"But 'tis true," Nuala continued.

"When my mother asks me where he is, I say that he's probably in some monastery somewhere, praying."

We all laughed.

"Well, it's a joke, but Des likes to pray. There's a lot of piety in the book, like he says he's praying for me because he thinks Chicago is more dangerous than Asmara."

"Were you after telling him about this nice boy you've been dating in Chicago?"

"I did. I thought I should. He says he knows him, met him at a couple of parties and he's totally cool."

"He didn't bat an eye?"

"Not that I noticed."

It was not all quite that easy, I thought. But Des had fair warning.

"Did Des seek you out?" Nuala asked cautiously.

"He sure did. Girls were all over him and he slipped away like he was a ghost. I thought they were disgusting. Scrawny, crazy little guy with a fake smile. Then one day in the Student Union he was behind me in the cafeteria line and he said something stupid like he thought I ought to talk more in Father O'Donovan's class because I had plenty to say and he was tired of carrying the conversational load. And I said that I thought he could carry a conversation in an empty room. Then that afternoon I got into an argument with Father about whether it was all right to imagine God as a woman. Back then the Jebs were a little uneasy about that. I won the argument."

"Of course!" me wife said brightly.

"Dessy congratulated me after class and I brushed him off. Then I began to notice that he'd turn up next to me in the Union pretty often and say something stupid and I'd laugh at him."

"Then didn't he take you out to supper one night at the best restaurant in Milwaukee, if they have one?"

"Me wife is fey," I explained.

"You don't have to be fey to know something like that," Nuala said with a sniff.

"He didn't put any moves on me," Siobhan explained, "never did. Yet he really did like me and I liked him."

I had finished my crab cakes and Nuala, skillful from much practice, deftly slipped her second cake over to my platter.

"And his parents liked you?"

"They would have liked any woman who didn't have tattoos and pierced lips."

"Where does this sister of his fit into the picture?"

"She's the quiet, thoughtful type, the very opposite of Dizzy Dessy. She adores him but doesn't fight her parents about it, just sort of stands on the sidelines and silently cheers him on. She's as smart as he is. I talk to her on the phone once in a while and tell her that he'll be back as crazy as ever."

"She's a senior?" I asked.

"She is and she's not doing the Peace Corps. She's doing Teach America instead. Wants to go to New Orleans."

"Won't her parents love that!"

"They're not bad people, Nuala, just very conservative. They must have been desperate to ask for your help."

"Aren't they now, poor dear folks."

We drove her back to her home in south Oak Park and then returned to Sheffield Avenue. Despite frequent calls to our house, Nuala was impatient to return and see if anyone had misbehaved.

I drove the car and Nuala and Siobhan sat behind me, talking about Ireland. Me wife deigned to join me in the front seat on the way home.

"A very nice young woman," I said as we steered onto the Congress Expressway (as we Democrats call it).

"They were in love, Dermot. They just wouldn't admit it to one another."

" 'Tis true."

"Do you think she should have pushed a little harder?"

"Like I pushed you?"

"I didn't say that."

"Go long with you, Dermot Michael Coyne, you were thinking that. And I didn't have to be fey either to know what you were thinking . . . Anyway it wouldn't have done any good and himself an illusive leprechaun fella."

"But not mean, like the real ones."

"No not mean at all . . . I want to cry for the two of them."

"It won't help them."

"It will help me."

"She'll be a wonderful wife and mother and a great psychologist," I said.

"And what will he be?"

"He may regret all his life what he lost."

"You don't say he will regret it."

"I don't know, Dermot Michael, I just don't know."

The childer's behavior had been exemplary, Ethne reported.

Ethne was technically our nanny, though in fact she was a substitute for the little sister whom Nuala never had. She was in the final phases of her doctoral work in educational psychology at DePaul University and was "practically engaged," to Brendan our sometime dog runner and now an affluent artist.

"Brendan was here tonight."

"Why am I not surprised at all, at all?" Nuala asked.

"He says he wants to marry me."

" 'Tis about time, isn't it now?"

" 'Tis."

They both sighed loudly.

"And what did you say to him, Ethne?" I asked.

"I wanted to tell him that I needed a couple of months to think it over."

"It would have been good enough for him . . ."

"It would have."

"But that's not what you said?"

"I just said yes."

"And he seemed surprised altogether?"

"He did. I told him that he would have to ask you, Dermot, and my parents dead and buried!"

"Me! I'm too young!"

They both laughed at me.

— 12 —

"You understand, Timothy," the Minister for External Affairs whispered in his usual soft voice, "that Ireland is neutral in this foolish war."

"I do, sir."

"But we certainly don't want that madman to win, do we?"

"No, sir."

"And this a Catholic country!"

"Yes, sir."

"So we must be absolutely and totally neutral, right?"

"Absolutely, sir."

"But neutral on England's side, eh?"

"Naturally."

"Your da isn't going to take command of his regiment again, is he?"

"Only if England gives us back the six counties."

"That'll be the day . . . So we won't let the Brits use our treaty ports, which will drive Winston crazy."

"Perfectly fair."

"We will tell our people that the state does not approve of them volunteering to serve on either side in the war. We will not, however, be able to prevent our citizens from crossing the Irish Sea to seek employment of whatever kind, will we?"

"That would violate their rights, sir."

"And we'll intern all military personnel, sailors, airmen, spies whom we apprehend within our borders."

"We'll have no choice, sir."

"It may just happen that the English we intern may slip away on us into Northern Ireland. That isn't our fault, is it now?"

"Neutrality, Irish style."

He looked at me intently and sighed.

"You'll send your signals to us in our usual code?"

"I will, sir."

"It's not our fault that the Brits might intercept them."

"They'll need someone who has the tongue."

"You'll be sending them in the official language of our nation?"

"Naturally, sir."

"Aye, then the Brits will need someone to translate, won't they?"

"Yes, sir."

He sighed again.

"I would imagine that they'll be able to find the odd Irish speaker somewhere on the island."

"It would not be impossible."

"Well, the long fella will be pleased to read them in our traditional language, won't he?"

"Yes, sir."

"You'll be running some risk."

"The most they'd do is deport me. Neutral embassies are important in the game the way it is played now. Both sides need them to do their behind-the-scenes negotiations."

"I think you have the right of it, Timothy, but be careful, just the same."

"I will, sir."

I would then be a cautious but attentive spy for the British Empire in Berlin. This assignment did not surprise me. Quite the contrary, I took it for granted. I was surprised that the minister had made it so explicit and even more that he did not make me promise to treat his observations as a deep secret. He might indeed have believed that such a warning was quite unnecessary.

I spent the weekend with my parents, who doubtless figured out the double role I was to play. They promised prayers and bid me Godspeed.

The war had turned into a rout for the Führer's enemies—Poland, Denmark, Norway, the Netherlands, Belgium, and now France. Just as Claus had predicted, Guderian had crashed through the impenetrable Ardennes and driven to Boulogne, thus cutting the Allied armies in two and surrounding the British Expeditionary Force around the port of Dunkirk. The Allies expected that the Germans would follow the same route to Paris as they had in 1914—through Belgium and the Netherlands. They were utterly unprepared for the Blitz through the Ardennes. Paris fell in twelve days and France was effectively knocked out of the war. The Brits managed to evacuate most of their army by using an armada of small boats along with their regular navy units. France formally surrendered on June 22 at Compiègne, where the 1918 armistice was signed, indeed in the very same railroad car. The Germans occupied the northern half of the country. Marshal Pétain, the hero of Verdun, took over the government in the south, which became a German puppet regime. Everyone in France assumed that England would be next, that Hitler would launch a Blitzkrieg across the Channel against a battered English army, which would soon collapse. Many in England wanted to negotiate a peace, including a majority of the inner cabinet in Winston's government. He gave his famous speech about fighting on the beaches and promised that England would never surrender. He is supposed to have added after the microphone was turned off, "And we'll have to fight them with sticks because we don't have any guns."

But they did have the Royal Navy up in Scapa Flow in Scotland, secure from the Luftwaffe which couldn't fly that far, and from subs which rarely were able to break through the nets that protected the big ships. If Hitler were about to launch his barges into the Channel, the Navy would appear and blow them out of the water. Many ships might fall prey to German planes and submarines, but the Wehrmacht would suffer horrendous losses.

I bet the Old Fella that the invasion would never happen. Later, much later, I would collect the thousand pounds we had wagered.

Thus I arrived in Berlin the day of the Compiègne surrender. I was exhausted after a long and circuitous flight from Dublin to Lisbon to Madrid to Berne and then a train ride through celebrating cities till I reached Berlin, where the streets were filled with delirious Germans. Versailles had been avenged. The war was over, this time a quick and easy war. Peace had returned. The Führer had triumphed. The choice now was either England or Russia.

I unloaded my baggage at the musty three-story building on the Friedrichstrasse, which had served as both the embassy and the Residence. I phoned the couple who were my staff, a butler/driver and a cook/housekeeper. They sounded like they had just come in from the celebration.

Much of the German government arrayed itself along the streets running parallel to the east end of the big park called the Tiergarten in the center of Berlin and around the bend in the Speyer River north of the park. The embassies clustered in this area, the most impressive on the wide parkway called the Unter Den Linden or at the edge of the park on what was once the Ebertstrasse but now was the Hermann Goering Strasse. The Den Linden ended at the famous Brandenburger Tor. The Tiergarten was the old royal hunting ground and the Den Linden, originally the path the kings' road to the hunting ground.

The next street in from the Tiergarten was Wilhelmstrasse on which stood most of the government buildings, including the Old Chancellery and the New Chancellery with a bunker for the Führer in the basement. The narrow and gloomy Friedrichstrasse was a block east of the Wilhelmstrasse. The headquarters of the SS and the Gestapo was on the Albertstrasse, one of the cross streets between the Friedrichstrasse and the Wilhelmstrasse. I was therefore close to the headquarters of all the leading Nazis—the Führer in the Chancellery, Goering in the Air Ministry and Himmler in the Albertstrasse—too close for comfort I often thought as my time in Berlin went on.

Fortunately for me, this section of Berlin—the mitte or middle—was the cultural center, from the Den Linden down to the Potsdamer Platz. Both the U-Bahn and S-Bahn came into the station north of my house on Friedrichstrasse and there was another station on the Potsdamer Platz. The latter was one of the main shopping districts and the other, the Kufürstendamm, was on the west side of the Tiergarten, a couple of stops away on the U-Bahn.

A few streets farther east of Friedrichstrasse one encountered massive German culture—museums, galleries, churches, libraries, concert halls, and the campus of Humboldt University. Truth to be told, there wasn't much work to do, as Irish ambassador to Berlin. The embassy was open three hours of the day, two in the morning, one in the late afternoon. Our offices were on the ground floor, several bedrooms on the first floor, and our communications room on the second floor with the coders, decoders, and other secret means of communications, should the people of Ireland need to hear from me. I would listen to the radio, read the papers, attend the diplomatic functions and, disguised by my youth and my smile, talk to people in the beer gardens, wine gardens, and coffeehouses of my intensely active neighborhood.

And I would spend my free time finishing my book on the relationship between Germany and England. The trouble, I would argue, began when Germany decided it had to have a navy to be equal to Royal Navy. Blasphemy!

I would also on occasion walk by the Air Ministry in case I might encounter Annalise.

I would not know what to say to her if I did.

Yet she was always just a stone's throw away.

After I had done the preliminary work of unpacking I walked over to the Foreign Ministry and presented my papers to a clerk who didn't seem to know exactly where Ireland was. However, he stamped them and told me that I would be informed when I would be summoned to present my credentials to the glorious Führer.

"Heil Hitler!" he shouted, throwing his arm into the air.

I nodded politely, a response I would offer on every occasion during my term in Germany.

"You do not salute our glorious Führer?" he said, glaring at me.

"My leader," I said very gently, "is in Dublin, not here."

"Heil Hitler!" had a certain alliterative appeal. "Up the Long Fella!" would cause one to be laughed out of every pub in Dublin. "Up Dev!" on the other hand would lead to a fight with the followers of the Big Fella—Michael Collins, poor dear man as the Galway woman would say.

It took me several days to unpack and organize. Herr and Frau Winter were efficient and respectful. My predecessor had assured me that they were good Catholics who did not like the Nazis. I had resolved to assume they were spies and told them that I would double their salary.

My family had a bank in Berne from which I could routinely withdraw Reichmarks without any trouble—or anyone noticing. Thus I had available much larger resources than my predecessor, happy in the thought that it was English money I was spending and that there was a lot more of that where it had come from.

We hoisted the tricolour on the flagpole in front of the building, put up the sign which identified us as the embassy of Eire (Ireland) and hooked up the aerials on the roof, which enabled me to pick up the news from Radio Ireland and the BBC and send my dispatches to Dublin. I also hooked up the encoder which would transmit my dispatches to the Ministry. Magda Winter pressed my morning suit and my evening clothes so that I was ready for formal appearances. Franz Winter serviced the Benz touring car, filled it with petrol at the station where diplomats were able to obtain it, cleaned the cover which was supposed to protect us from rain, and affixed the flags on the front of the car— the tricolour and the foreign office flag which, alas, had a Swastika in the center. Later we were ordered to paint the Swastika on the right-hand side and the tricolour on the left. There was now a highly visible Irish presence in Berlin.

I was ready to go.

I sent my first dispatch to Dublin, reporting the general jubilation in Berlin and the assumption that the war would soon be over. I observed that judging by the propaganda on the radio, the German people were demanding an invasion of England. I asked Dublin to confirm reception, which they did promptly.

Franz called the tennis club where the embassy had a membership and informed them that I would present myself the next morning for a match and a swim.

Ja, ja, all was in order.

My opponent was Herr Hauptman Claus Graf von Stauffenberg.

The attendant introduced us formally.

Claus winked and bowed.

"Ja, Herr Ambassador."

"Ja, Herr Hauptman."

I beat him easily. "Tomorrow afternoon," he whispered, "a café just down the street from the Adlon Hotel, on the right-hand side of the street as you face the Brandenburger Tor."

"Ja, ja, Herr Hauptman!"

"There are too many ears in this place."

"Ja, ja."

The Adlon, on the Pariser Platz, was the social center for the diplomatic corps, as fine a hostelry as one could find anywhere in Europe. I avoided it because I didn't want to seem to be wasting the money of the people of Ireland, though in fact it was my father's money, taken from his trust fund for me.

The 1932 Benz, however, in which Franz would drive me everywhere, even a block away, when I was on official business, belonged to the people of Ireland.

The morning after my arrival I called at the Foreign Ministry to try once again to pay my compliments to Reichsminister Joachim von Ribbentrop, the architect of the Hitler-Stalin nonaggression pact which sealed the fate of Poland and divided that poor country once again.

I presented my calling card to several guards at the various portals one had to pass to approach the office of the Reichsminister. Finally, I reached the outer office, my diplomatic patience wearing thin. After all I had the dignity of Eire-Ireland to protect.

Ribbentrop was a former whiskey salesman whose foreign experience had consisted of sales trips around Europe and Canada. Like so many of the people around Hitler, he was grossly incompetent.

"The Reichsminister is very busy today, Herr Ridgewood," his secretary, doubtless a veteran of Wagnerian opera, said, looking down her nose at me. "I'm afraid that he will be unable to see you. These are glorious days for Germany, you know."

I turned on my Celtic charm.

"I understand perfectly. I merely wanted to present my card so that he would know I was serving in the Irish Embassy."

Her expression was that of a farmer at an Irish country fair facing a notorious gombeen man.

"I will give the card to the Reichsminister."

"Thank you." I bowed.

"Heil Hitler."

I nodded.

I had already left the outer office when she caught up with me breathless.

"The Reichsminister will see you briefly, Herr Ridgewood."

Von Ribbentrop (the von was fake) looked for all the world like the Protestant cleric near Castle Ridgeland—tall, skinny, pinched face, thick glasses, little hair.

"Heil Hitler."

"Good morning, Herr Reichsminister. I am sorry to have disturbed you. I merely wanted to leave my calling card as a courtesy."

I had sworn a solemn oath the day before never once to say Heil Hitler during my term in Berlin, less as a matter of principle than as a matter of Gaelic stubbornness.

"Not at all, Herr Ridgewood," he said, standing up and extending his hand. "I commend you on your excellent command of the German language, a Swabian accent, I believe. Do sit down please."

"I studied at Heidelberg, sir. German history and literature. I am writing a dissertation at Trinity College in Dublin on the long history of cooperation between England and the German states, which I assume is why the Ministry for External Affairs has sent me here."

No point in telling him that it had begun as a paper at Oxford.

He was intrigued. Blarney works with these folk, I told myself.

"It is most unfortunate"—he removed his spectacles and began to polish them—"that England chose to unite itself with France in this century. Now it finds itself defenseless against the military genius of the greatest leader in human history."

"There can be no denying that the Reich has won a series of victories unparalleled since Alexander the Great or Bonaparte."

Over weak enemies, I did not add.

"England's army was destroyed in France. Its air force barely exists. The Führer has ordered Operation Sea Lion to send an occupying force into England. We will, of course, recognize the neutrality of Ireland."

The hell you say.

"It need not be that way," he went on. "The Führer has great admiration for England and its people; after all we are of very similar racial backgrounds, are we not?"

"And very similar languages."

"The Führer's final ambition is to eliminate Bolshevism and thus introduce a thousand-year Reich of peace and prosperity free of Jewish control. With a proper government in London and a treaty of nonaggression between our two countries, there would be no need for more than a thousand of our officials in London . . ."

The dummy was dreaming of the Ribbentrop-Eden treaty. I thought Anthony Eden was a handsome neurotic without much ability (because that's what the Old Fella thought). However, the image of him sitting down at a table across from this fool was high comedy.

"An interesting idea, Herr Reichsminister."

"I presume the Irish government has a sense of how things are in England."

"Ireland is totally and absolutely neutral, Herr Reichsminister," I lied.

"I understand, I understand. Yet you must have some sense of the morale of the English people? Presumably the aristocrats, led by Churchill, want the war to continue and the ordinary people hope for peace."

"I can offer only my impression, Herr Reichsminister. But it is rather the opposite. The aristos want peace and the people are typically stubborn Brits whom Churchill has rallied in favour of the war. The real aristos don't consider Winston to be one of their number at all."

My Old Fella certainly didn't, but he admired him.

"Interesting. Interesting."

"However I will, with your permission, pass on your reflections to my government. They have certain liaisons with the British Foreign Office."

"Excellent! Excellent! Churchill has to go, of course, but the English can keep their fleet and their colonies so long as there is no blockade of Germany."

"I will mention that to my superiors at the Ministry for External Affairs."

I did not laugh in his face, behaviour which demonstrated that I might still have some future as a diplomat.

However, I did laugh as I recited our dialogue that afternoon to Claus at the Café Linden, where we sipped tea under the shade of the trees and under a clear blue sky. He laughed with me.

"I assume, Claus, that he is one of the less competent of your Führer's ministers."

"Quite the contrary, Timmy, he is one of the more competent. They are a group of trash, criminals reveling in power that they do not know how to use. Goebbels is superb at propaganda but he is quite mad with anti-Semitism. Goering is a pervert and drug addict. We must sweep them away."

We had already discussed his family. He and Nina had three children and perhaps a fourth on the way. Nina was flourishing, more beautiful than ever. It was necessary that Annalise marry. She had no family and in the present days, she needed a protector. Paul was harmless and adored her, though he was still living the Flying Circus experience. She was working at the Luft Ministry in a senior staff position. She was very efficient and respected by everyone. She did not seem unhappy.

I told myself that my heart was not breaking.

"You will present your credentials to the Führer the day after tomorrow at his annual reception for diplomats?"

"Your contacts are very good, Claus."

He waved the compliment away with his usual self-deprecating smile.

"The Führer will speak about England. He will denounce their treachery, but then he will in effect offer them peace, not unlike what the Reichsminister proposed to you. How will the English react?"

"They will laugh at him. Will they really attempt an invasion?"

"That is why I am in Berlin instead of with the Sixth Panzer on the coast of Normandy. The OKW—the General Staff—is formulating plans. Since I am considered an expert on the problem of logistics, it is my task to point out the many obstacles. In general the OKW has grave reservations. Von Rundstedt, Hitler's favourite after our victory in France, will command Sea Lion. He has very grave reservations. Personally he does not like the Nazis—at the proper time he might well be with us. He also sees that an invasion could easily end in disaster."

"Why is that?"

"Your impressions here will go back to your government?"

"At a very general level, no one will be identified."

"Very good . . . They will share them with the English?"

"I shouldn't be at all surprised."

"Good. Gerd—von Rundstedt—knows that our success is the work of our Panzers. He wonders how you can put one of them, say from my division, on a barge, tow the barge across the Channel and then put it on the shore in England when you have no experience with amphibious landings. I estimate that the chance of any given Panzer landing in England less than one in ten. For that matter, I'm not sure how many of our men we can put ashore. Those who favour the invasion dream of our paratroops seizing a port, Southampton perhaps, and bringing the Panzers ashore from something bigger than a barge. Gerd says that England is not Norway. Finally, and most seriously, Gerd insists that he will never lead an invasion unless the Royal Air Force has been destroyed."

"The first battle of Britain will be fought in the air!"

"The Reichsmarschal—Goering is the only one with that title—says his Luftwaffe will destroy the RAF in four days."

"I rather doubt that."

"The Luftwaffe has yet to face a moderately effective enemy. It has had considerable success in supporting ground troops and terrifying a retreating foe. But it has only one truly modern aircraft—the Me-109—and that can spend ten minutes over England before it runs out of fuel. Goering is mad."

"And dangerously so, it would seem."

"Moreover the Abwehr, our intelligence group, warns us that the English already have three lines of defense prepared that are ready to slaughter advancing troops which have little or no Panzer support."

"I doubt that, Claus."

"So do I. Yet Admiral Canaris, the head of the Abwehr, has had a long history of providing Hitler with false information. He may approach you at the reception. He is to be trusted."

"One of yours?"

He looked around to make sure no on was close to us and nodded silently.

The chief of intelligence was on Claus's side. Ja, ja, interesting.

"Germany rearmed very quickly," he continued. "We concentrated on Panzer forces. That's why we won. We have not made much progress in other matters. The Stuka is an old plane with gull wings, struts, and fixed landing gears. The noise they make in their dive terrorizes ground troops, but they do not carry heavy bombs and their gunner is in the rear seat, firing in open air as they go down. Moreover, they often break apart at the end of their dives. We have a thousand of them in our Stuka wing. The RAF has new fighter planes about which Goering does not seem to know . . . If they are any good, the Luftwaffe will be repulsed."

"They are called the Hurricane and the Spitfire. My Old Fella's friends in the airline industry in Northern Ireland tell him that they are very good indeed."

"Paul" — he shook his head sadly — "thinks that it's 1918 and the Stukas are Fokkers. Like everyone else he thinks that we are military geniuses and invincible. So far we have been lucky."

"Do you want an invasion, Claus?"

"I want the Führer to lose just once so his reputation for invincibility will be shattered. Better in the English Channel than in the snows of Russia. Yet I don't want to see my own men drowned. But I don't want to see them frozen to death either."

"You can hardly launch a coup when he's riding high."

"Our chances would be small. Even though many in the Wehrmacht hate him, it is hard to argue with repeated victories. The Antichrist is clever, Timmy. We knew that."

"Yet your group is intact?"

"Loosely organized but in place. Powerful and important men."

"The Secret Germany?"

"Many of them."

I sent off a minute to Dublin which suggested that there was considerable debate in Germany about invading England and that the principle issue was the Royal Air Force. Everyone was quoting Goering that the Luftwaffe would dispose of the RAF in four days and England would then be at Hitler's mercy.

We had not talked much about Annalise. Perhaps Claus was upset with me for not saving her six years earlier. Or maybe he considered the matter closed. She had a husband and that was that. The husband, however, would be flying an obsolete bomber against the best fighter planes in the world, a point which Claus had emphasized in his discussion.

I was a good enough Christian not to hope that General Major Paul von Richthofen would die. Yet if that should happen . . .

I banished that thought as best I could. I didn't deserve a second chance.

The diplomatic reception at Hitler's brand-new Chancellery was like a grotesque version of Gilbert and Sullivan—men in a wide variety of uniforms, all very Germanic, which did not quite fit them. Most grotesque of all was the Reichsmarschal, corseted into a buff Luftwaffe dress uniform, wearing makeup and laughing constantly, like a man who had too much to drink or too many drugs. They were all drunk, in fact, with the intoxicant of victory.

The wives of many of the guests were there too, in long and modest gowns. Their makeup was exhaustive. Only a few of them would attract a second glance from a young celibate male like me.

Frau von Richthofen, as I tried to think of her now, was certainly not present. She would be dangerous in such a group.

The Führer himself, in gray battle dress, might have been an innocuous waiter serving refreshments. He was a strange-looking little man with his funny mustache and his slick hair draped over his forehead. There was no hint of the charisma he was supposed to exude and which presumably generated the awe and the reverence of those who spoke to him.

The greatest Reich ever, stretching from the North Cape to Africa and from the Bay of Biscay to the Vistula. Rome eat your heart out. Yet somehow I thought that Rome had more style, more class. Perhaps even the Hapsburgs did too. Triumph, if Claus were to be believed, because of luck and the war weariness of the others.

How durable this triumph? There was still Russia. And the United States.

Determined not to be ignored in the midst of the splendour I expected, I wore my green linen cummerbund AND my tricolour lapel pin. The Irish are here, folks!

The new diplomats would present their credentials to the Führer, then he would give his talk. I was the last of the four, not because Ireland was unimportant in the room (though it surely was) but because I was the most recent arrival.

When the Führer accepted my credentials, I caught just a slight hint of the charisma, a flash of light in his eyes, a hint of a smile on his face. He was not Michael Collins surely, but I had the sense that men and women might worship for this smile. The smile of the Antichrist? Maybe.

"Ja, green for Irish," he said, "brave people."

"Thank you, my Führer," I whispered.

His performance during his talk, a manuscript in front of him on the podium but rarely consulted, was quite different. He spoke proudly and confidently about his new Reich which would last a thousand years at least. It would ennoble and purify the continent and protect it from any onslaught from future barbarian hordes. He thanked the brave armed forces of the Reich, for their quick and efficient victories. He hailed the prospect of peace for all of Europe. The only nation that had not gratefully accepted the peace and purity of the new Reich was England. Then the tone of his voice changed and the volume rose. We were at Nuremberg and the hysteria of the Führer spread to everyone present. His indictment of the English as weak, cruel, oppressive was one with which it was difficult for an Irishman like me to disagree. I might even have been able to overlook the anti-Semitism of his assault on the International Zionist conspiracy. Yet the virulence of his call for the destruction of England scared me. As a mick, I might want to see perfidious Albion cut down to size. Yet I thought the world would be a worse place if its respect for the rule of law and human rights (though not in Ireland) were crushed by this visceral hatred.

The tension and fury in the room as he screamed about the offenses of our neighbours across the Irish sea was orgiastic. England must be destroyed. It would be destroyed. Its army no longer existed. Its air force had never existed. The British Empire would be obliterated forever. It would collapse before the onslaught of German vengeance. Salt would be poured on its fields as it had been poured on the fields of Carthage.

I wondered how this speech would play on the BBC that evening. I had a feeling that it would have no impact on English listeners. In Dublin people would laugh.

Then his voice became calm and reasonable. He proposed something like the solution of the Reichsminister. A permanent armistice, a friendly government which would accept the victory of the Reich, a restoration of German colonies, free trade on the high seas—there would be no need for an invasion of England if a friendly government would agree to accept the triumph of the Reich honestly and humbly.

Would the pro-peace party within Churchill's war cabinet eagerly accept such terms? Would Lord Halifax insist again that Mussolini or perhaps the Pope be asked to act as an intermediary?

In my minute that night I expressed the opinion that the glove under the iron fist would only reveal a steel hand. The talk was not such to persuade the English people to overthrow Churchill and the other aristocrats as to spill venom on England. Perhaps his words would frighten the English but I didn't think it likely.

A handsome, white-haired man in the uniform of the Kriegsmarine, the War Navy, approached me. He was wearing a considerable number of decorations, including the highest grade of the Iron Cross.

"Canaris," he said almost unnecessarily.

"Ridgewood."

"Should I say Viscount Ridgewood?" He smiled.

"Not when I'm in the diplomatic service of Eire," I replied, with my own smile.

"Do you credit our Glorious Führer's view of the present strength of England, especially of the Royal Air Force?"

We both accepted champagne glasses from a tray.

My heart was beating rapidly. This handsome admiral with the seductive smile, the smooth voice, and twinkling eyes might be setting a trap for me. I had better be careful.

"I agree," I replied dodging the question that he had asked, "that operation Sea Lion will not succeed unless the RAF is taken out of the equation. If it survives, the Royal Navy is only two days away from the Channel."

We sipped cautiously from our glasses as the conversation continued and simultaneously made faces of displeasure.

"Is there great fear in Castle Ridgeland about the future of the House of Lords?"

"Castle Ridgeland is not a place that is easily frightened."

"And Lord Ridgeland has great confidence in his friend Winston?"

"Only when he is not interfering in Irish matters."

A brief nod, a concession to my point after he had made the point that he knew all about me. From Claus perhaps.

"Our dashing Reichsmarschal thinks he can eliminate the RAF in four days. Would you agree?"

"Hardly. They have some new planes which I am told are excellent."

"The Spitfire especially," he said.

"And some excellent tracking systems."

"Radar."

"And some quite able leaders."

"Dowding, Leigh-Mallory, and Park."

"The Abwehr is well-informed, Admiral. I presume that your dashing Reichsmarschal has this information and the Führer too."

"Both have elements of it. They will never be able say they weren't warned. However, they simply do not believe it."

"Ah . . . do you want them to fail, Herr Admiral?"

"I know that they will fail, Herr Ambassador."

"They will never reach the defense lines the English have established."

His frosty blue eyes twinkled.

"They will never test the possibility that those lines do not exist."

"And then?"

"Russia of course. It will be a great disaster for Germany. We will lose this war for the same reason we lost in 1918, not enough manpower. Too many of our young men died. Our enemies were exhausted too. Then the Americans arrived with many more young men . . . Does your experience in America in these recent years lead you to believe that they will arrive again?"

"It is a complicated question, but the answer is 'yes.' "

"Then"—he sighed—"the thousand-year Reich will not last five years."

"You do not sound unhappy about that, Admiral, not as unhappy as you probably were when the Royal Navy sank the Dresden off the coast of Chile in the last war."

Again the frosty eyes twinkled.

"The captain of the ship did manage to escape," I added. "A very clever man."

"August 13," he said, "is Eagle Day, the day when the Reichsmarschal begins to destroy the RAF. We will see what will happen when the Stukas encounter the Spitfires."

"Is the Stuka commander here today?" I asked.

He glanced around the room.

"Ah yes, he is the handsome younger officer close to our dashing Reichs-marschal, though not so close as to pick up any of his germs."

"I have a personal message to deliver to him that has nothing to do with the matters of our conversation."

I don't know why I said that. It was an impulsive, ill-considered example of Irish romantic folly. Now I would have to act on it.

"It is well that you deliver it to him today. His life expectancy cannot be great. God grant that he survives. He is a good man even if he still lives in the world of the Flying Circus. Germany will need men like him after the disaster is finished."

"The Secret Germany?"

"Ja, Ja, Herr Ridgewood." He smiled slightly. "The Secret Germany."

"You will, of course," I continued to be reckless, "intercept my dispatches to Dublin."

"That is one of the services the Abwehr provides to the thousand-year Reich. In your case we have no one on our staff who can translate your lovely Irish language and cannot afford to search for someone who could. I would imagine that our English counterparts will not have that trouble."

"How very interesting, Herr Admiral."

"I too have found this conversation very interesting, Herr Ambassador. Perhaps you will have time to visit my home out in Gruenwald. We could dis-cuss German literature, at which I hear you are an expert."

"I am only a student, Herr Admiral."

"And we also share a distaste for thousand-year champagne. I will be in touch with you."

We bowed politely to one another and parted.

He had told me in effect that he knew what I was doing and that I could continue to do it. No, he wanted me to continue. He wanted his information shared with the Foreign Office in London. I would be a go-between for him and Winston.

I tried to clear my head for my meeting with Paul von Richthofen. Pure ar-rogant folly on my part.

"Herr General," I touched his arm, distracting him from his careful atten-tion to the words of the intoxicated Reichsmarschal.

He turned around in some surprise.

"Tim Ridgewood, I'm a friend of Claus Stauffenberg."

He was about my height and had the same kind of tight wavy hair as mine, though blond, the tense, alert posture of a professional athlete or fighter pilot, and the broad smile of the natural leader.

"Ja, ja, Herr Ridgewood. Paul Richthofen. Claus has spoken often about you and praises you greatly. Also my wife, Frau Richthofen. I was hoping to meet the new Irish ambassador." He gestured towards my green cummerbund. "I did not want to seem forward."

"I especially want to congratulate you on your marriage and to wish you and Annalise all possible happiness and a long life together."

A happy flush formed on his face. Now he looked liked the descendent of a Viking who had learned how to play Irish football.

"Thank you very much, Tim," he said. "My wife is an astonishing woman, beautiful, intelligent, and often very comical. I am a most fortunate man. After this little affair with England about which the Führer has just spoken, we must all of us have dinner at our home in Wannsee, Claus and Nina, Annalise and I, and the ambassador of Ireland. Perhaps in a green suit."

"And wearing a leprechaun hat . . . Give my very best to Frau Richthofen and, Paul, be careful."

"Ja, ja, Tim, thank you very much."

I turned away to leave him to his slobbering boss, a man who probably knew a little about the Spitfires and had not warned Paul about them.

Well, I'd done my Christian duty to be a good sport and in thoroughly Irish style, a loser being gracious to a winner after a rugby match. I wished I felt better about it.

I rode back to the embassy and drank a large glass of the Irish whiskey, of which my predecessor had left a supply that might survive the thousand-year Reich.

As the Galway woman had insisted, I said the Rosary every day before sleeping. That night I prayed for Paul von Richthofen and fell asleep with the Rosary still in my fingers. I repeated it the next morning, just in case God and the Blessed Mother had any doubts about my sincerity.

— 13 —

"THE RAF did win that battle, didn't they?" Nuala Anne asked me the following morning in my office, after she had read the most recent segment of Timmy's diary.

She was dressed in shorts and an exercise bra for her daily struggle in our little gym room. I had already taken the beasts for their run and performed my workout requirement and hence was filled with a sense of virtue, distantly related perhaps to that which Timmy had experienced that dreadful day in 1940.

"They did indeed. On 'Eagle Day' they gave the *Luftwaffe* a bloody nose from which it never recovered. The battle went on till October, when the Germans switched to night bombing of English cities. The RAF lost some nine hundred planes and about four hundred pilots out of approximately three thousand. The *Luftwaffe* lost over two thousand planes. Some of the experts after the war said that if the Germans had sustained their attacks, they would have won. But Hitler and Goering needed the planes and the pilots for their attack on Russia in the spring."

"Three thousand men stopped the Glorious Führer and his dashing Reichsmarschal?"

"That's why Churchill said that never before had so many owed so much to so few."

"Your man Timmy is having a great time for himself, isn't he now?"

"And feeling very pleased with himself for his generosity of spirit."

"Give over, Dermot Michael Coyne! Would you have been so generous if someone had taken me away before you worked up enough nerve?"

"I would have killed him."

"No you wouldn't. You'd be after dying of a broken heart."

" 'Tis true."

"It would make a great film, wouldn't it?"

"Film" is pronounced "filum" just as my nephew Colm's name is pronounced "Colum." Don't ask me why.

"We'll have to see how it ends. What if they all die? We know Claus died and the Herr Admiral. And Hitler and the rest."

"WELL, certainly your man didn't die or he would not have written his memoirs."

" 'Tis true."

"And those funny old planes, whatever do you call them?"

"Stukas. Goering pulled them out early. The Spitfires were shooting them down in large numbers every day."

"I wonder if she loved him at all, at all."

"He sounded like a nice man."

"Lots of charm like Timmy. But I can't see your man hanging around someone like what's his name?"

"Reichsmarschal Hermann Goering."

"We got him at the end, didn't we?"

I didn't point out that Ireland had nothing to do with getting him.

"He was convicted at the war crimes trial and killed himself the day he was to be hung."

"He wasn't any less dead . . . Do you think Timmy went to Germany to have another chance to marry Annalise?"

"And to see Claus again?" I suggested.

"And to help kill the Antichrist?"

"Your man," I suggested, "is like our friend Des. He was looking for adventure. Maybe he encountered more than he expected."

"And lived to write this . . . and married someone."

"Who maybe settled him down?"

She thought about that.

"I don't think the Galway woman settled his father down."

"You probably have the right of it, Nuala Anne . . . What do we do next?"

"Well, first of all you talk to Jennifer Doolin and set up a time and a place for an interview."

"By myself?"

"She wouldn't feel free to talk to me about her brother, not at all, at all."

I didn't argue. I never did with Nuala's decisions in these matters. She would make the point that it was obviously the right decision and didn't require an argument.

"And second of all?"

"Haven't I been thinking that we need a day of swimming?"

When we had married and moved into our house on Sheffield Avenue, we had not sold my studio apartment in the John Hancock Center. It was, I argued, appreciating every month, and it gave us a getaway place when we wanted to get away, and a swimming pool. And, I hadn't added, a site for intense romance, free from dogs and children, subjects which had yet to enter my romantic imagination.

"At my apartment?"

"Well, where else do we have a pool?"

We hadn't been there since the presence of Patjo in my wife's body had become evident, almost a year ago.

"It wouldn't be daycent!"

It was apparently decent at Grand Beach, but what did I know.

"'Tis a ded friggin' bril idea!" I agreed.

So I called Grace Doolin and reported that we thought we were making progress and that we had begun to suspect that Des was still alive.

"Why hasn't he been in touch with us then?" she said with passive aggressive asperity in her voice.

"Perhaps he cannot, for one reason or another."

"It doesn't make sense to me. I knew we should have forbidden him to attend Loyola Academy. The Jesuits ruined him. We should have insisted on New Trier and then Notre Dame, just as we did for Jenny."

She was not particularly happy about my request for an interview with Jenny, but she acceded to it with very little grace. A handsome, pleasant woman, Grace Doolin would make herself old long before her time.

Jenny phoned us a half hour later. She would be in Chicago on Saturday to take some of her friends from Seattle shopping at the Water Tower and the Mag Mile and could easily escape for lunch. I proposed Rosebud on Rush Street at noon. If our promising spring weather continued we could eat outdoors. She accepted my invitation with what I could call guarded enthusiasm.

Our "getaways" had acquired a certain ritual through the years of our marriage. In midafternoon on Friday we'd go to the studio and engage in some preliminary activity, including some moderate lovemaking, a swim, and dinner at either Tru or the Four Seasons. We would not talk about any work we were doing and maintain only minimum essential contact with home—which meant a call every two hours or so to calm down the "hellions" who are usually pretty well behaved in our absence, even Socra Marie. The next day, we talked, read, swam, and made love, much more than just moderately. If weather permitted we might walk along the lakefront. Sometimes Nuala did a "little shopping" in the Water Tower. We ordered pizza in at the end of the day, drank red wine (Barolo preferred) and enjoyed quietly the rejuvenation of our love. Before going to bed we said the Rosary (as Timmy had done in his flat in the Friedrichstrasse in Berlin) praying for all married people, especially those who could not take a day off or could and would not (intention furnished by me wife). The next morning we ate breakfast in the Coffee Shop at the Ritz-Carlton and then went home to the hellions, whom we were already beginning to miss.

This time, herself went home, and I walked down to the river and back before my lunch with Jenny Doolin. At the first sign of a real spring day, the Mag Mile and environs erupt with women in spring dresses. It would have been a perfect day for me wife to sashay down the street in various kinds of light blue dresses. For meself, despite an interlude of intense sexual play the sights on the street were exciting, though I was careful not to stare—too obviously.

God had done a marvelous job in designing women and matching them with spring.

Exhausted from my exertions and feeling the heat and my old age and telling myself that I was a dirty old man, I sank into an umbrella-protected chair on Superior Street and tried to recoup my resources by sipping slowly on a spice-soaked iced tea. I had promised Jenny that she could recognize me by my old Golden Dome windbreaker and a stack of my wife's disks on the table.

"Mr. Coyne," a gentle voice said. "I don't mean to wake you up."

"Mr. Coyne is my grandfather," I said as I opened my eyes, "I'm Dermot and I was only resting my eyes a bit."

I jumped out of my chair, as my mother had taught me to and grinned my best Irish grin.

"I'm Jenny," she said shyly, a trim young woman, below medium height with the darkest brown eyes in all the world and short brown hair, a tentative smile that would break many a young man's heart, and an aura of fragile strength. Her thin beige dress revealed a figure that would contribute to the heartbreak. You wanted to take care of Jenny Doolin and yet you were quite certain that in her own low-key way, she could take care of herself.

She was surprised that I had attended the Golden Dome, even more surprised that I had quit the football team and left the school, well, flunked out because of poor grades.

"You must not have studied very hard, Dermot."

"Quite the contrary, I studied very hard and learned a lot. Unfortunately, none of it was in my assigned courses. Then I went to Marquette for two years and didn't graduate there either. My family bought me a seat on the Board of Trade where I was also a failure. Next I made a couple of million by mistake, retired, sold my seat, turned my money over to a wise investor, went to Europe, encountered my wife in a pub in Dublin, married her, and we have four children, whom she calls with some exaggeration, hellions."

I showed her my wallet picture of the five of them.

"Nuala Anne," she said with an approving smile. "Your good luck continues, Dermot."

"If she were present, I'd disagree. She sent some of her disks."

"Which she autographed! Isn't that sweet? . . . glad I can talk to you alone, because I'd be intimidated if she were here. Still next time, when Des comes home, I'd love to meet her."

OK, this lovely little woman had won me over completely with a few sentences. She'd also confirmed me wife's instincts.

"He's coming home, is he?"

"Of course he's coming home. My parents don't think so anymore, but they've never understood Des. I try to tell them that he's up to something special and he'll come home when he's finished and explain everything."

Her faith was absolute and simple. No doubts, no questions, like an elderly nun's faith in Jesus.

"As me wife would say, Jenny Doolin, I think you have the right of it."

"You can take notes if you want," she said shyly.

"I have a photographic memory, Jenny. You'd think I should have done well in school, but I didn't know then that I had such a blessing. It gets me in trouble with Nuala Anne, because I remember exactly what she has said."

"And she tells you that you should listen to what she means, not what she said."

"And yourself not even knowing her personally," I replied, liking this quiet young woman more and more. "So you admire your brother? The only one in the family that does?"

"I think Dad does too, but once Mom makes up her mind, he doesn't argue. Her brother went to a Jesuit high school in New York and to Fordham and then spent a year as a novice. When he left the novitiate, he started to drift and has been drifting ever since, in and out of work, in and out of marriage. So it's the fault of the Jesuits. She's afraid that the same thing will happen to Des, know what I mean?"

So that's the family dynamics.

"Is Des at all like his uncle?"

"I certainly don't think so. Uncle Joe is a dreamy sort of man, not much energy or enthusiasm. Des is bundle of enthusiasm and energy, too much maybe, but not passive aggressive. Uncle Joe could never figure out what to do next, Des always knew the next and the next after next. Mom sees only two men who look kind of alike and won't settle down with the right kind of young woman."

"Do you agree that Des should settle down?"

"When he's ready and poor Mom won't like her because she won't be a creep like Mattie . . . I shouldn't have said that. Mattie is fine for Conor. Des would never marry someone like her."

"Someone like Shovie, maybe?"

"Shovie adored him, but she is smart enough to see that there's probably no future there. She's looking for a husband eventually and she should. I'm different. I adore him and he's my brother and always will be, know what I mean?"

"You think he'll come back from Iraq?"

"Whenever he's ready to."

She dug into her Italian salad and I started working on my fettuccine Bolognese. Both of us ordered iced tea to drink.

"Did he talk to you about it before he left?"

"He came down to the Dome to watch a football game. He told me when we were walking back to his car that he had a big deal coming up and he'd be out of touch for a while and I shouldn't worry about him. I asked where he was going and he grinned and said that it was a big secret. He always loved his big secrets."

"Did you tell him that your parents would worry about him?"

"Of course I did! He really loves them too, always making excuses for them. He said he'd not be gone for long and that they would worry about him wherever he was and whatever he was doing."

"Wasn't that a kind of cavalier attitude?"

The pasta was truly excellent. I tried to slow down my consumption of it because Jenny was very deliberate in eating her salad.

"I have to say, Dermot, that he could either act that way or give up his life because they would take it away from him. Mom's worries about Uncle Joe were a form of emotional blackmail."

"You asked him how long he would be gone?"

"He grinned like a little leprechaun, and said, 'Peace Corps more or less.'"

"Two years, give or take?"

"Except that was before the war started," she frowned. "That might have changed his time frame."

"Did you notice any unusual behavior before he left?"

"No, not at all, not by Des's standards of unusual."

She frowned thoughtfully.

"Well he seemed to trade in the Lebanese for the Assyrians."

"Huh!"

"Des used to spend time with the Arab merchants around town, talking to them in their own language, which pleased them greatly. Then he began to spend more time with those Assyrians, Iraqi Christians I guess. You know, the kind of handsome people who run all the camera stores around the city."

"Also called Chaldees."

"Except that they don't like that name as much as Assyrian because they claim that they're descended from the ancient Babylonians and some of them speak the same language Jesus spoke, know what I mean?"

"I've heard of it."

"Des said that most of them speak Arabic too, but the ones from northern Iraq around Mosul also speak Aramaic as do some of the Kurds up there."

This was the first solid hint we had of where in Iraq he might have gone.

I changed the subject. "Did you exchange e-mail often?"

"A couple of times a week usually. He sort of felt that it was his responsibility to help me to resist Dad and Mom—they'd already picked out a 'nice young man' for me. The guy was a prime nerd. I didn't mind Des giving me advice. It was good advice usually but I made my own decisions."

"Did he send e-mail from Africa when he was there?"

"They didn't have the facilities. Now they do in Iraq but maybe he can't use them . . . He'd be in touch with me if he could."

"You have a lot of faith in him, Jenny."

"He's never done anything which would cause me to lose faith in him, Dermot. He'll come home, sooner rather than later."

"And then?"

"Mom will cry and Dad will be very stern and Conor will talk about the joy of marital happiness and none of that will make any difference. He's immune to them."

"And then?"

"He'll probably go back to UIC and get his doctorate."

"And then?"

"I don't know, Dermot. I don't have a clue. It will certainly be something that will be generous and good."

So we turned to the important question of the Notre Dame team next year and she expressed surprise and approval that I had quit the team and talked about her plans to do Teach America when she graduated.

"Will your parents like that?"

"They won't but at least I will be with Americans and they can check up on me every night."

"Mexican immigrants more likely."

She grinned impishly.

"I won't tell them that."

Back at my house, I found Nuala playing with the kids, young Patjo clinging to the back of the delighted Maeve, who barked approvingly at her charges' efforts.

"Whose idea was that?" I demanded.

"Mommy's," Socra Marie said all too quickly.

"Really?"

"Really, Da!"

Maeve rose up to stroll across the room. Patjo grew uneasy and began to wail. Nuala swept him off his mount. Maeve, upset that the game was over, stood up on her hind legs and nuzzled me wife, just to make sure she wasn't in trouble.

"It's all right, Mae-Mae," she assured the white hound, hugging her. "The little fella isn't quite ready yet. Isn't that true, Socra Marie?"

"Yes, Ma."

"Nelliecoyne, I have to put this little sleepyhead down and then Daddy and I must have a little chat. Can I leave you in charge?"

"Certainly, Ma!"

"I'll turn on the monitor, so you can yell if you need help."

"Yes, Ma."

"That one," Nuala Anne protested to me, "is entirely too responsible for her age."

"She'll probably rebel when she's a teen and run away from home."

"Give over, Dermot Michael, she won't give up the time to boss me around."

I rehearsed my interview with Jenny.

"A bright young woman, isn't she now?"

"And herself a Domer."

"Who can't figure out why you ever left there?"

"I didn't leave. They threw me out."

"That was before I was around to settle you down," she said with a wicked laugh.

That was the conventional wisdom in my family and not without an element of truth. Nuala rejected it flatly.

"You didn't need any settling down at all, Dermot Michael Coyne, at all, at all," she would say. "Wasn't it yourself that was settling me down?"

"A work in progress," I said.

"Beast," she said, pounding my arm gently or at least more gently than she used to. "Where is this Mosul place? Who are the Kurds? How would one get hisself there?"

I spun the huge globe I keep in the office.

"Here is Iraq, between Iran and Syria and Kuwait. Up there in the north is the place where a few of the remnants of the once enormous Church of the East still survive. Here is Mosul where the Neo-Aramaic-speaking Christians live. It contains the largest oil field in the country. The Assyrians share the land with Kurds and Arabs and are a tiny minority. Many of them have left and migrated to America, especially to Chicago and Detroit and Los Angeles. They are intelligent, hardworking, and dedicated people. The Muslims in Iraq don't like them because they are so successful and because they are infidels. Saddam protected them because he was running a secular state. His foreign minister was one of them. Now that the religious Muslims tend to be in charge, life over there is very dangerous for them. They do very well here, another boon to America from immigration. They are usually merchants who run small shops, like many of the early Jewish and Chinese immigrants. They are a handsome folk, characteristically with very dark skins. To the bigoted eyes of Americans they often seem sinister because they look like the bad guys in the old movies. In fact, they are very nice and friendly folk, especially if you ask them whether they're Assyrians. They will insist, sometimes in anger, that they are not Arabs. They are rather, they will say, descendents of the ancient Babylonians. They claim that the real name of Baghdad is Babylon. Their women tend to be gorgeous . . ."

"Och, Dermot, aren't you the brilliant one, and yourself knowing practically everything? I don't think I ever saw one of them folk."

"When you bought that digital Nikon for me at the camera shop over on Halsted Street, you met some of them. They own a chain of camera and electronic stores. Instant jobs for immigrants."

"Them folk are your Assyrians, are they now? You have the right of it, Dermot love, they are handsome and very well educated. The young woman who waited on me was terribly beautiful and darker than most of your African-Americans. She made me feel like I was an ignorant peasant and meself with a degree from a school for peasants like Trinity College."

"I think the Jesuits have or maybe had a college in Baghdad."

"Your Jesuits, is it now?"

"That suggests something, doesn't it? . . . I suppose there might be a link here somewhere?"

" 'Tis the first clue we've got, thanks be to God and Mary and Brigid!"

In Nuala's coterie of saints, this is the first string.

"Now who are your Kurds?"

"A fiercely independent Islamic people who got squeezed out of having a country of their own after World War I. They're spread out all over the Middle East—Turkey, Iraq, Iran, maybe some of them in Russia. They're always revolting against someone. The revolutions are usually bloody disasters, but they keep trying. Their wars with the Turks are especially fierce, there are ten million of them in Turkey, maybe a fifth of the country. The Turks hate them and they hate the Turks, though they're probably a Turkish people. During the first Gulf War, they set up an enclave up here north of Mosul and the CIA moved in to support them. With the help of the United States, they drove Saddam's army back and have had a free Kurdistan up there, an American beachhead, so to speak."

"Why would America ever need a beachhead in that part of the world?"

"The idea was that if we were to fight Iraq again, we'd move a division or two through Turkey and attack from the north as well as the south. The Turks agreed and we maintained an airfield up in Izmir here on the Turkish coast. Naturally they cooperated at a price and naturally we paid it."

"Did we do that?"

"We did not. The Turks wouldn't stay bought."

"These Kurds speak Arabic?"

"No way. They have their own language, a version of Iranian Farsi."

"So if your man is wandering around up there, he would have to know three languages?"

"He could get by with Arabic of which everyone in Iraq knows some.

Being the kind of language freak he is, he'd probably be working on Farsi and Assyrian by now."

"From what we know, Dermot"—she slowly spun the globe as she thought—"your man would love a situation like this place . . . Do the Kurds hate the Christians?"

"As a matter of principle, they hate everyone. However, they may have allied themselves with the Christians to drive the Shiite Iraq out of Mosul, whose oil fields they have commandeered. They also currently like Americans because we helped them set up their little Kurdistan up here. They expect to be betrayed by everyone. Once we get out of Iraq we'll indeed betray them. The Turks as you might imagine don't like the enclave because it will encourage the Turkish Kurds to revolt again . . . On the other hand if the Turks want to get into the EU, they'll have to provide the Kurds with some kind of autonomy."

"Will that be enough?"

"I doubt it."

She sighed her most agonized Connemara sigh.

"Och, Dermot, the world is in a terrible mess, isn't it?"

"'Tis, woman, a terrible mess altogether. Makes Ireland look simple."

"I had a nice conversation with your Assyrian woman after she noticed me St. Brigid Cross."

My good wife does not leave our house on Sheffield Avenue without some token of identification with that great saint of poetry and spring and new life and, as Nuala maintains, song.

"She tell you anything useful?"

"Well we bonded because we're both immigrants, strangers in a foreign land. Like meself, she loves this country. They have their own businesses, their own homes, their own churches, and they don't have to worry about the police or fanatics or Saddam's planes with poison gas. She hopes that all her people can get out of Iraq and come to Chicago."

"Doesn't everyone!"

"They even have two dioceses of their own, one in Detroit and one in Los Angeles and they expect to have one here soon . . . Dermot, is there any way we can tell whether your man is up there?"

"Well, we can find out which way he flew. I had always assumed that he flew to Kuwait—the Kuwaiti airline has worldwide services—and then hitched a ride with GIs or Marines into the country. But he might have flown Turkish Air into Ankara and hitched a ride into northern Iraq, that might have been more dangerous . . ."

"Can we find out which way he chose?"

"I'll call Mike Casey."

"Would the Turks let him in?"

"As an American citizen he wouldn't have much trouble getting in. As a scholar working in Middle Eastern languages, they might be glad to have him. Getting from Ankara to Mosul might be more difficult unless the CIA was helping him, but there would have to be a good reason for doing it, at least good from the CIA's point of view."

She thought a minute.

"Nelliecoyne, why is it so quiet down there?"

"Didn't I put Socra Marie down and aren't the doggies taking naps with them? And don't the Mick and I like to do our work quietly?"

"Thank you very much, Nellie. Aren't you the wonderful one?"

"Sure, Ma, don't I like hearing you say that, even if it's true?"

Nuala switched off the button.

"Isn't that one a handful?"

"Matriarch in training."

"In five years, Dermot, she'll be a teen. Do you think she'll be after turning into a rebel?"

"Since she's her mother' daughter, won't she become a manipulator?"

"'Tis true. It will be hard, Dermot. I'm scared thinking about it."

"Won't it be glorious fun altogether, woman of the house?"

"You have the right of it, Dermot Michael. That's the only way to think! . . . Now call that nice Mr. Casey and find out how your man got into Iraq."

On Saturday afternoon, Mike would be at the Reilly Gallery (the proprietor was his wife, Annie Reilly), not at the office of Reliable Security.

"It will take a couple of days, but we'll do it, Dermot. Is herself tuning in to the spirits?"

"That comes only when all other matters fail . . . Would you ever find out how he might have got across the border into Iraq?"

"We'll try. It will have to be informal and I might have to pay a Turkish official to find out. That's the way of it over there."

"We'd appreciate any information."

To Nuala, I said, "A couple of days."

"You're not going over there, Dermot Michael Coyne, do you understand that?"

"I wouldn't go to northern Iraq, Nuala Anne McGrail, even if you ordered me to do so!"

"And ourselves with a preteen in the house!"

I took advantage of the preteen problem to shift a little bit of the investigation onto her shapely shoulders.

"Tell you what, wife of my youth, while I'm waiting here for Mike's call on Monday, why don't you go over to the camera store and talk to your good friend. Show her the picture of your man and see if he ever came in to talk about the Assyrian church in northern Iraq."

"You know, Dermot love, she was wearing a diamond even bigger than mine."

"On an erotic exotic it might be appropriate. On an Irishwoman from Carraroe, wouldn't it be vulgar altogether?"

"Wasn't I saying the very same thing to meself?"

— 14 —

"Ja, ja, Herr Ambassador, I said it could not be you, when the attendant said you were down in the gun room."

"Just making sure I'm not rusty."

Three targets popped up simultaneously. I nailed them with a .25mm bullet between the eyes in 1.5 seconds.

"A little slow."

"The Wehrmacht could use you as an assassin. So could the Secret Germany."

A curt phone message suggested that we meet for lunch at this target practice club just below the Potsdamer Platz.

"If I had brought my own .25, I might have been quicker."

"You shoot targets for fun."

"I like to imagine that I'm a cowboy in Dodge City—or Wyatt Earp in Tombstone, even if you couldn't stop a varmint with a .25 unless he was pretty close to you . . . Let's eat."

"Did you not tell me in Heidelberg that you do not hunt animals?"

"Gave that up, much to my Old Fella's surprise and to the Galway woman's delight. So I took up small arms, just to prove I had a good aim. If I were faced with a human, I'm sure I'd freeze."

I had taken up handguns when the IRA were burning homes of English lords during the troubles. I was young enough to think my revolver would deter a group of drunken gunmen.

Only drunks would have attacked us. We were known as Catholics who provided work for Catholics in our linen mills. As I grew older, I began to wonder whether I could shoot anyone, even a gunman. I did win a marksmanship prize at Oxford, but now it had become a sport rather than a tool of self-defense.

"Would you," he whispered, "consider killing a Führer for us?"

"Not my war," I said. "I would have made a very bad soldier."

We sat on a wooden bench at a wooden table on which were placed almost immediately two large steins of beer, a loaf of dark brown bread, and a large platter of sausages.

"Sausages?" I said.

"Ja, but very good sausages."

They were.

"You are a strange man, Herr Ambassador."

"Call me Herr Viscount, please."

He laughed, that wonderful infectious, self-deprecating laugh of his, which enabled him to say almost anything and not make another angry.

"You are a man of astonishing grace."

I knew what was coming. I would be embarrassed. I must, as the Galway woman said, accept praise modestly, but without denial.

"All right, but he was a nice man and I thought it was the thing to do. I figured he'd tell Annalise and she'd tell you and I'd be able to pray for him every night when I say the Rosary. It was the Catholic thing to do."

"She wept for joy."

"He knows I was a rival?"

"Such a thought would never occur to Paul von Richthofen."

"Your good friend Admiral Canaris says he will be in jeopardy in the air battles over Britain."

"Goering would be mad to send the Stukas against the RAF. However, Goering is mad. Even if they demolish the RAF, von Rundstedt would not want to invade. He fears the casualties would be heavy. If the RAF survives, and as you know Canaris says it will, Gerd will resign rather than risk a blood bath of the finest troops in the Wehrmacht, including my division. In the OKW only the Führer's toadies like Jodl and Keitel want the invasion. The Führer nonetheless hesitates. He knows he will need the men and the planes for his Russian adventure."

"And that would create the catastrophe which would make it possible for the Secret Germany to rise."

"A bloody defeat in England would too. Russia, however, is certain defeat. Our fighting men are better than the Russians, but there are so many more of them. They are like the previous Asiatic hordes. They will keep coming, no matter how many of them we kill."

"The General Staff would resist such an invasion?"

"It would not be successful in that. The Secret Germany would win more allies. But the Führer has always been determined to drive to the Pacific, outdo both Napoleon and Alexander the Great."

I raised the platter to seek more sausages.

"You like our sausages, Timmy?"

"I think I might get tired of them after a few years, but they are better than the ones we have in Ireland . . . What will happen to Annalise if her husband dies next month?"

"She will grieve deeply. She will believe that men who love her are doomed to die. It will not be good. Even if he survives England, I fear he will die. He is not flying a Fokker like his cousin."

"So the ideal time for the Secret Germany will be when Hitler suffers a terrible defeat in Russia?" I said as I finished my stein of beer.

Knowing that I would sleep all afternoon, I signaled for another.

"The invasion will occur next spring, 1941. They will stop us short of total victory. The war will drag on. In the winter of 1942 we will suffer a great defeat. In 1943 the Russians will begin to move against us and it will be clear that they are winning the war. Then it will be our hour."

"You will have enough force to win?"

"We will have to eliminate the Führer. Then we will have a good chance of winning. No one can predict anything more than that."

That was, I thought, a fairly grim assessment. Not only would von Richthofen be dead, but so would Claus and Canaris and lots of other good people, perhaps millions of them.

"You are continuing to build your network, Claus? Is that not dangerous?"

"I'm careful about those to whom I speak. One has no choice but to take chances. Incidentally, you can trust Canaris as long as he is in power over there at Abwehr. Your dispatches will be destroyed. If the situation changes there, either he or I will let you know."

"Have there been any previous attempts to kill Hitler?"

"Seven! Some of them involving field marshals or colonel generals and approved by chiefs of staff. None of them have been successful. The Antichrist has powers of his own."

"Which you can overcome?"

"I must try, Timmy." He flashed his most disarming smile. "I have no choice."

It would be four years before the final desperate attempt.

I listened to different accounts of the Battle of Britain on both German radio and the BBC and learned the truth during my chess matches with Admiral Canaris out in Gruenwald. On Eagle Day, postponed to August 15 because of the weather, German radio claimed that the Glorious Luftwaffe, under the direction of the heroic Reichsmarschal, had virtually destroyed the Royal Air Force, caught on the ground at its sector stations. In a few more days England would lose its last air protection. The BBC reported that enemy attacks had been repulsed with scores of German planes shot down. Conflicting reports continued for the next week. The BBC observed that the Germans had already claimed to have destroyed more planes than the RAF possessed. Clearly, Goering had not delivered on his promise of a four-day Battle of Britain.

"The English are giving us a bloody nose," Canaris told me with unconcealed satisfaction. "They are knocking down Stukas like ducks on a hunt. The junior commanders say that they cannot afford the losses of pilots or planes. The English may be an inferior people but they are also surprisingly tough."

"I should believe the BBC?"

"*Both sides exaggerate, but the truth is that for every one of their planes we shoot down, they shoot down two of ours and their aircraft production is now twice ours. This is no way to win a war.*"

"*Operation Sea Lion?*"

"*It will continue as a plan perhaps till October, then we begin to prepare for Russia . . . Check, Herr Ambassador.*"

"*And the Stukas?*"

"*Your friend von Richthofen was at the Air Ministry today. They discussed pulling them out of combat. He was overruled by Goering himself. However, another week of such losses and his request will be granted. They have already lost a third of their planes.*"

"*You're in check now, Herr Admiral.*"

"*Ja, ja, you tricky little Irishman.*"

The radio reports continued the same for several more nights. The RAF was still getting its Spitfires and Hurricanes into the air.

Then one night a mournful announcer on German radio reported the glorious death of a great Luftwaffe hero. General Colonel Paul von Richthofen had been killed in action while obliterating the English airfield at Biggin Hill. Realizing that his Stuka was going to crash, he piloted it into the fuel reservoir which exploded and destroyed the entire station and two squadrons of English fighters. The Führer himself personally promoted Baron von Richthofen to the rank of Field Marshal General and awarded him the posthumous award of Knights Cross of the Iron Cross with Swords Diamonds and Oak Leaves. "*The whole of the Reich expresses its sympathy to Baroness von Richthofen and his family. England will pay for this tragic loss in blood of RAF pilots. We will have vengeance.*"

I turned off the radio, lifted the shade in my tiny bedroom and stared out at the darkened sky. I reached for my Rosary and prayed for all who would die in this war and all who they would leave behind.

Eventually I closed the shade and returned to my office. I turned on the light and sent off a coded minute to Dublin in which I reported that rumors around Berlin indicated that many suspected the Luftwaffe was having a difficult time with the RAF and that the posthumous promotion of the commander of the Stuka wing to Field Marshal General was a sign that the morale of the German people was being prepared for another glorious defeat against great odds.

I hoped that my minute would be on Winston's desk the next morning.

Claus called me the following morning. Rarely did I speak to him directly on the phone.

"You heard last night?"

"I did."

"There will be a memorial Mass at the Catholic Cathedral tomorrow morning. The Reichsmarschal will be there, but not the Führer. Nina and I will walk down the aisle with her."

"Would it be appropriate for me to attend?"

"Definitely."

"You're sure?"

"Yes."

"I'll be there."

I called the Foreign Office and talked to Ribbentrop's secretary.

"Would I need a ticket for the funeral tomorrow of Field Marshal General Paul von Richthofen?"

"One moment, Herr Ambassador."

She returned quickly.

"The Herr Reichsminister is grateful for your respect for our glorious hero. You will receive a document before noon."

I thanked her.

The Catholic Cathedral is a strange, distracting pseudobaroque monstrosity with a large dome, a poor second-place finisher compared to the nearby Protestant Cathedral. It was unspeakably hot and stuffy that dreadful August morning. The church was filled with people, Nazi officials in their black SS uniforms in the first rows, then high officers of the Luftwaffe, then the diplomatic corps, then ordinary Luftwaffe officers, then the ordinary people of Berlin come to honour a hero.

On the catafalque, draped in black rested both the baton of a Field Marshal and an Iron Cross decorated with the doodads and a Swastika.

I felt clammy and then sick to my stomach as I waited. What the hell was I doing in this city during a war?

Then Annalise walked down the aisle, her face covered by a thick black veil with erect head and a firm step, the fat Reichsmarschal festooned with jewelry in front of her and Claus and Nina on either side. She did not lean on either of them.

The Mass went on forever, accompanied by dour Bach music, heavy incense, and the bowing and scraping of the clergy in attendance around the Clement August Cardinal von Galen, Prince Bishop of Berlin, a tall striking man who was known to have no sympathy for the Nazis.

His sermon was, as I might have expected, long and difficult to hear. It seemed to be a plea for peace so that other brave men would not have to die. Clearly the words of a man who didn't give a damn about the Nazis.

At Communion only the widow and her cousin and cousin's husband went up to the altar rail. Thus the Reichsmarschal was not embarrassed.

At 12:45 we escaped from the Cathedral, walking down the aisle after the Reichsmarschal, swinging his baton like a clown at a circus, the widow and her attendants and the Luftwaffe dignitaries. Annalise walked with the same firm dignity that she had displayed at the beginning of Mass. The veil hid any possible tears on her face, but her shoulders did not shake with sobs.

What else did I expect from my Gothic princess?

My morning suit was soaked. We'd have to get it cleaned immediately.

Several days later I met with Claus in the café on the Den Linden.

He still seemed depressed.

"It was gracious of you to attend the Mass, Tim. Frau von, pardon me, Annalise asked me to express her gratitude to you."

I nodded.

"She grieves more deeply than I would have expected. Apparently he had visited her only a few days before his death and she found herself loving him."

I nodded again.

"She now is the widow of a fallen hero. That will require her to grieve for a year or perhaps longer. She has no taste for romance in any case. She believes that men she loves are cursed. I am reluctant to say these things to you, Timmy. I know that you still love her and I suspect that she loves you. I am merely saying . . ."

"I understand, Claus."

"Time changes people, and may change them again."

"I understand that too."

"Thank you for being so sympathetic . . ."

"Indeed, I do still love her. I probably always will," I said, words rushing out of my mouth ahead of my thoughts. "I can wait."

Once more his devastating grin.

"I'm sure you will. It is all in God's hands."

We heard the drone of planes high in the air.

Claus looked up.

"Twenty of them," he said. "Looks like Dorniers."

I studied them.

"More like Blenheims to me, Claus. It looks like there is an air raid on Berlin."

"No air raid siren!"

"The RAF is sending a message about its destruction."

Small specks like tiny insects detached themselves from the silver planes in the sky and tumbled lazily towards the earth. They grew larger and darker and more ominous as they fell, then they disappeared behind the trees of the Tiergarten. Then a line of black clouds surged over the trees and became large plumes on the horizon. A rumble of thunder raced across the park and hit us like a quick slap in the face. The teacups on our table rattled.

"They're bombing the government buildings," Claus said in wonderment. "Very accurate. Maybe they will save us the effort."

"The sound of the antiaircraft fire is important," I said.

"There wasn't any antiaircraft fire, Tim!"

"That's why it is important. The raid is a complete surprise and it hit the right targets."

"The Führer will be furious. Tomorrow we will bomb London. Then it will start. City after city will be destroyed. Unrestricted bombing of civilians. More horror!"

"Terror bombing," I said.

"It is the theory of strategic air attacks, they developed during the war in Spain, Tim. One destroys the morale of the civilian population and the war effort fails. Total war."

Claus stared at the sky, his face drawn, his eyes sad.

"The Antichrist grows stronger."

As we listened to the sound of the fire engines and of the belated wail of the air raid sirens we realized for the first time that if the bombardiers on the Blenheims had been a little less accurate the bombs would have fallen on us.

I shivered.

"They might have hit us," I murmured.

"In France I would have taken cover," Claus replied calmly. "In Berlin I did not expect danger. We must drink a little beer to calm our bodies."

He laughed at his own shivering.

"We were talking about Annalise," I said.

"She needs time, Timmy. I cannot tell you how much time."

"I'm not so insensitive as to push."

"That is wise."

Perhaps not, I thought to myself. Perhaps I am a coward.

"She knows I'm here, Claus. She will have to send a sign she wants to see me again."

He nodded solemnly. I knew he would pass the information on to her. Maybe we would meet by chance. Maybe I'd never see her again. Maybe either or both of us would be killed in an air raid.

Many times during the subsequent raids I would stand near the Tiergarten and listen to the bombs and the antiaircraft guns and watch the flames, still idiotically confident that I would not be hit. I was a neutral, was I not?

The next day the Luftwaffe flew up the River Thames in a much bigger raid on London. They inflicted heavy damage in the East End docks. Hitler had his revenge. The day after that, the English were ready with large wings of Spitfires—seventy in each wing. The Luftwaffe formations broke open and ran.

As Canaris told me later, that was the final mistake the Germans made in the Battle of Britain. The two days of respite at the fighter stations gave fighter command the needed respite to recover from the attacks against them and to rise to the sky to meet the Luftwaffe when it renewed the attack on the fighter stations. Again the German losses were heavy. The Germans turned to night raids on London, the "blitz" those who lived through would never forget. Then the raids tapered off as the Germans withdrew their planes to preserve them for the attack on Russia. Except for an occasional attack, London was safe for the time being.

However, the RAF accepted the theory of strategic bombing and prepared to respond in kind. As the war went on, their "Lancaster" bombers, big black, freight car planes, wiped out one German city after another with fire bomb raids that eventually killed six hundred thousand civilians, many of them in firestorms. Claus's prediction had been correct—more horror than we could have imagined that day on the Den Linden.

It was only that night as I listened to the ranting on German radio that I realized that the Air Ministry building had been heavily damaged. Either the English bombardiers were very lucky or very good. I wondered if Annalise had returned to work.

Nineteen forty became 1941. The OKW, however reluctantly, began the planning for Operation Barbarossa. Everyone seemed to know about the plan, even the day of the attack, May 22, even the Pope. Hitler was so confident of success that he didn't worry about security.

I found out that the Pope knew in March when the Ministry suggested that I go to Rome to pay my respects to the Pope. Pius XII had been Nuncio to Germany and wanted my opinion of the situation. I was happy to escape from the gloom of winter and war in Berlin. I wrote long letters to the Old Fella and the Galway woman, which I would mail at the Vatican Post Office, where they would not be censored.

Italy had entered the war against France when it was almost over, a "stab in the back," Roosevelt had called it. Small English contingents began to clean up the Italian empire. They encountered little resistance and captured thousands of prisoners. The second Roman empire faded away. Italians wisely were not ready to die for Mussolini. In North Africa, the Brits also chased the Italians out of Libya. Then Hitler sent two Panzer divisions, the famous Afrika Korps, commanded by Erwin Rommel, the "Desert Fox," which chased the English back to the outskirts of Cairo. The English counterattacked and armies swayed back and forth across the desert and piled up once again at the gates of Cairo. After the invasion of Russia, Hitler spoke to the General Staff of pushing through the Caucasus and a rendezvous with Rommel in Mesopotamia. India, he was convinced, would rise to welcome him, just like Austria had.

"He sees himself as emperor of all Europe and Asia." Claus laughed.

When I arrived in Rome, however, I encountered no grief about the loss of their empire. "Let the Germans fight in Africa." And no worry about the Italian prisoners in North America. "They will eat well and grow fat," a Roman matron bragged to me.

Despite my large tricolour button, they thought I was an American.

The Roman women were as lovely as legend had it. Alas for me, I was in love with a grieving Gothic princess.

I managed to be in the Piazza Venezia when Il Duce gave one of his performances. A lot of folks were shouting "Duce! Duce!" but a lot of others were laughing. Did it always end in bad comedy?

"What of Germany?" Cardinal Maglione, the Secretary of State, asked me in his marble office. "Do the German people still support that madman?"

"Some do, Eminenza, some do not. Right now he is popular because of his quick and painless victories. As the war grows worse, he will lose much of that popularity."

"And the Widerstand?"

"Ah, you know about that, Eminenza?"

A ruffle of silk as he brushed aside my surprise.

"It is my business to know things, Lord Ridgewood."

"Mr. Ridgewood, Eminenza, when I'm representing neutral Ireland."

"Of course," he said with a gentle smile. "And the Widerstand?"

"The German Resistance is not large, but it is very intelligent, deeply dedicated, and incredibly brave."

"You know them?"

"Some of them."

"You believe they will eliminate Hitler?"

"When they think it is the right time, they will try."

"You know that His Holiness has blessed their project?"

"I did not know it, but I am glad to hear it."

"The British ambassador has notified his Foreign Office about the Widerstand. We believe that some of their bureaucrats have buried his reports."

"I will inform my government of this fact. They might well make inquiries at higher levels."

"I thought that Ireland was neutral, Mr. Ridgewood?"

His gray eyes twinkled.

"Absolutely and totally neutral, Eminenza. But also pro-British. If you know the Irish at all, sir, you know that it is not a contradiction."

"Certo!"

I was then ushered up to the fifth floor of the Vatican Palace to meet Pius XII, a slight, intense, fragile man with thick glasses. He asked about Lord and Lady Ridgeland and my brothers and sisters and wondered whether I was married.

"I am in love with a wonderful young woman, Sanita, and I have strong hopes that we will be married."

He smiled, a gentle, beatific smile.

"May God grant your hopes."

"She is Catholic, of course," I added.

He nodded, as if he took that for granted.

"Tell me about the Jews. They will die? The Gypsies too?"

"That is the goal about which they are talking. They will make definitive plans shortly."

"This must not be permitted."

"I quite agree."

"You know Graf von Stauffenberg?"

"We went to school together at Heidelberg, Sanita."

"What is he like?"

"I assume you know Der Ritter in the Bamberg Cathedral?"

"Certo."

"Claus is like him, Sanita, the last Catholic knight of Europe."

"God bless and protect him."

He blessed me too.

"Bring my most special blessing to Graf Stauffenberg and his family."

"The Russian war will begin in May, I understand?" he remarked as I left his office.

If the Pope knew the order of battle, everyone in the world did.

Later in the day, I wrote a letter on Vatican stationery to the Old Fella.

"Tell your good friend Winston that some of his Foreign Office people are *burying reports from the British Ambassador to the Vatican about the Wider-stand in Germany. I assume they may be burying mine too."*

I sent a similar minute to my government along with a summary of my con-versations at the Vatican. They would raise hell with the British Foreign Min-ister too, though very polite and very neutral hell.

I marveled at the beauty of Italy as my train carried me through Italy and up to the Brenner Pass. God protect it from the ravages of war.

That prayer wasn't heard. After the invasion of Sicily in 1943, the king of Italy dumped Mussolini and appointed Marshal Bagdolio as prime minister. Italy then withdrew from the war. For the Führer that was intolerable. He sent German troops into Italy and resisted the Allied march north till the end of the war. It was another foolish mistake. The men who fought in Italy might have been used to end the retreat from Stalingrad or resist the Americans in France.

I encountered Claus after my return from Berlin at the shooting range, My task that day was to face away from the range, listen for the sound of the tar-gets appearing, then whirl and dispose of all three of them.

I didn't succeed. The third one I missed each time.

"Ja, ja, Herr Ambassador! The aim is not so good today, nein?"

"I try to imagine that they're SS men and they will shoot at me. Want to try?"

"Not today, Timmy. I'm a father again, a lovely little girl."

"Congratulations!"

"The line will continue, no matter what happens to me . . . Come let us eat and drink and celebrate!"

"Your man in Rome sends his personal blessing to you and your family through me."

"Rome?"

"The guy in white. He also blesses the Widerstand and its efforts to remove Hitler."

"Did Our Most Holy Father speak of me personally?" He seemed surprised and, indeed, awed.

"Sure, he agreed with the comparison of you and your man in the Cathedral."

His blush was painful.

"The silly fantasies of a silly little girl."

"And how fares that young woman now?"

"She does not weep, she prays often, she works hard, she does not smile anymore."

"Is she safe at the Air Ministry?"

"Goering is a fop and a pervert, but he is still loyal to his colleagues, particularly after they're dead. Frau von Richthofen is as safe as she would be in a convent. She now has major responsibilities there in the coordination of communications."

"And in May we march on Moscow?"

"Guderian says his tanks will be in Red Square within a month. Stalin refuses to believe there will be a war."

"And your role?"

"I am to be supply officer for Army Group South. Our goal is to reach the Volga River and the oil fields in the Caucusus."

"Will you get there?"

"Not this year at any rate."

We were momentarily silent.

"Timmy Pat, you are a very good friend."

"As are you, Santa Claus."

My new name for him.

"I must ask you for a very great favour."

"I'll do it, whatever it is."

"If I should die in the service of the Secret Germany, will you take care of Annalise for me?"

"Naturally."

"Here is a letter to her. It commands her to obey you. You will not read it of course."

"Naturally."

"It only applies if I die in an attempt to kill Hitler. There is no way I can prevent her from being part of the Widerstand. Despite Goering's protection, they will torture her to death. Not my family. They are part of a long and distinguished line. Annalise is no one important and she speaks very strongly. She is already involved with some of the young women in the Kreuzer Circle."

"*What must I do with her?*"

"*Get her out of the country.*"

"*I think I can do that.*"

"*She will go with you, of that I am quite confident.*"

"*This will happen soon?*"

"*I think not. And I hope that I survive. Yet one must prepare.*"

I hid the letter in my private safe at the residence. It was absurd fantasy. The Gothic princess and her Irish Parzifal on the run in Hitler's Germany.

On June 22 a month later, the Wehrmacht *swept into the Soviet Union. Within a month Guderian had captured Smolensk. His advance patrols were already probing around Moscow and found the city unprotected. But the Führer decided that he wanted to capture Leningrad and Kiev at the same time, so he curtailed Guderian's fuel supply. Kiev did fall to Claus's Army Group South. Leningrad held out through the whole war. Moscow was never seriously threatened again.*

At the end of 1941 Hitler made another enormous blunder. After the Japanese attack at Pearl Harbor and the American declaration of war on Japan, Hitler quite gratuitously declared war on the United States.

"*Now,*" Canaris said, "*the Americans have an excuse to come to England's aid. They will crush us before they go after the Japanese. What do you think, Timothy?*"

"*I think you're in check again, Herr Admiral.*"

He muttered a few Germanic curses.

"*And the Americans?*"

"*I lived there for four years. Hitler is even more insane than you realize. The sooner you folks get rid of him, the better.*"

On January 20, 1942, in a meeting at Wannsee, a Berlin suburb on a lake, the Nazis completed the planning for the Endlösung, *the Final Solution to the Jewish problem. They would eliminate all Jews, Gypsies, Slavs, homosexuals, undesirables (the blind, the lame, the deaf), and decadents. This would be a vast exercise in purification carried out by the SS and the Gestapo. The victims would be eliminated in gas chambers, and reduced to ashes in giant ovens. It would be a huge and costly project, but none of the men at the meeting doubted that German organizational skill could carry it out. Canaris, who was there,* could not believe what he had heard. I reported it to Dublin. Whether Winston would see my minute or not I did not know.

The Russians counterattacked in the winter of 1942 and drove the Wehrmacht back in the snow. The Afrika Korps was stopped at the edge of Cairo again. Then before the end of the year the tide seemed to change. The English routed the Afrika Korps, the Americans landed in North Africa, the American Navy sank four Japanese carriers at Midway Island. And Hitler lost the war at Stalingrad.

— 15 —

I WENT back to the store where the woman with her big diamond had sold me a camera for my poor Dermot and meself
wearing jeans and a Chicago Bears sweatshirt on this lovely
spring day. I would begin by purchasing another camera, a less expensive
one for Nelliecoyne's birthday. She recognized me at once and apologized
for not knowing that I was the famous singer. I dealt with that the way I
usually do and gave her a couple of discs I had packed in my large shoulder bag. She gave me a big discount on the camera, which I had to accept
or I would have been rude. I then showed her our picture of Des—the
one with the smile.

"He speaks Arabic?" she said dubiously.

"And Eritrean and Ethiopian and a couple of other languages. We suspect he may be trying to learn Aramaic too."

"God's language!"

"No, actually God speaks Irish of course, but Jesus and his mother spoke Aramaic."

We laughed and laughed at that.

"We think so."

"Why would he go to Iraq, especially at this time?"

"We think he had already planned to go to study languages, perhaps around Mosul or Kirkut, and decided that he wouldn't let the war discourage him."

"Well there are many languages there. If he really liked diversity, he could have had a good time, if there wasn't a war and so many people didn't hate one another."

"Whom do the Assyrians hate?"

"Everyone of course, perhaps the Kurds less than others because we are their allies against the Iraqis. It is so much better in this country, you just make mean jokes about them, instead of hating them."

That morning Mike Casey had called us.

"Well, Nuala Anne, he flew from Chicago to Ankara on Turkish Air and then on to a place called Kars way out on the east end of the country near Russia and Iran. The people there are mostly Kurdish."

"Suppose our friend wanted to get into Kurdistan inside Iraq," I asked the Assyrian woman, whose name, I had learned, was Mary. "Could he do it by flying to Kars?"

"Yes, though it would be a long ride through the mountains and he would have to speak a little Farsi, which is a dialect of what the Iranians speak. Could he do that?"

"He might have learned some of it when he was in school."

"It would be very dangerous."

"You've been to college in this country?"

"Oh yes, I have attended Loyola and in another year or so will graduate. Our parents studied with the Jesuits in Baghdad before they were thrown out of the country. We had to learn to speak English before we came here."

Her husband came into the store, a giant of a man with a book bag over his shoulder. They kissed the way your typical Yanks don't in public, creepy Prots that they are.

She introduced me to Joseph, her husband. He bowed respectfully.

"We are honored that we have become your regular camera shop."

"He's studying to be a lawyer."

"Dangerous business," says I.

"Not as dangerous as in Iraq," he said with a big smile. "I want to work as a defense lawyer."

"You know a woman named Cindy Hurley?"

"I have the honor of being an intern in her firm. She is a very nice person, though I argue with her only rarely."

"Well, I have the honor of being married to her brother and isn't she my defense lawyer?"

"I cannot imagine you need that much defense."

"The Feds want to pick me up occasionally as an illegal. If they come after you, sign her up."

"I know that the United States Attorneys for the Northern District of Illinois are very much afraid of her."

His wife told him our story.

"How very interesting. This young man must be extraordinary."

"He has the glint in his eyes."

"He does indeed. Our people over there will surely love him. They appreciate the glint in the eye . . . May I borrow this photograph for a moment?"

"Certainly . . . Mary, I think I'll take along one of those printers I looked at. The childer will have fun making pitchers."

Despite me poor man who is a Nazi about words, I always pronounce "pictures" as though the word was "pitchers," a distinction which doesn't bother us in the West of Ireland at all, at all.

Joseph came back with a perfect copy of my pitcher of poor Des.

"With your permission, Ms. McGrail, I'll fax this to all our stores. Someone might recognize him. You won't have to worry about establishing credibility with them."

"Isn't that wonderful altogether! Would you ever think of coming over to our house for supper some night?"

"I will have to ask Ms. Hurley if she would be offended. I think not. Only prosecuting attorneys offend her."

"That's fine. Thank you very much for the help. You may be seeing me often now that you're me very own camera people."

I called me man on me modular and told him what I'd learned.

"OK, he certainly was headed for Mosul or that part of the world. You want to try a few more stores?"

"The childer?"

"Himself is sound asleep with Maeve guarding him. The others are over at school still."

"I'm having fun, Dermot."

"That's what pro football players always say."

"But won't it be unnecessary for me to visit any more stores? Didn't your man fax a copy of me picture to all the Assyrian camera shops in town?"

"Why would I ever not realize that something like that would happen?"

So I drove home feeling very proud of meself.

Me man greeted me at the door of our house with a big hug which meant a) he was very proud of me and b) he wouldn't mind making love with me at all, at all.

"You bought a printer too."

"Didn't I figure that my Nelliecoyne should have all the equipment she needs?"

"We will now have a little camera nut scurrying around the house taking pictures of everything and then printing up copies."

"Won't it keep her out of trouble?"

"My Nelliecoyne is never in trouble."

"And when she is, she becomes my Nelliecoyne."

He was still hanging on to me like he was half about to seduce me. That's an upsetting situation. I was halfway seduced meself, me body busy creating the hormones that would settle the matter altogether.

"Dermot Michael Coyne, you don't have to hang on to me that way at all, at all!"

"I will if I want!"

Then he began to play with me the way a man does when he wants to set a woman on fire. I was already on fire as it was.

"I hope you weren't planning to fuck me here in the parlor with the windows open."

"I was planning to do just that, no one will see you on the couch."

I pretended to struggle to escape from his arms which is, of course, part of me act. If I didn't want to make love, it would have been a different struggle.

I had seen the signs in his eyes that morning when I left that he was besotted again. Ah, well, that's the way of it, isn't it?

Me poor man was now absolutely out of his mind with desire. I would resist just a little more to increase his fun. So I got in the way of his taking off me tee shirt. Then it was the end of it for me too. He took off the rest of me clothes, laid me on the couch like I was a delicate figurine and went into an advanced stage of playfulness, the kind of stuff at which he is very good.

"Finish me off, now, Dermot," I begged, "I'm losing me mind."

All the time, Fiona, who had greeted me at the door, lay curled up on the counter, oblivious as she always was to human sexual activity. She knew my screams were categorically different from other screams.

Finally, me poor husband and meself collapsed into a soft lake of soothing pleasure and grace.

"Fiend," I said to him as I nibbled at his ear.

We managed to get our clothes back on before his son began to demand attention and the doggies restlessly came to the window to await the other childer returning for their lunch.

"I'll go get them," I said. "You're too worn-out."

"Woman, I'm not."

He took the leashes out of my hand and I went upstairs to the other male rapist in the family, if you believe Freud.

We gave Nelliecoyne her early birthday presents and she went off the wall with excitement.

Her sister and brother looked envious till I promised them that when they were the same age, they'd get the same presents.

"Till then," said Nelliecoyne, "you can use my camera and printer whenever you want."

"Me too?" asked Socra Marie.

"Sure!"

"Ma, after school can I take Patjo down to Katiesue's house to take a pitcher of him and Johnnie Pete?"

"So long as I can come with you."

"Me too?"

"So long as you have a good nap, Socra Marie!"

"Hokay."

I felt I understood the problem of Baron von Frankenstein and his monster.

Dermot and I did our exercise and then sat and talked about our investigation.

"I think," I said, "maybe we should go down to the Cathedral tomorrow morning and talk to the little bishop about Mosul and the Assyrians and the Jesuits and such things."

"Excellent idea."

"Maybe we could ask him whether there is a school or parish or a monastery there where he might be staying."

"An equally excellent idea."

"Usually, I bring one of the younger kinder along, but they could be disruptive."

"And Socra Marie has school."

"She does indeed."

"Still, he hasn't seen him since he was baptized."

"But he can't climb into his lap."

" 'Tis true."

"You know what, Nuala Anne, I'm exhausted altogether."

"What else would you expect, Dermot Michael, after all that exercise? I could use a nap too, so long as it is a nap-nap."

"And individual showers afterwards?"

"Well, this time anyway," I conceded the point.

I think joint showers are wonderful, prolonged luxuriant play. However, sometimes a couple needs to sleep.

So we did.

So the next morning we presented ourselves at the Cathedral. Archbishop Blackie opened the door.

"No childer?" he said.

"The little girl is in school," I said, "and we would not dream of violating the discipline of a Catholic school."

"Remnant that you are of a former era," Archbishop Blackie said with a sigh, which while not as deep or as loud as my husband says mine is, nonetheless could indicate either the advent of an asthma attack or deep despair on the condition of the world.

He was wearing his current uniform of a black clerical shirt without a Roman collar, black jeans and a Chicago White Sox cap. Is that not, he had asked, the usual garb of a coadjutor Archbishop with right to succession?

"And Patjo is a little too young for a rectory office in the absence of one of your Megans."

"I now list their job description as porter persons and rectory babysitters . . . Actually and despite my dignity, I am answering the bell because our housekeeper is sick and the good Crystal Lane is in church praying, odd behavior for a member of a rectory staff."

Crystal Lane, the youth minister, is also a mystic.

So we sat in the rectory counseling room, which had been gussied up to look like an American living room.

"Actually," me husband said, "herself and I are not here in search of counsel."

"Why am I not surprised?"

So we told him our mission and showed him our pictures of Dizzy Des.

"Fascinating," he said, his pale blue eyes blinking rapidly behind his Coke bottle lenses.

Me husband insisted that the glasses were part of the persona and that behind them were perfectly good contact lenses.

"It is all speculative, Your Riverence."

"Save for the airplane flight to the border of the Kurdish country."

"His parents," I said, "believe he's a wastrel."

"Oh, clearly not. He's a wandering monk of the kind we produced in the very early Middle Ages and whom we now replace by missionaries who stay in one place."

"Monk?" Dermot asked.

Because my poor Dermot is totally brilliant, he is less confused by Archbishop's Blackie's elliptical manner of speech than most other folk.

"Not necessarily one in holy vows, much less holy orders. In the early Middle Ages, before the Canon lawyers took control of the Church, such itinerant doers of good, some more honest than others, some saner than others, wandered about the land. Today, alas, they'd be arrested as vagrants or incarcerated in mental institutions, even if on occasion they worked miracles."

"Folks like Himself?" says I.

"You have the right of it, Nuala Anne," says he, and himself imitating the way I talk.

"Des is a Jesus figure?" me Dermot asks.

"I wouldn't recommend that you tell his parents, but that might be a useful model to keep in mind. Such folk do come along, now and again."

"You think we should stop looking for him?" says I.

"To search for the missing is your profession, is it not?" says he.

"I'm a wife and a mother," says I.

"She sings occasionally," me Dermot adds some sense to this conversation.

"As I understand your story," Blackie began again, "you're wondering if there might be some Catholic organization around Mosul with which Des might have affiliated?"

" 'Tis true."

"I believe there are seven Catholic dioceses in Iraq, one of which is the Archdiocese of, you should excuse the expression, Babylon, as Baghdad is properly called. I am not acquainted with my Most Reverend brother in that see. There is also a papal nuncio who, as a canon lawyer,

can hardly be concerned about itinerant monks. The Jesuits had a college there too, but I believe that the former president of the country
closed down all such Catholic institutions. Might there be a small and
informal Caldee monastery in the Mosul area? It is not unthinkable because the once glorious Church of the East had a strong monastic tradition, building such as far away as China."

"So," says I, "maybe Des finds out about such a place in one of these
camera stores, establishes contact with them, and goes over there to
learn some more languages and help the people and promote peace and
have fun?"

"Not likely, Ms. McGrail," says he, "not likely at all, at all. But not impossible."

"How can we," me Dermot wants to know, "interview the papal nuncio?"

"Dermot Michael Coyne," says I, "you're not going to Babylon!"

"That worthy would hardly talk to one as lowly as a coadjutor Archbishop, but he would respond immediately to a Cardinal Prince, even
one who is so infirm that he needs a coadjutor."

Cardinal Sean of course is not infirm at all, at all. He has a coadjutor,
he claims, to be sure that the Vatican does not assign Blackie anywhere
west of the Des Plaines River, "Beyond which my very survival would become problematic."

"So we hire Cardinal Sean?" says I.

"I'm not sure you could afford his hourly rate. However, since 'tis yourself that wants the information, he'll probably do the research gratis."

I removed from me purse the two most recent photographs of me
brood, the four kids and the two doggies. Poor Poraig is at the center of
the picture with a huge grin as he accepts the worship of everyone else.

"Well, Your Riverence, here's his stipend and a fee for yourself as his
agent."

"Fascinating!"

"A pleasure to do business with you!"

We stood up to leave.

"You might also visit Father Ibrahim Ibrahim at St. Ibrahim's Church.

That is the local parish for the Assyrians. He doubtless has some informal communications with those remaining in Iraq. I shall warn him of your advent. He is one of the few priests in the Archdiocese who takes seriously my dignity."

"Ask Cardinal Sean if this monastery in Mosul has e-mail connections with the rest of the world."

"Nuala Anne," me husband says to me as we drive back to our cottage in his car (and meself driving), "do you realize how high the odds against our finding him in a monastery or even finding a monastery?"

"'Tis all we have, Dermot love . . . Now let's get home and see what mayhem our eldest has caused with her new camera."

— 16 —

In February of 1943, the remnants of the German Sixth Army surrendered at Stalingrad. Almost a million Germans had died. Of the ninety thousand who had laid down their arms, less than five percent survived. It was the worst military defeat in the history of Germany, a disaster that should have been avoided. A Russian counteroffensive had swept around the Sixth Army's siege of Stalingrad and besieged the besiegers. Hitler had lost interest in Moscow and Leningrad. He had decided to drive across the Volga River and wheel south into the oil fields of the Caucasus and then across to the Caspian Sea. He was, as Claus suggested, in his "Alexander" mode as opposed to his previous "Bonaparte" mode. The General Staff had argued against the offensive. The Sixth Army was powerful, but it would extend its communications and logistics network beyond all sensible limits. Despite Hitler's argument that the Red Army had been destroyed in the summer's battle, it was still capable of huge winter counteroffensives. If the Sixth Army should be stalled at Stalingrad, it would be at grave risk of falling victim to a massive counterattack on its flanks.

Hitler would accept none of this. The time for the German army to end the war in Russia was now—before the Americans became fully involved. Through August and September Army Group South (in which Claus had served) pushed across the steppes of southern Russia with ease. Hitler was pleased with his brilliant strategy and sent half of the group into the Caucasus to the oil fields—which Hitler bragged would solve the German oil shortage. In early August the Sixth Army was on the outskirts of Stalingrad. Hitler proclaimed that victory was at hand. However, the Red Army poured reinforcements into the city. Behind the Russian front lines stood other soldiers with orders to shoot anyone who ran. House by house, block by block, the Germans fought to the banks of the Volga in early November. The General Staff realized that the inferior Hungarian and Romanian armies, which protected the flanks of the Sixth Army, invited a Russian encirclement. They begged Hitler to send troops to throw back any Russian counteroffensive. He was not interested in the flanks, but only in the city itself. In mid-November the Russians launched two massive attacks on both German flanks and surrounded the Sixth Army. General von Manstein, who had withdrawn his troops from the Caucasus to escape a trap there, was ordered to break through to relieve the Sixth Army. At a decisive meeting with his generals, Hitler almost ordered the Sixth Army to launch an attack to break out of the siege. The generals argued that they could no longer provide supplies for the Sixth Army. Then Goering promised, "My Führer, the Luftwaffe will easily supply Stalingrad." Hitler went into a tantrum. "German soldiers do not retreat!" he screamed.

That moment, according to my chess partner, determined the outcome of the war.

"We lost ten percent of our army in Stalingrad, Timothy, a million men."

Hitler fired his chief of staff, General Halder, a great supporter of Claus, and appointed a puppet. Now the Führer was the only voice at headquarters in East Prussia. His "no retreat" policy slowly reduced the size of the German army so that it was not able to prevent the march to Berlin two years later.

The German people knew nothing of this story. Hitler forbade any reports of the scope of the disaster, though Goebbels, as always the shrewd analyst of public opinion, urged that the government should tell the truth. Listening to the

BBC every night, I had some notion of what was happening. Nonetheless, I was shocked.

"What is to be done?" I asked.

An ambassador tends to identify with the people of the country to which he is assigned—at least if he is a good ambassador. Images of the Red Army destroying Berlin frightened me.

The admiral puffed on his pipe.

"We must make peace with the English and the Americans. Everyone who knows what has happened—Goering, Himmler, von Ribbentrop—will immediately rush to betray Hitler. The General Staff will support Claus's little movement. Perhaps it will succeed."

"What will Stalin do if the West makes a separate peace?"

"Most think that he will continue the war. Personally I doubt it. If there is anyone who fears the Red Army as much as we do, it is Stalin himself. He worries that they will come back to Moscow and destroy him. He will probably pause at the Vistula to see what happens. He knows that his General Staff is as eager to kill him as ours is to kill Hitler. He is already seeking terms for peace in Sweden, negotiating with Ribbentrop and Goering. Himmler also has contacts in Berne and Stockholm."

"Rats on a sinking ship," I said, citing a cliché which was particularly appropriate for these men.

That night I sent a minute to Dublin, describing as obscurely as I could what some well-informed people in Germany were thinking.

"Winston," I murmured, "I hope you are still sharp enough to read between these lines."

I did not worry about our Minister for External Affairs. He would certainly understand.

Claus was not in Berlin when Field Marshal von Paulus surrendered. His friends and admirers in the OKW were uneasy about his rhetoric. Such comments as, "Is there no one on his staff who will not shoot that man . . . If not, I will!" were dangerous, though they indicated the kind of courage which would be needed to lead an anti-Hitler Putsch.

So, at Halder's suggestion, he was transferred to the Tenth Panzer Division in the Afrika Korps, a place to keep him out of trouble for a time.

We had dinner at the Adlon Hotel by the Brandenburger Tor before he left. His easy charm did not fail him, it never would. However, he was angry.

"You know that they are planning to kill all the Jews and the Gypsies and the degenerates and I think all the priests?"

"The Brits tried that in Ireland and it didn't work."

"I have seen with my own eyes what they do in Russia. The Slavs are treated just as Himmler treats the Jews. They are Untermench, they have no right to live. We will pay a terrible price for that in years to come. I was in Kiev when the Wehrmacht rounded up a hundred and fifty random people on the street and hung them on the lampposts. One twisted head I will never forget. A young woman, perhaps Annalise's age when you first met her, she was wearing a new blue sweater set. She must have dressed in it for the first time before she went out that day, expecting people to admire it. No idea it would be her shroud. We will be punished for that."

"God will punish us?"

"I leave that to God. Our enemies will do the same thing to our young women, only worse."

"Not the Brits or the Yanks."

"They will not capture Berlin. The Russians will . . . I welcome Africa. I will die there perhaps. Then I will not have to kill Hitler. Or the Americans will capture me. They do not hate us enough to kill us, not yet."

"The Afrika Korps seems to be in trouble."

He waved that problem away.

"Rommel is the best general we have, a Swabian by the way. He will fight the Americans and then turn on Montgomery who, as they say, is always a day late, and defeat him again. We will live to fight another day. The allies will crush us eventually of course, and drive us into the sea. As gallant as the Afrika Korps and Rommel are, they—we, I should say perhaps—are a waste of manpower."

"You will survive and wear proudly your Afrika Korps medallion to a ripe old age!"

I didn't believe that, not for a minute.

"We still must eliminate Hitler."

Then his mood changed again.

"At least in Africa we do not massacre civilians as a matter of policy. All war is dirty, but in Africa it is less dirty than in Russia . . . Have you seen Annalise yet?"

"No, I am following your counsel that I should wait for her to take the initiative."

"Yes, but she has been a widow now for a long time, two years?"

"Three."

"I see her occasionally in Bamberg. She is as beautiful as ever. She does not smile . . . Nina says that her problem is now despair more than grief."

We shook hands as we left the table.

"God go with you, Claus."

"Include me in the Rosary you say every night."

"I have ever since our Easter together."

"We will be young again." He smiled, filling the whole dining room of the Adlon with joy.

He was wrong, I told myself. We would never be young again.

Rommel had pulled off another miracle in Tunisia. He had chased away an inexperienced American division attacking at Kasserine Pass and then turned on the British Eighth Army and stopped them cold in their tracks. Even the BBC admitted a "setback" at the hands of the Desert Fox.

It was all playacting. The Germans would soon be fighting a three-front war. There could be no doubt about the outcome, no matter how brave the German soldier was and how wily the occasional German general was when he was free from Hitler's supervision.

On a lovely day in early May as I was preparing a minute for the Ministry, the phone rang in my office.

"Ridgewood."

Silence for a moment.

"It is Frau von Richthofen who now speaks."

"Annalise," I said, as calmly as I could. Her English was much more stilted than it had been eight years ago.

"It is necessary that I tell you some unfortunate news . . ."

Claus!

"Herr Oberstleutnant von Stauffenberg suffered serious wounds in

Tunisia. He is gravely injured. He has lost one of his eyes and his right arm and two fingers on his left hand. He is in the hospital in Tunis."

"Annalise," I said again.

"It is most unfortunate. Frau von Stauffenberg, who now expects their fifth child, and all the children pray fervently. They ask for your prayers. I pray that he will be captured by the Americans . . ."

"A wise prayer."

"It is proper for me to bid you farewell now."

"May I take you to supper some night?"

"It would not be correct. Farewell, Herr Ridgewood."

I was angry at myself. I had blown it all.

The phone rang again.

"Ridgewood."

"It is again Frau von Richthofen who speaks."

"Changed your mind, Annalise?"

"You know me too well."

"Nineteen hundred on Tuesday evening at the Kepinski."

"Ja, Herr Ridgewood. Farewell."

I resolved as I hung up, my fingers nervous, my stomach uneasy, my mouth dry, that I would proceed cautiously, very cautiously. I didn't know who she was. I would respect her virtue as I had in the past.

But this time I would not lose her.

The Kepinski was an elegant nineteenth-century hotel just off the Kudamm shopping district, which kept its charm by pretending that Bismarck was still alive and Germany still ruled by a kaiser. I paused at the entrance of the dining room and looked for Annalise.

My heart stopped beating when I saw her. Dressed in stylish black, her blond hair partly obscured by a black veil, she was beautiful beyond my dreams. No, I would not let her get away this time.

She looked up as I walked towards her table and smiled. My heart skipped several more beats. For a smile like that men would go to the end of the world and back.

She stood up.

"Herr Ambassador."

"*Annalise.*" *I bowed and kissed her hand.*

Her smile turned into the wicked grin I had known so long ago.

"*You are not changing,*" *she said cautiously.*

"*And you are far more lovely.*"

She blushed and turned her face away.

"*I possess news about Herr Oberstleutnant Stauffenberg. They evacuated him from Tunis, one of very few. He is too important to the General Staff to leave behind. He and Marshal Rommel and a few others. He is now in a hospital in Munich. I do not say it is good news. God has his ways. I'm sure that Frau Nina thinks it is good news.*"

"*I must visit him.*"

"*Perhaps one should wait till he is home. They have returned to the Schloss in Jettingen. He is very fortunate that he still lives.*"

We turned to German when the waiter came to our table.

"*My English is now very poor and your German is now excellent.*"

I ordered a white wine. She nodded in approval.

On closer inspection and despite skillful makeup, Annalise showed the strain of the war years. Her habitual expression, one into which she returned after a smile or a quick grin, was melancholy, the light in her eyes died quickly, her fingers grew tense as we talked, then relaxed. She was, I thought, trying to recover the mask of the sixteen-year-old that I had rowed across Stauffenbergersee. I found that effort both hopeful and sad, hopeful for my cause and sad because of her suffering.

"*May I talk to you about my husband, Herr Ridgewood? You met him once, I believe, and he said that you and he liked one another. He was proud of that.*"

"*He knew I was a rival?*"

"*I don't believe that he could think in those terms. Perhaps he did, sometimes he was quite surprising. He would, I think, have been flattered. He truly thought you were wonderful. He spoke of your dancing green eyes that took in and understood everything. I observe that they still do.*"

She lowered her own eyes and blushed.

"*I have written about my husband. I wanted to record it properly. May I read it to you?*"

"*If you wish.*"

"*Paul was not what one could call a sensitive man. Neither was he ever harsh, much less cruel. To me he was always respectful. I did not love him, but I did not dislike him. He did not love me either, but he did worship me. Is that possible?*"

"*Surely.*"

If pressed at the moment to say how it was possible, I would not have been able to do so.

"*His life for him were his planes and his pilots and his memories of the first war. Baron Manfred was his patron saint and the Flying Circus was his Church. I do not ridicule this. On the contrary I found it understandable and acceptable. He was proud of his lovely and gracious wife, as he was proud of his Iron Cross and his Stuka. I did not expect more of him. With him I was safe and, I will not say respected, but venerated.*

"*He was very proud of his triumphs in France and Poland. To me his Stuka was an ungainly, old-fashioned thing, when compared to the sleek, modern and deadly Messerschmitt fighter. Naturally, I did not say this to him. It seemed from his words that the plane was useful for killing retreating troops and terrorizing refugees. From what one hears at the Luft Ministry that is what other pilots say.*"

Our white wine arrived. We ordered fish and beef tenderloin.

She continued.

"*He was eagerly waiting for the attack on England. His Stuka wing would destroy the Royal Air Force in a couple of days, then eliminate the English airplane industry, and then fly above the Panzers as they consumed England. Then the war would be over and we could retire to his Schloss in Bavaria and begin our family. He went off to war with a swagger which might have embarrassed his cousin Manfred, who was a shy and modest man and, I thought, a man who took much less delight in killing other men than my brave husband did.*"

The pulse in her delectable throat was throbbing as she read and her fingers shaking.

"*Then he came home briefly after the Battle of Britain began. He was not the same person. Rather, he was an anxious broken man. As he lay in my arms, he told me his story.*

" 'We are losing, Anna. The English are beating us. My planes are crashing, my pilots are dying. They have better planes, better pilots, better technology, better tactics, better leaders. My poor Stukas are no match for their damnable Spitfires. The Führer and Goering have lied to us. We have Blitzkrieg on the ground, but we are obsolete in the air. If this continues for long, there will be no Stukas in the air. We could kill defenseless soldiers with them, but not destroy Royal Air Force Fighter Command stations. We were cowards and murderers and God is now punishing us.'

"My Flying Circus hero was weeping in my arms.

" 'But what about the Messerschmitts?'

" 'After ten minutes over England they have to leave because they run out of fuel. Can you imagine that Goering did not know that!'

" 'What will they do?'

" 'Some generals, like Kesserling, wish to remove the Stukas from the battle and save them for other wars. That means we have lost the Battle of Britain. I will tell them that as long as the English have Spitfires in the sky, Stuka pilots are doomed, but I will not request that they be withdrawn.'

" 'What will happen?'

" 'They will wait a few more days and then they will take us out, if there are any of us left. Can God forgive me for what I have done? I have betrayed my men.'

"I then realized that he was confessing his sins to me and seeking absolution. I was not a priest. I had no power. But nonetheless I gave him absolution. He fell asleep in my arms. I knew when he kissed me the next morning that I would never see him again."

I interrupted her reading to say that Thomas Aquinas argued that laypeople could give absolution.

She smiled and went on.

"I realized then for the first time that I had come to love him the night before.

"I was not surprised when Goering called to tell me that Paul had died destroying the Biggin Hill RAF station and that he would be a German hero for centuries. Later I learned at the Luft Ministry that a wing had fallen off his plane and that the crash destroyed one Spitfire and damaged another."

She folded the paper and returned it to her purse.

"So I grieve for him and for all those good men who have died because of bad equipment and poor leadership in an evil cause."

I had heard much of the same story from Canaris. It was much more moving in the mouth of a Luftwaffe widow. The war was not over yet. It would go on for perhaps two more years, perhaps less if Claus could do away with the Antichrist.

"I wanted you to understand," she concluded.

"I do understand, Annalise, as best as someone who has never known such a loss can."

"So now"—she dabbed at her face with her makeup—"I am part of the Widerstand. There are three young Catholic women in my apartment building in Charlottenburg who are working with the Kreuzer Circle. We type for them, deliver messages, help them organize their meetings. It is not much, but we must do something to fight the Antichrist."

The fish dishes were delivered with great ceremony.

Annalise consumed her food like she was ravenously hungry.

"Forgive my bad manners, Herr Ridgewood. I do not eat much these days."

"It is said that the Kreuzer Circle is very theoretical," I said tentatively.

"Very theoretical—priests and pastors and some politicians and aristocrats. They want to design a post-Hitler Germany before Hitler is gone. However, they are now in touch with some important members of the General Staff. They now need a leader and an organizer."

"I wondered who that might be."

"Who else? Either he will free us or we all will die."

I didn't like that.

"I'm not planning on dying," I said, "and I don't think you ought to either." She considered me very carefully, almost clinically.

"Perhaps not, Herr Ridgewood. Perhaps not."

I suspected that my Gothic princess had a strong impulse for sacrificial self-destruction. I would not tolerate it.

The rest of our dinner was pleasant and amusing, the happy sixteen-year-old returned to tell amusing stories about her colleagues at the Luft Ministry. Gradually she relaxed and enjoyed herself. How many dates had she experienced during her life?

"May I take your picture?" I said, removing my Leica from my jacket pocket. "I have often wished I had one."

She shrugged her shoulders indifferently.

"If it amuses you, Herr Ridgewood."

"It does."

There was not much natural light, but, with a small flash, probably enough for a picture that would look persuasive on a passport. She smiled politely for me.

When we finished our custard—how I hate custard—we walked out on the street. Berlin was blacked out now, but you could still sense your way down the street.

"I will escort you back to Charlottenburg," I said.

"That will be unnecessary," she snapped. "I can ride the U-Bahn by myself."

"I want to establish one factual matter, Annalise. It is not my intent to seduce you, not for the present at any rate. Should it ever be my intent I will give you due warning. Nor do I intend to force my way into your apartment tonight or any night. I think you should know me well enough to understand that."

Silence for a long moment.

"My apologies to you, Herr Ridgewood. Ja, I do know you well enough to understand that. Certainly you may escort me to my apartment."

At the door of the stately and ugly building I brushed my lips against hers.

"It was a lovely evening, Annalise."

"Thank you very much, Herr Ridgewood. I quite enjoyed it. Perhaps when Claus has returned to Jettingen we could visit him there."

"That would be very nice," I agreed, and took my leave.

The air raid sirens sounded as I went down the stairs to the U-Bahn. I ignored the siren, rode to the Potsdamer Platz, climbed over the sleeping people in the station and then went above ground to walk along the Friedrichstrasse to the embassy. I had promised that I would never let the RAF chase me underground. I hesitated about that promise, now that I had a clear goal in my life. What if I were caught in a firestorm?

Then I would be caught in a firestorm. Someone else would have to protect my Gothic princess. It was all in God's hands.

Back in my apartment, I entered the small darkroom I had created in a closet and developed the film in the Leica. There were two excellent pictures of Annalise. I printed small copies of both, just enough for a passport photo. When they were dry I would put them in the safe with Claus's letter. Then I said my Rosary and examined my conscience. I was still playing the role of the gentleman with Annalise. I looked forward eagerly to the day when I would not have to. Those were not appropriate thoughts when one was saying the Rosary.

"Dear God," I concluded. "I love her. Help me to take care of her."

I considered that and decided that I should amend it a bit. "Help me to be the man she needs."

In July, while the biggest tank battle in history was happening in Kruz in Russia—another German mistake approved reluctantly by Hitler—I received another phone call.

"Ridgewood."

"Annalise, Herr Ridgewood."

"Good morning, Annalise."

"Gräfin von Stauffenberg says that her husband is now well enough to receive guests and would like to see both of us. However, I do not think it proper that we ride the train together."

"As you wish, Annalise."

"I will take the night train on Friday and return on Sunday night."

"That will make Saturday night the only test of my virtue."

She said nothing for a moment and then laughed.

"Your virtue is not in question at the present, Herr Ridgewood. Nor is mine."

"Point taken. For the present. I will ride down Friday morning and return Monday morning."

"Ja, ja, all is good."

"I trust you will instruct Nina to put us as far apart as possible."

"Good-bye, Herr Ridgewood."

We were flirting. Again. How long could I wait? The Americans, I supposed would land somewhere in Europe next year. Claus's Putsch would have to happen in the summer, June or July. After that?

It was all in the hands of God.

Claus was waiting at the station with three of his children, attractive, chattering, grinning little blonds (like their mother) with mischievous eyes and great affection for their father.

Despite the black patch over his eye and the empty right sleeve and the two fingers in his left hand with which he shook mine, Claus did not look like a wounded veteran. If anything, he seemed stronger, more radiant than ever, as if fatherhood had canceled out the unfortunate encounter with the American P-40 in Tunisia.

"Let me carry your bag," he said, gripping the handle firmly. "I need some practice."

With practiced ease, he took my bag with his left hand and hoisted it up against his thigh.

The children applauded.

"They take great credit for my recovery," he said. "Not without some considerable reason."

"You will be returning to war?"

"The Wehrmacht's manpower resources are so limited that any soldier capable of walking," he said grimly, "is on active duty. For me it will be a staff assignment at the Bendlerblock in Berlin."

"Not far from the Irish embassy."

"I will be the chief of staff to General Fromm, commander of the Home Army, which is mostly replacements for those who have died in any of our three wars. Ja, Ja, you will call me Herr Oberst, please Herr Ambassador. Moreover in that role, I will have access to the Führer himself in the Wolf's Lair in East Prussia, where all his brilliant strategies are devised."

A colonel already. He still had powerful friends.

Access to Hitler! What he had always wanted!

I shivered despite the hot summer day. So many things could go wrong and indeed had gone wrong. The Antichrist takes care of his own, as Claus often said.

Yet he was in high good humour, reveling in his recovered life and the love of his family!

"Is it proper to call you, Herr Ambassador, Herr Ambassador?" young Berthold, save for the blond hair a replica of his father, asked.

(I interrupt this text to note that Berthold Graf von Stauffenberg was the first general in the Federal Republic's Bundeswehr.)

"My name is Timothy, Bert, or Tim. Would Uncle Tim be acceptable?"

Claus laughed joyously.

"Ja, ja! *Wunderbar!*"

As we entered the Schloss, he whispered to me that there might be some embarrassment tomorrow because Aunt Hannah would be present.

"Who?" I demanded.

"The Kinder call her that."

"I won't be the first one to blush."

"You are friends now?"

We had remained outside the Schloss absorbing the warm sunlight as the kids rushed in to tell their mother and grandmother that Uncle Tim was here.

"And alas for me, no more than that. I took her to dinner once and we talk on the phone occasionally, yet we keep our distance because, I suspect, she is very conscious of her role as the widow of a great hero of the war."

"Ja, ja, doubtless that is true. She is also afraid of you, Timmy. You are too attractive, too powerful."

"I don't see myself that way at all, Claus."

"She does and that is part of the attraction . . . You love her still?"

"More than ever."

"And though she doesn't say it around us, she loves you more than ever."

My heart began to pound at that confirmation of what I dared not dream to hope, but which I knew to be true.

"I fear that once again I will have to wait."

"Why, Timmy? Life is short."

"She is deeply involved in your resistance movement."

"Nonetheless, if you courted her, she would not reject you."

"I think that is true, yet it is not time."

"Perhaps, you are right, Timmy. It should all be finished in a year . . . But we will talk about that after supper. Nina knows, of course. I can hide nothing from her."

"I would hardly think you could."

"You remember your promise to take care of Annalise if my plans go wrong?"

"Naturally."

"You have not read my letter to her?"

"Claus . . ."

"Forgive me, I should not have asked."

"It is in my safe next to a photo which will look quite striking on an Irish passport."

He laughed.

"I should have known you'd be planning. I don't want to know any more . . . Come, the good Karoline and my good Nina will wonder why we are tarrying."

Claus's mother had aged in the years, but she was as vital and vivid as she always was. She wondered if I had made any progress in reading Thomas Mann, he was essential if I wanted to understand the Nazis, all of whom, she averred, were homosexuals even if they deny it.

I agreed that this was a distinct possibility.

Nina, however, had not changed at all, still tall, confident, and now content with and proud of her children. Her anxieties about Claus were obvious—and how could a wife not be anxious, if she were married to the last knight of Europe.

So quick and deft was Claus with his fingers and his arm, that one hardly noticed that his procedure for eating was different from everyone else's at the table. He must have worked with great persistence and determination to master his new style of consuming food. Karoline had told me once that he had been a weak child, almost dying as had his twin brother. He had stayed alive and grown to a strong man by constant effort.

During supper we talked about Aunt Hannah and her tennis rivalry with Uncle Tim. Also her swimming rivalry. The children were fascinated. Their mother warned them that we would pretend to fight but it was only pretend fighting. The Kinder divided by gender as to which one they would cheer for.

"It's all right," I said, "half the time when I'm playing against her, I cheer for her too. But if I don't do my best to win, she becomes very angry at me."

"You will win?" Bert asked.

"Oh yes," his father said, "even when I had all my fingers, Uncle Tim beat me. However, it will be a close match."

The food was less spectacular than at Easter years ago—potatoes, vegetables, sausage, a glass of wine and some fruit. However the spirit around the table was the same. Respect, laughter, and prayer.

As we finished the meal we heard a deep rumble as of a distant volcano, heavy, thick, hard.

"Lancasters," said young Bert, "their engines throb, the engines on the American B-17s hum."

"Where are they going?" I asked.

Bert frowned. He looked so much like his father that it hurt me. I had yet to father kinder who would look like me.

"South and east of here. Leipzig, Wiener Neustadt, maybe Munich, but I don't think so."

"I hope not," I murmured.

"Tim," Claus said in his most serious of tones, "there are none of us in Germany who are not in danger of sudden death. A flaming Lancaster crashed into a farm only fifteen kilometers down the river and killed everyone."

"That's hardly the brave RAF of the Battle of Britain," I murmured.

"They are very brutal," Nina said somberly, "but no more brutal than we were and are. And we started it."

"And we must stop it," Claus ended the conversation.

My life could end just as dramatically, especially if I persisted in my refusal to enter the bomb shelters in Berlin. Not so tragically, however, because I would leave no one behind. Only a distant memory to be listed once a year in the memorial mass of the Irish Diplomatic Service.

"Annalise will not arrive until midnight," Nina complained over coffee and tea, the youngsters having departed for their chores or their games or their beds. "That young woman can certainly be difficult."

"I presume," Claus replied, "that she felt she had to work most of the day at the Luft Ministry."

"I will meet her at the train," I volunteered.

No one vetoed my suggestion.

"She is very, very difficult." Karoline continued the discussion. "Von Richthofen was a pleasant man and she now has a name and an income, but he was doomed from the day the war began. Now she persists in grieving for him as if she loved him, which I don't believe she ever did."

"She seems to believe that every man she loves is doomed to die—her father, her brothers, her husband," Nina said. "It is not a Catholic way to think."

"Given her life story, it is," I said, defending my love, "what one might expect."

There was no doubt that the women in the family had arranged this weekend as another opportunity for Annalise and me to realize that we were in love. I appreciated the opportunity.

Yet I would have to give her more time if she wanted it. Someday, perhaps soon, I would insist.

If I could work up the nerve.

After coffee, Claus and I went for our walk in the woods. The comforting smell of harvest was in the air. The sky was still bright in a long dusk that reminded me of the Weltschmerz of a Richard Strauss opera.

"Nina knows what we're talking about," I said.

"She worries, with good reason . . . I wish we were ready this year. Now the Secret Germany must rise in 1944. The Americans will be ashore in the spring. The Red Army will push towards the Oder. It will be our last chance. It may be too late. Why should they negotiate with us? We should have struck after Stalingrad or even before the first bad winter in Russia but we weren't ready and then I was wounded . . ."

"You personally will kill Hitler?"

"There is no choice. As the leader I must take the lead, all the other attempts have failed. It is for this that I survived in the desert. I will leave a bomb underneath the table at the Wolf's Lair in East Prussia. . . . You really know Churchill personally?"

"Yes."

"And he's seen your dispatches?"

"I believe so."

"We need his support—at least his passive support. Would you go to London and describe to him who and what we are—no names of course . . ."

"Clergy of both denominations, intellectuals, aristocrats, generals, non-Nazi political leadership?"

"Precisely. And if we dispose of Hitler, more will join us."

"All right, what will the General Staff do when they gain control?"

"We will arrest all war criminals. We will free those in the camps. We will appoint a president and a prime minister from the pre-Nazi era. We will pull back our troops to the Rhine and the Oder and the Alps and announce a unilateral cease-fire. We will offer to negotiate unconditionally to respond to their terms. We will agree to return Germany's boundaries to their pre-Hitler borders."

"Austria?"

"An independent republic again, perhaps with a Hapsburg duke as president."

"The Sudeten?"

"Back to the Czechs."

"Poland?"

"Nineteen thirty-nine borders—Europe as it was before the Munich surrender of the English and the French."

"And the Russians?"

He shrugged.

"Who knows what they will do? We will concentrate all our forces east of Berlin. Stalin will know that we may very well be able to beat him along the Oder Line. He will not want a battle with the Americans, who will be able to advance into the heart of Germany without resistance. He is a cautious man. His ambassador to Stockholm has been negotiating a separate peace with Himmler and Ribbentrop for over a year."

"Thin, Claus."

"I know that, Timmy. I know that. Yet, should we succeed, many lives will be saved. Three million Jews in the concentration camps, a million German soldiers, a million and half Russian soldiers, a half million perhaps British and American soldiers . . . We will say these things when we go on the radio if we are successful."

"Risky, you're saying, but it's worth the risk?"

His response was in the tone of voice one would expect from Der Ritter in the Bamberg cathedral.

"At least they will know in the years to come that some Germans were willing to give their lives in a struggle against the Antichrist."

"And Nina and the kinder?"

"They may kill them if they choose for blood revenge. I think not since Himmler wants to make peace as much as we do. Our family has endured martyrdom before in its history."

So had mine as far as that goes, but not with such pious intensity.

"I shall tell all of these things to Winston and to him only."

"They will let you see him?"

"I think so, especially if he's seen my dispatches. Moreover, perhaps I have not said it before, but my Old Fella has enormous influence with Winston, more than anyone else in the House of Lords. He sends the prime minister a case of the best Middleton's Irish Whiskey and Winston sends him a case of the best Glenlivet Scotch."

"And they both consume the entire gift?"

"We have a dozen cases stored in the cellar of Castle Ridgeland. I don't think there are any such at 10 Downing Street."

He laughed, the same easy, relaxed laugh, I had heard so many years ago on the banks of the Neckar River.

"You will take care of Annalise. She is not enough of a noble to be immune to Himmler's wrath and she will be involved in the rising, there's no way I can keep her out of it."

"As I promised, I will do all I can, even if that means carrying her away by force."

He laughed again.

"I don't believe that will be necessary, Timmy."

On that note he returned to the Schloss lest Nina worry in his absence and I walked on to the old railroad station.

It was 2230 and the train from Munich was due in at 2330, a schedule which meant very little even in times of peace. I had been shown the door to Annalise's room—discreetly distant from mine but not impossibly so—and given an old key to the Schloss which weighed more than one of my .25s.

Everyone had claimed that they needed sleep to prepare for the weekend. Patently, however, they wanted Aunt Hannah and Uncle Tim to have time together.

I said the Rosary sitting on the single bench of the station, my eyes on the bright moon and the clear sky. A bomber's moon it used to be called. Now the mass bomber formations of the RAF preferred overcast skies. After the first wave of bombers had outlined the target with fire bombs, all the remaining waves had to do was to drop their bomb loads within the fiery rectangle.

In the great distance, I saw occasional beams of red light that mean fire or might only be the aurora borealis. I thought I heard explosions too, far, far away. Maybe only a summer storm. I did hear planes overhead, perhaps returning home, flown by sergeant pilots, because His Majesty's Government would not risk commissioned officers on flying coffins like the Lancasters.

But as Friday turned into Saturday, the sounds went away, save for an occasional chirping cricket, a peaceful summer evening during the worst bloodbath in human history.

One o'clock, 2:00, 3:00 . . . still no train. I was sleepy. My love had been incinerated in Munich. Perhaps a Messerschmitt night fighter would do the same to me.

"It is you who sleeps here on the platform?" Annalise asked. "Would they not accept you in the house?"

"What time is it?" I asked, my tongue thick as though I had been drinking.

"A little before four," she said. "The train was late, as always. I was sad that they had sent no one to greet me. Then I noticed this bundle of clothes on the bench and I asked myself whether it might possibly be His Excellency Timothy Herr Baron of Ridgewood and the ambassador of the Republic of Ireland."

She was laughing at me. How wonderful!

"Not quite the Republic of Ireland yet, Aunt Hannah . . . Give me your case. I'm sorry I failed in my duty to welcome you to Schloss Stauffenberg . . . I was afraid you had died in an air raid."

If I had been wide-awake and thinking clearly, I would have embraced her, quietly and moderately of course. As it was I could only stumble and bumble as we walked down the street to the Schloss.

"*God has not seen fit to call me home,*" she said seriously, "*though I am always ready to answer such a call.*"

"*You'll live into the next century, Aunt Hannah.*"

"*Why do you call me that?*"

"*That's what the children at the Schloss call you. I warn you that I am Uncle Tim and they are placing wagers on the outcome of our tennis match tomorrow.*"

"*That is not proper,*" she protested without much vigor.

"*Complain to their parents. I urged the little girls not to bet on Aunt Hannah in the match.*"

"*That was very improper. Of course I will win . . . I trust our rooms are properly distant.*"

"*I would characterize them as properly but not impossibly distant.*"

She laughed again.

"*You Irish are terrible!*"

"*We do our best.*"

Yet another laugh.

I opened the door to the house.

"*And certainly not to be trusted with the keys to a house.*"

"*Alas, it won't open bedroom doors.*"

A third laugh. I was doing pretty well for someone who was still probably dreaming.

She was wearing a plain black dress and her blond hair was tied up in a black scarf. It didn't matter. My Gothic princess was still impossibly lovely.

I showed her to her room, opened the door, placed her bag on the floor, put my arm around her and brushed my lips against hers, somewhat more slowly than I had at the door of her apartment in Charlottenburg.

"*Good night, Annalise.*"

She leaned her head against my chest, all too briefly.

"*Good night, Herr Ridgewood. Thanks for welcoming me.*"

"HE WILL neither propose to her nor proposition her," Nuala Anne said wearily. "You Irishmen are faint-hearted lovers."

"Frightened lovers."

In the midst of a heavy spring downpour we were driving (i.e., she was driving my car) into the Northwest Side, an obscure no-man's-land with old two-story houses, often two flats, always nicely painted and flawlessly landscaped, searching for St. Ibrahim's Church and its pastor Father Ibrahim Ibrahim.

"Frightened that the woman will say yes or that she will say no?"

"Both . . . Anyway, our mutual friend is quite incapable of propositioning his Gothic princess."

"I know THAT. But he should have offered marriage and left that dangerous country."

"For Ireland?"

"Where else?"

"She would have turned him down."

"You think so, Dermot?"

"She had to be around for the grand sacrifice."

Silence from me wife as she pondered.

"You may have the right of it, Dermot Michael Coyne. She's a strange one, that Gothic princess. I know her and I don't know her."

Changes of mind are rare for me wife.

"You still think she'll end up in Ireland?"

"Even if he has to drag her there."

We pulled up in front of a small, nondescript church of brown brick, next to a school which seemed to have four rooms and a tiny parking lot with the inevitable basketball backboards. Did Assyrian kids really play basketball?

The church, Nuala Anne had informed me, had been Russian, which was in fact, a branch of the Ukrainian Catholic rite from a different spot in the Carpathian Mountains. The congregation had moved west to Jefferson Park and built a new and larger parish "plant" and the Cardinal had turned this one over to the eager Assyrians.

The rectory was a small house made of similar bricks, almost a lean-to attached to the sacristy—all very compact and tidy, designed I suspected to resist incursions from the Poles, immediately higher in the food chain, and especially the Irish from downtown (the Chancery).

Father Ibrahim Ibrahim, pastor of St. Ibrahim's parish, was a tiny young man who fit perfectly into his limited space. He wore a small beard, a small pectoral cross, and spoke in a staccato voice with small gestures. His skin was lighter than that of the Assyrians we had met and his waving hands and accent suggested some French influence. He was inclined to be uncooperative until he saw Nuala and then he smiled and became a charming gentleman. Such is me wife's impact on most clerics.

"His Eminence Sean Cardinal Cronin asked that I talk to you," he said, dipping his head at the mention of the local Prince of the Church as he would halfway through the Nicene Creed, "so I will be happy to do so."

His smiles were like the rest of him, small and neat.

"Desmond was indeed charming," he rushed on, "and remarkably fluent in several languages, especially Arabic, which he spoke with a strange, but not unpleasant accent. He asked about an ecclesiastical institution in northern Iraq that he might work with. He wanted to learn Aramaic, which is the language of Jesus himself as well as ours, though to be honest, I'm not sure we could have understood the Lord, since languages change so much across time. He also wanted to learn Kurdish Farsi, which is a barbaric version of the Persian the Iranians speak, also barbaric. I did my best to discourage him. There would certainly be another war in Iraq and it would be very dangerous in the Kurdistan as the Kurds hate everyone, especially Christians."

He paused for breath. His recitation had obviously been carefully prepared.

"Even Americans?"

"They hate the Americans less because the Americans helped them to build their little enclave. However, they do not trust the Americans."

"With good reason," I said.

"How did Des react to your discouragement, Father Ibrahim?" Nuala asked in her thickest Galway accent.

"Like the Irish do! He listened politely and smiled. He was a little crazy of course. He had made up his mind."

In the background young voices began to sing hymns in a foreign language, Assyrian I assumed and doubtless very old hymns. Father Ibrahim ran a typical American parish, a fact certified by the scuffed basketball in the corner of his office.

"I told him that all our efforts now are to get the Assyrians out of Iraq. Saddam—a vile degenerate—nonetheless was secular. He protected us from the Muslims. Now there is no one to protect us but the American army, which realizes we are Christians like themselves, though very strange Christians."

He waved his hand as if to dismiss the American skepticism. The rural and small-town folk who were fated to fight the war had doubtless never seen an Assyrian before, much less a Babylonian which was a very bad place.

"So after ten millennia we are finally forced to leave and gather our people elsewhere in the world, some to Lebanon or Egypt, some to Britain or Spain, but most to this wonderful country which does not want us because of our skin color but lets us in anyway."

"You have a typical American full-service parish here," I observed.

"Yes, naturally. We are eager to learn, especially from the Irish. The Irish priest next door at St. Odelia has been very helpful. Unlike our Polish neighbors he approves of our dark skin. Indeed he says our people are probably the ancestors of those from the West of Ireland. He is very good. So is Cardinal Cronin, of whose sympathy and support I cannot speak high enough praise. Yet our young people are dying every day in Iraq. We are fighting against our own little holocaust."

Nuala had suppressed a giggle at his comparison with the West of Ireland. Yet the farmers and fishermen wandering her Connemara peninsula were often as dark-skinned as the Assyrians.

"So, finally," Father Ibrahim Ibrahim charged on, "I gave him the name of the Bishop of Mosul, who might be able to help, promised him my prayers, and blessed him. He surely needed the blessing and prayers. He was such a delightful young man. Mad of course, but delightful."

"Fits the picture," I said to me wife as we entered my ancient Benz.

"It does indeed, Dermot Michael. We know where he went and why he went."

"But not how he got there or whether he's still alive."

"Oh, he's still alive, Dermot love. 'Tis obvious, isn't it now?"

"Is it?"

" 'Tis!"

"I suppose you're going to write down on a piece of paper the solution, seal it in an envelope, and give it to me to hold until it becomes obvious to everyone else?"

"How much will you bet?"

"I know better than that!"

So as soon as we got home, we went to my room, she sat down at my desk and on my stationery wrote several lines. Then she grabbed one of my envelopes, folded the stationery, slipped it inside and sealed it. Then she demanded some of my Scotch tape to seal it a second time.

All of this ritual was performed with great solemnity, as if it was ritual for a papal conclave. Then with an enormous grin she gave it to me.

"Sign it, Dermot love, and put the date and time on it."

"Why do I always fall for this trick?" I said as I signed the envelope.

"Because you never believe me, no matter how many times I'm right."

"You're not sending me to Iraq?"

"Dermot love, wherever in all the world would I find a better husband?"

"How are you going to find him then?"

"I have a couple of ideas, but I'm not ready to try them yet . . . Och, Dermot love, won't this be my most brilliant solution altogether!"

The doorbell rang. The implicit rule of the house is that Nuala never answers the doorbell when I'm in the house. She violates the rule sometimes, which is all right I guess because isn't the lawgiver above the law. However, after her last encounter with the man in black, didn't she refuse to open the door ever again.

I went down to answer it. Tom and Grace Doolin. They both looked aggrieved.

"We would like to talk with you, Mr. Coyne," Tom Doolin said.

"And your wife," his wife snapped.

Nuala in a light brown sweater and a dark brown skirt, looking like nothing if not a professional woman, appeared in the parlor. She had already banished the curious doggies to their room downstairs.

"Won't you sit down?" I said.

Despite the spring warmth outside, the temperature in our parlor had seemed to decline to well below freezing.

"That won't be necessary," Grace said curtly.

"We have come to ask you for your bill for expenses and services and to request you to end your search for Desmond," Tom said, awkwardly. "We feel it's time for closure."

"You've been *talking* to people," Grace said angrily. "We want that to *stop*. We want you to *stop*."

"All our work is pro bono," me wife said calmly, "and the only way we can find someone, which you asked us to do, is to talk to people."

"We would prefer that you stopped," Tom said, hating the situation into which we had been forced by his angry wife. "I have made out a check for $5,000 to cover your expenses. If any more is required, please tell me."

Nuala took the check. An Atlantic storm was rising and about to assault the coasts of Galway.

"You have made our grief even more intense with your foolish questions. Father Gerard, our parish priest, says it's presumptions to hold out any more hope. Desmond is dead. We should never have trusted the Jesuits. I was not told you were a Marquette graduate."

"I didn't actually graduate," I said.

"We plan a nice quiet memorial mass with Father Gerard as the celebrant and we ask only that you leave us alone."

"I sympathize with your grief," my wife said softly. "Have your memorial mass with your Father Gerard and find your closure. We will not aggravate your pain."

"We appreciate your understanding," Tom Doolin said, his embarrassment now both obvious and painful. "We are grateful for your efforts."

"Well, I'm not!" Grace insisted.

"However," Nuala continued to speak softly, "we did nothing more than you asked. As for expenses, five thousand dollars covers much less than a half minute of my time."

She tore the check in half and permitted it to fall from her hands on the floor.

"And," she continued, almost in a whisper, "we never give up on a case until we solve it. Now please leave my house before I sink to your level of nastiness."

"I'm sorry." Tom Doolin tried to smooth the conflict over . . .

"Better leave before the dogs come up the stairs," I suggested.

They left.

"That focking bastard," my Nuala exploded. "That pissant gobshite, that focking nine-fingered shite hawk, that focking shite-faced lying son of a bitch!"

I usually edit Nuala's words, but I present these so that you have some slight hint of what she's like when the dignity of a Celtic warrior countess is offended.

The two white wolves appeared in the parlor and paced around nervously. Nuala was upset. Therefore, they were upset.

"I'll report him to Cardinal Sean, that's what I'll do. He's unfit to work with young people, he's a lying, focking pervert, that's what he is!"

Her target was patently the chaplain of the Newman Club.

"Tell Blackie. He'll do it more discreetly."

" 'Tis true, Dermot love, you have the right of it altogether, and yourself always having the right of it. I'm sorry I sounded like a fishwife at the edge of Galway Bay."

She sat down on the most comfortable couch in the room and began to sob.

The pooches climbed up on the couch to console her.

"Poor dear doggies, wasn't I terrible altogether and meself saying awful things about the Galway fishwives, poor dear women."

Then more sobbing.

"If a husband's vote means anything, I thought you were wonderful."

"You're only saying that, Dermot Michael, because you love me."

"Love you I do . . . Fiona, do you mind if I sit next to my wife . . . Thank you . . . However, I said it because it was true."

"Dermot Michael Coyne, have I ever pushed you around like that woman pushed around her poor husband?"

"Woman, you have not and you'd better not try."

A lot of folk were being labeled "poor," not, however, Grace Doolin or Father O'Halloran.

He was, I might mention in passing, subsequently translated to a parish so far north in Lake County halfway to Milwaukee.

"I feel terrible sorry for them and I understand that they are terrible sad, but why take it out on us, and ourselves knowing where Des is and bringing him home, safe and sound, one of these days."

The next day was Holy Thursday and the McGrail family, as I like to call it because that makes my wife furious, moves its base to Old St. Patrick's Church, where Nuala sings in the choir, much to the delight of the rest of the choir, the local clergy, the childer, my family, and the congregation.

"And for free too," I complain to my brothers and sisters.

Nelliecoyne is permitted to join her in the choir if only for the hand-clapping in one of the Easter hymns.

Then we go to my parents' house for the Easter dinner, a festival taken over by our childer's cousins. I think our brood, save perhaps the irrepressible Socra Marie, are the best mannered of the lot. But I'm prejudiced.

Monday afternoon, all of us, recovering from the Easter exertions, settle down.

"I'm not angry at poor Grace Doolin anymore," Nuala informed me in the shower, "and meself acting like a banshee."

"The poor woman has created most of her own troubles," I suggested.

" 'Tis too bad that something in her own past made her unable to enjoy poor Dizzy Des."

As we were dressing, Joseph from the camera store called and asked if he and Mary might come over to report on the results of his distribution of the faxes to his colleagues. Might they also bring their child who was too young to be left in charge of the store.

"I bet he's a little boy named Yeshua," I suggested.

"Don't be blasphemous, Dermot Michael, they're not Mexicans and themselves speaking the same language Jesus spoke."

"It's not blasphemous for the Mexicans!"

" 'Tis not but these people must be his relatives."

The child's name was Therese and she was as beautiful as her mother and the same age as our Socra Marie, who was called from the play yard with her unindicted coconspirator, Katiesue Murphy. The three little girls took one look at one another and, as such entities do, bonded for life.

"Now be nice with Therese," Nuala warned.

Socra Marie glared at her mother with her "you-gotta-be-out-of-your-mind" expression, which she had acquired from her two older siblings.

"Your daughters are very sweet," Mary marveled.

"Only the tiny one is ours. Katiesue is from down the street. Her father teaches at Loyola and her mother is an officer in the United States Coast Guard. Don't worry, they'll be nice to your daughter."

Joseph removed five pictures out of a file.

"The first one, my colleague James, as you would call him, owns a shop on Wabash. He says your young friend came into his shop often to purchase various electronic material. He found him charming and sympathetic and very interested in the Assyrian experience in America. He did not mention Iraq."

"Very interesting," Nuala said.

YOU'RE GOING TO HAVE TO VISIT ALL OF THEM, SPEAR-CARRIER. AND STOP OGLING THAT OTHER WOMAN'S TITS. NUALA MAY LOOK UP AND CATCH YOU.

"The next one, Michael, owns a shop on Taylor Street where many students from the university shop. He likes them all, especially this young man, though Mike was evasive about religion. He still fears the Shiites, unnecessarily it seems to the rest of us."

"We won't have to see him then," I said.

Nuala frowned at me. She didn't grasp that the Irish are not the only long-oppressed people who keep the best till the end.

"Ephrem's store is over on Southport, near the Music Box Theatre, he is my nearest rival and my closest friend."

"He witnessed our wedding, back in Iraq before we escaped," Mary added.

"He recognized your man, but he was more relaxed than his usual yuppie customers, so he didn't trust him. He feared he was from the police because he was so different. I did not argue with him, but I thought he was being silly. Yet Ephrem has had much trouble with the police. Mrs. Hurley has him as a client."

"Then he has nothing to fear," Nuala said firmly.

"Fourth is Marco, who works on Chicago Avenue just west of Clark Street. He is very successful and very suspicious. He did not want to say anything about the Assyrians, though he admitted at first he was a member of St. Ibrahim's Church."

"I can understand why they all might be suspicious. I'm an immigrant too and I've had my trouble with the Feds. Fortunately your Mrs. Hurley routed them each time."

"She is a woman of great power and great beauty," Mary said with feeling.

"Finally, we come to the most interesting of all. This is Tariq, my cousin. He has much to do with bringing refugees to America. He works with Father Ibrahim in these matters. He admits he gave the young man directions about how to get into Mosul but he refused to describe them to me, though we came out through the same way. He will talk to you, but that is all."

"You flew from Kars to Ankara," Nuala said.

Both Mary and Joseph gasped and looked very frightened.

"My wife," I said, "is very sensitive to these matters. Do not worry, she and my sister are great friends and Nuala is a woman of absolute integrity."

"Isn't that the route we traced from the airplane records? Presumably friends of Tariq escorted him through the mountains and across the border, that's all we need to know. Assure him that he has nothing to fear from us when we talk with him. Where did you say his store was?"

"Way out west on Pulaski Road."

We West Side Irish bigots always called it Crawford Avenue because our parents and grandparents refused to accept a Polish name, regardless of what Pulaski did for George Washington's army. In the northern suburbs it's Crawford too.

"Do you know where that is, Dermot?"

"Woman, I do."

WHAT KIND OF FOREIGNER IS THIS THAT YOU MARRIED? SHE DOESN'T KNOW ANYTHING BETWEEN SOUTHPORT AND HARLEM AVENUE.

Neither do most yuppies.

"Joseph, will you call your cousin Tariq and see if you can make an appointment to see him. Assure him of our discretion. Tell him we already know the general path that Desmond followed and we need no more information about his journey. We want merely to know where he might be and if there is any way we can get in touch with him."

"I will speak to him," said Joseph. "You must understand I can make no promises."

"Of course."

"May we meet your other children?"

"Certainly, they always love to show off."

She turned on the monitor system.

"Are all you wretched rascals being good down there?"

"Yes, Ma!"

And then, confirming what they said, Nelliecoyne spoke, "They really are, Ma."

"Is the baby awake?"

"Yes, Ma, and I changed his diaper."

She put her hand over the speaker.

"Do you people like dogs?"

"Oh, yes!"

"Peaceful but large dogs."

"The larger the better."

She removed her hand.

"Would youse like to meet Therese's ma and da!"

"Yes!"

"Bring the doggies, but keep them under control."

"Yes, Ma!"

The thundering herd streamed up the stairs, Nelliecoyne and the doggies trailing behind.

"Ruffians, this is Therese's ma and da. Reading from left to right, they are Nelliecoyne and in her arms, Poraig Josefa, Micheal is the one with the hounds, and Socra Marie whom you have already met. The one next to her is Katiesue Murphy whose ma works for the United States Coast Guard and her da teaches at Loyola University.

"Doggies, introduce yourselves to the guests."

Fiona and Maeve walked over politely and offered their paws for shaking, they curled up in front of me wife, the alpha female in the house. Unbidden, Nelliecoyne—the vest pocket witch that she is, handed Patjo over to Mary. The child, show-off that he is, smiled happily.

"I will have one of these in about seven months. I hope he is as cute as your little brother."

"I'm sure he will be," Nelliecoyne assured her.

The other kids, laying on their training for all it was worth, came up and shyly shook hands.

"OK, you ragamuffins can go back downstairs."

"Therese, dear, it's time to go home."

"Can she come again?" Socra Marie begged.

"If your ma and da want her to."

Nuala Anne nodded approval.

"We'd be delighted that you want her to come back. I'm sure we'll see you all again."

The kids went back to the playroom. The doggies stayed with us. Mary and Joseph, we still did not know their last names, and little Therese, already sleepy-eyed, left quietly. Nuala promised that we would see them again, in her tone that goes beyond courtesy and becomes commitment.

NOTE, DERMOT COYNE, THAT YOU SAID NOTHING.

Why should I when she handles the formalities with so much grace.

YOU'RE USELESS.

She doesn't think so.

The Adversary, as I call the "voice" is my "bad" self, whose control of my actions ceased long ago.

I'M REALLY NOT THAT BAD, NEVER WAS.

"Dermot!" my wife said, embracing me. "We've almost solved the mystery. Now all we have to do is to find out where he is and get him back here if he wants to come."

"Will it really be a boy child?"

"Certainly!"

"Nelliecoyne knows too?"

"She's her ma's daughter, isn't she?"

"On the subject of Des, finding out where he is and asking him if he wants to come back are major issues."

"We'll find him and I know he wants to come home . . . Now I must go down to the kitchen and help Danuta prepare tea for those starving childer before they organize a protest against us."

— 18 —

I called my Old Fella from Lisbon.

The Galway woman answered, under her principle that you don't impose on a servant to deal with the telephone.

" 'Tis meself," I announced, as though I had talked to her only yesterday.

The conversation continued in a code designed to avoid tears on both sides of the conversation.

"Did they throw you out of Germany?"

"Woman, they did not."

"You're in trouble with your Ministry?"

"Not as far as I know. I asked to come home and report."

"You won't have any time to come up here?"

"I will."

"When?"

"Weekend."

"I'll have to see what himself is doing. You know what he's like."

"When I'm in Dublin I might stay in the row house on the park. This is a short walk to the government buildings. If you and the Old Fella came down, we might have dinner at the Lafayette Restaurant at the Royal Hibernian . . ."

"Well, we'll see what himself wants to do. You know what he's like."

"By the way, is he around the premises?"

"I'll see if he wants to talk."

The Old Fella was on immediately.

"Where the fock are you!"

"Lisbon. That's in Portugal."

"Is anyone listening in?"

"I'm at the Irish embassy here. Supposedly we have a secure line. Nowadays you can't tell."

"What the fock you doing there?"

"Waiting for the BOAC flight tomorrow."

"They shot one of them down."

"Only because they thought Winston was on it . . . I need a favour."

"Name it and you got it."

"I need an hour with Winston tomorrow morning. Just him, no Foreign Office wallahs."

"I imagine that I could arrange that. Urgent, is it now?"

"Extremely."

"I'll ask him to have a limousine pick you up."

"Smashing!"

My second weekend at Schloss Stauffenberg was, I hate to admit it, fun. The much-heralded tennis match between Uncle Tim and Aunt Hannah had attracted everyone in the Schloss, servants included. What was it that Welleseley said about Waterloo, "It was a damn fine run thing."

"I'll have no trouble beating you this time, Herr Ridgewood. I am younger than you are and in better condition."

"A little younger," I had admitted, "and I delight in your better condition."

She was slimmer than when we had played the last time and in her tennis whites, more breathtaking. However, I was willing to bet that the poor nutrition of wartime food had deprived her of the energy she would need. I was willing to accept a one-set match, she had insisted on two out of three.

She overwhelmed me in the first set 6–2. She was stronger than she had been at sixteen. Lots of practice and self-discipline, both traits impressed me. My beloved was serious about such matters. However, she was panting at the end of the set and I was breathing easily. I had been overconfident. Never again with this woman. I became aggressive immediately and broke her first and second serves 4–0.

She then broke two of my serves and I had to be content with a 6–3 victory. However, she was exhausted, partly because I had volleyed to force her to run across the court. Her wet tennis clothes clung to her body in a most distracting way. However, I was determined to win.

I did—6–0.

She glared at me, shook her racket in general displeasure, and then ran to the net to hug and kiss me with considerable affection.

"Better than the last time."

"Older." She laughed.

Then with the kids we adjourned to the swimming dock. Her bathing costume was much more abbreviated this time—bra and panty, green matching her goddess eyes. It looked new. Bought especially to please me? I felt like weeping, sentimental mick that I am.

I noticed that she was not wearing her wedding ring anymore.

"I owe you a brief row on the lake," I said when we trudged back to the Schloss.

"I need a small nap. I would have beaten you if I'd had more sleep."

"I'm sure you would."

Dinner—the main meal at noon—was a delight. The little girls were upset with me for beating Aunt Hannah. I had cheated because I made her chase the ball all the time.

"Herr Ridgewood did not cheat," Annalise said solemnly. "He is always un gentilhomme parfait."

"I blush modestly at Aunt Hannah's compliment," I said. "However, I did make her run a lot. She's so much younger than I am."

More laughter and applause.

"Sixteen hundred for the boat trip?" I said as I showed her to the door of her room.

She nodded.

"Very well.

"Pleasant dreams, Aunt Hannah."

"For you also, Herr Ridgewood."

There is no point in recounting my dreams, except to say they were pleasant.

She was still wearing the green swimsuit, this time with a white shirt over it to protect herself from the sun. She insisted that I go back to my room and don a shirt too.

"Irish skin."

The summer heat had abated somewhat. The lake was glass smooth again. She sat in the bow of the boat, safely away from me.

"You are wondrous in your swimming costume, Annalise," I said.

She blushed.

"I don't mind you admiring me, Herr Ridgewood. I didn't mind the last time either, though I pretended I did."

My turn to blush.

"I must say something serious to you, Herr Ridgewood."

"I will listen carefully."

She hesitated, searching perhaps for the right word.

"You are a very attractive man, Herr Ridgewood. Also you are a very good man . . . I need more time."

"How much more time?" I asked as gently as I could.

"Not much, a year perhaps. I cannot ask you to wait. Still . . ."

"I will wait gladly, Annalise. But I promise you that in a year, I may carry you off by brute force."

She laughed, the rich, full laugh of a happy woman.

"And I will resist your force!"

"That will make it very interesting. Your gentilhomme parfait will become a Viking berserker."

This time she had giggled.

The thought of Viscount Ridgewood as a Viking rapist rated only a giggle.

I had escorted her to the station for the train to Munich early in the evening. There was lightning in the distant sky. A summer storm. The Lancasters *would not be flying tonight, thanks be to God. As we heard the train huff down the track, we embraced and kissed passionately. At long last.*

"Good night, Herr Ridgewood," she said as she boarded the train.

"Good night, my love."

She turned towards me for a moment and smiled.

That smile still remains with me.

On the flight to London, I thought of nothing but our final embrace. Talking to Winston would have to take care of itself.

So the next afternoon after my father's call, precisely at 11:00, I found myself in his tiny office in the bunker beneath 10 Downing Street, a room filled with the aroma of cigars and whiskey. Winston looked older and tired. But the glow of battle was on him. Or maybe only the whiskey. A bottle of Middleton's and two tumblers rested on his desk. Good sign.

"Who are you working for, young man?" he demanded with a fierce, Winstonian growl.

"Ireland," I said.

"You're absolutely and totally neutral."

"And because my ancestors repealed the principle of contradiction, we are also pro-English."

That line reminded me of Annalise, from whom I had heard it for the first time.

"You won't let us use the treaty ports."

He meant Cobb and Dun Leary as we called them, now that they were ours. The treaty Mick Collins had signed promised them to Britain in time of war.

"You didn't ask politely. You know us better than to demand anything."

He growled again. He knew I was right. I'm sure the Old Fella had told him the same thing.

"I've been reading your dispatches. They're brilliant. Very informative. And you're out of your mind to take such risks. You are crazier than even your own father. You're the best spy we have in the whole damned country."

"I write them in Irish. Abwehr would have a hell of time deciphering that. I've been more careful recently because there's been a change of administration there."

"You should receive an OBE for this work, maybe after the war."

"Thanks but no thanks. It wouldn't go down well with my superiors. Just the same I'm honoured."

He threw up his hands in resignation. He always knew that we Irish were crazy. Alas for Winston's problematic career among us, he never did comprehend that brilliance and imagination were comfortable companions of our craziness.

He filled the two goblets with the creature. Winston might have sloshed through the war as someone said much later. It did not, it seemed, interfere with his judgment.

"Your very good health, Timmy."

"And to victory, Winston."

"Indeed yes." He smiled, raising his fingers in the "v" sign which he had made famous.

He finished his drink during our conversation. I had only a sipeen or two.

"I suppose you're here to tell me about this resistance movement in Germany, whatever they call it."

"Widerstand, it means resistance."

"I don't like resistance movements," he thundered.

"No de Gaulle in this group," I assured him.

"I'm glad of it."

"This is all between us, Winston. The Foreign Office wallahs should not hear of it. There are some English Communists in MI5. They will pass this information on to the Russians."

He raised his huge eyebrows a bit and then nodded.

I relayed to him Claus's message, virtually word for word.

He listened impassively.

"When?"

"Shortly after you and the Americans land."

"Hmm . . . What do they want from us—guns, tanks, planes?"

"Nothing at all, only your belief that they are what they say they are and your willingness to negotiate with them when they are firmly in control."

"That does not seem an unreasonable request. You may tell them that I said that if they declare a cease-fire and begin to release the Jews and to arrest the

criminals, I would have no choice but to talk to them. . . . What do you think the Russkis will do?"

"The hope is that they will stop to figure out what will happen."

"That's what Stalin will do all right. He is a very cautious man. The Red Army is in no mood for another war and its generals hate him."

"I believe that too, sir. He's been negotiating a separate peace with Himmler and Ribbentrop for some time."

"You sure of that?" he growled again.

"Quite sure."

"My old friend, Admiral Canaris, is alive and well?"

"Alive, sir, but fallen from power."

"I am genuinely sorry to hear that. Sometimes I hear his voice in your words. You must give him my very best . . . Did they really think they could destroy the Royal Air Force in four days?"

"Only Goering."

"Fools . . . Your estimate of the plotters' chances, Timmy?"

"Slim, very slim. All other attempts to kill Hitler have failed. The Antichrist takes care of his own, one of my contacts says. If they kill Hitler and Himmler at the same time, their chances improve. Most of the General Staff will support them, some already do."

He nodded.

"Does the Pope know? Has he truly blessed them?"

"He knows in a general way and, yes, he has blessed them."

"God grant them success," he murmured. "It could save millions of lives."

"Thank you for listening, Winston."

I stood up to leave.

"If they fail, how long will the Nazis continue to fight?"

"They're running out of manpower . . . No more than a year after you and the Americans land."

"Just as we all did the last time around . . . God support those brave men you have described. You will stay in touch with us, Timmy?"

"Of course, Winston."

I stood up, glancing quickly at my watch. Fifty-five minutes. Not bad.

The Prime Minister was lighting a cigar.

"You'll be going home for a couple of days?"

"I must report to my minister."

"Give my very best to your mother."

"The Galway woman," I said.

"Yes, the Galway woman."

The weekend at our Schloss was great fun. I beat both of my brothers at tennis. Annalise would have no trouble with them either. They accused me of practicing too much. I said that there was not much else to do in Berlin, though dodging bombs offered some exercise too. Both of them were officers in the Irish Army, exercising Irish citizenship this time around. Since we were technically on the north side of the border of what me da called "the rump state of Protestants, Puritans, and pookas," they didn't wear their uniforms. In the midst of the laughter, I wondered how my wife—for so I permitted myself to think of her on occasion—would fit in with this madcap crowd. At first she would be shy and they would be in awe of her Gothic queen's beauty. Then she'd say something funny, probably at my expense and she'd be part of the crowd.

My parents drove me down to Dublin. We ate each night at the Royal Hibernian's Lafayette Restaurant which the Old Fella said was the best in all of Ireland. In those days of the Emergency (as we called the war) and the folly of Dev's mercantile economics there wasn't much competition.

"You shouldn't go back," the minister said to me. "One of them bombs might decide to hit you."

I had given him a briefing like the one I had presented to Winston.

"I'll come home after the Rising," I said. "If it fails, then there will be nothing left for Germany but death and destruction and rape—millions of each. By your leave, I'll get out of there in a hurry. If it works, then it will be safe again in Berlin and everywhere else."

"Winston knows what you told me?"

"In substance, yes."

"You know, Timmy, I probably ought not to tell Dev about the plot. He has enough to worry about . . . What if your good friend Winston tries to take over the treaty ports?"

"I told him that if he had asked politely, we probably would have gone along with him under some limitations."

"Even the best of them don't understand Ireland. They probably never will."

"'Tis true."

"All right, Timmy. We'll want you back here a year from September in any event. We'll need to have you do a little work here before we send you off to Washington as ambassador."

"That would be a very interesting posting, sir."

"I hope you can keep out of trouble there, Timmy."

"I'll try."

"I'm not sure you will, but you'll do a good job, of that I'm confident."

Thank you, sir."

I was dazed when I left the office. I had enough sense not to ask whether Washington was a settled matter. I knew already, since I understand the way we Irish talk.

I walked down to the passport office, where a very good friend presided happily over a very dull job.

"Would you ever be able to create a passport for this young woman?" I asked, using again the Gaelic subjunctive of polite request.

"It will be a pleasure and herself so lovely . . . Diplomatic passport is it now?"

"'Tis," I agreed. "Anne Elizabeth Ridgewood."

"And yourself married to her when next you come home?"

"With the grace of God and a little luck."

"I'm sure God will be on your side, Timmy, and yourself always the lucky one . . . All kinds of stamps on it, like showing that she came into Germany say a week hence?"

"That would be brilliant altogether."

"Won't I be making it so that all the border guards in Europe will think it's authentic, but it will cost you when you come back."

"Whatever it costs . . . "

"One visit here so I can say hello to Lady Anne."

"She would insist on it even if I didn't."

"You'll be back here tomorrow morning to talk to some of the other staff and then off in the afternoon to Holyhead?"

"I will."

"We'll need stamps from Switzerland, Spain, Portugal, and bloody England. Anyplace else?"

"Italy."

"Easy as cutting butter with a warm knife. Then when she's back in Ireland, and herself a citizen, won't we make everything legal like."

"Thank you."

"Glad to help . . . Tomorrow about 12:30, convenient for you?"

"Perfect."

If he were more ambitious, he could make a fortune on false Irish punts, not that they were that valuable back in those days.

I stopped at a jewelers across from the green and bought the biggest and most brilliant rings they had.

I collected the passport the next morning. It was a work of sheer genius. Now I had all the materials I needed to smuggle a new wife out of the country.

If the "Rising," as an Irishman would call it, were a success, all of this would become optional. I prayed to God every night as I said my Rosary that it would be a success. If it failed, it would fail the first day and I would have to move quickly to get Annalise out of the country. Would she escape with me? Would she feel bound to stay and let the Gestapo rape her to death? I hoped the words in Claus's letter were strong enough. Would she hate me for forcing her to live when she wanted to die?

I should not worry about such things.

As it was, I would have to leave the country pretty quickly myself because the evil men on the Albertstrasse would discover my relationship with Claus. Irish diplomatic immunity would be scant protection.

My ma and da drove me over to the ferry docks in the Liffey. We stayed in the car until the very last minute.

"You'll be coming back soon?" the Old Fella asked, not quite sounding casual.

"Probably within the year."

"Um."

"You'll go to the bomb shelters during the raids?"

"Naturally."

That was what my Jesuit teachers would have called an equivocation.

"I don't suppose you'd be bringing home a nice German girl, would you now?" the Galway woman asked.

"And if I did, would you be wanting a German daughter-in-law around the house?"

"I might get used to her if she were a nice young woman . . . It would be easier if she were a Catholic, now wouldn't it?"

"It would," I said.

She and my hoped-for new wife would quickly bond together against the rest of us. Still, it would be interesting to be present at the meeting, if the meeting should ever happen.

More daydreams as we crossed the bumpy Irish Sea on the way to Holyhead.

The trip back to Berlin was not without some excitement. Me-109s followed our BOAC Dakota, buzzing us periodically just for the fun of it. The unspoken agreement against shooting down airliners was violated only once—the Germans thought Winston was on the plane. The pilots in the 109s would shoot us down only if they had orders to do so, and then they would have done it immediately. They were only playing, though it was scary playing. They departed rather quickly, their fuel tanks notoriously too small. Then a flight of three snub-nosed planes joined us. They looked like sawed-off Folk-Wulfes. When they came closer I saw a white star on their wings. They escorted us to Portuguese air space and then saluted us with a wag of their wings and peeled away.

"What were those Yank planes that escorted us?"

"Grumanns. F4F. They're from the baby carriers the Yanks use on convoys these days. Merchant ships with flat tops. They're killing off the U-boats. I called our Coastal Command to see if they could provide any escorts for us when the 109s showed up. They sent the Yanks."

"Nice of them."

Only while I was struggling through the Madrid immigration procedures, did I ask myself whom the Yanks were trying to protect. Probably the Irish ambassador.

That scared me.

I would have to lay in a supply of food shortly before the Rising and fill the auxiliary fuel tanks I had Franz install. Nonperishable food. Fruit at the last minute. Straight from Berlin to Nuremberg and then cut to the west and Basle. Four days, five days, probably under the hot summer sun.

A bomb from the RAF could wipe out this problem completely.

The day after I returned, Claus's voice said on the phone, "One-thirty at the Adlon. If it is not raining, café outside."

"Ja, ja."

At that time the elegantly Edwardian Adlon was arguably the finest hotel in the world. Later the Russians would burn it to the ground for their newsreel cameras. I was punctual. Claus was waiting for me. He was certainly anxious, but his charm precluded any hint of it.

"It was nice to be home again?" he asked with his usual broad smile.

I yield to no one on our island of indirection in putting off the matter in question till after all the bullshit was over. Not this time.

"Winston listened sympathetically. He called upon God to grant you success. He wanted to know if the Pope had blessed you. He promised that he would issue no condemnation or dismissal. Once you were in charge and had begun to institute your reforms, especially withdrawal to the Rhine, he would be happy to hold conversations with you."

"That is good, that is very good." He sighed. "You are an excellent diplomat."

"And, yes, to answer your question, it was good to see the Galway woman and the Old Fella again."

He chuckled.

"I should understand the Irish by now."

We ordered our standard beer and sausage, which I thought would be an insult to the world's greatest hotel until I tasted the sausage.

"You have prepared a method for removing Annalise from Germany?"

I told him what I had done.

"You even bought the rings!"

"Naturally. I won't propose real marriage as opposed to fictional until we are out of Germany. I would much rather, however, propose when the new government is in power."

"Do you think that will happen, Timmy?"

"Churchill asked me that. I said there was some chance, greater if Hitler is eliminated."

"He agreed with that assessment?"

"Yes."

"Both of you give it more chance than I do . . . But speaking of Annalise, I have a second letter for you. Again you must not read it."

He removed another letter, with seal on the envelope.

I signed my name over the seal.

"Does this replace the previous one or supplement it?"

"Reinforces it," he said.

"Good," I said. "I promise you, Claus, I will do my best, though I hope that I will not have to."

"We have an addition to the plan," he said, cutting the sausage so nimbly that one hardly noticed the absence of arm and fingers.

"It is called Operation Valkyrie, a plan for the army to take complete control of the country in a national emergency—like spreading revolt of foreign workers or a plot by the SS to seize total power. Once Hitler is dead, we send out the Valkyrie signal to all units. Even those leaders who are not with us will obey the plan—once a plan is ordered the Army will seize all SS leaders, all Gestapo leaders, all Nazi Gauleiters. In twenty-four hours the army will be in complete control. Marshal von Beck will be named as president and the socialist Julius Leber will become Chancellor. Everything must be organized in every city and province of the country, we must know who our enemies are and who our friends are, whom we can trust and whom we cannot be certain about. There is an enormous amount of work to be done so that we won't fail after we succeed. I'm sure you can guess who is supervising the preparation of the organizational issue, but so much behind the scenes that she is invisible; she even wears gloves when she types so there will be no fingerprints."

"I'm glad she is invisible."

"Ja for twenty-four, perhaps thirty-six hours . . . what do you think of our plan, Timmy? No one will ever say it was a Putsch of a handful of disorganized madmen."

"They will have to say that it was brilliantly organized," I replied.

"It will work despite the cries of the Nazis and the viciousness of the SS. The *people now want the war to end. They want to be protected from the Russians. There is but one small point . . . "*

"The Führer?"

"Ja. He has to die. If he lives, millions would rally to him. Is he not the Führer? Otherwise we fail. And a couple of thousand of us will die horribly. At least we tried."

"And you must be the one to kill him."

"There is no one else. All other attempts have failed. I may fail too. I hope not . . . I know that he who acts will go down in German history as a traitor, but who can and does not will be traitor to his conscience. If I did not now act to stop this senseless killing, I should never be able to face the war's widows and orphans."

"God go with you," I said fervently.

I walked slowly back to the Friedrichstrasse, my heart heavy. The Antichrist takes care of his own. The rising was typically Germanic—planned in elaborate detail and depending on one problematic and indeed mad act. It might be the best-organized rebellion in human history, but before it could even get started one brave man had to strike down a madman to change the course of history.

And my love working every night somewhere in Charlottenburg or Gruenwald to build the organization, with gloves to cover her fingerprints. I did not like that at all, but she had to work out her own destiny.

Late in the afternoon I took both my .25s and walked to the gun club.

Claus had killed in battle, though likely no one face-to-face. If I had to use these weapons for face-to-face killings, my shots must be deadly accurate to the center of the forehead. The .25 makes a small sound, like a tiny firecracker. The man I killed would hear it and then be dead.

I almost vomited on the sidewalk.

Yet if Annalise was in grave danger, I would have to do it.

My quick turnaround shots to fire at the head were accurate that day. But I was shooting only at lifeless targets.

Could I protect Annalise if someone was about to do her harm?

Hell, I'd tear him apart with my bare hands.

The raids continued almost every night, some of them heavy, others relatively light if an air raid can ever be called light.

In early December, I was feeling bored, homesick, lonely and sorry for myself—perhaps in reverse order. My morning mail contained an elaborate invitation from the Spanish embassy to a Christmas celebration at the Adlon Hotel. I was told that I might bring a guest.

I liked the Spanish diplomats. They had been around a long time and seen a lot, including their own civil war. They had no illusions and disliked the whole Nazi scene.

I would invite Annalise to be my guest at the Spanish Christmas party.

Grand idea! But I had never learned her phone number. Nor did I have Claus's number.

So I had to wait for the usual mysterious call from Claus. A week later, time running out for a response, he was on the phone.

"I need a swim this afternoon."

Then he hung up. No mention of time. I went over to the club at 12:30, fired my pistols for an hour and a half, becoming more deadly as I became more angry.

Damn Germans, always organized and always inefficient. We Irish were congenitally tardy but never by more than a half hour.

Did I really want a German wife?

Yeah, I really did.

I went into the beer room and ordered a stein and a platter of sausages.

Claus showed up at 3:15.

One look at his wounded body and his gaunt face exorcised my rage.

"What time did I say I would be here?" he asked cheerfully.

"You said afternoon."

"I was not more precise?"

"Doesn't matter," I said with equal cheer. "I practiced my shooting."

"I'm sorry. After I called you I had to see the doctor who supervises me. He said I should not swim this time of the year. There is much flu and I am subject to many infections because of my wounds. He tells me I must be very careful."

I was glad I hadn't said anything and felt guilty for what I thought. That's what love does for you.

"I was thinking of inviting Annalise to the Spanish embassy formal Christmas party at the Adlon."

"*Splendid! Now you begin a courtship, nein?*"

"*I don't have her phone number.*"

"*She refused to give it to you?*"

"*I never asked.*"

"*Ja, I write it out for you.*" He removed a pocket notebook from his pocket and then wrote out the number, smoothly, efficiently, as though he had never been wounded.

"*If she asks who gave you her phone number, you say I did. I don't think she'll ask. You will have a wonderful time at the party.*"

If we go, I thought.

"*How are the plans developing?*"

He sighed.

"*It is not easy being a revolutionary, Timmy. So many things to worry about. General Fromm, my superior, is one of us. He is a coward. If anything goes wrong, he will have us shot. Then the next day, he will be shot himself because he is too deeply involved already. He expects to be made a field marshal if we are successful.*"

"*What will you be?*"

"*Undersecretary of War. I will accept nothing higher. I am not leading this affair for power. Only to save the Secret Germany.*"

His eyes took on the usual faraway mystical look that appeared when he mentioned the Secret Germany. Then the look faded.

"*Yet sometimes I think that we will have to lose this war and be obliterated before there can be a new Germany born. We are a new country, only seventy years old, bound together by conquest. Perhaps the real Antichrist was Friedrich der Grosse. It might be that we must suffer more death and more rapes to be free to reshape our nation. Then and only then would the Secret Germany be free to emerge.*"

[Looking back from the perspective of time, the Federal Republic has its imperfections. It may not be the Secret Germany of which Claus dreamed. Yet Prussia and part of Brandenburg are now in Poland. Militarism seems to be dead. Germany is a functioning democratic country, a little dull and boring, perhaps, but it is not a Fourth Reich and I think never will be. Was all the suffering of 1945 and after necessary? God knows, I don't. However, if the Rising had been a success, as it almost was, the history of Europe would have been different. Better or worse? God knows, I don't. R.]

"Those speculations are beyond me, Claus. I know that Germany would be a better place if there were more people like you."

"I already have five kinder, Tim."

I hadn't meant that, but I let it pass.

So that evening after a lean supper of potatoes and vegetables, the best poor Magda could do with the supplies available even at the stores which served the embassies and before the air raids started, I called Annalise's number.

"Annalise," she said curtly.

"Timothy."

"You should not have my phone number."

"Claus gave it to me."

"What do you want?" she demanded.

Do you really want to marry such an authoritarian woman?

No.

"The Spanish embassy has a nice formal Christmas gathering every year. Would you ever be my guest this year?"

She didn't recognize the polite request form. It did not matter, however.

"That would be impossible, Herr Ridgewood. Good-bye."

Certainly not. She was a Gothic witch, not a Gothic archduchess. How could I ever love her.

The phone rang again. If it were my former love, I would tell her off.

"Ridgewood."

"Annalise, Herr Ridgewood, and I am weeping because I am such a fool. Yes, it would be wonderful to accompany you to the Spanish Christmas party — if you still want me as your guest."

I struggled for the right words.

"I was hoping you'd call back. Certainly I want you to be my guest."

"I have nothing to wear, however."

"That's what my mother, the Galway woman always says. I've learned to be skeptical about such protests."

Then the air raid sirens began and we said good-bye.

I keep my rule about avoiding the shelters. But I went down to the crude shelter that Magda and Franz had made for me in the basement. Happy man that I was, I did not even hear the all clear in the morning.

On the Sunday night before Christmas in 1944, Franz proudly drove me through the Tiergarten and up the Kudamm to Charlottenburg—named after the wife of Friedrich der Grosse. He had put the canvas top on the Benz and turned on the heat. A layer of snow covered the ground and the ruins. My date was ready at the door to her apartment in a simple white gown, if any off-the-shoulder gown, however professedly modest, can be simple. She wore a green sash around her waist and a small red pin shaped like a Tannenbaum on her breast.

I gulped, I fear audibly.

"I hope I do not discredit you, Herr Ridgewood."

"It's a credit to be with the most beautiful woman in the room." I helped her on with her cloak and conducted her down to the car. Franz, approving my taste, bowed deeply.

We returned through the Tiergarten and the Brandenburg Gate and stopped at the front entrance of the Adlon.

"Remember, Franz, there is a shelter for employees under the hotel." I gave him my card, complete with a large shamrock to show if necessary.

The Adlon and its employees were dressed in Christmas finery, the lights glowed softly. The Spanish colours of red and gold were everywhere.

"One advantage of this hotel," I said, "is that it has the best bomb shelter in Berlin."

"There will be no bombs tonight," my wide-eyed, luminous date said. "There could not be."

"How should I introduce you?" I whispered.

"Just call me Annalise."

She charmed everyone. Even the ambassador's normally disapproving wife congratulated me on her beauty. When we danced, she melted in my arms, though I felt the strength in her arms.

"I have never been in the Adlon. It is quite beautiful."

She was a little child in wonderland.

I did not hold her too tightly as we danced. I did not after all own her.

And never would, no matter what happened. But I did keep her close to me.

"Is it wrong for us to be here," she asked, "when so many in Berlin are hungry?"

"I don't think so," I said. "Remember, tonight you are Irish. Your green sash matches mine. The Irish are representatives of their country and only do their duty when they represent their countries at diplomatic receptions like this."

I learned a lot of casuistry from my years with the Jesuits.

Just as the roast beef was being served, the RAF proved that my date's convictions were wrong. The warning siren wailed and then almost immediately the more piercing scream of the "bombs falling" alarm followed.

Trust the Germans to have different sounds for different problems.

"I must ask all our guests to join us in the shelter below, where we will eat our roast beef and drink our wine."

With practiced speed, the servants moved our wine and beef downstairs and we went into the shelter, the most comfortable in Berlin, as well as the safest. There were electric lamps everywhere, easy chairs, small tables for each pair of chairs, drapery on the walls and soft music.

After I had led Annalise to a chair, I checked the servants' shelter to make certain that Franz was safe there, which was as well protected as ours but not so well furnished.

I returned to find my date, a glass of Spanish wine in her hand engaged in animated conversation with the ambassador and his wife. She acted as if she was at the Adlon almost every week. They were discussing the future of Germany.

Could it last another year?

"When the Yanks come," Annalise said, "it will be the end. We barely have the manpower to fight a two-front war, much less a three-front war. Many men will die. Many women will be raped."

She patted my place on the chair next to hers, indicating that I should sit down.

"It is well with the good Franz?"

"He's as safe as we are."

The roar of engines came closer, almost overhead. Bombs fell quite close to us.

"I think it possible that formation of the Second Reich was not a good thing for Germany. It was a union forced by Prussia and still has to some extent the aura of Prussia about it. The real Germany, say the Rhineland or Swabia, the Secret Germany if you will, has yet to influence the soul of this new and somewhat artificial country."

Annalise smiled faintly. She knew from whom my ideas had come.

The bombs were coming quite close again, perhaps aimed at the gigantic flak tower in the Tiergarten. It was alleged to be impenetrable. Some nights there were more than thirty thousand people in it, not counting the men who operated the 88 mm cannon on its top.

If several large bombs hit it at the same time, there would be horrific casualties. Another great triumph for the Royal Air Force. Finally, the cacophony of plane engines, 88mm fire, exploding bombs, sirens, declined—slowly at first and then definitively. The tension lifted from our cozy shelter. People woke up, stretched, and stood up. There was another day ahead, another day of walking or riding by smoking ruins, checking on one's family, and friends, struggling on. And hoping that they survive the next night or the night after or the night after that on and on till the war ended, if it ever did.

Didn't the RAF wallahs remember how the stubborn people of London had stood up to the Luftwaffe blitz and actually became more stubborn in the process? Did they think that Germans were any different? Or did they believe if they killed more people than the Luftwaffe did, German morale would collapse? There were worse crimes in this war, but was not the indiscriminate killing of civilians also a war crime? Since the Allies are now certain to win the war, the leadership of the RAF will not be subject to trials. But can we call this justice? Will history think that it is justice?

That would go into my dispatch to Dublin before the day was out.

So there, Winston.

Franz drove us back to Charlottenburg. Animals from the destroyed zoo were wandering in the Tiergarten, the Prince William Church was in ruins. The Kepinski had vanished. Long blocks of the Kudamm had been devastated. All military targets?

"I am very grateful to you, Herr Ridgewood, for your invitation. It was a most interesting evening. I met very many nice people. I ate good food and drank good wine. I know the Irish are lucky people, so I felt safe with you when the raids began."

"And you did dance a little."

"Fortunately for me, with a very skilled dancer."

Dawn was turning into sunrise. Charlottenburg had been damaged seriously too. However, her tower still stood.

"Good! I still have a home. I must bathe and dress properly and return to the Luft Ministry."

I walked with her to the door of her building. She turned and kissed me, a sign that I was not to go up to the door of her room.

"A very lovely young woman, Herr Ambassador," Franz observed, "and a very nice one too."

"I had noticed that, Franz."

The BBC informed me that the RAF had made the largest raid yet, fourteen hundred planes had leveled large industrial areas of Berlin.

I wrote a passionate dispatch to the Ministry for External Affairs.

"The industry of Berlin, located mostly in the suburb as is the industry of Paris continues to hum, relatively undamaged by the RAF raid last night. Most of the bombs fell on a central swath across the city, where tens of thousands of people live, many thousands died, and many more are homeless. Also many of the animals at the Berlin zoo are dead or wandering around the park near the zoo where they will be dead tomorrow. It seems obvious that the Royal Air Force's goals in these raids is not to destroy industry but to kill people. It is successful in that goal. It killed many last night. How many more do they have to kill before they realize that such murder has no effect on Hitler or the Stormtroopers?"

I then filled in the rest of my thoughts on the subject, including the charge of war crimes, translated it into Irish, and fired it off.

I didn't imagine Winston would like it very much. I wasn't sure that my minister would like it either. However, he sent back a two-word minute.

"Brilliant altogether."

I had not written so passionately in any of my earlier dispatches. Why now?

Because I was in love with a woman who, for all her hesitation, was in love with me. I did not want to lose her to an errant Royal Air Force bomb.

I said a couple of Rosaries that night.

— 19 —

"SHE'S NOT going to die," Nuala insisted.

"Even if she survived," I said, "she'd be dead by now anyway."

"Dermot Michael Coyne, you have no romantic sense at all."

"Life is not a film on the Lifetime Channel," I said.

"Besides, she's not necessarily dead."

I calculated the numbers.

"She'd be almost ninety."

"A lot of people live that long."

"Is all of this fey knowledge like about Des?"

"No, it's just common sense—with maybe a touch of fey hunch in it."

"Where's the common sense?" I demanded.

"Give over, Dermot Michael! Your man is obviously in love with the
woman. He's not writing about a fading memory but about a living
woman. If she were dead or if he had lost her long ago, he wouldn't have

been capable of the book, would he now? We miss the dead, we miss them terribly, but we can't be humorously affectionate about them . . . And don't say that I've cheated and read ahead. I have a lot of faults, but would I be doing something like that?"

"Not all that many faults."

"Hmf!"

We were driving up to the distant regions of the Northwest Side, in Nuala's Lincoln Navigator with myself at the wheel. Me wife seemed to believe that the region around Crawford and Lawrence was some sort of outpost of civilization where we would need a tank to escape safely. I told her that it was the real Chicago and that River Forest and Lincoln Park West, our little enclaves, were not at all typical. The real Chicago, she insisted with no evidence, was "down below," her term for the Loop and the Mag Mile.

My poor wife was in a snit about Nelliecoyne. It had been a mistake, she insisted, to buy a digital camera and a printer for our eight-year-old. One genius is enough in a house. I requested clarity on who the other genius was. The problem was our daughter had the natural eye of a gifted photographer. She was now running wild taking pictures, some of them, as Nuala herself admitted, "brilliant altogether."

Two nights ago, the child had brought us two dozen of her photos, "the only ones worth looking at," she claimed.

"Are they any good, Da?" she asked me, which was a violation of the family protocol. You always asked the Ma first.

I worked my way carefully through the prints.

"This one of your baby brother and Johnnie Pete is marvelous, and the one with two doggies looking at the baby is wonderful."

"They adore him, Da, and he loves them."

Being a responsible husband and father, I quickly passed the prints into my wife's eagerly waiting hand. She gasped a couple of times as she inspected them.

"You have the eye, kid," I said. "It's a natural gift that many professional photographers would die for. Keep it up."

Nuala burst into tears and scooped up the eight-year-old in her arms.

Nelliecoyne responded as a girl child does to a mother when they both share the same wavelength—she sobbed too.

"They're marvelous, Hon. Isn't your poor da right like he always is! You have a lot of talent. I'm so proud of you."

Poor Da is always right, huh?

"The only one I don't like," the woman of the house continued, "is the one of meself nursing the little pest."

Nelliecoyne dismissed that complaint with a wave of her hand.

"You're only saying that, Ma, because you don't think you're that beautiful. You have to learn to accept that you're drop-dead gorgeous."

So saying, our daughter ran off, delighted with herself.

The words "learn to accept" were a direct quote from the little book of Nuala Anne, the unwritten rules in our house for child rearing. My wife was getting her own back.

"Where did she pick up 'drop-dead gorgeous,'" I said. "Mind you 'tis true."

"It's a Madonna and Child picture." My wife sighed. "She's seen too many of them over in that school. I'm not the Mother of God and the little punk certainly is not God and there's no mystical glow in me eyes. Besides there's too much boob in it."

"You know better than that, Nuala Anne McGrail. A nursing mother is a metaphor of God's maternal love for us. Haven't you been reading my poems?"

"Still too much boob."

I glanced at the offending print.

"I'd say it needs a little bit more boob."

"Wouldn't you be saying that?" She tapped my arm lightly in mock disapproval, an improvement over the solid punch with which she used to show affection.

I didn't realize that we had a full-blown family crisis on our hands until that night as we cuddled in bed, after I had amused myself by playing with her aforementioned boobs at some considerable length, accompanied by her squeals of delight, as a prelude to more advanced amusements.

"What are we going to do about our little girl, still?"

"I thought she has calmed down lately," I said half-asleep.

"I mean Nelliecoyne and herself a friggin' genius."

"We encourage her but don't push her. It's likely to be a phase, but if it isn't, so much the better. She can support us in our old age."

"I'm serious, Dermot Michael."

POST-COITAL SERIOUS DISCUSSIONS ARE NOT NATURAL.

Too right.

"'Tis a terrible thing altogether to be a parent."

"I agree."

"We can't tell her that her pitchers are no good because that would be a lie, wouldn't it?"

In Irish English the words for a photograph and for a receptacle from which one pours a liquid sound exactly the same.

"And it is what happens in some Irish families to prevent a talented child from getting a big head."

"Too true, Dermot love. But won't she neglect her schoolwork and make all her little friends envious and won't she drive people out of their minds and herself pestering them with her friggin' camera."

"As for the little friends, many of them well on their way to nastiness, she has already proved that she can deal with them like a precinct captain. She'll snap pitchers of them that are flattering. Our daughter can take care of herself."

"I donno, Dermot Michael, she'll be a teen in four more years."

"And will be as bossy as her ma."

"I'm SERIOUS, Dermot."

"I understand. A little kid might freak out with her new skill. We'll have to watch closely to see if that starts happening. But, to be fair, our Nelliecoyne is not the sort of child who freaks out."

"'Tis true." She sighed. "It's a problem still . . . You can go to sleep now, Dermot love."

"I already have."

Nonetheless, my wife continued to fret for the next several days and hence had to finish catching up to the Stauffenberg story as I drove the tank to the Northwest Side.

"Why didn't you tell me that this was such a nice little community, Dermot and all these nice shops and these friendly people on the streets?"

"And with every skin color under heaven . . . This is your typical Chicago neighborhood."

Tariq was a man about forty with graying hair and a paunch which suggested a sedentary life rather than too much beer. His face, not as dark as our friends Joseph and Mary, was lined with sadness. He was courteous to us but he did not smile.

"First of all," my wife began the conversation, "our daughter has become a camera enthusiast. She didn't ask for it, but I think we ought to get her one of them printers which will do eight-by-ten prints, something simple that you don't have to be a genius to operate."

"A man in my business is always happy," he said in a melancholy voice, "to hear about a new camera lover."

They picked out an appropriate printer and the paper to use with it.

"Will she need software to use with the printer?"

My wife had not the faintest idea what the question meant. She glanced at the family's computer expert. I nodded.

"Certainly. What would you recommend?"

"There are many different kind of software programs that are popular. They range from simple to moderately complex. This program"—he held up a box—"is somewhere in the middle. If the young woman is skilled at computer use, I would recommend it."

Again I tilted my head. It was nice to play a useful role.

Our merchant was an honest man. He didn't try to sell us high-end equipment, though he doubtless knew he could.

Herself paid with her own credit card. I leaned on my spear. She insisted on showing the merchant the print of Patjo and the doggies.

He raised an eyebrow.

"She is very talented. She is perhaps sixteen?"

"Half that."

The eyebrow went up again.

"We merchants need more children like that."

Again he did not smile. Had he lost family, a wife and children perhaps, in Iraq? Gunned down by trigger-happy soldiers?

Then herself got down to business while I continued to lean on my spear.

"We want to talk to you about our young friend Desmond. We don't want to know any secrets. We already have evidence from Turkish Air that he flew from Chicago to Ankara and then to Kars. We assume that he walked along the mountains to free Kurdistan in Iraq. We think you might have helped him."

"That part of the world is very wild and dangerous, ma'am. The map says it is in Turkey, but it has never been really under Turkish control. The Russians occupied it during the First War. There are Kurds and Russians and Armenians and Georgians and Chechens up in those mountains and they all hate one another. If Noah's ark really landed there, then they must have built the Tower of Babel in the same place . . . I beg you, madam, do not even think of going there."

"No way."

Tariq, clearly an intelligent man with a strong sense of irony, spoke in a low, emotionless monotone.

"Most of the people, especially in the southern end of the mountains, are Kurds. They will never accept Turkish rule. Thus far the Turks will not discuss even limited autonomy, though it may be a price they will have to pay for membership in the EU. Of all the hates in those mountains, none is stronger than that between the Kurds and the Turks, except perhaps between the Armenians and the Turks. Although I am Assyrian, I was born in those mountains. No one hates the Assyrians because we are too few to matter. That was true in Iraq until the Americans came and the religious fanatics began to hate the Assyrians because they are infidels. The mountains are very beautiful. However, I much prefer Chicago."

"Galway Bay is beautiful too," Nuala commented, "but I too much prefer Chicago."

"There are groups of bandits up in those mountains that band to-gether regardless of their religion or ethnicity for their own protection and for their own livelihood, something like the Mafia in Sicily, I sup-pose. They are, however, more honorable than the Mafia, they keep their word. And also more ruthless. I know some of the men in one of these groups. I grew up with them, some are my relatives. When Assyrians in this country want to bring out their relatives in Iraq or Iran, my friends bring them out. I pay my friends and the relatives pay me. With the dan-gers in Iraq increasing for Christians, there is more of a demand for, such ah, transfers. I make no money on it, this I swear . . ."

"We believe you," my wife assured him.

"So far they have never failed me. Everyone they have contracted to bring to Kars has arrived safely. After that the relatives must arrange for the plane fare and get them safely into another country. Your Homeland Secu-rity people try to stop us, but they do not even know how to begin. I assure you, madam, sir, we Assyrians have had seven thousand years of practice in deceiving governments. No one is better than us at this activity."

"We Irish are probably high on the list," Nuala said. "Trouble is it be-comes a habit and we deceive even our friends."

True enough.

"So your young friend Desmond comes here to buy some materials for his computer that he sees in the window. He speaks fluent Arabic. The accent is African because he was in the Peace Corps in Ethiopia. He knows all the little nuances and the allusions that would mark him as a pious Muslim. He tells me, however, that he is Irish Catholic. I should have known that. He is so charming, though sometimes I do not under-stand what he is saying."

"We never say what we mean or mean what we say."

I continued to lean on my spear.

"Yes. That is it. He says a few words to me in our language, Aramaic, which is the language Jesus spoke, as I'm sure you know. He tells me that he will soon have a doctorate in Eastern languages and he wants to learn our language. He even speaks a few words. He asks about our monaster-ies. The Church of the East, he says, had many monasteries in Persia and

Afghanistan and India and even China when your St. Patrick was bringing religion to Ireland. I am not an especially religious man. I believe in
God because all we Assyrians do, but I have never had an opportunity to
study religion. He tells me that we are the last remnant of the Church
of the East. He wants to spend some time in one of the remaining
monasteries. I tell him I don't know of any. Well, someone has told him
that there is one in Mosul. He has charmed me into admitting that I
know ways to get people out of Iraq. He asks if I can get him into Mosul.
I tell him that there will be a war and it is quite impossible. He persists.
I should have refused, but he is so charming . . . Even as I talk about it, I
feel guilty. It is true, I tell him, that he speaks Arabic well enough and
knows Islam well enough that he could deceive people for a time. But it
would be very dangerous. He begs me, he has the money. My friends are
always ready to help. I agree. They say that they delivered him safely to
Mosul and even that they enjoyed traveling with him. I suppose he is
dead now. He was a fine young man. I am sorry."

"He's not dead, at all, at all," Nuala assured him. "Thank you very
much, Tariq. We will keep this conversation confidential. I myself have
had trouble with the Department of Homeland Insecurity too. God bless
your work."

He made the sign of the Cross.

I shook hands with him, picked up Nelliecoyne's printer, lifted my
spear, and followed herself out into the dull sunlight, filtered through disapproving clouds.

Herself was in a buoyant mood.

"Look at this street, Dermot love, all the different restaurants. We
must try them out. Don't we spend too much of our time in the narrow
world down below."

She's not being ironic.

Don't bet on that.

"Won't I be driving us home?"

She reached out for the keys to our M1A3 tank.

"Will you give that printer to Nelliecoyne?"

"Why else would I buy it?"

"But won't that encourage her to waste a lot of precious time and become a nuisance?"

"Our sweet little Nelliecoyne a nuisance? Give over, Dermot Michael! She has the talent and we should encourage her so that she knows we are on her side."

Right!

With her usual skills and finding her way around, she steered us back to the Kennedy Expressway and towards the closed world down below. I didn't tell her that she might want to take Lake Shore Drive. Save that for the next time.

"Well, I was right all along, wasn't I?"

"Yes, ma'am."

"We know exactly where Des is."

"Was."

"And we know what he's doing."

"Learning Aramaic and charming people."

"And we will get in touch with him and see if he wants to come home—just like your man in Berlin wants to take his Annalise home."

"Des will have an Assyrian bride on his arm when we extract him?"

She thought about that.

"I don't think so."

"So all we have to do is find a way to talk to him."

"You must learn to be patient, Dermot love. One step at a time."

She's not being ironic.

The hell she's not.

The kids and the dogs charged into the house when school let out, Ethne, proud of her huge diamond ring, in command.

"Nelliecoyne!" me wife called out. "Come here this minute!"

"Yes, Ma," the young woman replied, not troubled by Ma's preemptory summons.

"Your da thinks that you're so skilled with your pitcher taking that you should have a printer to make enlargements and the software necessary for . . ."

"Cropping," the da said.

Ma's statement was pure fiction. It was her idea to use a better printer as a ploy for dealing with Tariq. Da, however, went along with the fiction.

"Hooray!" Nelliecoyne clapped her hands and jumped up and down.

"However," Nuala continued to speak in her sternest of tones, "there is one condition. You must absolutely finish ALL your homework before you begin to play with these things. Is that understood?"

"Och, Ma, would I ever neglect me homework and meself a responsible and mature young person!"

I produced the gifts.

"Like totally cool! How did you know to pick the perfect stuff! Thank you, Ma!"

And then as if in afterthought, "Thank you, Da!"

She could have carried the whole charade off if she hadn't giggled.

"I'll get started on my homework, so I will have all day tomorrow to print my pitchers. Course, don't I always have me homework finished by Friday evening?"

"Stop laughing, Dermot Michael Coyne!"

"Am I laughing?"

"You are inwardly. Stop it."

Then, after some consideration, she added, "That one knows how to kill her parents with responsibility. She'll be the death of us still."

"Woman, she will not."

"Won't I go upstairs now and feed me poor starving baby!"

"Nuala Anne, you'll just have to learn that the child sees right through us and loves us just the same."

"Hmf!"

The next morning we were sitting in "our" office as Nuala tried to think of a way to get in touch with Des. She wasn't making much progress. Nelliecoyne arrived with an eight-by-ten print held against her chest.

"I'm having a little trouble using the new printer, so I do proofs on plain paper before I waste a sheet of the good paper. This is the first one that turned out kind of all right."

"How frugal of you," Nuala said, glaring at me so I would stop my interior laughter.

She turned over the print and revealed, not to my surprise, the image of a mother nursing her baby. The cropping was exquisite.

"See, Ma, we see the mystical glow in your eyes as you feed the poor little punk. God adores us even before we adore God."

Nuala Anne, to give her full credit, resisted the temptation to assert for the record that she was not a mystic.

"The Ma behind Ma," I said.

"You have the right of it, Da."

Nuala's always ready floodgate of tears opened and the tears streamed down her face.

"Hon, I'm so proud of you. It's wonderful! And so are you!"

After our daughter scampered away, me wife said, "Fair play to you, Dermot Michael, you were right all along. You can laugh at me publicly now."

"I'd never do that, wife. It's no fun. I'd much rather laugh at you behind your back and yourself knowing that I'm doing it."

We went back on Sunday to Old Saint Patrick's Church where Nuala reprised some of her Easter hymns. Her current platinum recording was *Nuala Anne Sings for Spring Festivals*, a combination of Catholic, Protestant, and Jewish Passover songs with an Islamic hymn thrown in for good measure. She even wore a veil over her head when she sang the Muslim hymn. I told the pastor at OSP that he owed us a fee for the performance and he said that we owed him a fee for the public relations value. He laughed when he said it because herself was one of their top contributors—though it was none of my business how much she gave and I never asked.

We went back in the rain to our house on Sheffield Avenue to read the papers and relax because, "After all, it's still a day of rest and them awful NFL games over."

I was deputed to read the "funnies" to the children with my older daughter assisting in the womanly voices.

The phone rang. No one answered it, so I played my usual role of backup switchboard operator.

"Dermot Coyne."

"Hi, Dermot, it's Megan Kim. Cardinal Cronin wants to talk to herself."

Me wife was sleeping on our bed, her child cuddled up next to her.

"Wake up, woman, isn't your man on the phone?"

"Which man?" A clear violation of the Irish rule that you have to guess who your man is.

"His Eminence Sean Cardinal Cronin, Archbishop of Chicago."

"Glory be to God and meself sleeping. You take it downstairs and I'll talk to him from here . . . And you be quiet, small child, do ya hear. Won't your ma be talking to a Cardinal Prince of the Holy Catholic Church."

Our son continued to sleep, notably unimpressed.

I picked up the phone in the parlor, just in time to hear her say, in her best Dublin Irish, "Nuala Anne McGrail Coyne."

The addition of "Coyne" was a new gimmick.

"Hi, Nuala, Megan Kim here. Cardinal Sean would like a brief word with you."

There were four Megans who acted as porter persons at the Cathedral rectory.

"Hi, Nuala." The Cardinal's rich baritone voice was on the line. "I hate to bother you on a Sunday, but I have some news about your good friend Desmond Doolin. Incidentally, my spies tell me that you were like totally cool at the parish this morning."

"I did me best, but haven't the childer worn me out altogether!"

"How is the youngest?"

"Fat and sassy, just like his da."

"I hope that your handsome and gifted spouse is on the line."

"He is."

"Hi, Dermot."

"Hi, Cardinal."

GET OUR SPEAR, ME BUCKO, YOU'VE GOT MORE LISTENING TO DO.

Got it.

"I have some very interesting news for you. My brother bishop, the nuncio to Iraq and a notorious anti-American, has dodged and weaved and equivocated. So I put my Coadjutor, Archbishop Ryan, whom I believe you know, on the case. The good Blackwood, who has a very low tolerance for bullshit, forced the admission that there was an American monk up in Mosul who was 'singularizing' himself by meddling in political affairs, by which Blackie took it to mean making peace every time there was a bad situation up there. That sound like your friend, Des?"

"Exactly."

"He says that he fears an incident in which Shiite activists might blow him up and the whole monastery with him. He didn't say how many monks were in the monastery, didn't seem to care. He said that such an incident would be very bad for the Church. To which Blackwood replied that doubtless it would be bad for the monks too."

"Sounds like him."

"Is this kid as good as he seems, Nuala Anne?"

"He is astonishing, Cardinal Sean. And himself speaking Arabic and Aramaic—that's Jesus own language—and Akkadian and . . . Dermot?"

I stirred from supporting my spear.

"Tigre, that's an Ethiopian language. Also Eritrean."

"And understanding all the history of the Church of the East and also practically a doctor in Arab language and literature. And a peacemaker too."

"Blessed are the peacemakers, as Blackwood says, for they shall be shot at from both sides . . . Look, I don't want to stand in the way of the Holy Spirit, but with all the people from the Middle East pouring into Chicago I need a point man. If you talk to him, tell him he's got a job with me when he comes back."

"Did you get his phone number?"

"Blackwood says that the monastery does not have a phone and that while the Bishop of Mosul does have one he wouldn't be of much help. I don't know if they do cell phones up there, though I guess the American military has them. They probably don't have e-mail either."

"Och, won't we find him and bring him back to Chicago where he belongs? Won't we, Dermot?"

"Woman, we will."

I didn't even bother changing the spear for that comment.

"Well, then see to it, Nuala Anne. Stay in touch with Blackwood. Bye, Dermot. Take good care of her."

"I do my best."

He laughed his boisterous West Side Irish voice and hung up.

"All right, Dermot Michael Coyne, give me your damn spear. How do we learn his address?"

"Well, we don't ask Jenny because she's bound to secrecy. Do you still have Siobhan's phone number?"

"Cell phone. Isn't she a child of the twenty-first century too?"

We found Shovie in her apartment studying for her final exam.

"That's a good idea, Nuala. Des couldn't live without the Internet. Congratulations!"

"Me man thought it up!"

"Tell Mr. Coyne, I said congratulations."

Mr. Coyne, I felt like saying, is me da.

'Twas ever thus. Nuala was one of them. I belonged to the older generation.

"He changed his address often to avoid pests. But it was always some variation of Des or Desmond and Dizzy. Like Dizdes or Desdiz. He always used AOL, said he could no more give it up than leave the Church. He's still alive then? Didn't they have a memorial service for him?"

"Didn't his mother want closure?"

"She would, poor woman."

Me wife bounded off her bed.

"Let's go, Dermot, we have work to do."

"Woman, not till you do your exercise and have a cup of tea. I don't want you coming down with a migraine."

"I don't get migraines."

"You will if you don't stop thinking too much."

So she did her exercises, drank a glass of iced tea, and prepared tea for the mob—ham and Swiss on rye with the crusts cut off the way they are in Ireland.

There was also milk and iced tea and ice cream for dessert. Nuala does not hold with child-rearing practices which prohibit ice cream.

"We found him, Dermot, and isn't he alive and acting like himself."

"As we knew all along."

After the children were safely asleep, we sat at my computer and began to hunt for Des. The process was slow despite my broadband link and high-end computer. We used the same message: "Hiya, Des, What's happening?"

Then we sent it out under each successive address we were able to cook up—all at AOL:

Dizdes, Desdiz, Desthedis, Dezdediz, Dizzydes, Desdizz.

The sending party was on Nuala's account mgmpa—McGrail, Marie Phinoulah Annagh.

Each time the system bounced the message, telling us with austere haughtiness that there was no such member and asking us to correct the address. Nuala departed for a moment and returned with the bottle of Middleton's we keep for special occasions and two Irish crystal tumblers.

"Isn't this to prevent migraine headaches?"

"Does it work?"

"It deals, Dermot love, with every human problem."

We tried every variant of everything we knew about Desmond David Doolin—Loyola Academy, Marquette University, Chicago, Illinois.

We were interrupted by a wailing baby. Nuala went to feed him. He was decisively not hungry. She changed his diaper. That didn't help. Both doggies appeared in alarm.

"Sing some lullabies to the little monster," I suggested.

The little monster wailed more loudly. The doggies glared at me reproachfully.

Nuala began to sing. The sound of her voice calmed him down enough so that he decided that maybe he would take a little food. "Maybe there's enough of the crayture in me milk to put him to sleep."

However, he decided that he'd had enough mother's milk laced with whiskey and closed his eyes, however tentatively.

Nuala continued to croon. My rival relaxed in her arms. She tiptoed into the nursery, the pooches followed stealthily. Nuala returned. "The poor little guy just wanted some attention, like men always do."

"Aren't you spoiling him rotten?"

"Give over, Dermot, I'm just providing unconditional love."

We returned to our task. AOL seemed annoyed with our ineptitude because it periodically shut down.

"Tomorrow is another day," I said.

"We gotta find him, Dermot Michael."

"We're not going to find him tonight."

"We might try to talk to Jenny."

"Bad idea."

That was that.

"I can't see the frigging screen anymore."

"It's a twenty-four-inch screen."

"I don't care if it's a twenty-four-foot screen," she fired back, "aren't me eyes blurring?"

"You should have used your reading glasses."

"I only need them when I'm readin'."

"That's what you were doing."

"I don't care. I'm going to bed."

When my Nuala Anne crashes, she like totally crashes.

I turned off the computer and joined her in bed. She was dead to the world, totally. Not that I was much better off. I fell into the land of Nod before my head hit the pillow.

Then, much latter, I woke with a start. I had an idea in my dream. Des was marching with a huge band of monks into a monastery that looked like Cluny. That's silly, I told myself. Cluny is in France. Des is in Iraq or Kurdistan or whatever.

I struggled out of bed, careful not to wake my wife, and stumbled into the office. I booted up the computer, waited impatiently for it come alive, then demanded attention from AOL which came slowly. Finally I sent our message to DESMONK.

AOL insisted that it knew no such person.

Damn! It was such a good idea.

I DO MY BEST TO HELP YOU.

Shut up, this has nothing to do with you.

Then I knew for sure the right address.

DESMUNK.

AOL accepted the message.

There was someone out there in virtual reality who thought that was a cool name.

What time was it over there? Let's see, early afternoon, maybe.

Then the computer told me that I had mail. I almost opened it. Then I realized that this better be a joint enterprise.

"Nuala," I shouted.

No answer. So I bellowed again, at the risk of an awakened baby.

"Dermot, are you all right?"

She appeared at the door of the office in a splendid state of dishabille.

"I've got a response!"

She darted back into the bedroom and reemerged instantly with a throw around her shoulders.

"Lemme see! . . . DESMUNK . . . You're a friggin' genius! What does he say!"

"You know I never open your mail, even when there's money in it!"

She eased me out of the chair and opened the mail.

She shifted into the instant message utility that she often used to talk to her own ma or her siblings around the world.

— 20 —

On June 6 the Brits and the Yanks landed in Normandy. As usual, Montgomery was one day late and then a month late before he achieved the assigned positions. The Brits thought he was a brilliant hero. Everyone else, including German intelligence, knew he would always be at least a day late. The Germans had been caught by surprise by a make-believe army under Patton's command and by constant "leaks" from Brit intelligence about a landing in the Pas de Calais. The Americans, however, were surprised by the accidental concentration of two divisions, one withdrawing and one replacing, near their landing at Omaha Beach. There were heavy American losses.

Or so Admiral Canaris told me during one of our now long and hard-fought chess matches the day after the landings.

"How long will it last, do you think?" he asked me while pondering a move.

"Less than a year. You have no more men to fight, only old-timers and Hitler youth. Hitler has destroyed the Wehrmacht."

"Ja, the Americans will fight Blitzkrieg style. They'll be on or near the

Rhine by Christmas and then on the Elbe by April. They will leave Berlin to the Russians."

Even though he was no longer director of the Abwehr, he still went into his office every day.

"Most of it I pick up from their faces."

The dull roar above us signaled the inevitable return of the RAF. An air raid siren wailed. The admiral and I always ignored it. Now that I had a woman to worry about I felt guilty. Yet, as Canaris said, we would all die sooner or later, a notion which correlated with the fatalist component of my Irish soul.

"Damn fools have bad maps if they bomb Gruenwald again. They will spoil lovely houses and miss the machine tools and the railroads."

"And the Widerstand?"

"Young Claus is a great leader. There could be no better. Only it is too late, much too late. The evil has already been done to Germany."

"You think they will fail?"

He moved a knight and looked up at me.

"If they kill Hitler, they have a chance. However, I think it is written in the stars that only the Russians or the Americans can kill him. Or perhaps Himmler. Should they win, they still have to make peace. That will be very difficult. The Red Army smells Berlin, blood and rapine, and will not be satisfied until it drinks the last dregs of victory here. Check."

There was a tremor in his hands as he moved his queen. The poor old man was losing it.

I made the move I had been planning in response to his.

"Check," I said.

"You Irish are diabolically clever."

"Then how come we moved next to England? And if they don't kill Hitler? If, as Claus says, the Antichrist continues to protect his own?"

"Then many of us will die, perhaps thousands. I will be one, so will Beck, Leber, Gordeler, Pastor Bonhoeffer, Tresckow, perhaps that young blond woman who compiles all the plans, Claus and his brother of course. Not you. You are far too clever. You combine recklessness with ingenuity. Irish trait I suppose."

The 88s were firing very near to us. Bombs were falling even closer.

He moved his queen again.

"Checkmate," I said.

The next bomb seemed to explode just down the street.

"Damn," he murmured. "Someday your Irish cleverness will destroy you, though I hope not."

The bombs stopped falling and the 88s were quiet. He emptied the winebottle into my glass. The all clear sounded weakly.

"They will be back, Timothy. You'd better go home."

"Ja, ja, Herr Admiral . . . For the sake of history, did you tell them that the landing would be in Normandy?"

"Only to confirm their choice of the Pas de Calais. No one but a fool would have thought that it wasn't Normandy."

We shook hands as I left the gracious old house.

"We will meet again, Herr Ambassador. I don't know where or when. But we will meet in happier times."

"Ja, ja, Herr Admiral."

"It will of course not be in this world," he said, laughing sardonically as I walked down the footpath.

"We have a saying in my country that wherever old comrades meet it is always this world."

I don't know whether he heard me or not.

I found my way to the S-Bahn and rode back to the Friedrichstrasse. Blazing ruins lined the Speyer River and then vanished in the darkness. There were fires on my own street too. However, the Irish embassy had been spared. My passports, revolvers, map, and letters from Claus were still safe.

The bombings continue, I wrote in my dispatch. Berlin continues to survive. Life goes on. Many Berliners who understand military matters say that the war will be over within a year as the Americans and the Russians lock Germany in a vise and squeeze. No one knows for sure how the Americans will fight, they say. One more lesson of 1918 that is forgotten. Some people are whispering that the more of Germany the Americans occupy the better will be the fate of Germany.

The next day I met Claus at a Weingarten just off the Potsdamer Platz. Most of the buildings on the little street were in ruins.

"Well," he said, his face taut and grim, "I spent the last three days out at the Wolf's Lair in East Prussia with the Führer."

"An exciting time, I imagine."

"You can't imagine how ugly it is," he burst out as soon as were seated. "A scattering of huts, some concrete, some wooden, in a setting of scrub trees and rocks. I wonder why the Russians or the English don't bomb it. I can't imagine that they don't know where it is. There are usually some Me-109s in the air above. From the air it probably looks unimportant. It feels decadent. Goering is there, of course, where Hitler, who no longer trusts him, can keep an eye on him. The smell of his cologne fills the concrete hut where the remnants of the OKW meets every day. They are all servile and sycophantic Keitel, Jodl, Zessler. The dregs of the General Staff.

"They tell the Führer only what he wants to hear, not what he needs to know. I am presented to him as the chief of staff of the Home Army, he nods and stares at me, the hypnotic expression that frightens most of those whom he meets for the first time. It frightens me, but I don't drop my eyes. I know I am looking into the eyes of the Antichrist. I say an Ave Maria to fight off the evil. He looks away. I win. Worthless victory.

" 'Where were you wounded, Colonel?'

" 'Tunisia, by the Americans, my Führer.'

" 'They are not very good fighters, not like my brave German soldiers.'

"I realized that was a compliment, so I nod, and say 'They learn quickly, my Führer.' "

Claus falls into silence, his dark eyes deeply troubled.

"Sorry for exploding at you." He smiles and is himself once again. "You can't imagine the shock of realization that the fate of the German nation is in the hands of these degenerates. Goering is just barely conscious. He can survive a day only by filling his veins with narcotics. The others are corrupt and know they are corrupt. Yet they hunger for a word of approval from Hitler and cower at his hostile stare. The building stinks with fear. I could remove my Luger and kill him on the spot. But we are not yet ready."

"When will you be ready, Claus?"

"July 1 is our target day . . . Timmy, the Führer is half-dead already. He is bent over, one of his arms does not seem to work, he blinks constantly, he smells of defeat. His face is twisted from terrible headaches. His mistress, Eva Braun, is not permitted at the Wolf's Lair because sex is forbidden. Naturally you can't forbid sex to men like that. Even the Führer flies back to Tempelhoff periodically. No one knows if he and Eva have sex. Or even if he is capable of it anymore. Or ever was."

"A long way from Friedrich der Grosse."

"Ja, ja. It would be so easy to kill him, Timmy. Yet none of the plots have succeeded. Why should I think I am the one who will be able to kill the Antichrist?"

I always became uneasy when Claus talked about the Antichrist. We Irish believe in fairy forts and pookas and banshees and other wicked or ambivalent folk. But a creature of cosmic evil . . . That's a little much for us. Yet if there was or could be such a being, it might well be Adolf Hitler.

"You laid out a plan to dispose of him?"

"It would be absurdly easy. The Führer has usually been obsessive about his personal safety, as well he might be. But the situation out there in East Prussia is remarkably lax. The Russians or the English could land a parachute regiment and destroy the place in a single day. I don't know why they don't do it."

"Probably they don't believe it would be as easy as you say."

"I would fly out there with one assistant. We would have a dispatch case with two shells in it. In one of the latrines we would activate the ignition liquid. I would go into the headquarters building and put the dispatch case under the table, wait ten minutes and then leave. The explosion would kill everyone in the room. We would fly back to Tempelhof and activate Operation Valkyrie."

"Sounds easy, Claus, but I don't like it. Too easy. And too risky. You're the leader of the Rising. If you get killed, it's all over."

"No choice, Tim. No choice. We must take the risks. If I fail, I will be blamed for the deaths of others. I hope their widows will forgive me and that God will forgive me."

Then our conversation turned to Nina and the children and the good times we had enjoyed during my all-too-brief visits. Nina was doing well in her sixth pregnancy and happily expecting her child. He was for a few brief moments the delightful young man I had met in Heidelberg.

As we rose to leave the table, he said to me, "If the worst happens you will take care of Aunt Hannah."

"Everything is prepared," I said. "I will save her or die trying."

"Ja, ja, that is good. I will let you know the day before."

We shook hands.

"You have been one of the great graces in my life, Timmy."

What does an Irishman say to that?

I quote without attribution the words of Admiral Canaris.

"We will meet again, Claus. There will be better times and better places. If not in this world then in another."

I'm not happy with those words, but they were the best I could do.

I invited Annalise to supper at the Adlon.

She accepted.

"If I say no to your invitation, Herr Ridgewood, I will have to call you back and apologize. However, I will meet you there and return to Charlottenburg on the U-Bahn. You should not be seen with me near my apartment."

I did not argue.

It was a pleasant enough meal. She had put on her comic mask, which meant that she made gentle fun of me.

"Ja, it is good to take supper with a rich Irisher. I eat where I would never dream of eating. If I did this often I would become very gross. I cannot resist temptation."

"I'm not rich, Annalise."

"Surely you are. I'm sure the Irish government cannot afford to pay for all your expenses . . . That lovely Benz you drive."

"It's an old car, Annalise. Moreover, the government of the Free State insists that the only women who ride with me be beautiful blondes."

"You must have found many of those in Berlin."

And so it went, an evening of bantering and laughter in which I was hardly the winner.

After we left the Adlon, I walked with her to the U-Bann and kissed her good night at the entrance to the station.

"Good night, Annalise. Be careful."

The air raid warning siren on the Platz started to wail.

"Good night, Herr Ridgewood." She was leaning against me and trembling. "You take care of yourself."

She thinks that she will never see me again. She expects to die. I may have to talk her out of that.

On June 29 Claus called me late one night as I was listening to the BBC reporting a very different version of the Normandy situation than Berlin radio.

"July 15," he said crisply, and hung up.

The next day I gave Franz and Magda three months' pay in Swiss marks and told them to return to their home in the Schwartzwald until I notified them to return.

They thanked me and asked no questions. I then filled the gas tanks and hooked up the auxiliary tanks I had hidden in the basement of the embassy. I also packed into the trunk enough dry food to last us for the days it would take to drive to Basle. Fruit and milk would wait till the day before the Rising—as I always thought of it.

A week later, Claus called again.

"July 19 or 20, depending on the weather. I have been to confession."

Claus had told me once that, while he was a Catholic, he did not believe in such things as confession. Now, faced with death, he did. He had also insisted that he had never been unfaithful to Nina. That I did not doubt.

I walked over to the Foreign Office, showed my credentials, and went to the desk for diplomats. I gave the clerk the undated minute I had cajoled out of my minister before we had left Dublin. The clerk stamped both passports several times, and said, "I should see if the Reichsminister wants to speak to you. He is very busy, but he would not want to seem rude to such a distinguished diplomat."

Yes, he did want to see me. I had anticipated such a summons.

"Herr Ridgewood, it is good to see you again, especially on such a happy day for the Reich."

"Ah?"

I had learned the rhetoric of the regime long ago. He meant that a new official line had developed to account for the bad news.

"Yes, the brave soldiers of the Wehrmacht have won great victories on both fronts. In the east we have driven the Bolsheviks back towards Warsaw, which we expect to recapture any day now and in the west we have sealed the Americans back in their beachhead, which is now quite precarious."

Bullshite, I thought to myself.

"I'm sorry that I must return to Dublin before August 1. I would like to be present in Berlin when these victories come to full fruition. However, I can assure you that Ireland intends to sustain its embassy here permanently."

True enough.

"I understand, Herr Ambassador, I understand. To facilitate your journey I have written a letter of passage for you."

He rose from his desk, walked over to me, and handed me a letter and an envelope. I folded the letter and put it in the envelope.

"Please read it, Herr Ambassador."

It was handwritten. It confirmed that I was the accredited Ambassador to the Third Reich of the Republic of Ireland and was traveling under the special protection not only of the Reichsminister but also of the Führer himself. Everything possible should be done to facilitate the journey of the Herr Ambassador and his wife.

His signature filled half the page.

"Thank you, Herr Reichsminister. This will surely help us in our journey in the present troubled times."

"Sit down for just a few moments, Herr Ambassador."

I knew what was coming and had my answers prepared.

"These are very troubled times for Germany, Herr Ambassador. It is time, I believe, to reach out to the West in a search for peace which will satisfy all legitimate desires of the countries involved. I have had some communications with the American intelligence people in Berne. If you would not find it inconvenient, I would ask you to continue the conversation, Herr Ambassador."

"I stand ready to be of any assistance to the cause of peace."

"The Führer is a very tired man. I believe that he is willing to step down in the name of peace. My colleagues and I are ready to accept a return to the borders of 1939 and sign nonaggression pacts among all the nations involved."

This was certainly audacious from the man whose nonaggression pact signed with Molotov in Moscow had led to the dismemberment of Poland.

"Including Poland?"

"Naturally!"

He didn't even blush.

"And the Sudeten?"

"If necessary . . ."

"Herr Reichsminister, I am asking only the questions I will be asked."

"Naturally, Herr Ambassador. I understand."

"And the criminal elements in some agencies of the Reich?"

"Believe me, Herr Ambassador, I will rest more easily than most Germans at their elimination."

"Finally, I must ask, because I will be asked, about the Endlösung."

"Naturally you must ask. I will say that I opposed the 'Final Solution' from the beginning and will be delighted to bring it to an end as soon as possible."

"Thank you Herr Reichsminister for your candour. I believe that I can present an accurate picture of your position to the Americans in Berne."

We shook hands; his was wet as it well might be.

The dirty son of a bitch, I said to myself, as I walked back to the embassy. He's selling out everyone in the cause of his own political power. Yet all the others would do the same thing.

His surrender terms are virtually the same as those of the Widerstand. But there's no way he can deliver on them, while if Claus is successful, he will be able to deliver.

I would pass on the terms to the Americans, should they be interested. Then it would be their problem about the millions of lives which might be saved if such a deal could be cut.

On July 20 I finished packing the car. All it needed for us to leave for Switzerland was Annalise in the car with me.

It rained on the nineteenth.

I had not slept for several nights. I thought I had calculated all the possibilities. But the great imponderable was Annalise. How could I reach her if the Rising failed? Would she call me? If not, how would I find her?

— 21 —

Who are you, what do you want, how did you find me?

I'm Nuala Anne. I'm a detective and I figured it out. Jenny didn't tell me. My husband who is a genius guessed your Internet name. I want to know whether you think it might be time to come home.

Why would a beautiful popular singer need to be a detective?

To make ends meet.

Blarney.

'Tis true, but you're pretty good at that stuff yourself.

'Tis true too . . . My parents hire you?

They did, but didn't they fire me, right before the memorial service Jenny told you about, like she told you about our interview with her.

I used to play basketball with your husband. He's a big guy and strong and bright. Nice man.

'Tis true, but besides the point.

Marquette.

Again besides the point.

I forget what the point is.

Whether you want to come home to Chicago.

I think the other monks here would like to get rid of me, but are too polite to say so. They say there's a contract out on me. They say it's time to go home.

So are they right?

Could be. I never did want to be a monk, though I've learned a lot from them.

Course not. You want to be a parish priest in the Archdiocese of Chicago.

You're one of the dark ones?

Sometimes.

From halfway around the world?

You know that has nothing to do with it.

'Tis true.

I could get a deal for you. Pick up a few markers.

How long you been in Chicago?

Ten years.

Who can you pick up the markers from?

Whom.

All right, whom.

Cardinal Sean, Archbishop Blackie.

Why?

Cardinal Sean thinks he needs a "point man" to work with Middle Eastern immigrants and Muslims. He figures you'd be good at the job. He doesn't know about the parish priest bit, but he'll like that even more.

You have the authority to make that offer? No, don't answer that. It's a dumb question . . . Is Dermot there?

Certainly.

Hi, Dermot.

Hi, Dez.

I suppose that I'd have to go to the seminary for a couple of years? Probably be a good idea.

They know how to deal.

Dermot, does she talk with the brogue?

All the way from West Galway to Trinity College, depending on the game she's playing. What's it like over there?

Up here it's pretty good. A lot of professional people come up here for vacations from Baghdad. The Kurds are good at security. Not many Sunnis around. You move down to Kirkut you've got more trouble. The Kurds are driving out the Shiites that Saddam planted up here like the Brits replaced Catholics in the Island with lowland Scots. The Turkomans, not to be confused with their cousins the Ottoman Turks who live in Turkey, are a presence up here in Kurdistan too and they've been pushed around a lot. Our guys, the Assyrians, claim very little land since there's not all that many of us. Occasionally someone kills a few of them in the name of Allah the merciful. Farther south towards Baghdad you have bloody chaos. The Americans destroyed the old social order and don't know how to make a new one. The Shiites have been pushed around for a couple of centuries, NOW they want to push back. The Sunnis think they rule by divine right. Americans try hard and work hard, but they don't know anything about Iraq. They don't have enough troops, enough equipment, enough training, enough experience.

What have you been doing in Mosul?

Praying, learning languages, studying religion, putting out fires, usual stuff. Fun mostly. Tho there's always the madman with the rifle-propelled grenade, most of the people are good people. I even get along with the local Muslim clergy. Sometimes they come to liaise with the Americans. That's how I got in trouble with the CIA and why they won't talk to me.

Won't talk to you?

Well I worked out a deal between the Kurds and the Americans about not throwing Shiites out of their homes. There was a hardhead colonel who was furious. So when he went home to the Pentagon, he complained about me and they ordered the CIA to pretend that I don't exist. Ironic because the army guys still get along with me.

So if you want to get out, how do you manage?

I suppose you talked to Tariq.

Yes.

That's one way. Truly scary. Or I could put off my monk's robe and try to make it down to Baghdad. It might take forever to persuade someone to let me on their plane down there. Dangerous too.

And the CIA?

They have daily chopper flights from here down to Kuwait. I could buy a ticket and fly home from there, though they'd probably want to hold me for questioning. Still, it's the best way out but not with me under interdict. I think maybe I'll ask Jenny to talk to Tariq.

How much time do you have?

The monks would like me to leave this week. I probably have more time than that.

We will talk to Archbishop Blackie in the morning. Can we print out this conversation?

Why not? Your husband has a photographic memory anyway.

'Tis true . . . When will we be able to get in touch with you again?

Seven tonight your time.

We'll do it, Des.

Somehow I don't doubt it for a moment.

Bye, Des.

Bye, Nuala. Bye, Dermot.

Bye, Des.

Nine o'clock the next morning we were in Archbishop Blackie's office in the Cathedral rectory. Crystal Lane, the youth minister and, in Blackie's words, "our resident saint," was playing with our youngest in the "counseling room" next to the office. Patjo, as always, was delighted to discover a new worshipper.

The "Arch," as the Cathedral teens called him, read the transcript of our communication with Des for a second time. He placed it gently on his desk.

"This young man will make a fine priest," he said softly. "He is not seeking a personal identity like so many of the applicants we encounter these days. He is seeking to serve God's people. Indeed, he appears to have rendered more service in a few years than most of us priests do in our whole lives."

He was silent for a moment.

"This ban on him will not continue."

He picked up a phone on his desk, turned on the speakerphone, signaled us to be silent, and punched in a number.

"Walter speaking."

"This is Father Ryan."

"I hear rumors that you are an Archbishop now."

"You may discount the importance of those rumors. I am calling about a certain Chicago Catholic whom the CIA apparently has placed under interdict, one Desmond Doolin."

"I can't talk about him."

"Walter, you will talk about him nonetheless. The media, especially here in this city, will find it passing strange that the CIA refuses to acknowledge the existence of a young man who has been accepted as a candidate for the priesthood in this Archdiocese. They will also find it strange that this ban is imposed at the orders of the Pentagon. Since when, Walter, does the Central Intelligence Agency take orders from the Department of Defense?"

"I am not unfamiliar with the case."

"I would assume that to be patent. Otherwise, I would not be harassing you."

"We don't make these kinds of decisions anymore. There have been changes in personnel. The people at DOD have short memories . . ."

"I presume that the Reverend Doolin has done excellent work in Iraq."

"We should give him a medal, he's saved so many lives. He's a legend. The trouble is no one controls him."

"And over there the Pentagon controls everything."

"That's the premise."

"It has been called to my attention that Reverend Doolin's life is in danger because some of the more agitated people, as we say here in

Chicago, have put out a contract on him. We deem it essential that he be extricated from this situation immediately. Just now live priests are more important to us than martyrs, especially when the martyring agent is the United States government."

Walter was silent for a moment. In the meantime, the Cardinal himself appeared at the door of the office. The only signs of his office were ruby cuff links on a collarless shirt and a ruby ring. His snow-white hair, his broad shoulders, and his dangerously flashing blue eyes, as Blackie once put it, "create the presence that all such churchmen should have but most lack, myself notably so." Leaning against the doorjamb, a casual Renaissance prince on Wabash Avenue, he was reading the transcript he had snatched from Blackie's desk.

"Does he want out?"

"Walter, if he didn't want to, I wouldn't be harassing you. More to the point Milord Cardinal Cronin wants him out."

The Cardinal grinned and winked at us.

"How soon?"

"Yesterday would not have been soon enough."

"You're in touch with him?"

"It is safe to assume that we are."

"I'll see what I can arrange."

"We wish to settle the matter to our satisfaction by the end of business today. Reverend Doolin's life is in grave danger. We will await your response."

The "Arch" replaced the phone with infinite care.

"Like I always say, Blackwood, I'm glad you're on my side."

"Arguably . . . These men are worse fools than your very good friends over in Vatican City. But then, unlike the Secretary of Defense, the Vatican is infallible only in certain limited matters."

Crystal appeared, sleeping boy child in her arms.

"You poured the sacred waters on this young man, didn't you, Cardinal?"

She passed him over to Sean Cronin, who accepted him with the practiced skill of a Chicago politician.

"You're growing into a pretty big guy, Poraig Josefa," he said softly.

Our kid opened his eyes at the sound of a new voice, frowned, and then went back to sleep.

Crystal took him back. I figured it would not hurt the rest of our day if he continued in the arms of a certified, bona fide mystic (which me wife insists is not the same as being fey, well not exactly the same). Nuala Anne smiled contentedly.

"Are we going to get our guy out of there, Blackwood?"

"It would seem so."

"You did everything but call him Father Doolin."

Blackie sighed.

"I would have done that if necessary. It is an old Irish custom to use the term of anyone who has enrolled in the seminary."

"'Tis true, but before my time." Nuala confirmed the folk tale.

So we collected our baby from his admirers and returned to the much-less-hallowed halls of Sheffield Avenue.

"Now we wait," Nuala said, never a woman who was very good at waiting. "And pray."

"What will his parents say when he comes home?" Nuala asked.

"His father will be delighted to see him," I replied. "His mother will never forgive him. He humiliated her by coming home alive after her silly memorial Mass."

"Won't she be proud to have a son a priest?"

"With all the troubles the priesthood has these days, people like them aren't always proud of the priest son. Heaven knows my parents are proud of Prester George, but they're different. They're even proud of their son the poet who married the gorgeous colleen from Galway."

"Hmf."

Time passed as though one were sitting in a hospital lobby waiting for the doctor to report on the surgery he was performing. Neither of us had any sense when the end of business was in Langley, Virginia. We had to presume that Blackie knew when to send his last and best warning. If there were either good news or bad, we would hear immediately.

Surely Walter—whoever Walter was—knew the risks of playing hardball against the apparently harmless little prelate. Could he convey these risks to whoever had to make the final decision?

After "tea" the family assembled in the game room to say the Rosary, an event which occurred when herself was not altogether sure that God was awake and listening. Socra Marie always prayed with great fervor but without sufficient speed. Thus her "at the hour of our death. Amen" trailed the communal expression of these same thoughts and thereby caused merriment among her older siblings. The latter were fixed with a murderous glare from their mother. Promptly at seven we turned on my computer and Nuala sent out the message to Desmunk.

> Are you there, Desmunk?
> Right on time.
> We're leaning on CIA right now. No news yet. How long can you stay at the Internet café?
> Two hours. Maybe a little longer.
> We'll be back to you as soon as we hear.
> Thank you. Pray.

"He sounds worried," Nuala said.

"He does indeed. Maybe there's something going down that he didn't want to tell us."

So we said the Rosary a couple of more times. Nuala sang hymns which I could join without too much embarrassment. She saw to the bedding down of the children, brought Patjo back to the office and fed him. At first he was more interested in sleeping, but like most males he could not turn down good food. Then he returned to his dreams.

At 8:45 the phone rang.

"Nuala Anne."

"Blackie here. The issue is still in doubt. There has been little debate all day about extracting—their quaint word—Des. The debate is whether they should serve notice on the Pentagon of their intentions. Our man said this would be absolute folly. He questioned whether news of the removal of a single innocuous monk from Mosul would ever reach the upper levels of the Pentagon. Still, the debate goes on for such is the nature of bureaucracy. I told him that the issue would become moot at 9:00 Chicago time because I would then summon the local and the national media for a press conference in which Cardinal Sean Cronin, by the grace of God and favor of the Holy See Archbishop of Chicago, would blame the Director of Central Intelligence, the Secretary of Defense, and the President of the United States for risking the life of an American citizen because of bureaucratic infighting. I warned him that I was not bluffing and that in fact I never bluff. As you both know on occasion I do bluff. In any case I will be back to you at 9:15. Are you still in touch with Father Desmond?"

"We are. I'm afraid he's in some imminent danger. We will ask him to give us fifteen more minutes."

Nuala returned to AOL:

> Des, can you give us fifteen more minutes?
>
> Sure, some of my friends are hanging around here.
>
> Who are these friends?
>
> Some very tough Assyrian youth who would do well as security guards at the court of Nabucco, a few Kurdish cops and a squad of American paratroopers.
>
> We'll be back to you.

"They must be expecting an attack if they have their own gang out to protect him," Nuala said fretfully.

"I think we can assume that Des would put together his own gang."

"Suppose they drive a car bomb into the café?"

"I think his gang will be prepared for such an attempt."

"Dermot love, you need a splasheen of the crayture."

THAT MEANS SHE NEEDS THE SPLASHEEN.

We both do.

Nuala rushed back with the ravaged bottle of Middleton's and the two goblets, scrupulously clean from all traces of the previous night's consumption. At 9:10 the phone rang.

"You answer it, Dermot, I'm too nervous."

WHAT'S THE POINT IN BEING FEY IF SHE GETS THAT NERVOUS?

"Dermot Coyne."

"Father Ryan here. I believe it's safe to say that we have won. Here are the details to transmit to the valiant Father Desmond. In mid-afternoon local time, an official of the CIA named Steffan, obviously a code name, will wait on Desmond and confirm the extraction—sorry if their slang would be more appropriate in a dental office. Sometime later in the day, probably after nightfall, he and his personal effects will be lifted to Baghdad by helicopter. Thereupon he will be transferred to the Ramstein Air Base in Germany. Thence he will be moved to the Frank-furt Airport and flown to Chicago, along with Steffan and another CIA officer. They will arrive at O'Hare about noontime . . . Thereupon he will be driven to your home, where he will be handed over to the custody of Milord Cronin and my undistinguished self. You will be notified of the time of this meeting. Is that all committed to your usually reten-tive memory, Dermot?"

"'Tis."

"Excellent."

I moved me wife aside and repeated the Arch's narrative on the computer screen.

For five long minutes there was no response from Des.

Got it, guys. I know Steffan, informally of course. He's a good guy. Sorry for the delay. We had an incident down the street. A group of unpleasant people tried to blow up this café. They were diverted from their goal. I'm going home now to sleep—home still being the monastery.

You have a cell phone?

I'm American, am I not? I never use it much.

Phone us from Baghdad and Frankfurt—312-773-2525.

Will do. Good night and good luck.

"He thinks he's Edward R. Murrow."

"Or Sinbad the Sailor," Nuala said with a vast sigh of relief.

I reached for the Flight Guide and checked flights from FRA to ORD,

American Flt 83 left FRA at 1410 and arrived at Chicago at 1730—2:10 and 5:30.

"Five-thirty tomorrow afternoon!" my spouse, who had virtuously put the bottle of the water of life back in its cupboard, exclaimed. "And the house such a terrible mess. I won't have time to clean it."

Fiona ambled into the office, yawned, turned around a couple of times and settled into the carpet.

"Day after tomorrow. And the house doesn't need cleaning."

"And I'll have to make a few bites for our guests . . ."

"And insult Danuta? I won't hear of it!"

"Sure, don't you have the right of it . . . I'd better call the Arch."

"'Tis Nuala Anne, Your Grace. We've passed on all your information to him. Apparently there was a little dust-up at the Internet café—that sounds like one of your Clint Eastwood filums, doesn't it, but everyone on his side is all right . . ."

"It is well that we acted expeditiously!"

"'Tis true . . . He'll try to call us from Baghdad or Frankfurt if they'll let him. He'll be here probably tomorrow at five-thirty. We'll have a bite here at our cottage . . . Ah no, me husband tells me it will be the day after tomorrow . . . We poor West of Ireland folk tell time by the shadows the sun makes on our fields, don't we now?"

"I have required my good friend Walter to keep me informed about the progress of this mission. I will call you as soon as I learn anything. Probably early tomorrow afternoon."

"Do you think them fellas over at the Pentagon will try to make any last-minute trouble?"

"They are capable of anything—if they find out. We must get Desmond into the boarding area of the Frankfurt Airport . . . You might have your virtuous sister-in-law meet the plane. I will, of course, be there too."

"Good idea."

"My best to all the childer. I will look forward to sharing a bite with them the day after tomorrow."

I called my sister, who was delighted at the prospect of a battle with federal bureaucrats.

"Is there anything more we can do, Dermot?"

"Do our exercise and get a good night's sleep."

"I'd rather have another jar."

"It would not be good for you. We both have to run for the tension."

"Why must you always have the right of it, Dermot Michael Coyne?"

"Because me wife is smart enough to know that I'm occasionally correct."

She leaned against me.

"Please?"

"No way."

— 22 —

I woke up early in the morning of July 20 and turned on Radio Berlin and the BBC . . .

The bomb exploded at 1242.

The BBC had the story first, naturally at 1442.

"We have just learned that there has been a tremendous explosion in the hut in Rastenberg in East Prussia which has served as a briefing room for Herr Hitler. Our sources tell us that the structure has been completely destroyed."

So the bomb had exploded. What next?

I would later learn that Claus and his aide, Lt. Werner von Haeften, had arrived in midmorning at the Wolf's Lair and, having passed all the checkpoints, attempted in a washroom to rig both bombs—artillery shells actually—in a satchel. The presence of a curious sergeant major permitted them to rig only one. Acid was supposed to eat away a wire and detonate the bomb in fifteen minutes. They had no time to rig the second. They walked into the briefing hut. Claus was introduced to Hitler. The Führer nodded and suggested that in the next phase of the briefing, Colonel von Stauffenberg report on the condition of the Home Army. Claus sat about five chairs away from Hitler and slid the bomb under the table towards Hitler. Von Haeften placed his bomb under the table, hoping that the live bomb would detonate the other.

Claus whispered a request that he could sit closer to the Führer because his hearing was poor. He managed to inch up the table. Then, with only a few minutes remaining, he and von Haeften slipped away and began to run. They made it to a car which had been left for them and began to drive away. Then the bombs detonated in a thunderous explosion. A signal officer who was part of the conspiracy reported to the other conspirators at the time that the explosion had been successful. Then, when he had seen Hitler emerge from the wreckage, he suggested that all communication links be cut, so that Operation Valkyrie could continue.

When Claus arrived back at the Bendlerstrasse (the location of the war office) he did his best to sustain the momentum of Operation Valkyrie. With cool and dignified wit, he continued to give orders that it should continue.

But it was too late. General Fromm, the commanding officer of the Home Army, lost his nerve. The building was in chaos for several hours. At 6:45 Radio Berlin announced that Hitler was still alive and would speak to the nation shortly (only six hours later was the Führer able to speak). Fromm tried to retake control of his office. There was shooting in the building. Claus was hit in the arm and bled profusely. He prevented his men from killing Fromm. Desperate to save himself, Fromm convened a "people's court," which ordered the immediate execution of five conspirators, including Claus and General Beck. Fromm demanded that the two of them kill themselves and placed pistols in front of each. Beck went off to another room and shot himself twice, though a coup de grace was still necessary. A hapless sergeant was ordered to finish off the most popular commanding officer in the German army.

Claus shoved the pistol away.

"General Fromm," he said calmly, "I have no intention of killing myself."

He and the only three others who had not tried to escape were dragged down to the courtyard and shot. Claus's last words were, "Long live our Secret Germany!" About midnight their bodies were buried in the courtyard. Several days later they were removed from their graves and burned.

The Antichrist had survived again and millions more would die—Germans, Russians, Jews, Americans and English.

When the Nazis took control of the war office the next day, the first thing they did was shoot General Fromm.

Fromm was a coward and a traitor. Yet once the world learned that Hitler was still alive, the struggle died, save for the torture and murders in the weeks and months ahead.

The street and the building are now called the Stauffenbergstrasse. There is a memorial plaque in the courtyard where he died. The Russians and the East Germans, of all people, changed the name of the street and built the memorial.

I knew by 1900 that Hitler was still alive, that the plot had failed, and that Operation Valkyrie was ended. I assumed that Claus was dead. I hoped he was dead.

Where was Annalise? Would she call or would I have to search for her?

"Claus," I prayed, "make her call me."

Then the phone did ring—2100.

"Ridgewood."

"Annalise, Herr Ridgewood. He is dead. He was already bleeding from a wound. They shot him in the courtyard of the Bendlerstrasse. Young Werner Haeftin threw himself in front of Claus. They reloaded and fired again. I was there. His last words were 'Long live our Secret Germany.'"

"I'm so sorry, Annalise."

"He and those who died with him were the only ones who didn't run away. I want to die too."

"They were fortunate to die that way. The others will be tortured to death by the Gestapo."

"I don't care."

"Annalise, I have two letters for you from Claus. Please come over here and read them."

"What do they say?"

"They are sealed. I did not read them."

"I want to die."

"I know you do. That means you will be raped at least a hundred times on the cement floor of the basement in the Albertstrasse and then hung on a meat hook to slowly strangle. Do you want that?"

"I don't care."

"Before you do that will you come over to the embassy and read the letters so that I will have fulfilled my promises to Claus . . . Where are you now?"

"In my apartment."

"Pack a bag with enough clothes for a week and ride over there in the U-Bahn. I will meet you at the Potsdamer Platz entrance. You have a sacred obligation to read Claus's last letters to you."

"Very well, Herr Ridgewood. I have such an obligation."

That's how you deal with Germans. You talk about sacred obligations.

A half hour later, a full moon above us, she came up the stairs from the station. I would not have recognized her, if she had not said, "Good evening, Herr Ridgewood."

She was wearing a gray wig, a very effective wig as one would expect of Annalise, and a long, ugly gray dress under which there appeared no womanly form.

"Very impressive disguise, Annalise."

"You did not recognize me, Herr Ridgewood?"

"Not till you spoke."

"Claus ordered me to disguise myself. He also ordered me to escape and to call you."

I removed from her hand the small bag she was carrying.

We walked silently down the street to the Irish embassy, both living with our own grief.

We went up to my quarters and I turned on the light and opened the safe. I removed the letters and gave them to her.

"You note that they are sealed."

"I trust you, Herr Ridgewood."

I gave her a letter opener. She sat at my desk, opened both letters, and placed one on top of the other. Typical German love of order. Perhaps, please God, I would have to get used to it.

She sighed, folded the letters, and put them in their respective envelopes, having made sure that she had everything in the right order.

"Do you wish to read them, Herr Ridgewood?"

"No," I said, "they are private letters to you."

She sighed again.

"Claus orders me, for the sake of the love he and I have for each other, to permit you to save me. Of course, he was never unfaithful. We never spoke of love . . . Yet we loved one another. Does that surprise you, Herr Ridgewood?"

"No, it would be very hard not to love Claus."

"How would you save me?"

"I have created a fiction. Before I describe it to you, let me insist that it is fiction and nothing more. When we reach Berne, the fiction will end."

"What is that fiction?"

"The fiction believes I have a wife named Anne Elizabeth, for whom I have these passports and papers, which you will note have been stamped very recently by Reichsminister von Ribbentrop, who has furnished me with this very generous endorsement."

She studied the passports and the papers.

"Does this mean I am now Irish?"

"Hardly. It means only that you have proof that you are Irish."

"You are a very clever man, Herr Ridgewood. You have been planning this for a long time, haven't you?"

"Claus made me promise to save you."

She nodded as she put the two letters in her purse.

"I will now say, Herr Ridgewood, what needs to be said. I trust you."

"Thank you, Annalise. Now we have a room for you with a bath, should you want to bathe."

"And perhaps a glass of strong Irish whiskey, so I may sleep."

I provided a jar of the best.

"The wig and the dress must be destroyed," I warned her as she went into her room.

"Ja, Ja, Herr Ridgewood."

As I tried to sleep that night, I ran over in my mind all the things that had to be done before we set out for Basle.

When I woke in the morning, I remembered that I must send a minute to our embassy in Berne. I dressed in my morning suit because I figured that

I should look like an ambassador if I was going to claim to be one. In my office on the ground floor, I sent the note to Berne telling them that my wife and I would arrive there in about five days. I also sent one to Dublin, briefly summarizing the story of the failure of the "Rising."

I glanced out the office window and saw a black limousine pull up. The flags on the hood of the car told me it was Reichsführer-SS Heinrich Himmler himself coming for breakfast. I removed one of my .25s from my desk, slipped it into a pocket in my suit, and went to answer the bell.

"Heil Hitler," said the handsome young thug waiting at the door. He was wearing the black uniform of the SS. "The Reichsführer-SS wishes to have a brief word with you, Herr Ambassador."

"Ja, ja," I replied, nodding as I always did in return to the salute.

The driver and another thug stood at attention next to the car. The SS was close to running the whole country now. I had better be careful with my words.

Hell, I was Irish. I was always careful with my words—when I was sober, which was practically always after I left Cambridge.

The first thug opened the door, and said, "Heil Hitler" again. I nodded once more.

I sat down next to Himmler.

"Good morning, Herr Ambassador," he said in the careful tone of a man who was carrying a terrible burden but was determined to be polite. Like his thugs, he was wearing the black uniform of the SS.

"Good morning, Reichsführer," I said pleasantly.

I know what you want, I thought. I won't have to kill you.

"You have chosen a good day to leave Germany," he said, shaking his head as if he were sad and troubled.

He looked much like a ticket clerk at a rail station, wearing a funny uniform.

"My instruction to return for consultation came last week," I said. "So it is not related to the events of yesterday."

"I understand, I understand," he said soothingly. "I came early because I expect a very busy day. Those foolish aristocrats have disturbed my most careful plans. We must first restore some sense of order before I can proceed with them. I hope that when you arrive in Berne you will speak with some of my contacts there."

"*Naturally, I will relay any message you wish. I trust the Führer is recovering?*"

I had guessed right, no need to kill you now, Herr Reichsführer.

"*Yes, he is, though the pace of his recovery is slow. I must govern the country in his absence.*"

"*A very difficult task, Herr Reichsführer.*"

"*Indeed. However, the Führer has not been himself for some time, not since Stalingrad. The German people should permit him to rest and relax, one might even say retire.*"

"*Ja,*" I said approvingly.

"*I know that you are discreet, Herr Ambassador. You will understand the need for confidentiality in these matters?*"

"*Naturally.*"

"*Graf Stauffenberg's goals were the same as mine. His tactics were absurdly naïve. This foolish war must end before the Red Army pollutes the sacred soil of the Fatherland. We must persuade the English and the Americans of our mutual interest in preventing this new Asiatic horde from sweeping all the way to the Atlantic . . . I personally have established certain contacts in Switzerland, ja, with the Americans. I am asking you—not ordering you naturally— if you would be able to renew those contacts. They will be in touch with you when you arrive there.*"

"*I will be honoured to serve as an ambassador of peace. We Irish have a great respect for peacemakers.*"

Please don't remind me that we kill the peacemakers like Michael Collins.

We then went down the same catechism that I had recited for Ribbentrop. Did they both know that the other was playing the same game? I suspect that Himmler knew about Ribbentrop but the latter didn't know about the former. What a terrible way to run a country!

I loathed them both. But it wasn't up to me to make decisions for the Allies, but only to report the messages for the Americans in Berne.

Let the gobshites make their own decisions.

"*I believe,*" Himmler continued, "*that I am the only man in Germany who has sufficient power to hold the country together and guarantee a peace which may not be accepted universally in this country.*"

I added my warning about the families of the conspirators.

"What I said yesterday was aimed mainly at the Führer," he said. "I am not Stalin. However, your comment is sensible. No blood vengeance."

"Candidly, Herr Reichsführer, such vengeance might well destroy the confidence of the Americans in Berne."

"You may assure them that as of this morning, the blood vengeance plans will cease . . . and as a token of my gratitude, I have written this laissez-passer message for you and your wife. I don't think I have had the pleasure of meeting her. Perhaps when you return, you will introduce her to me. Please God when you return we will have peace."

"I too hope for that, Herr Reichsführer."

"Please read the letter."

"Ja, ja!"

It was even more exaggerated than the document the Reichsminister had given me. I was a distinguished and respected diplomat and I should be treated as if I had the future of Germany in my hands.

"Was Himmler looking for me?" Annalise was sitting in the office, a mug of tea in her hand and two hard rolls for breakfast on a plate. She was wearing a long robe with the collar held together with one hand. She smelled of spring flowers.

"No, he was allegedly looking for peace. He had a message for the Americans in Berne. I had the same conversation with Ribbentrop a couple of days ago. They are negotiating with Russians up above in Stockholm."

"Himmler would have a better chance than anyone else in Germany of imposing peace," she said as she poured me a cup of tea. "But surely you will not tell the Americans they should negotiate with him?"

"My job, Annalise, is to be a disinterested diplomat who relays the substance of the message he was given without intruding his personal opinions. Both Ribbentrop and Himmler accepted terms not unlike Claus's. Peace now would save millions of lives. I persuaded Himmler to drop the blood vengeance promise as essential to peace."

"Nina and the children will be safe!"

"Let's hope so. Both these men are pathological liars and traitors to the Third Reich. The Americans will insist on knowing what I think."

"And what do you think?"

"I'll say that if I were in their position, I would proceed with further negotiations only when and if Himmler's thugs kill the Führer, end the Endlösung, and release everyone in the concentration camps."

"Will he do that?" Herr Ridgewood.

"I doubt that he could do it even if he wanted to. But he knows that will be the price of peace . . . Oh, he gave his own laissez-passer to us."

She read it carefully.

"It is much better than the other one . . . When do we leave, Herr Ridgewood?"

"Ten-thirty. We should try for an early start. Are you packed?"

"Of course."

"Here is how we'll do it. You collect the passports and the letter from Ribbentrop and put them in your purse. You have charge of them for the whole trip. I will take your bag down to the garage and put it in the car. Then I will drive by here. You'll be standing inside the door with your purse and the key to the house. When the car pulls up, you come out of the door. And close the door, making sure the lock slips into place. Then you will walk down the stairs casually and get in the car. You open the purse and show it to me. Then we will leave for Berne. We'll head right down the Autobahn towards Nuremberg. It will be the easiest drive of the trip . . . OK?"

"Yes, Herr Ridgewood. You will forgive me if I cry a little today?"

"I may weep too, Annalise. We are both leaving a lot behind."

She lifted a package she had tied with a piece of string.

"My wig and dress. You will dispose of it?"

I'd forgotten that.

"Thank you for remembering."

I returned to my radio equipment and sent a final minute to Dublin.

In the wake of the abortive attempt of the OKW to establish a new government that would seek peace with the Western allies, there are rumors here of other negotiation attempts to open channels of communication between the Reich and its enemies. Unofficial feelers have been extended both in Switzerland and Sweden. It is also understood that Russian officials are in contact with German emissaries in Stockholm. This sudden hum of peace activities will probably lead nowhere. In Germany the plotters will have to eliminate Hitler because he will never agree to peace nor step down voluntarily.

A'chiara.

I scrambled the decoder so that the Abwehr would not be able to decode my dispatches, if they had kept any of them around.

Annalise brought her suitcase to the ground floor and placed it next to a bag which contained six bottles of springwater.

She was wearing dark blue slacks and a matching jacket, very much a former code clerk at an embassy. That reminded me of one last item. I rushed upstairs to retrieve the rings from my safe. I had to spin the combination three times before it opened. I put the rings in my watch pocket.

I returned to the door. Annalise was waiting patiently.

She opened her purse and showed me all four documents. I nodded briskly.

"There's one more point I have missed. I note that you are not wearing your wedding ring."

"I put it in the candle box at a church in Charlottenburg. I will always feel grief for Paul. But the mourning is over."

I wasn't sure what that meant.

"These rings are part of the fiction and nothing more. However, they were purchased in Dublin as any expert jeweler would realize immediately."

"They are quite lovely, Herr Ridgewood, but I cannot wear them. I will not wear them."

"Then our pretense that you are my wife and enjoy the privileges of a diplomat's wife will collapse. We will find it difficult to escape from Germany without a plausible sign of marriage."

She looked at me, searching my face.

"Very well, Herr Ridgewood. I will wear them."

Yet her lips were reduced to a thin line, as if the very act of putting on rings was abhorrent.

"Go for the car now, please."

It would be a difficult, perhaps impossible journey if these spats recurred often. Our worst enemies were not the Gestapo or the SS. The strains between us could destroy us. I was an eejit, as the Galway woman would have said, for dreaming of such a scenario. Once we crossed the bridge at Basle, the fiction would come to an end, a permanent end. I loaded the trunk and the backseat of the car, paid the garage owner three months in advance, and said that it was not unlikely that I would be back in Berlin by the end of September. Summer vacation in Ireland, I explained. He wished me good luck and said he and his wife would pray that my trip would be safe.

I threw her dress and wig in a dustbin.

I fastened the canvas cover in place. It would protect us partially from the hot sun and a pounding summer rain.

I felt like a rat leaving a sinking ship.

I was not a Berliner, I told myself. I had no obligation to stay here and die with the others. Besides, I had another life to protect.

I drove by the embassy to make sure there were no obvious surveillances. The Gestapo's most skillful gumshoes would be after bigger fish, though if they knew who the young woman whose hair was concealed by a green scarf was — nice touch — they would never let us out of Berlin. I went around the block past several smoking ruins and stopped in front of the former Irish embassy.

Without the slightest sign of haste, the young woman walked down the steps towards the car, as though she were going for an afternoon ride in the Tiergarten. I opened the door for her, she bowed slightly and settled into the front seat. I closed the door.

— 23 —

SO WE exercised and slept through the alarm and went into panic mode to prepare for our distinguished guests.

"Should we invite his family?" I was asked when I brought tea and toast up to our bedroom after I'd led the kids and the pooches over to the school. Daffodils were beginning to pop up in Nuala's garden and the grass was turning green two weeks after Easter.

"Why would we ever do that?"

"They are his parents. Still."

"Not in my house," I insisted. "Let them work it out by themselves if they ever work it out."

"Do you think he told Jenny he's coming home?"

"Maybe, but that's none of our business either."

"He should have told his ma and da where he was going, shouldn't he?"

"They would have stopped him. They've had him arrested before. If he was convinced that he should go to Iraq, the only way he could have done it was to run away from them. They brought it on themselves."

She nodded, her maternal conscience not completely satisfied, but she knew that I was right, though this time she didn't admit it.

Blackie called in early afternoon.

"Our monk is safely out of Iraq and on the way to Germany. He escaped one step ahead of the bailiffs. The defense department wants to hold him for questioning on matters of national security. I have already alerted the good Cindy Hurley. She plans to seek relief, as she describes the process, by requesting an injunction in the Federal District Court here in Chicago on the morrow. Needless to say, I will appear there."

"Will they pick him up at the airport in Germany?"

"The CIA has diverted the plane—it belongs to them, not the Air Force, to another airport, location unspecified, where they have a safe house. They hope to get him on the plane tomorrow afternoon before the defense department finds out where he is. They may have to smuggle him on the plane."

"Bastards!"

"Well, yes. We have one more weapon in our arsenal which I plan to invoke before the day is over."

"How ultimate is it?"

Blackie sighed.

"Pretty ultimate."

I went to the kitchen to report to my wife.

"You mean they might try to arrest Des up above at O'Hara? Them friggin' gobshites!"

My wife shares with the late Mayor of Chicago the propensity to call the airport by its wrong name.

"Sure, it ought to be called O'Hara!"

Which settled the matter.

Ethne, Danuta, and the woman of the house were bustling frantically on the preparation of a meal which would put a massive Christmas dinner to shame.

"How many can we expect, Dermot love?"

"You and me, the Cardinal and Blackie, Cindy and Tom, Des, and Steffan—eight altogether."

"Sure, isn't that a brilliant crowd for a dinner party? You must remember, Dermot Michael Coyne, not to talk too much!"

"Woman, you are full of shite!"

She thought that was funny.

"I'd better call Cindy and make sure that Tom knows he's invited."

As we were about to begin our "tea"—pretty lean fare compared to the planned meal for the morrow, Blackie called again.

"I have here in my hands, Dermot, a restraining order from the United States Court of the Seventh District enjoining the United States of America or any and all of its offices or agencies from interfering with the return of Desmond David Doolin to the said United States. We know, however, that some of the officials of the federal government believe firmly that they are not bound by such orders in a time of war. Thus there is the possibility that there will be some contretemps at O'Hare when American Flight 83 lands tomorrow afternoon. I believe that the good Hurleys will have some United States marshals present to enforce the restraining order. Also some private security, ah, assets, arguably the employees of Mike Casey's Reliable Security. The Chicago Police Department is hardly likely to be deterred by the Department of Homeland Security or the Department of Defense."

"Messy," I said.

"Indeed. Your valiant sister has prepared what she calls a writ of habeas corpus and also a citation for contempt of court for any and all agencies and officials who violate the original court order—including if necessary some of the highest officials in our battered but resilient democracy."

"Didn't the United States Attorney appear against the restraining order?"

"He did not. He is apparently too busy hunting for political scalps."

"He'll certainly be in court tomorrow morning."

"Perhaps, but he will have to contend with the good Cindy. Also my ultimate weapon is now in play. Incidentally, Father Des, soon I suspect to be assigned to the Cathedral staff, is safe in the safe house, at least for the moment. The CIA plans to sneak him on the plane in such a way as to avoid the American Military Police who may be searching for him. It is not beyond belief that the MPs may try to remove him forcibly from the plane. I fondly hope not. It could be a national scandal."

"A point that Cardinal Sean will make at the highest levels in the land."

"Oh he won't bother with the vice president . . . You will inform your valiant and virtuous wife of these developments, letting her draw her own conclusions."

I did.

"The Cardinal will speak to the Secretary of Defense, the vice president, and the president," she said, as if she knew it all along. "On second thought, he won't bother with the vice president."

The doggies were well aware that something unusual was happening in the house. They paced around nervously, sniffing and snooping. The kids demanded to know why they couldn't sit at the dinner table. Nuala explained that they would meet the guests and after that they would find the conversation BORING! She also promised Nelliecoyne that she would ask if the Cardinal objected to a quick portrait by a very talented young photographer.

At eight the next morning Des was on the phone.

"Hi, Dermot! Good to talk to you!"

"Likewise, Des. Where are you?"

"Admiral's Club at Frankfurt. Some odd things happening. Apparently the DOD wanted to arrest me at the airport. We evaded a dozen MPs coming in with the help of some of the CIA friends here. But then they tried to force their way into the boarding lounges and the German police stopped then. For a moment it was like Checkpoint Charlie then our guys backed off. Just like the Russians did at Checkpoint Charlie."

"After a secret agreement with us."

"Really! Gosh, you know a lot of history, Dermot."

"That's why I didn't graduate from Marquette. Now let me tell you about the drill at O'Hare when you get here. There'll be a reception committee, including Archbishop Ryan, my sister Cynthia Hurley and her husband Tom. They have court orders restraining any and every American agency and official from preventing your entry. There will be a band of Irish pipers and an Irish dance group to pipe you in . . . That was me wife's idea . . ."

"Won't she be there to sing!"

"No because she'll have been busy the better part of the last two days preparing tea for us all tonight, that's tea in the Irish sense of the word, meaning supper, though actual tea will be available. This will all be at our cottage on Sheffield Avenue. Steffan is invited . . ."

"That's a good idea. He really has taken good care of me."

"The Cardinal will be here too. And I wouldn't be surprised if he's at the airport."

"Gosh!"

"Have you talked to Jenny?"

"Yes."

"So she knows you're coming home?"

"Yes."

"Your parents don't know?"

"No."

"I see."

"She'll tell them tomorrow. She says that it will take time for them to get used to it. Mom especially. Then we'll see. I would have told them what I was doing, but they would have tried to stop me by force. They have to accept that I make my own decisions. I have to take the chance that they never will. I have to find a place to stay tonight."

"There's a room waiting for you at the Cathedral rectory . . . You still planning on going to the seminary in the autumn?"

"If they'll have me."

"Then the room at the Cathedral is yours till then. I'm sure they'll find plenty for you to do with our Middle Eastern immigrants."

"Gosh, Dermot, I can hardly believe it. I'll never be able to thank you enough."

" 'Tis herself you should thank. I just carry the spear for her."

I went downstairs and demanded breakfast from my wife. She produced bacon, English muffins, tea, orange juice and a waffle.

" 'Tis time to be good to Dermot again."

She kissed me.

"I tell the kids that we must always be good to poor Da . . . Was that your man on the phone?"

"It was. Apparently Cardinal Sean's clout worked again. The MPs in Frankfurt were ready to storm the plane and then they backed down."

"Good on them! Call Blackie and tell him."

I did just that.

"Arguably it worked the way it should. I will hear the full story eventually. However, you can depend on it. They didn't do it because they are nice guys. In any case we will deploy all our assets at O'Hare just the same. My information is that the plane will be airborne shortly and will arrive at O'Hare on time."

— 24 —

I made the sign of the Cross as we drove down the Friedrichstrasse, as the Galway woman had insisted we do when we were beginning a trip.

"An American force has landed in southern France near Marseille," she said. "If one is to believe Radio Berlin, German and French troops have driven them into the sea."

"Just as they did in Normandy."

"Herr Ridgewood, I'm sure that Claus did not expect you to be responsible for a foolish little child. You should drop me at the Potsdamer Platz and I will take the U-Bahn back to Charlottenburg."

"No, I will drop you off only when we cross the Rhine at Basle."

"I deserve to be punished like an unruly child."

"No, you don't. You've endured a terrible event."

"I said I trusted you and I meant it. Then I became juvenile. I am wearing the fictional rings and wear them with real pride. They are quite lovely. Please forgive me."

"Whatever there is to forgive, I have forgiven. I should have been more sensitive."

"All the documents are in my purse. You will inspect them at the next traffic light."

"All is in order."

We drove south, by the Schloss Schoenbrunn, which would become later the city hall of West Berlin where my friend Jack Kennedy would give his famous "Let them come to Berlin!" speech, just west of the Tempelhof airdrome where the Berlin airlift saved the city, and then out of the city across the Teltow Canal and on to the Autobahn to Nuremberg under a blazing summer sun. It was not an easy drive. We were stopped frequently by southbound Panzer traffic. The Führer was pulling troops out of the Eastern Front to cope with the American invasion of southern France, which, according to Canaris, the Americans had scheduled to coincide with the Normandy landing. The two forces were supposed to junction near Tours and cut off the German army in southern France. By now, however, there were only garrison forces in the south. They would be cut off and the Reich would lose more manpower, even if they were not the best of troops. Presumably the Führer still adhered to his conviction that German soldiers never retreat. There was no such thing as a strategic retreat.

American B-17s flew over us in massive numbers, headed perhaps for Wiener Neustadt. German fighters doggedly attacked them. American escort planes, which looked like the Me-109, destroyed many of the German planes. It was a terrifying battle in the sky—cowboys and Indians chasing each other at three hundred miles an hour. The Indians were falling out of the sky. Germany was losing again.

"Everyone of those falling planes has a pilot whom someone loves," Annalise sobbed next to me. "It is madness."

Suddenly, a plane skimmed just above us with a terrible roar and a slash of wind. It seemed that it was only a few feet above us, a bird of prey about to snatch us into the sky. It exploded into the fields, not fifty meters away from us. Our car seemed to jump off the road and into the air. It then landed again in a jarring bump. Only when the burning plane disappeared in our rearview mirror did I worry about our extra petrol tanks.

Well, if they were going to explode, they would have exploded by now.

"A man died in that plane," Annalise cried out.

"Maybe he was able to bail out."

"Please, God."

We did not make it to Nuremberg that day which was a good thing because the RAF attacked it that night. We stopped at a small Gasthaus on a side road which bypassed Nuremberg and would lead us eventually to the Autobahn towards Munich. We were given a room with twin beds, which was a relief to me. I did not want to have to sleep next to Annalise, not that night, not ever. She had been, however, a self-possessed traveling companion save for the time we encountered the crashing Me-109. It could have been an American P-51. But they don't have Iron Crosses painted on their fuselages.

It was a difficult night for both of us. We were both grieving for our losses. We were worn-out from the heat and the travel. We were tense from the strain of sleeping in the same room. The distant explosion of bombs seemed to rock our beds. How could we last four more days?

Annalise woke first in the morning. She came back to our room with a cup of hot chocolate and some "good, German bread, with butter." She was wearing a brown skirt and white blouse with sandals instead of shoes and bare legs. She had somehow found time to bathe and use perfume.

She looked cool and lovely and rested. I would not be able to keep up with her.

"I must bathe and shave before we leave," I said. "Diplomats shave every morning."

She merely giggled.

The proprietor of the Gasthaus told us that there had been a terrible raid on Stuttgart, that the Gestapo was still hunting down the conspirators, all of whom would pay a terrible price for their crimes, and that the Americans were falling back in both the north and the south of France and that there was no more talk of blood vengeance.

"Do you believe all those reports?"

Our host said that he never believed anything on the radio and that it was too bad they didn't kill the madman.

One of their sons had died at Stalingrad and another had been wounded in Normandy. In their judgment Count Stauffenberg was a great hero.

That day was long and hot, though there were no air battles above us. We had enough food, enough water, enough petrol. We said the Rosary several times in both the morning and afternoon. But sadness dominated our ride. We were realizing now for the first time that Claus was really dead, that we would never see his smile, never hear his laughter in this world. We were overcome with frustration and guilt. If only we had done more, if only we had more faith in him, perhaps the outcome would be different. At least that's what I thought. I could only surmise that Annalise was thinking the same thing.

Military police, the SS and the Gestapo had established roadblocks all along the Autobahn, checking papers, comparing what we looked like with pictures on clipboards. Each time I pointed to the Irish flag on one side of the car and the foreign ministry flag on the other. Then after some protest I showed them our passports and our endorsements by the Reichsminister and the Reichsführer-SS. The last always worked. The troops who had stopped us invariably apologized and gave us the Heil Hitler salute, to which we both replied with a nod.

"I always wonder," Annalise said wearily, "when one of these roadblocks will have my picture."

"If they don't have it now, I don't think they know yet who the elderly woman in the gray dress was. Those who would know, I presume, are already dead."

What would we do if we were pulled out of the car and brought to some commanding officer? I would demand that the officer would call the Reichsführer-SS and ask if his laisez-passer was valid. I didn't think anyone would take that risk, except a high-ranking officer in the SS or the WaffenSS. As the sun began to sink behind the mountains to the west of us, the roadblocks seem to have been recalled. Later we learned that the three young women who had worked with Annalise in Charlottenburg had been arrested and then released. There was no evidence against them, they were all Catholics, beautiful, and upper nobility. Their haughty contempt for their interrogators had proved very effective.

Yet they were certainly as guilty as Annalise was. Perhaps the Gestapo had decided that the German public was not yet ready to see young women aristocrats hanging by wire from meat hooks. Or perhaps Himmler was concerned about the reaction from England and the United States. His foolish political ambitions may have saved many lives.

Were the Gestapo and its allies looking for Annalise, the widow of a war hero? Probably not.

I suggested that possibility to her as we left the Autobahn for a small Gasthaus set back in the woods.

"I have thought of that too, Herr Ridgewood. Yet it is better this way. In two more days we will be out of Germany. Please God."

Perhaps better and perhaps not. Had I let my love for the woman weaken my judgment? It would be a restless night.

They had only one room free at the Gasthaus. And that had a double bed.

"We both knew that this might happen, Herr Ridgeland, didn't we? I will not distract your sleep tonight."

"Nothing would distract my sleep tonight," I said.

Only the torment of hideous dreams of roads not taken.

She was a quiet sleeper. I hardly knew she was next to me. Well, that's not altogether true. But I was not seriously tempted.

The next morning she asked if she might drive the car. We slipped through Munich with little trouble and then headed south into the hills and low mountains of the Schwarzwald with its picturesque little towns and villages tucked like Christmas presents beneath a tree. We left the Autobahn and took side roads that would put us below Stuttgart but above Ulm at the end of the day, avoiding Jettingen and its memories and dangers. Single airplanes crisscrossed the skies above us, perhaps scouting for possible oppositions to the American Seventh Army as it moved up from its beachheads in southern France and into Alsace and finally to the Rhine.

"You were wise, Annalise, to choose a cooler day for this pleasure ride through the Black Forest."

"Ja, Herr Ridgewood. I know this part of Germany."

I was content to let her do the work. I was worn down and did not trust myself on winding, mountain roads.

Then, suddenly there was trouble. We rounded a bend in the road and encountered two men in the uniforms of the WaffenSS, the SS's military unit of Hitler fanatics. They leaned against a motorcycle and sidecars, their uniforms open, and wine bottles in either hand. When they saw us they raised their machine pistols and pointed them at us.

"Out!" they ordered. "Or we kill you. Maybe we'll kill you anyway."

They meant it.

They were delighted at the sight of Annalise.

"We take her a couple of times, make him watch, and then kill them both, nein?"

They found the suggestions very funny.

They were dangerous men, drunken thugs who had probably deserted their unit and stolen the wine. Empty bottles lined the road. Now I would be put to the test. Could I really kill another human being?

"We have a letter from Herr Reichsführer-SS Himmler," I protested.

"Fuck Herr Reichsführer-SS Himmler." The bigger of the two seized Annalise and kissed her violently. She fought back and he hit her. She continued to fight.

"Into the woods, Kurt," he shouted. "We will have a little party in the woods, a picnic with this lovely morsel." He dragged a struggling, screaming Annalise into the woods. She fought him every inch of the way. The .25 fit comfortably into my hand. They both were doomed. The man who had captured Annalise threw her on the ground, fell on her and tore at her clothes.

"Ja, Ja, Fritz, stick it to her. Save some for me."

In his delight at the prospect of a brutal rape, he focused his attention on Fritz fighting with Annalise and ignored me for a couple of dangerous seconds.

"Ja, Ja!"

I shot him between the eyes and he died soundlessly.

"Kurt!" Fritz sensed that he was alone and he turned his head looking for his buddy. I killed him too. He also died soundlessly. I pulled his body off Annalise and threw it on the ground. The .25 makes a sound like a very small firecracker. Both men had barely heard a sound and died.

I lifted Annalise to her feet.

"They are both dead. There will be time later for sickness. Now we must move quickly. Drive the car to the edge of the bridge and stop there."

"Ja," she said as she looked at both the bodies. "They are both dead?"

"They both are dead. Now do what I say."

She did. I considered throwing the dead men over the edge into the racing stream below. But that would call attention to them. Let them rot in the wood *and the bugs and the birds and foxes feed on them. I was in a very dangerous mood. I had better be careful. I must not hurt Annalise.*

I loaded the wine bottles in the sidecar, started its motor and drove it slowly towards the edge of the valley. Then I turned off the motor and pushed the motorcycle over the edge. It tumbled straight down and fell into the rapidly rushing waters and immediately sank beneath the waters. In a moment it disappeared, just as had the lives of the men who had occupied it. I threw the gun after it.

Requiem aeternam dona eis, Domine.

Then I realized that my heart was pounding and my body shaking.

I climbed into the car.

"Can you drive, Annalise?"

"Naturally."

"There is another way to Freiberg?"

"Yes. We could have turned at the last crossroad. It is longer, though not much longer."

"Can you back us up and turn around?"

"Naturally."

She turned us around and drove back to the previous signpost.

Several kilometers down that narrow road there was a parking space, overlooking the same plunging stream.

"If you wish, this would be a good place to change your blouse."

"Thank you, Herr Ridgewood."

She climbed into the back of the car. I stared firmly down the road, watching for other cycles. In a couple of minutes she returned to the driver's seat, her hair brushed, her face clean, another blouse in place.

"Thank you, Herr Ridgewood. I now feel more myself."

"You look fine."

"You killed those two men with the gun you threw in the river?"

"Yes."

"You have another gun?"

"Yes."

"I am happy to know that . . . I heard no shots."

"A .25 makes a noise like a small firecracker. Your screams drowned out the sound."

"You must have shot very quickly and very accurately."

"I learned in Ireland when I was afraid that a gang might assault our house. I knew that I could never kill anyone with it."

"But you did?"

"I understand now that killing is easy when someone you love is in danger."

"Those poor men would still be alive if we had not taken that road."

"To kill and rape others and to die eventually in the war."

"Do you feel sick, Herr Ridgewood?"

"Yes. And my heart is still pounding and my muscles still quivering."

"I also."

We proceeded down the road to a valley where the stream rushed into the Neckar and towards the Rhine. An occasional car passed us. Farmers were working in their fields, reaping an early harvest. The peace of a gentle summer day slowly returned to our weary bodies. We had kept the rules that ours was a fictional marriage. We had not embraced one another and shared the horror of what happened. Nor would we exorcise death with life creating love that night. Not until we were safe in Berne. If then.

My comment about killing to protect someone you love had escaped my lips. She had not reacted to it.

"Sharing mortal danger is no guarantee," the Old Fella had told me once, "nor a sign of permanent friendship after the danger is over."

He was talking about battlefield danger and not about a man and a woman. Still he was right. There had always been a bond between me and Annalise. Now it was much stronger. Yet we both had doubts about the strength of the bond. At least I did. I was well on my way towards the fate of the traditional Irish bachelor.

Yet I had learned much about this young woman. She was brave and tough and resourceful. Perhaps I had learned nothing new. I would want her next to me in a bar when the lights went out.

"Despite this unfortunate incident, we are ahead of our schedule, are we not, Herr Ridgewood?"

I noticed for the first time that we had been speaking English through most of our journey. Was that a sign of something? Perhaps only that Frau Ridgewood must speak English when someone questioned her.

"Yes. We should be able to arrive at Lake Constance by tomorrow afternoon, without any difficulty."

"There is a nice hotel thirty kilometers down this road. It might be useful to spend the night there. We both need to rest . . . It used to be a nice hotel. I do not know what it is like now."

Excellent idea.

Then a flight of four planes appeared, flying very low. I did not recognize them. What were they doing here at this time of the day?

They ascended rapidly and one of them turned and skimmed the treetops as it inspected us.

"Folk-Wulfe?" Annalise asked.

She gripped my arm with her strong fingers.

"P-47."

Were we to die, just as Claus had been wounded? It was too late to jump out of the car. We waited for the bullets, too frightened to scream.

The plane flew over us, the white star on his wing clearly visible. He turned and ascended again. He wagged his wings and the four planes quickly disappeared.

"An American Stuka?"

"Yes."

"How ironic!"

"Americans are sentimentalists, Annalise. He may have seen that there was a woman in the car. Or perhaps he had caught a glimpse of the Irish flag. Irish-Americans are especially sentimental."

She removed her fingers from my arm.

"We both need to rest, Herr Ridgewood."

[I would learn many years later in Washington what had happened. At a dull cocktail party, an Air Force colonel approached me.

"You're the Irish ambassador, aren't you, sir?"

"Some people think so."

"Perhaps you can solve a mystery for me. I was leading a reconnaissance flight in '44 over the Neckar valley. We suspected the Panzers were rushing to the front to resist the Seventh Army."

"Herr Hitler always argued that German soldiers never retreated."

"We were able to break up one Panzer formation and to report that indeed Hitler was diverting some of his forces to resist on the Alsatian side of the Rhine. We spotted what looked like a German staff car with a Swastika painted on one side and what looked like Irish tricolour on the other side. A blond woman at the wheel. I had no idea what the Irish might be doing in the Neckar valley. But my Irish ancestors would not permit me to strafe the tricolour. Any idea who it might have been?"

"Maybe an Irish diplomat driving to Switzerland to escape the Gestapo after the attempt to kill Hitler, in which some of his friends were involved."

"Yes, sir," he said, puzzled.

"As I remember, Colonel, you wagged your wings in salute as you ascended. Permit me to return the compliment, however belatedly."

I saluted him and we both laughed.]

The hotel, probably built before the Great War, was still open, though with a small staff and only a few guests. We were greeted with a mix of grave formality and smiling delight. They gave us a room with two large beds and a balcony overlooking the Neckar. Annalise insisted that the Herr Ambassador's morning suit needed cleaning and pressing and that there was also other laundry. We must leave in the morning . . .

"But of course, Frau Ambassador . . ."

Annalise laughed at the title.

"First time!"

We bathed, dressed properly (I in the one suit I had brought, she in an elegant blue dress with a white sash), and sipped sherry and ate cake on the porch overlooking the Neckar as the sun slipped into the hills across the river. She had now become the efficient and gracious Frau Ambassador, who carefully supervised the details of our schedule. She would indeed be a good wife for a diplomat.

"It was an interesting day, Herr Ridgewood," she said. "We must say a Rosary tonight in gratitude to the good God for keeping us alive."

"All the angels too."

We did not discuss the details of the day. There would be many dreams in the days to come about these events. Nor did we discuss our own future after we crossed the Rhine at Basle late the next afternoon. We maintained the fiction that our "marriage" was a fiction. As we ate supper, I felt intense sexual desire. I wanted her desperately. I had to have her. After killing the enemy, the male must have a woman.

If I treated her that way I would be a rapist like the man who had thrown her on the ground of the Black Forest. I must continue my discreet and respectful pursuit. If she refused me in Basle, I would continue my pursuit.

I had not been a particularly effective pursuer before. Would I give up the chase now?

We said the Rosary and then went to bed. We must, she said, leave at ten in the morning. I agreed, but overcame the temptation to call her Frau Ambassador.

Nothing happened during the night except that we both enjoyed sound sleep, so sound that it was difficult for me to struggle out of bed. We did not leave the resort till eleven, entirely my fault because I couldn't organize myself. My fictional wife did not nag or complain, perhaps a very hopeful sign for the future.

It was another intolerably hot and humid day, with thunderstorms that only added to the humidity. I drove till three and then she offered to take over. We should arrive in Basle by seven. Our flight from Nazism was coming to an end.

Then the roadblocks began again. The Gestapo was searching for people like us—refugees from the terror. Our documents were impeccable, especially our laissez-passer from Himmler. That earned us smart salutes and apologies at every roadblock—and smiles for the Frau Ambassador as she was now called by everyone, excepting me.

Then, just as I was falling asleep after passing the last roadblock, I was jolted away as the car bumped and swerved and ground to a halt.

"The tire is kaput!" Annalise said, covering her face in mortification.

"Ja, ja is kaput," I said, climbing out of the car and looking at the left front wheel.

"You know how to change a tire, Herr Ridgewood?"

"Every man knows how to change a tire," I snarled.

I'd even done it once or twice.

So I began the long and tedious effort necessary to change a tire on a 1933 Benz. It rained several times. After the rain, the humidity hung all around us like a thick curtain. I was mean, nasty, angry. It was all her fault, why didn't she watch where she was driving, why did she have to spoil the whole trip almost at the very end. I swore, I cursed, I used every foul word in the Irish vocabulary (mostly English words) and was in every possible way an idiot.

My fictional wife wiped the sweat and grease off my face, brought me water to drink, and, I am certain, prayed for me.

Then I saw that she was laughing at me.

"You think I am amusing, Frau Ambassador?"

"Ja." She grinned. "I know it's not funny, Herr Ridgewood. But it is funny. God will take care of us."

"He'll have to make this friggin' pump work if we're ever going to make it to Basle . . . I am sorry, Annalise. It wasn't your fault, it wasn't God's fault. It's probably my fault for not asking Franz to show me how to do this before he went home."

"It is not required that you apologize, Herr Ridgewood."

"Yes it is."

God probably took pity on me then. Or one of the angels. The pump finally worked. The car was no longer kaput.

By the time of our arrival in Basle it was dark and the rain was constant. The city on the German side of the border was dark and foreboding because of the blackout, though the lights were shining across the river in the Swiss city. We had a difficult time finding the border gate on the German side of the Rhine. We drove up and down dark, rain-drenched streets and searched in vain for street signs and directions.

Why had we ever left Berlin?

Though I had reinstalled the canvas top, it was useless. We shivered like we had caught the flu. Indeed I became convinced that I had caught it.

"There is the sign for the border post, Herr Ridgewood." Annalise, intolerably proud of herself, pointed down a street. "There, to the left."

She would be a know-it-all Frau Ambassador, though she would never say, "I told you so."

Just the same, she would think it.

She unfolded an umbrella and we huddled together as we went to the lighted station.

A young man opened the door, glanced at our documents, and shouted, "No it is not permitted! This station is closed! It is too late! Come tomorrow morning! Leave now!"

"We are diplomats! There is a letter from Herr Himmler!"

He grabbed our papers!

"Tomorrow morning! Leave! It is not permitted!"

He reached for his machine pistol.

Nazi, failed SS trooper, no doubt.

"It is raining."

"You come late! Leave! That is an order!"

We covered ourselves with a rug, and hunched together in the car in a vain attempt to stay dry and warm. I was aware that there was a wondrous woman in my arms. But it didn't make much difference.

Tom Linehan, the chargé in Berne, was probably across the bridge waiting for us. Alas, there was no way to communicate with him.

We were fated to fail.

Nonetheless we both surrendered to deep sleep.

Much later, it seemed like a half of eternity, an older guard with a pleasant face nudged me gently.

"What is this? A diplomatic car? Why haven't you crossed? May I see your papers?"

"They're inside the hut, Herr Hauptman. The sergeant confiscated them last night. This is Herr Graf von Ridgewood, the Ambassador of Ireland. I am Hannah, Frau Ambassador."

"Why did he refuse to permit you to cross?"

"He said it was not permitted because we had come too late."

The sun was rising behind us, creating a rose gold glow on the Rhine.

"Pig-Dog," the captain said. "Damn Nazi! Come, I'll get your papers and stamp them! I have made tea! You spent the night in the rain! This is terrible!"

Our papers were on the desk where the Nazi had thrown them. The captain glanced at them. God in heaven! Letters from Himmler and Ribbentrop! He stopped to pour us each a cup of tea, then began to stamp both our passports

with the important-looking Swastika and eagle mark which said we had left
Germany for Switzerland.

"You may go, Herr Ambassador, Frau Ambassador! I apologize in the
name of the real Germany, the Secret Germany."

So!

"You drive us across, Annalise."

"If you wish, Herr Ridgewood."

And so we drove to freedom and a new life, or so I hoped. Tommy Linehan
greeted us warmly. Tommy rolled his eyes at me when he shook hands with
Anne Elizabeth. I was proud of her. A night in a car during a rainstorm had
not dimmed her grace.

"So," said the American intelligence officer as he glanced at me later in the
day at the American embassy with a superior and artificial smile. "Let me begin by asking who precisely you are."

I was sitting on a hard chair in a small barren and windowless office, an in-
terrogation room.

"Timothy Ridgewood, sir," I said, "Ambassador of Ireland to Germany."

"How can Ireland have an ambassador? It's not a real country, is it?"

I had spent most of the day sleeping in my room in the luxurious hotel suite
that the Irish embassy had booked for us. I was groggy and in a very bad mood.
Anne Elizabeth and I had had harsh words. Then she had gone shopping, with
the money from the Old Fella's account in a Zurich bank.

"I'm afraid your education has been inadequate, sir . . . Princeton I presume . . . In any case by the States of Ireland Act of 1922 it became in effect
one of the English dominions. Like Canada or Australia."

"But how can you have relations with Germany when you're part of England?"

"Shall we stipulate that we can. We make our own foreign policy."

He was a sleekly handsome young man, twenty-two at the most, with hostile brown eyes and a built-in smirk.

"Isn't that ungrateful to England after all the things England has done for
you?"

"I am unaware of any need to defend Ireland in this conversation. Shall we
discuss the reason for this conversation?"

"Well, as I understand it, you are acting as an agent for Herr Himmler and Herr Ribbentrop in regard to a separate peace. Is that an honourable role for you to play?"

"You do not understand the role of a diplomat. It is our job to relay, whenever asked, messages between the governments of countries at war with a view to establishing peace. This does not mean that the diplomat endorses the views of either country or of the government officials who are conducting these indirect negotiations."

"But these men are killing millions of Jews."

"If there should be peace between the two countries, one essential condition would be the release of all those in concentration camps."

"Do you really trust Himmler? If you do, you're a fool!"

"Then I yield to your superior judgment."

"You're a Catholic, aren't you?" he sneered.

"Most of us Irish are Catholic."

"Then I suppose you approve of that notorious anti-Semite and Nazi who tried to kill Hitler."

I stood up.

"I am terminating this conversation, sir. You have insulted my nation, myself, my religion, and a true German hero. I will not deal with the Office of Strategic Services in the future or any other American agency until a full apology is forthcoming. I will also send a minute about your insolence to my government and suggest they protest to the American government."

I stalked out, proud of myself. Then I remembered my argument with Anne as I must now call her. I had given her a pack of Swiss franks I had drawn when we had arrived at the hotel yesterday and told her to do whatever shopping she needed.

She accepted the cash reluctantly.

Then, in the flush of my excitement about our successful escape, I had done a very foolish thing. I had proposed marriage. Too abruptly.

"I know a very nice priest here in Berne," I had said. "If you wish we could regularize our marriage tomorrow."

"There is no marriage to regularize, Herr Ridgewood! It is outrageous to suggest that there might be. I am grateful that you helped me to escape the Gestapo.

That does not give you any claim on me. It is most improper. You should know better than that. It is disgraceful. You are an irresponsible, evil man!"

She was just warming up.

"I'm sorry, Annalise. I did not mean to offend you."

"You have offended me deeply!"

She removed the rings from her finger and slammed them on a lamp table.

"Never speak to me this way again."

"I had better go to the American embassy now. I'm not sure when I will be back."

"I do not care whether you ever return. I will seek lodging in another hotel where my honour will not be violated."

It seemed pretty definitive.

She had divorced me even before we were married.

After my tussle with the OSS man, I walked to the Irish embassy, which was near our hotel. I told Tommy Linehan my story.

"They have some odd people over there, still sorting things out. The colonel will still want to talk to you, I'm sure."

"I don't know why he turned me over to a fool."

"Everyone makes mistakes. He's out of town, heaven knows where. The Brits want to fly you to Dublin in a couple of days, via Lisbon still, I'm afraid. The way the Yanks are traveling, next time it will be through Paris."

I sent a minute to our Ministry in Dublin, informing them that I was safe in Berne and that I had carried peace proposals to the Americans from both Ribbentrop and Himmler.

So I walked back to our hotel, heartbroken, to tell the truth. I had been a complete fool. I'd better postpone moving her to another hotel till tomorrow morning. A pile of packages in the parlour of our suite indicated that her fury had not hindered her shopping expedition. What was I to do with her? Should I leave her in Berne? Were there any schoolmates in London who would welcome her while she found a job and a place to live? Or would they intern her as an enemy alien? Well, that was not my problem.

I heard the shower coming from her room. She had become addicted to showers.

Only, of course, it was my problem.

One of the packages had been opened to reveal a lovely white frock. I looked at the end table. One of the rings was still there.

How could I have been so stupid? I must have misread the signs completely. It would be a long time before I worked up the nerve to court another woman.

The door opened. Annalise emerged, wrapped in a large towel and drying her hair with another towel. She was quite delicious.

Then I saw she was wearing the engagement ring again.

"I didn't hear you come in, Herr Ridgewood . . . Is that not a lovely frock? Look at the label!"

"Irish linen—County Donegal, the Old Fella's company!"

"I thought it might be a nice dress for a wedding . . ."

My heart beat much faster and spread warmth through my body.

"We have changed our plans?"

"If you will forgive me, Herr Ridgewood, for being a stupid fool. Naturally I knew you would propose marriage when we reached freedom. I eagerly awaited such a proposal. When I heard it in your typical casual fashion, I lost my nerve. I ran away from it in fear."

"Not so much that you didn't go forth on a shopping expedition?"

She was quite near me now, the warmth of the shower, the smell of the soap, the glow of her skin assaulted me.

I drew her into my arms.

"You will ruin the press of your suit . . . Oh, please say that you will give me one more chance . . . I swear I will never do anything like that again . . . You knew I would change my mind, did you not . . . I hoped you did as soon as you left . . . Please forgive me . . ."

She leaned her head against my chest. I could take her right then.

Don't be a fool. She'll be even more delicious tomorrow night.

"I note, Frau Ambassador, you have spent some of the Old Fella's money on Parisian lace. It would be a shame to waste that. So we'd better have a wedding."

She blushed, the flush spreading over her face and then down to her throat and over her shoulders.

"You forgive me, Herr Ridgewood?"

"Of course I forgive you, Annie," I said touching one of those shoulders.

Truly delicious. "I will always forgive you as I'm sure you will forgive me."

"Thank you, Herr Ridgewood."

"Now put on your clothes and we'll go see the priest about a wedding."

We were married at Mass the next evening, with the priest's sexton and cook acting as witnesses. Annie had found a veil somewhere and I a bouquet of flowers for Mary's altar. He preached about the mystery of love. God, the ultimate love of all is shrouded in mystery. Married lovers, no matter how close they are to one another, always live enshrouded in the mystery that envelops each of them. You must never permit one another to cease to be a mystery. When the mystery is gone, your love must be renewed. Never forget these words of mine.

My new wife had been serious and quiet through the service, though she never released her grip on my arm. We ate at a restaurant reputed to be the best in Berne, ate steaks from Argentina (beef, she told me, gives one more energy). We toasted each other in rich Italian wine and devoured strawberries and heavy cream.

I promised her another wedding in Donegal for our family and friends.

"I hope they like me." She sighed.

"Count on it, they will."

We returned uneasily to our hotel room.

"You will wish to remove my garments, Herr Ridgewood?" she asked, as I closed the door.

"Well, it would be grand altogether," I said, "but only if you permit it."

"You have seen through me ever since those lovely Holy Week days. I have never been able to hide from you. Why should I be afraid of giving you all that I am?"

I had no idea what that meant.

Despite our brave talk we were awkward and nervous as we began the consummations of our union. Then I was so overcome by the beauty of my wife's body, her generosity, and her shyness that I filled up with sweetness. Then grace prevailed.

Afterwards while we were sliding into happy sleep, she pressed herself against me.

"Timmy, Timmy, Timmy, I will be your loyal and devoted and loving wife for all my life and even after."

"*Thank goodness that I am not Herr Ridgewood anymore.*"

"*But I am still Frau Ambassador!*"

The next morning I went to our embassy to do battle with the American OSS.

The colonel tried to take over the conversation at the very beginning.

Flush with conquest in bed (though perhaps I had been conquered long before), I interrupted him.

"*Excuse me, sir, I will do the talking. Roisin over there will transcribe my remarks and I will later send it to my government, which can decide whether to pass the document on to Washington. You have shown contempt and incompetence by assigning a briefing officer who is not only uneducated but gratuitously rude. He said that Ireland was not a nation and was disloyal and ungrateful to England for maintaining its neutrality in the current war. He insulted me by suggesting that I was immoral because I was acting as an agent of Himmler and von Ribbentrop. He insulted the Catholic Church because he suggested that it was Catholicism which made me anti-Semitic, and finally attacked the honour of my late friend Claus von Stauffenberg as a well-known anti-Semite and a Nazi count.*

"*If this is the best the United States of America can do, then it should withdraw from the intelligence business.*

"*I will rehearse briefly the proposals of Herr Himmler and Herr von Ribbentrop. They add to their previous undertakings their willingness to suspend the Endlösung, their term for the Final Solution to the Jewish question, open the concentration camps and free those held in them. They will withdraw the German armed forces to their 1939 borders, including that of Poland and Czechoslovakia, they will order a cease-fire on all fronts. They believe that Stalin will suspend his attacks on the Eastern Front. They are fully aware that he is attempting to negotiate a separate peace with Germany through his agents in Stockholm. I note that if, through some miracle, an agreement like this could be reached, similar to the one to which Graf von Stauffenberg was committed, millions of lives will be saved—Jewish and Gypsy lives in the camps, German and Russian lives on the Eastern Front, German civilian lives saved from the tender mercies of Air Marshal Harris, American lives on the Western Front.*

"You will ask if I recommend that you proceed further with these negotiations. It is beyond my charge to respond to such a question. I will say, however, that I personally deem the Jews in the concentration camps are the key issue. When Herr Himmler or Herr von Ribbentrop order the killing to cease and begin to release the prisoners, then one might begin to believe they are acting in good faith.

"That is all I have to say, sir, except that I worked in the United States for five years as Vice Consul in Chicago. I am fond of the American people. They deserve to be served better."

"Roisin"—I turned to our grinning stenographer—"type that up, if you will. I'll translate it into Irish and send it off tomorrow to Dublin."

"I'm Irish too, sir," the colonel began . . .

"Irish-American, Colonel. There's a difference."

"I admire your Irish spunk."

"Don't give me that shite, Colonel. I don't give a good fuck what you admire."

"I want to apologize . . ."

"In writing, Colonel, with guarantees that it will never happen to any other representatives of the Irish government . . . Good day, Roisin. You can leave out the last dialogue, I don't want to shock the minister. Good day, Mr. Linehan. Good day, Colonel."

"I'm not without some powerful Irish friends . . ."

"Roisin, put the dialogue back in and add this reply: Don't you ever, ever threaten me again!"

Later I told my Annie the story as she lay in my arms.

"You're a desperate man altogether, Timmy . . . Is that the right idiom?"

She clung to me whenever she could. She held my hand when she could not cling to me. I was not at all embarrassed. At the Zurich airport of Swissair, she held my hand as though she would never let it go.

"Haven't you been on a plane before, my love?"

"No, and I'm frightened. However, we will die together." The plane, a small Lockheed, much like the one to become famous in the film Casablanca, took off in the darkness. The sun came up over the Alps through whose mountain valleys we were picking our way.

"Isn't it beautiful, Timmy Pat," she said as she held my hand more tightly. "I think I'll love flying . . . Is this the way it looks to the bomber pilots?"

When they have time to notice.

She had learned that Timmy Pat was my "real" name and decided that it was "sweet." Indeed I was "sweet," especially when I played with her body. Often she gazed at me in shameless adoration which I did not deserve.

I had better enjoy the adoration and hand-holding. It would not last for long.

In this hasty judgment, I was wrong.

We refueled in Madrid and then landed in Lisbon. Everyone in the airport looked like they were an agent spying on everyone else. Using the embassy phone, I called Castle Ridgeland and found the Galway woman at home.

"I'll be home for a few days."

"Not for long, I suppose."

"They'll want me to work at the Ministry for a while."

"You're coming alone?"

"Won't I be bringing me wife home?"

"Will I like her?"

"Can't tell."

"What she look like?"

"A Gothic princess, willowy, shapely, long, pale blond hair."

"Glory be to God! Won't you be the death of me!"

"Try to be nice to her; she doesn't speak English very well."

The result of this conversation was to assure me ma that me wife would not be boring.

I repeated the conversation to Annie.

"I know she'll hate me."

"She loves you already."

After a layover of four hours, during which my wife continued her determined efforts to read through all the novels of Charles Dickens, while clinging to my hand, we boarded a Douglass Dakota for the trip to London. The plane was painted white with the letters BOAC written in large letters so British patrol planes would know who it was. The Luftwaffe had long since disappeared from the Bay of Biscay. Still clutching my hand, Annie slept all the way to London.

A limousine from Downing Street met us on the runway.

"By your leave, Sir Timothy, we'll be taking you to Number 10. We assume you won't leave for Ireland till tomorrow, so we have made a reservation for you at the Connaught."

"Formerly called the Coburg," I noted, "when England was proud of its relationships with Germany."

"What's in a name, eh, sir . . . Perhaps Lady Anne would want to rest there until you are finished talking to the PM. We will take care of the reservation formalities."

"Fine, except we will pay . . . Annie, this is just in case you should need some money."

I gave her a hundred-pound note.

No charity from the British Empire for me.

"Well, Timmy, that was a splendid minute you sent about the OSS," Winston began. "Needless to say, I was also impressed by your story of the failure of Graf von Stauffenberg. Tragic loss of brave men that Germany would have needed in the years to come."

"I quite agree, Winston."

"Can you tell me the story in greater detail . . . lest your throat become dry."

He pushed a glass of Middleton's at me.

I recounted the story carefully. Winston would remember every word of it, perhaps write it down.

"Sad, sad . . . So many great men lost . . . Like your father's friend Michael Collins for example . . . I'm told you brought a beautiful woman with you, Timothy. German? Enemy civilian?"

"Lady Anne is my lawfully wedded wife and hence an Irish citizen and by your own rules English too, though you won't let her vote in this country . . . More to the point she is also Lord Ridgeland's daughter-in-law."

"He knows about her?"

"Yes, though he has yet to meet her. She is also the only survivor of the Bendlerstrasse bloodbath."

"A match for you then?"

"I'm afraid so, Winston!"

"Congratulations to the two of you. I will look forward to meeting her someday."

I was a little more uncertain about the reaction of my minister the next day.

"I hope you don't think those last two minutes will interfere with your appointment to Washington, Timmy."

"I hadn't considered them in those terms, sir."

"Good. Our current man there said that he showed the material on the OSS to the Undersecretary of State, who said he would take appropriate action. I doubt that they will discipline the colonel. He may well be an enemy when you do arrive in Washington."

"That would be unwise of him, sir."

"The only other item is when do I meet this fabulous wife of yours."

"Whenever you wish to, sir."

"We'll arrange that as soon as you get back from your vacation . . . and we will take care of any possibility of questions which might arise later about the validity of her presence in Ireland."

"She is an Irish citizen by marriage to me, a valid marriage in a Catholic church, she is also a survivor of the Stauffenberg Rising. This is a copy of our marriage certificate."

"You think of everything, don't you, Timothy?"

"I try, sir, but I often fail."

I returned to the Royal Hiberneian to find my wife awake and recovered from the sea sickness she had acquired during a particularly rough crossing from Holyhead.

She did not seem happy.

"I do not want to meet your parents, Timmy Pat. I won't do it. Call them and tell them that I am sick and they should stay away."

"No."

"Why not?"

"Because if I do you, you'll change your mind in five minutes."

"You're right . . . Will you make love with me, so I'll look radiant for them?"

"You will look radiant anyway, but I will never reject such an offer."

"Ma, Pa," I said to my startled parents in the Lafayette dining room, "this is me wife, Anne Elizabeth . . . Anne, these are me ma and pa."

My lovely Gothic countess took a deep breath and smiled. The words cascaded out of her mouth.

"I have heard so much from Timmy Pat about the Old Fella and the Galway woman that only with difficulty have I waited to meet you. I talk stilted now because I am a little nervous. My dress, Lord Ridgeland, is I believe from your mills. It was my wedding dress . . . You may call me, Annie. I hope you do."

The eyes of the Galway woman and the Swabian woman linked and, as often happens in such contacts, they bonded instantly and permanently. Against me of course.

"Annie," the Galway woman said, embracing her daughter-in-law, "welcome home to Ireland!"

SOME ADDITIONAL NOTES

The war ended nine months later. More humans died, more women were raped than in the previous five years of the war. Germany was destroyed, but quickly rose again, too quickly for those who believed in collective guilt.

Herman Goering committed suicide the day he was to be executed. Joachim von Ribbentrop was thus the first Nazi war criminal to be executed, first at last. Heinrich Himmler was captured by English troops after the German surrender as he desperately tried to find someone to talk to. He is alleged to have committed suicide, but it is always suspected that his captors shot him on the spot.

Admiral Canaris, Julius Leber, Pastor Bonhoeffer, and many others lived into 1945 and were executed only when American guns were heard near the prison.

There was, however, no blood vengeance against Claus's family or anyone else.

We were in Washington and I persuaded friends at the Pentagon to order that the American military take good care of Nina and her children. When we returned to Germany later, we visited Schloss Stauffenberg with our children. It was still a happy place, with many memories. Once again I defeated my wife at tennis. The match was much closer, however. We also went to Berlin to place flowers at the monument to Claus. On the same trip we also placed flowers on the grave of Field Marshal General Paul von Richthofen in the small cemetery at the now closed Biggin Hill fighter station. Annie and I wept both times.

We would return many times to Germany. The Federal Republic presented me with a medal for my "Great service to the New Germany" the year I was President of the General Assembly of the United Nations. My wife and I continue to love one another. She still holds on to my hand, calls me "Timmy Pat," and on every possible occasion avers that I am sweet. The mystery has never gone out of our love.

She never did show me the letters from Claus ordering her to permit me to lead her to freedom. But then I never asked to see them.

Ridgeland.

— 25 —

SO THE rest of the story is anticlimax. The two limos and the two security cars arrived twenty minutes early. Nelliecoyne, who happened to be in the parlor, opened the door. The rest of the kids swarmed into the parlor. And the doggies instantly bonded with Des, himself wearing one of those funny stovepipe hats that the Greek priests wear, a flowing robe, a dangerous black beard, and a cross around his neck. Blackie picked up Socra Marie. Des swung the Mick in the air. Nuala and I arrived, herself with the baby in her arms. He loved the noise and the excitement, assured as all tiny ones are that it was for him. Nelliecoyne snapped pictures right and left. I shook hands with "Steffan," who had been a contemporary at the Dome. Des hugged Nuala and they both wept. The rest of the evening was like that. Laughter, tears, stories, songs.

"So how did you know that Des wanted to be a priest all along, and a parish priest here in Chicago?" I asked my wife as we lay in bed, exhausted

after our party, the biggest we'd ever had in the house and one that escaped completely from our control, especially when Cindasue and her
mob arrived, followed almost immediately by Mary and Joseph and their
little flower—last minute ideas of Nuala Anne's about which she hadn't
warned me.

"I didn't have to be fey to recognize that, Dermot Michael." She
sighed patiently, as with Patjo when he had shit in perfectly clean dia-
pers she had just put on him. "When you think about Des's life, he was
always rushing around helping people and getting involved in religion.
His mother may be right that your Jesuits corrupted him with religion
when he was in high school. After that he had a mission. He took theology courses at Marquette and took them seriously. Who else does that
unless someone who wants to be a priest?"

"Maybe he just wanted to teach at some university?"

"Give over, Dermot love! If he wanted to be an academic, why did he
run off to the Peace Corps?"

"Maybe he was just an idealist."

"But he spent a lot of time healing wounds and bringing people together, just like good parish priests do, His Riverence, for example?"

"'Tis true," I admitted, though her frequent praise of my self-
proclaimed big brother always offended me.

Giving the divil his due?

I never said he wasn't a good priest.

"But, Nuala Anne, then he returned to Chicago and went to graduate
school in Arabic."

"And appointed himself de facto chaplain there. That should have
been the decisive clue. He liked being a parish priest. Why else cool
things off with the perfectly presentable Shovie, who would have been a
fine wife for your Catholic intellectual."

"Then off to Iraq! Why not the seminary then and there?"

"Because he wanted to see what monastery life was like and pick up a
couple more languages. Praying at that strange place while people were
shooting one another convinced him that this was not his vocation.

Then he made up his mind that he belonged here on the shores of your Lake Michigan. You'll remember how quickly he agreed when I said his vocation was to be a parish priest in Chicago. Then we made him an of-fer he couldn't refuse. 'Tis a good thing, Dermot Michael, that we know Cardinal Sean and Blackie, isn't it?"

"'Tis . . . So you knew that Tim Ridgewood would be faithful to his love because Des was faithful to his love?"

"Och, Dermot, don't be a complete eejit altogether. Wasn't it the other way around? Your two men with the glint in their eyes were lovers, I realized that the glint showed that they would be faithful and impla-cable lovers. Timmy told us a lot more about himself than we know about Des. He made up his mind that Holy Week in Jettingen that someday he would carry that woman off to Ireland and display her as a prize to his wonderful parents. The poor thing never had a chance, especially be-cause she loved him too. He just never gave up. Then I says to meself, self, who is the lover that Des is chasing. It was perfectly clear as soon as I thought about it that way. Like I say, I didn't have to be fey to figure all that out."

"As the Cardinal says to Blackie, I'm glad that you're on my side."

"And as Blackie says to the Cardinal, arguably."

I was on the edge of sleep, but our conversation wasn't over yet.

"That woman is still alive, Dermot. She's only ninety or so. Her hus-band has gone home, but she's alive and still loves him. We'll have to pay our respects to her when we're in Galway this summer. It's a brilliant love story and it should be told, shouldn't it? Why else was it sitting there waiting for us in His Riverence's church basement?"

"I can't argue with any of that, Nuala Anne. I'd like to meet her too. She was quite a woman."

"Is . . . But don't you understand why I'm an expert on men with the glint in their eyes?"

"No . . ."

YOU REALLY ARE AN EEJIT.

"Didn't I meet a man with the glint in his eyes one night in O'Neill's pub just off College Green and didn't he devour me altogether, body and soul, and didn't I know I'd never escape from him."

As Blessed Juliana predicted, all things were well, all manner of things were well.

— Afterword —

Claus Graf von Stauffenberg was one of the heroes of the twentieth century. He alone had the courage, the energy, and the intelligence to put together a vigorous plot against the Third Reich. The Gestapo analyst who created the dossier against his memory did not hesitate to praise his nobility of character. The Russians and the East Germans built a shrine to him in the courtyard where he was executed and changed the name of the Bendlerstrasse to the Stauffenbergstrasse. The English historian Trevor-Roper sang his praises. Yet the charges of the fictional OSS agent in my story represent the image of him created in the American press, which somehow has stained his reputation in the United States. He was not a Nazi count, he was not a fascist, he was not an ambitious power seeker, he was not a rebellious renegade. He was politically a Social Democrat and religiously a committed, if not always devout, Catholic, a man of enormous personal charm, intellectual brilliance, and dedicated bravery. If his carefully planned plot had worked, history might have been very different.

However, an ideology emerged in the United States after the war that insisted on the collective guilt of the whole German nation. There could not have been a *Widerstand* against Hitler of any importance. There could not have been many Germans who resisted, nor many plots against him, nor this one last desperate and almost successful plot, nor one shining hero without an arm and without an eye and with only three fingers who almost carried it off. Theories of collective guilt or an evil culture do not help us to understand any society. As Hannah Arendt once remarked, "If everyone is guilty, no one is guilty."

Was it perhaps necessary that the war destroy Germany in order that the Federal Republic finally become a working democracy (albeit imperfect like all democracies), as Claus suggests in my story? Is the Federal Republic, particularly in its Bonn-based Western version, a manifestation of Claus's "Secret Germany"? At least one can say that it is more influenced by that ideal than any other social form since Germany became a nation in 1870. If the July 20 plot had succeeded, might a new Germany have developed not unlike the Federal Republic and much earlier?

At least one can say that some six hundred thousand German civilians would not have died in RAF raids and two million German women would not have been raped by the Red Army. The idea that Germans brought this suffering on themselves and therefore it was just punishment is morally repugnant. Who is entitled to make such a judgment?

(In the long and bloody history of the British Empire, six hundred thousand deaths is something of a record.)

I was astonished by the Stauffenberg who emerged from the literature I read. I've tried to create a picture of him based on firsthand descriptions of him in the books. I know he would have delighted in a real-life Timmy Pat. I believe with Annalise that he was the last knight of Europe, "the last and lingering troubadour to whom the bird had sung that once went singing southward when all the world was young."

I have pushed up the date of the American invasion of southern France by a couple of weeks in this story.

Books about von Stauffenberg and Berlin during the war:

> *Hitler's Spy Chief: The Wilhelm Canaris Mystery* by Richard Bassett
> *Battlefield Berlin* by Peter M. Slowe and Richard Woods
> *Stauffenberg: The Architect of the Famous July 20th Conspiracy to Assassinate Hitler* by Joachim Kramarz
> *Secret Germany: Claus von Stauffenberg and the Mystical Crusade Against Hitler* by Michael Baigent and Richard Leigh

The Internet encyclopedia Wikipedia also provides many useful and interesting articles on these subjects.